Western Skies

Majken Selinder Nilsson

Acknowledgements

I dedicate this book to my family and the loving support they have given me in my crazy endeavor to write novels. I thank you Mans, Lukas, Lena, Helene, and Erik, for always putting up with my late nights, my zoning out while writing and editing, and for understanding when I have to put off other things in order to meet deadlines.

As with my first novel, *A Good Kind of Crazy*, I am also grateful for my parents, who always encouraged me to try, my extended family who supported my efforts to read and learn, friends who helped me through tough times, and my teachers and professors who gave me the educational foundation on which I still stand. I cannot adequately express my thankfulness for my experience growing up in a small, Western ranching town in the middle of the Nevada desert, as well, where community was valued, everyone knew each other's names, and the friendships I made are still intact today. Indeed, I am incredibly appreciative of the hometown support I have received since embarking on this unplanned and unexpected journey of becoming an author.

I am grateful to my beta readers, Ms. Rachel March and Ms. Becky Garfield, for giving me valuable feedback and encouragement on those days when I struggled to find my voice. The support of good friends and mentors, such as authors Tammy L. Grace and David W. Thompson, also helped to make the experience less daunting and more fun.

Of course, I cannot forget the innumerable talents of Ms. K. C. Sprayberry, who was the driving force in the preparations of this novel for its original publication, my original editor, Ms. Melissa Manes, and all the other employees at Solstice Publishing who had a hand in making the first publication of this book a reality.

I appreciate the guidance, suggestions, and dedication to help me initially get *Western Skies* out there.

I thank Ms. Lori Collett, who, blessed with her incredible photographic talent, managed to capture me at my best. I am deeply grateful to friends and editors, Ms. Susan Daniels and Ms. Kimberly Vancoughnett, for volunteering to read through the final product as yet more pairs of eyes. I am also appreciative for Majken Longlade, who has put in countless hours helping me to produce quality content.

Most of all, I am grateful for God and the amazing life I have. It hasn't always been easy, but the journey has taught me to feel deeply, appreciate profusely, and love greatly.

Of course, none of this would be possible without you, the readers. I am so honored that in this busy, crazy world, so many people have spent their precious, limited time reading what I created. Thank you for allowing me the privilege of entertaining you. I hope that you find Sarah and Joe's story enchanting.

Chapter One

The wind blew forlornly over the rolling plains as the young widow stood beside the recently dug grave that was to be her husband's final resting place. She held the hand of her little boy, now fatherless at four years old. Her handkerchief was completely saturated and did nothing to remove the tears that were running down her face, so she just kept clutching it in her free hand, looking down into the mocking hole and the wooden coffin therein. Though her family members were trying to rally around her, she felt utterly alone, and the fact that they were all standing near was lost to her. She watched as the preacher commended her husband's body to the earth, but it was as if she had suddenly gone deaf, hearing nothing but the sound of her blood rushing through her ears. When she looked up, she saw that all the trees stood naked and lifeless in the late autumn sun, their progression toward winter apparent. She felt in that moment that even the trees had died and left her alone in her grief.

***

Sarah White had met her husband, George Johnson, on the playground of the local schoolhouse on her first day of class at seven years old. He had been ten at the time, and not at all interested in her. The boys were much more focused on their stickball game than on anyone of the female persuasion and didn't even look up as the little girl and her sister walked past. Sarah had been terrified, clinging to her big sister's hand, wondering how she was going to navigate this new, big environment. She wanted nothing more than to run home into the loving arms and voluminous skirts of her mother. However, all children in their town started school at seven, so she had no other choice than to follow her older siblings down the lane and over several hills on the mile-long walk to the pretty little red and white schoolhouse.

As soon as her sister, Ginny, had done what she had promised her mother by getting Sarah to school, she quickly dropped her hand and ran off to meet her friends. Being three years older, Ginny already had a long-established clique of girls who were thrilled to see her after the summer break, while Sarah stood on the grassy playground, not sure what to do or where to go. Suddenly, a ball flew right into her upper arm, which she quickly grabbed with an emphatic "Ouch!" as she massaged the area, tears of pain and humiliation stinging her eyes.

Her tears were about to spill over onto her cheeks when a bigger boy ran up to grab the ball that was now resting next to her foot, picking it up with a half-hearted "Sorry," before turning and starting the jog back to his friends. However, as he took the first step away, something compelled him to turn back and look into the little girl's face. When he saw the tears that had now spilled over, he had felt badly, but then had gotten annoyed that he was now going to have to attend to her, saying, "Ah, man. Don't cry! We didn't mean to hurt you! It was just an accident!"

Sarah stood looking up at him, unable to speak. Instead, she nodded slowly and then hiccoughed. She looked so sad and lost that George felt his protective instincts come out. He automatically wrapped his arm around her shoulders and pulled her along with him, toward the schoolhouse. Seeking comfort, she rested her head on his shoulder as they walked.

"First day here?" he asked her, knowing it was, but feeling like he needed to say something to make her feel more comfortable. She merely nodded at him in response.

"Well, you'll like it here a whole bunch. Miss Wilcox is real nice," he tried again, but she only nodded.

As they reached the stairs, she heard the taunting of the other boys as they saw what was happening.

"Ooooo! Lookie there! George has found himself a new sweetheart!"

"She's real cute, George. She probably doesn't have cooties at all!"

"Don't you come back here to play with us until you wash your hands! We don't want them girlie germs all over our ball!"

Sarah tried to ignore the jeers, but her little heart was breaking. No one had ever told her that she had cooties just because she was a girl! Now, on top of everything else, she was going to have to go home and ask Ma how to get rid of them.

She was pulled out of her own thoughts when she heard George respond, "Ah, shut up, you guys! She's new, little, and hurt. Say, why didn't any of *you* big mouth sissies go and help her?"

The other boys just stood around glaring at him for calling them names.

When they reached the front steps, George helped Sarah sit down. "Here you go, then! Miss Wilcox will be ringing the bell real soon, all right?"

Sarah could only nod at him again, her eyes pleading with him not to leave her alone. Feeling sorry for her and responsible that this had happened on her first day, he shook his head, angry with himself that he was letting some girl sucker him into sitting beside her to wait for the day to start. But once his bottom was beside hers on the stoop, he couldn't help but ask her, "So what's your name, anyways?"

"Sarah," she whispered her first word to him.

"Sarah?" he asked, having barely heard her.

"Yes," she said shyly.

"Well, it is nice to meet you, Sarah. I'm George."

Of course, she had seen him before, as their town was small, and they had all assembled at the same church, stores, and community events for years, but Sarah had been too young and too caught up in her own world to care much about people who weren't family or close friends. She certainly had never spoken to a bigger boy who wasn't her brother before. As her older brother was twelve, she rarely spoke to him, either, but instead worshipped him from afar.

"Thank you," she murmured so softly that he instinctively leaned forward to catch what she was saying.

"You're welcome," he told her with a cocky grin.

After a few more minutes of them sitting together, Miss Wilcox rang the school bell, and the rest of the children rushed inside, breaking the spell between them.

***

It didn't take long for Sarah to become comfortable and happy in the classroom, but she always had a soft spot for George, whom she regarded as her knight in shining armor. From that first day forward, he kept his eye on her, as well, always willing to lend her a hand when she needed it. Indeed, as the school year progressed, they were both keenly aware of the other, as if they had a sort of magnetic attraction to each other.

Almost a year after they met, they discovered by accident that they liked the same fishing hole. Though George had been going there for years, Sarah's father had just taken her for the first time over the summer while teaching her to swim. Once he was satisfied that she wouldn't drown if she accidentally fell in, he gave permission for her to go by herself. His only stipulations were that she always had to tell him or her ma where she was going, and she was to be back before suppertime.

So, on one particularly hot and humid summer day, little Sarah, taking her pole and her bucket, had headed down to her fishing spot, but then stopped short when she realized someone was already there. Feeling quite proprietary, she then marched down the embankment, her small lips pursed in annoyance. Hearing a stick snap on her descent, George had turned around, fire in his eyes, wondering what had broken the silence, potentially scaring away his fish. Seeing it was Sarah, he relaxed for a minute, before his anger built up and he spat out, "What are you doing here? This is *my* fishing hole!"

"Is not!" she responded, her voice full of contempt.

"Oh, yes, it is!"

"No, it ain't!" she insisted, stomping her little foot on the ground for emphasis. "I've been coming here with my pa all summer long!"

"All summer… that ain't nothing, little girl. I've been coming here for years!"

Sarah hiked the rest of the way to the downed log that was next to the water and settled in, deciding that she wasn't going to let any old boy make her leave. He was furious.

"Hey! What are you doing? I just said this is my spot!" he huffed at her.

"No, it ain't! This is my spot. Now, scoot on over and shut your mouth!"

"I ain't moving!" he hollered at her.

"Now who's scaring the fish?" she taunted him.

"You need to leave!" he told her gruffly.

"No way! You leave!"

"I'm not leaving!" he sputtered.

"Why not?"

"Because fishing ain't for girls!" He stood up to loom over her.

"Fishing ain't for girls? Is that what you just said?"

"Yup!"

Sarah didn't say another word as she gently laid her pole to the side and then thrust her arms forward, giving him a shove. George's face went from anger, to realization, then to shock as he stumbled backward and fell into the water below. When he came up, he pushed his wet hair back off his forehead with his hands and glowered at her as the water dripped down over his face. Sarah, in the meantime, couldn't contain her glee as she stood with her arms wrapped around her body and doubled over with laughter.

George knew he had to save some face. "You happy now?" he spat out angrily.

"Quite," she replied, her laughter unceasing.

He knew then that he had been beaten, fair and square. He was just happy that none of his friends had seen him get put in his place by a girl: a girl three years younger than him, no less! He shook his head out like a dog and began to climb back up as he was thinking of all the things he could say or do to her, but every time he came up with something, he heard his pa's voice echoing in the back of his head, telling him that he had to be nice to girls. Still, he couldn't resist one more barb.

"I hope you don't catch anything!" he taunted her once he was up on the dry edge of the water.

"Careful, George, or I may just have to shove you back in!" she gleefully jeered.

Humiliated and angry, he snatched his pole and bucket and began to walk back up the hill.

"Hey, where are you going?" Sarah called after him.

"Home!" he responded.

"Why?"

"Because you kicked me out of here!"

"No, I didn't," she told him, confused.

"Yeah, you did! You win! You can have the daggone fishing hole for all I care! I'm outta here!"

"Wait!" she hollered at him.

"What?" he asked her, turning around, annoyance etched in his face. His mind flashed back to the time when he had helped her after the ball had hit her. He began pouting to himself, thinking that here he had rescued her, and had even put up with the teasing from his buddies no less, and she was now treating him like this!

"Come back here, silly!" she told him.

"Oh, so now you're calling me names, too, are you?"

"I'm sorry. Please come back here, George! Is that more to your liking?" Sarah's experience with her older brother and sister had taught her to give as good as she got.

George was surprised that instead of his anger ramping higher, he began to feel a stirring in his chest; something was telling him that this girl was special! He began to think of her in a way he had never before thought about girls, and it scared him. Why, she was cute, with her blonde hair and pretty blue eyes!

She was fun, too! And she could fish! She could razz him as well as his friends! What was going on? He became even more determined to leave.

"Just leave me alone!" he muttered as he continued to climb the hill, scared of the reaction she was evoking in him. His thoughts were consumed by thinking that her sister, Ginny, was his exact age, but never acted like this. She was snobby and disinterested, and quite frankly a brat! So, who was this girl, and how could she be Ginny's little sister?

"All right, George. I will. If that is what you want."

Did she sound a bit sad and disappointed that I'm leaving? He wondered if he was imagining things.

"I just want you to know that I never told you that you had to leave; I just told you that you had to let me stay," she declared.

That stopped him short. He slowly turned around and saw her grinning at him even before he dared to meet her gaze, but when he did, he was greeted by a twinkle in her eyes. Shaking his head in defeat, he began to stroll back to her perched on the log. They then spent the rest of the afternoon fishing together, neither talking much, but just enjoying each other's company as their shoulders lightly touched. When evening was coming on, they finally decided that it was time to go back home, each grabbing their fish before heading up the hill. Neither said a word as they parted ways, but Sarah picked up her hand carrying her fish and waved.

The events of that day were never spoken of again. It was just understood that the fishing hole was now "their" place. Through the years, they went as often as they could, sometimes prearranged, sometimes just showing up. Whichever one of them was there first would greet the other with a welcoming smile that would light up his or her whole face.

As they grew, they spent their time together talking about everything under the sun. At first, it was about happenings at school, what their friends were doing, and the goings-on in their families.

However, as the years passed, their connection grew, especially once they began to share their hopes, dreams, and aspirations for the future. In particular, George's mother was a constant thorn in his side: while he wanted to get out and explore the world, she had already predetermined his destiny was to take over the family farm, and it seemed they were always butting heads.

At school and at church, Sarah and George were always polite to each other, but distant. No one outside of the two of them had any idea that they spent as much time together as they did, and they wanted to keep it that way. When they were younger, it had been a good way to save face and not get teased about kissing and marriage. As they got older, neither of them had wanted to break the bond they had formed by letting anyone else in. By then, each had become the other's only confidant, saving the most intimate details of their lives for when they were able to be alone together.

When George was about to turn eighteen and finish his schooling, he was considered a hot commodity by all the young local girls. Tall, dark, muscular, and handsome, he was the catch of the town, but he never seemed to be courting anyone, so people wondered what was going on with him. It became a game to see who could turn his head, and the harder they tried, the more outlandish their attempts at flirtation and flattery became. What no one knew, though, was that by that time, he had realized he was helplessly, entirely, and completely in love with Sarah, but was too shy to tell her. He had told her his deepest, darkest secrets, and she knew all there was to know about him, but he still couldn't bring himself to share his innermost desire that she would become his wife. She was only fifteen, and he had never even tried to do more than hold her hand if she was upset and crying about something that had happened in her life, but he knew without question that she was the girl for him. Sarah, on the other hand, truly believed that he loved her like a brother and was secretly devastated by that fact, but she, too, was always too shy and too much of a lady to try to pursue him.

Meanwhile, Sarah's older sister was quite arguably the best-looking girl in town, garnering more looks and flirtation from men than the rest of the young women her age combined. However, at some point, Ginny had made up her mind that she and George were destined to be together, especially after she had heard that upon his completing school, his father was giving him half of their farm. The Johnsons' farm had always been one of the most prosperous in the area, so it made perfect sense to Ginny that George would want her to be his wife and bear his strong, strapping sons to help run his portion of the land.

Ginny began throwing herself at George with more and more abandon as spring term was winding down. She would wait for him after class at the bottom of the stairs and hold out her books, giving him little choice but to ask if he could carry them for her. The first time it had happened, he had caught Sarah looking at him with an unreadable expression, but when he had taken Ginny's books, she narrowed her eyes and turned around, never looking back.

Soon his accompanying Ginny home had become routine, and Sarah stopped going to the fishing hole after her schoolwork and chores so she wouldn't have to see him. She also wouldn't look him in the eye anymore at school. Meanwhile, George was becoming more and more desperate for her to know that he was not happy about the current situation, but she never gave him the opportunity to get her alone to explain.

Two weeks before the term let out for the year, Sarah was walking toward the schoolhouse when she saw her sister standing on the side of the building, mere inches from George, laughing up into his face and running her finger seductively down the buttons of his shirt. Her stomach lurched as she noticed that he didn't exactly seem upset about the situation, either. In fact, if anything, he looked thrilled as he was smiling back down at her. Sarah decided then to just divert her eyes and pay them no attention. Her heart didn't listen, though, as with the jar of every step, it felt like it was ripping just a little further apart.

As she got closer to the steps, she overheard some of Ginny's friends talking scandalously about what was happening between George and her sister.

"Well, Samuel told me, in the strictest of confidence mind you, that George told him that he's in love with one of the White girls," Ellen said.

"Ginny told me at the church picnic last Sunday that she's fully prepared to ruin herself with him if that is what it takes to seal the deal," Mary replied.

There was a sharp gasp as all the girls considered the implications of what Mary had just said.

"They certainly look cozy enough that one might assume she already has," tittered Claire. "It is positively disgraceful how they're carrying on over there in full view of everyone. If she is that demonstrative with him in public, in front of schoolchildren, no less, can you imagine what they must be getting up to when they're alone?"

Chastising herself for being so stupid, Sarah forced herself to keep walking, her eyes downcast to hide the fact they were filling with tears, her heart broken, while kicking herself for never telling George how she felt about him. She also lamented that it wouldn't have mattered, anyway; she was nowhere nearly as beautiful as Ginny, so she knew she never stood a chance, regardless. Determinedly, she resigned herself to the fact that he had only ever cared about her as a friend, like a kid sister, and then stoically tried to convince herself that if she truly loved him, she only wanted him to be happy.

When the school term ended, Sarah continued to avoid George as much as she could. However, he continued to study her intently, especially whenever Ginny was not with him. Meanwhile, Sarah would always miss the look of longing in his eyes when he gazed at her, until one day at the mercantile, she just happened to glance up in his direction. He was so handsome that even though it was extremely painful to do so, she couldn't stop herself from habitually staring at him when she thought he wasn't looking. Thus far, she had been able to do so without

10

anyone noticing, but that day, when she gazed at him, she lingered a second too long, and their eyes locked. He gave her a weak smile and quickly turned away, hoping to hide the reaction she was evoking in him, emotionally and physically. Sarah looked down in embarrassment at being caught but was also trying to hide the desire rising up in her, having no idea that George was fighting the urge to sweep her up in his arms and kiss her in front of God and the entire town with everything he had. Sarah quickly turned on her heel and left.

That night at dinner, Sarah's father asked her if she would mind heading to the fishing hole the next day to catch some fish. She reluctantly agreed, after reassuring herself that George would be too busy on his newly acquired plot of land to break away and go there in the middle of the day. Then, she said nothing more for the rest of the evening, especially after Ginny proudly announced to the family that Samuel had told her that George was getting ready to ask if he could court her.

Sarah did her chores the following day, trying to appease her nerves before making her way down to the pond. She was relieved at first when the pond looked deserted that she had been correct in her assumption that George wouldn't be there, only to have her heart skip a beat just a second later when she saw him. She was starting to turn around when he called out to her, "Sarah?"

There was something in his voice, a sort of unsaid plea, that made her stop.

"Sarah? Please, Sarah, don't go! I have been wanting to talk to you for so long…"

She sighed deeply and began to pick her way carefully down the embankment, her anger rising with every footfall. As she got closer to him, her temper flared.

"Why? So that you could tell me you're going to ask my sister to court you? I'm surprised you would even care, seeing how she has already ruined herself with you!"

As she spoke the last sentence, his eyes widened in shock. He stood dumbfounded, unable to speak. She continued to walk toward him, fire in her eyes, until she was directly in front of him. He stood as if he was frozen in place until he reached up suddenly, grabbing her to him, before kissing her long and passionately.

When she recovered her wits about her, she pulled back and smacked him across the face… hard.

"How dare you!" she spat at him, her anger and frustration boiling over. "Do you think I intend to ruin myself with you, too?"

"No," he answered quietly. "I intend to make you my wife."

Now it was Sarah who was dumbstruck. She felt as if her brain was incapable of forming coherent connections; that she was rendered not only speechless but also unable to act.

"Sarah, I don't love Ginny. I never have. I only love you! *You* are all I have wanted since I was ten years old. You! No one else! I never intended to court anyone else, and I most certainly never had anyone ruin themselves with me. The only person I intend to do those things with is you, after we are married. All I have been waiting for is for you to come of age."

Sarah found her voice, "But Ginny said that Samuel told her that you were going to ask to court her next week."

He emphatically shook his head. "No! What I said to Samuel was that I was going to ask a White girl to court me. He never asked me which one! I was going to wait to ask you until you turn sixteen next week, because I figured your pa wouldn't let you court anyone before that. But after seeing you in the mercantile, I couldn't wait any longer to speak to you."

"So, you want me?" Sarah squeaked, still unable to fully grasp all that was happening.

"Sarah, you're the only one I have ever wanted. I love you! I want to marry you, and together we will build a farm and family to be proud of. I know you're still too young to marry, but like I said, I was planning on asking your pa next week if I may court you. I reckoned we could go together until you turn seventeen, and then I will ask for your hand."

"But what about Ginny?" Sarah's mind was still ten steps behind.

"I don't want Ginny! I don't love Ginny! I love you, Sarah White. You!" With that, he grabbed her again and kissed her with all the pent-up frustration and desire he had felt for her for as long as he could remember. His hand went behind her head as he held her in place to fit with his lips. His other hand was tucked firmly around her thin waist, pulling her tight up against his muscular physique. At first, she was unsure of what to do, but then she heard her pole and bucket hit the ground as she let go of them to wrap her hands around his body, running them up and down his back as he bent over her.

She wasn't sure how or was even aware that they had made it to the ground until several minutes later when they came up for air. She was surprised to find herself on her back, George laying prone beside her, both of them breathing hard. He leaned forward and touched his forehead to hers as he panted, "These will be the longest two years of my life!"

Chapter Two

Several things happened in the days between Sarah and George's kiss by the pond and her birthday, but Sarah was unaware. She felt as if her feet had not touched the ground in days, and any time anyone wanted her attention they had to say her name several times before she realized that she was being addressed. Her heart felt as though it would fly out of her chest whenever she thought about him, and when she recalled their kiss, she would absentmindedly rub her finger along her bottom lip, while feeling what could only be described as butterflies in her stomach. She could not believe that he wanted her, that he had declared his love for her. Her only worry was what would happen when Ginny found out.

She didn't have to wait long. On the evening of her birthday, she was surprised to walk into the house and see George sitting on the family's settee in the parlor in his Sunday best, sipping lemonade and looking very nervous. Her mother had sent her on an errand to town at the behest of her father, who had invited the young man as a surprise, and she was mortified that he had seen her state when she had gotten back. Her face was red and sweaty from the oppressive summer heat and her hair was falling from its knot at the back of her head. She hurriedly placed the basket with the items from the mercantile on the counter in the kitchen and then instinctively ran her hands over her hair, trying to push the unruly pieces off her face. It was obvious to her that she must look a fright, but by the expression on George's face, one would think that he had never seen anything more beautiful in his life.

Ginny was talking a mile a minute to him, still completely unaware that he was not the least bit interested in her, when he stood up and quickly crossed the room to Sarah, taking her fingers in his and lifting them to his lips. Ginny stopped speaking mid-sentence as her eyes narrowed in realization and anger about what she was witnessing. However, Mr. Miller was quick to jump in and explain, "Sarah, George came over here to speak to me about something a few days ago, and I decided to invite him to your birthday supper. I hope that you don't mind."

George knew at that moment from whom Sarah had inherited her spunk, as well as the mischievous twinkle in her eyes.

"No, sir, I don't mind at all. It's good to see you again, Mr. Johnson," she said, her eyes sparkling and the corners of her mouth tipping up slightly in delight that she was seeing him. Out of the corner of her eye, she could see that Ginny's face looked like thunder; her expression made it abundantly clear she was furious with this recent development.

"Well, given what George has been telling me, you are already aware of the fact that he would like to court you, then, I take it?"

"Yes, sir," she answered, watching Ginny silently seething in the corner.

"And I also gather from his and my recent discussion that you're agreeable to this proposition?"

Sarah merely nodded, her eyes not leaving George's face, her heart leaping at the silly, undignified grin on his lips, his elation openly apparent. "Yes, sir," she said. "I'm absolutely agreeable to the proposition. Thrilled, in fact."

"Well, then, there you have it. I expect to be seeing you around these parts quite a bit more in the near future, Mr. Johnson."

"Yes, sir!" George answered, glancing at Sarah's father briefly before returning his gaze to hers.

"All right, then, you two, since all is in order, let's eat!" Mr. White rose up off the armchair in which he was sitting and clapped his hands together as if an important matter had been settled and all was well.

The evening was wonderful and horrible at the same time. George and Sarah sat next to each other, exchanging small smiles and private looks between them. Meanwhile, Ginny sat across the table, shooting daggers with her eyes at both of them and taking every opportunity to tell unflattering stories about her sister. As the evening progressed, Sarah became almost frantic with worry that George would realize she wasn't worth the trouble Ginny was inevitably going to cause for the both of them as payback for her humiliation. At one point, after Ginny had made yet another cutting remark about Sarah, she looked into George's face with horror, to which he responded with a tight smile. However, he also reached down and found her hand hanging limply at her side in defeat, grabbing it to deliver a firm squeeze of solidarity and comfort, his eyes telling her all she needed to know: he loved her, and no one was going to be able to say or do anything to change that.

After dessert and tea, Sarah got up to escort George out the door for his lonely walk home. While her mother and sister washed the dishes, her father sat down in his chair, lit his pipe, and with a quick wink to her, raised his paper high above his face, effectively blocking his view of their goodbye, giving them privacy where there was none.

"Goodnight, Sarah. Happy birthday!" George said quietly as she opened the door and he stepped out, turning back to face her.

"Goodnight!" she replied.

He reached down and grabbed her fingers, intertwining his with hers. Looking back over her shoulder to ensure that her father was still shielded behind her, she quickly leaned forward and reached up to peck him on the lips. As he loomed over her, a smile spread lazily across his features as he realized what she had done. Ducking down to sweep his lips across her cheek, he paused close to her ear, whispering, "I love you, Sarah White," which sent excited shivers down her spine.

Behind his paper, Mr. White cleared his throat, giving them a second's warning before he lowered it and said pointedly, "Goodnight, Mr. Johnson!"

"Goodnight, sir!" George answered somewhat sheepishly, realizing that their goodbye had perhaps dragged on a bit longer than what might be deemed appropriate. However, he held onto

16

her fingers as long as he could, letting them slide slowly through his hand, unwilling to give up contact with her until the last possible second.

The summer passed quickly, with Sarah and George stealing as many private moments as they could together. They would walk to and from church arm in arm, dawdling behind her parents just enough that they could even steal a quick kiss around a corner or up a hill. Sarah's parents were aware of what they were doing but figured no harm could come from a few stolen seconds of intimacy. But their trips to their fishing hole were quickly curtailed, and they both felt the loss very deeply. They were, however, permitted to sit together in the warm, sultry evenings on the porch to talk, and every once in a while, even hold hands, but it wasn't the same as they were used to. Not only were they both very much aware of the fact that Sarah's parents were keeping a watchful eye over them, but Ginny was also often lurking where she was not wanted as a way to demonstrate her displeasure at what she perceived as George's snub of her in favor of her younger and less attractive sister.

Their saving grace came in the early fall, when the girls' older brother, Matthew, came home with his new sweetheart, a beautiful girl named Ruby McAllister, and her brother, Jacob, as their chaperone for the journey. Jacob and Matthew had met first when Matthew had left for Chicago and gotten a job at the bank where Jacob, who worked as a manager for the railroad, often came in to conduct business. The two men had hit it off, and eventually, Matthew had met Ruby when he was invited to their house in a thinly veiled attempt to bring them together. Matthew had ultimately asked if he could court Ruby, and then for her hand, which she had gladly accepted, leading them to take the journey to introduce her to Matthew's folks before the wedding, scheduled for late June the next summer.

Ginny had taken one look at Jacob and promptly forgotten all about George Johnson. While George was good-looking and had a farm, Jacob was dashing and sophisticated, had good employment, and was college educated. It hadn't taken long before Jacob was taking full advantage of his ability to travel the rails cheaply through his job and spending many weekends at the White's house, before asking the girls' father for his blessing in asking for Ginny's hand, which had been happily given.

Suddenly, the White household went from having three single children to two young adults who were soon to be married. Meanwhile, George was growing increasingly impatient to make Sarah his wife, and had secretly begun to build a small house, tucked away in a grove of trees on his property gifted to him by his father. He figured he would build it slowly when he had the time so that it would be ready when he would formally ask for Sarah's hand. However, once the crops were in for the year, he felt the need to hurry to enclose the little structure with walls, a roof, and floors before the snow fell, so that he could concentrate on working inside during the coldest winter months. It had all gone much quicker than he had anticipated, and as the Christmas holiday grew near, he was finding it harder and harder to leave Sarah each night, especially knowing that by the end of spring, he would have a home ready for his new bride but would have to wait another year to bring her there. He made up his mind to approach her father to ask his permission to propose to her on the holiday in hopes that he could carry her across the threshold by late summer at the latest. Whenever he thought of her, the idea of having to wait another full year after asking for her hand was too much to bear. He knew she would not be done with school by that point, but he figured that since he had his own plot of land and his family's farm was one of the most profitable in the area, he would be able to convince her parents that her certificate of completion would not be necessary. He was confident that he would always be able to provide a comfortable life for her.

Therefore, two weeks before Christmas, George brought Sarah's father to his farm and showed him what he had constructed. The man admired the fine workmanship and intricate details, such as a built-in pantry complete with a series of pull-out compartments of varying sizes for dry goods, from

18

flour to rice, to the large feather mattress on the bedstead than he had constructed himself.

"Well, George, this is a fine place you have built here, son."

"Thank you, sir."

"Are you living here now?"

George shook his head. "No, sir. Not yet. I don't want to live here without Sarah. I want this to be our home, not mine into which she will move. I built this for us. It just wouldn't feel right living here without her."

"I must say that I'm surprised, George, that you took this upon yourself now when you know that Sarah has the rest of this year and the next to complete in school before she will be able to marry you."

"Yes, sir. But that's what I wanted to speak to you about," George blurted before he lost his nerve. "I wanted to ask if you would allow me to marry her this summer instead of next? I'm fully running my own farm here and would very much love to have her by my side."

"I understand, but she still has a ways to go in school. Her mother and I feel it is important for her to finish her education."

"And I respect that, sir. Really, I do. But," George took in a deep breath before continuing. "I also wonder to what end, sir?"

"What do you mean?"

"I mean that I have the ability to support her, so I see no need for her to finish. She already knows how to read, write, and figure sums. Her place will be with me, together here in our home, raising our young ones and helping out on the farm. I guess that I see her certificate as unnecessary to be my wife and the mother to my children. I intend to take care of her until the day I die."

"But George, that's the issue. What would she be able to do without her certificate in case something were to happen to you? How would she support herself?"

"That's not going to happen, sir!" George said determinedly. He wasn't even going to entertain the idea that they would have anything less than a long, prosperous life together.

"You never know, George. There are no guarantees in this life."

"With all due respect, sir, I'm aware that there are no guarantees in life, but her certificate wouldn't allow her any more opportunity to support herself in case of my demise than she would have without it. There are no professions which require certification open to a woman who is a widow with children."

Mr. White thought for a few minutes, pondering what the young man had said. After what felt like an eternity to George, he spoke again.

"I suppose you're right in that. I can't think of any reputable profession which would allow her to work in those circumstances, either. Therefore, if you're sure, and she's agreeable, you may marry this summer. I can't really imagine she would learn that much more in her final year than what she already knows, anyway."

George was so elated he wanted to hug her father with joy. However, he instead stuck out his hand, offering it to the other man, who met him in a hearty handshake.

On Christmas morning, George arrived to walk with Sarah's family to church. Sarah was giggling most of the way about the smirk he had lighting up his face, but every time she would ask him why he was so giddy, he would merely squeeze her hand. After the service concluded, he came home with her family and spent the rest of the day with them. When it was time to read the Christmas story from the Bible aloud, Sarah was surprised when her father broke with tradition and asked George to read it instead of him, and she found herself being lulled into a sleepy stupor as she listened to his deep baritone voice washing over her. She felt completely at ease and at peace.

Jacob McAllister was also visiting the family, wanting to spend the holiday with his fiancée. He and George had hit it off nicely, and they seemed to enjoy each other's company. Since

Ginny was now enamored of Jacob and no longer felt slighted by George, the sisters had begun to repair their relationship, as well. A few weeks earlier, citing Sarah's extraordinary sewing skills, Ginny had even asked her to sew her wedding dress fashioned off one she had crudely sketched on a visit to a bridal boutique in Chicago when she had gone to meet Jacob's family, and Sarah had graciously accepted. All of the White women were decent seamstresses, but Sarah truly had a gift for not only the construction of a gown, but also the designing of one. Many of her personal creations had roused quite a stir in town through the years, even to the point of people asking her to make things for them. So far, she had resisted, but it was nice to feel appreciated for her craft. So, on the cold, windy Christmas day, the two young women sat with their mother at the family's dining table, their heads close together as they pored over Ginny's drawings and Sarah's patterns. After several hours of the men talking before the fire while the women communed over the styles and materials, Sarah felt a hand on her shoulder. She looked up in surprise and saw George standing smiling above her.

"Enjoying yourself?" he asked.

"Yes," she replied quietly. "Are you?"

"Yes. Very much so." George took a deep breath before continuing. "I suppose you're designing your wedding dress?" he inquired, his eyes sparkling.

Sarah looked at him strangely for a second, wondering to what he was referring. "No, we're working on Ginny's. I don't need one right now," she said, feeling slightly confused. They were courting, not engaged.

"I wouldn't be so sure about that," he stated, getting down on one knee before her, while grabbing a small box out of his pocket at the same time. "Sarah White, I love you and want to build a life with you. Would you be my wife?"

Her hands flew to her mouth in shocked amazement as she glanced around and saw her family gathered all around them.

"But… what in the world? What is going on?" she asked, looking to her father to gauge his reaction.

"I spoke with your father, and he has agreed to let us marry this summer, if you're game?" George said, still on the floor, now having opened the red velvet box to reveal a thin gold band with an opal on the top.

"But what about school?" she asked, confused.

"You are over sixteen, my dear, so if you would like to stop, you're legally free and clear to do so," her father told her. "Of course, if you want to continue for your final year, you may do that, too, and this will just be a really long engagement." He then looked pointedly in George's direction, his expression telling him in no uncertain terms that the decision about whether to marry sooner rather than later would be entirely hers.

"Sarah, if you want to finish up your last year of school, then I will absolutely wait for you to do so. But as I was telling your father, I don't see a reason why you need to finish. Our farm will provide for us all that we could ever need. I know, though, that I want to marry you, now or later, so if I have to be patient, I will."

Sarah knew that many local children of both genders quit going to school at sixteen, or even earlier, so it was certainly not unheard of to do so. However, her brother and sister had finished, as had George, so she had just assumed that she would, too. On the other hand, she knew that George was correct: the trajectory of her life would be one of housewife and mother, not scholar. She was well aware that she already knew all that she would need to know academically in that role, so it seemed foolish to wait another year when her certificate of completion would do nothing for her other than to feed her own vanity. She reasoned with herself that in all actuality, being George's wife and the mother to his children would give her far more to be proud of than a piece of paper ever would.

She met George's eyes and saw the desire that smoldered in there, just for her, and she remembered how he had made her feel on the bank of the pond several months back, a shiver then racing down her spine as she realized what all being George's wife would entail.

She then turned to her father and said, "Honestly, I would rather marry this summer. I won't need that certificate for anything important."

She then saw the look of joy that crossed over George's face when he realized what she had said. He grabbed her hand and slipped the ring over her knuckle as she stared down at her finger, now adorned with the outward symbol of George's claiming her for his own, and she couldn't feel prouder, or more importantly, lucky.

Ginny quickly grabbed her hand and drew it closer to her face. "Oh, that's a nice ring. Not a diamond like mine, but it will do for country life!"

Sarah pulled her hand back and looked at George. "I think it is the most beautiful thing I have ever seen," she said sweetly. In all honesty, she wouldn't have cared if it had been a piece of baling wire he had twisted together. He wanted her!

Chapter Three

The rest of the school year went quickly as the White household prepared for three weddings in the upcoming summer. Sarah was kept busy between her schooling, her work on the farm, and the sewing of her and Ginny's dresses. Ginny helped, but it quickly became apparent that Sarah had a special gift for maneuvering the expensive materials into something exquisite. She only saw George on the weekends when he would come calling for walks or buggy rides, and on Sundays, as he would always accompany her to church.

George had also purchased a buggy, and it hadn't taken long for the couple to discover that in it they could steal private moments together. When he came for her, they would always drive his team far away from any settlements, where they could picnic privately. As their wedding drew near, their need for each other grew, and many an afternoon was passed lying next to each other in the tall meadow grasses, reading poetry, or kissing and holding one another.

As Sarah's body grew more accustomed to George's caresses, she became more brazen in her attempts to drive him over the edge. She had quickly discovered what power she had over him, and it thrilled her to see how just the stroke of her hand and the length of their kisses could make him lose all reason.

One day, as they lay in the grass after a particularly exhilarating romp, her head on his chest and her arm slung over him, George finally realized what she was up to.

"You little vixen!" he exclaimed as she pushed herself off him and grinned at his half-shut eyes and dreamy expression before settling back down onto his warm body. "You're going to kill me, sweetheart!"

"How so?" she asked innocently, running her finger up the buttons of his shirt, then palming her open hand against his chest.

"You know how!" he answered, lifting his head a little, looking her in the eye, then kissing the top of her head.

"Why, Mr. Johnson!" she declared, opening her eyes wide in mock innocence. "I have no idea what you're talking about!"

"Oh, you don't, do you?" he asked, propping himself up on his elbows just a bit, causing her to roll down his body slightly. "Somehow, I don't believe that. I think you know *exactly* what you're doing, and furthermore, I think you're enjoying it!"

"And what would that be?" she asked, her eyes sparkling.

"Let me show you," he said as he took her hand and placed it on the front of his trousers. He then laughed at her shocked expression before leaning in for a kiss.

"George!" she exclaimed, genuinely stunned at what he had done. She had been enjoying making him squirm, but he had taken it to the next level. Moreover, she was shocked at what she felt under the material.

"What is it, sweetheart?" It was his turn to sound innocent.

"I… Well, I shouldn't… We shouldn't…" she stuttered.

"Shouldn't what?" he probed, his smile reaching all the way up to his eyes.

"I shouldn't… you know… touch you… there," she mumbled, her face turning red as her eyes automatically drifted downward.

"Why not?" he questioned her.

"Because we aren't yet married!" she explained stupidly, as if he didn't know.

"So?" he responded in a seductive tone.

"So?" she retorted, sounding exasperated.

"It isn't… proper!" she stumbled on to explain.

He threw his head back and laughed, pulling her tighter into his body. "No, I suppose it isn't," he solemnly agreed.

He then sat up and put his mouth right at her ear as he whispered, "But neither were those open mouth kisses you were giving me." His lips then delved down her neck, excruciatingly slowly, making her gasp.

"I think…" she whispered breathlessly, "I think… I think we need to head home."

"Why?" he inquired into the crook of her neck, nipping and sucking gently at the skin he could reach above the collar of her dress.

"Because otherwise, I think we may get into trouble," she moaned.

"What kind of trouble?" he prodded as his lips brushed along her cheekbone.

"You know what kind of trouble!" she whispered earnestly back to him.

"Is there any chance of that?" he tested, his voice low with a mix of humor and something else she couldn't quite discern. Whatever it was, though, she felt it down deep, all the way to her core.

"George!" she huffed at him, surprised.

Sensing her rising distress, he sat up and took her hands in his while he looked into her eyes. "I'm sorry, Sarah. I'm getting carried away. But no, there honestly isn't any chance of that happening yet. I won't let it. But I will admit that as we are only two months away from getting married, it's getting harder and harder to wait!"

"I know," she agreed, having felt the same way for a while. She just hadn't dared to voice it.

He leaned forward and placed his forehead on hers, while still clasping both of her hands in his, as he quietly confessed, "I do find myself thinking of and anticipating it more every day."

"Me, too!" she confided to him quite unabashedly, wishing desperately that they could just let themselves get lost in the moment.

He suddenly stood up determinedly and then offered his hand to help her. "I think the fact that you're leaving for Chicago next week for half a month isn't helping, either. Tell me again why we agreed to get married after both Matthew's and Ginny's weddings?"

26

"Well, you know the stink Ginny caused when she found out we wanted to marry first because she's older. And Matthew... Well, Matthew's at the mercy of his fiancée's plans. As he wrote to Mama, he just knows when and where he's supposed to show up and stand."

"I know. I'm just getting impatient! I wish that we would have fought your sister on her outlandish ideas instead of just going along with them. She's never happy unless the focus is on her!"

"George, you know as well as I do that it just isn't worth the fight."

"That's what you think!" he complained under his breath, making her smile.

She laughed softly at his response before answering him, "I promise you won't die from a few more weeks of waiting!"

"And if I do?"

"You won't!"

"But if I do? Just think of how long I have wanted you and all that wasted time!"

Sarah leaned over to him and put her head on his shoulder, reaching up to put a hand on his cheek, whispering, "I promise it will be worth the wait!"

He bent down and kissed her gently, slowly, before pulling back and saying, "I have no doubt about that, Sarah. I've been looking forward to that day for as long as I can remember."

"It would have been easier if you could come with me, but I know you can't get away from the farm. I don't want to leave you at home, but I don't want to miss my brother's wedding, either!"

"I know, Sarah," he answered seriously. "I'm just anxious to start our lives together! I am more than ready to call you my wife."

"And you will! I promise!"

Soon, it was August. Sarah's family's trip to Chicago had passed, albeit agonizingly slowly, but George had been waiting for her on the platform with a bouquet of wildflowers in hand upon her return. In the next few weeks, the flurry had instead shifted to Ginny and all of her desires for a perfect wedding. Soon enough, though, her trunks were packed to send her on her honeymoon, and then on to her new life in Chicago.

Sarah and her parents were then suddenly alone, and the quiet was deafening. Her mother and father were grateful that after all the hullabaloo, Sarah was satisfied with a simple country wedding, accented more by friends and family than any frills.

The night before their ceremony, George finally took Sarah to their new home, secretly and lovingly constructed as a wedding surprise. As they pulled up in front of the little house hidden within the trees, George laughed with relief when he saw her hands come together in delight as it dawned on her what she was seeing. She threw herself into his arms, exclaiming with joy at what he had created. She had asked him periodically about where they would live in the months since their engagement, but he had always been cryptic to the point that she began to worry that they were going to be living in a room of his parents' house. Relief now washed over her as her eyes sparkled in appreciation of the effort George had put forth, and she could hardly stop herself from tumbling out of the buggy before he stopped the team so he could come around to help her down.

They walked up the front steps and over the porch. Then Sarah let out a little squeak of surprise when George lifted her legs out from under her into his arms.

"What are you doing?" she cried breathlessly.

"Why, I'm carrying my bride over the threshold, of course," he responded as if it was the most natural thing in the world to do.

"But we aren't married yet!" she objected.

"Maybe so, but I'll just carry you over again tomorrow, anyway, so don't worry. No wife of mine is going to walk through the doorway of our home together for the first time, though, regardless. Now, close your eyes!" he ordered playfully, and she complied, turning her face into his neck as he reached the doorknob and twisted it open. She couldn't help but give his neck several small kisses while she was there, causing him to inhale sharply.

"All righty, then, sweetheart. You need to stop that before I drop you!" he exclaimed.

"Fine!" she told him, a pout evident in her voice.

"There will be plenty of time for that tomorrow, young lady, don't you worry. Right now, though, I want you to take a look at your new home!"

George gently placed her feet on the ground and held her steady until she got acclimated. Her utter delight was evident on her face as her eyes took in every small detail.

"Now, I know it needs a woman's touch…" he started in.

"Nonsense! I love it!" she broke him off.

His relief was evident. "I'm so happy you like it! My ma and sister made curtains and such, but it still needs you to make it feel like home to me."

He took her hand and led her around, showing her all the ins and outs of his unique and well-planned designs. Sarah was shocked at the amount of detail he had devoted to the project, and when she told him as much, he had merely blushed and explained suggestively that it had been a long, lonely winter.

Shyly, he took her hand and led her down a hallway, passing several closed doors along the way. When they came to the last one, he stopped and took a deep breath.

"This is our room. Do you want to see it now, or wait until tomorrow?"

Sarah didn't answer right away, suddenly feeling bashful, as she realized exactly what "our room" would entail. Both blushing deeply, they stood shoulder to shoulder in silence for several seconds, facing the door together. After what seemed like an agonizingly long time, Sarah figured she was going to have to be the brave one, so she stretched out her hand to the knob as she exclaimed, "Let's see it now!"

When she walked in, she gasped in surprise. Right in front of them was the large, inviting bed, fluffy and clean, beckoning to her. She dropped his hand and ran toward it, flinging herself over the mattress, landing in the middle with a satisfying "whoosh" as the quilts, sheets, and mattress all bubbled up around her, making her disappear from view for a few seconds. George could hear her laughing as she scrambled to push herself out of the bedding so she could see him and when she succeeded, he could only laugh at her hair that had spilled out of her topknot and was hanging loosely about her face until she took a hand and pushed it back off her forehead.

"Oh, do come up here with me!" she declared in delight.

"Uh, I don't think that's wise," he answered her wistfully.

"Oh?"

"I think I had just better stand here," he told her with a peculiar look on his face.

"Come on, George, I won't bite!" she teased.

"All right," he relented, realizing that deep down, there was nowhere else he would rather be than with her on their big bed.

He climbed up beside her and sat down. She took his hand, and together they sank down into the pillows, still holding hands and looking up at the ceiling for a long time, neither of them speaking. Finally, he squeezed her hand, and she propped herself up on her elbows to study the rest of the room.

On the outside wall stood a grand fireplace, ready for the cold, snowy nights they would spend together. There was also a good-sized wardrobe and two dressers for their things. A looking glass hung over her dresser, which was long and low, so that she could put out her toiletries and be able to see what she was doing while getting ready every morning. On either side of the big bed were small tables, just big enough for a lamp, a glass of water and perhaps a book, each with one tiny drawer. The space between the bed and fireplace was covered with a brightly colored woven rag rug, and the mantle above the fireplace was a darkly stained, roughly hued log.

As she looked around in awe, she grasped his hand again and exclaimed, "I love it! Oh, George, it is amazing! I can't believe you built all of this just for us!"

30

"I'm so glad you like it!" he answered, the relief evident in his tone. "I know that I can't give you a fancy church wedding in a cathedral or a diamond ring, but I can give you a sturdy home for us to build our family."

"It's perfect," she whispered, as she moved her head closer to him, his lips calling to her to be kissed. Together, they sank back down into the pillows, neither of them paying much attention until the room had grown significantly darker as the day drew to a close. George eventually looked up to notice the darkening shadows in the room and declared it was time to leave, as she whimpered into his neck, not wanting to let him go.

"I want to stay here with you forever," she pleaded.

"Tomorrow, sweetheart! I promise," he reassured her, while peeling her arms from around his neck, and bringing them down to her sides.

Reluctantly, they rose together off the bed, each of them instead longing to crawl under the covers and hold the other tight. They then silently straightened the quilts and fluffed the pillows, giving the bed the pristine, untouched look, it had a few hours prior, before they had lain together on it.

George gently took her hand and led her outside, shutting the door tightly behind him. "All set until tomorrow!" he declared with finality.

"Won't you stay there tonight, George?" Sarah asked in surprise.

"No," he answered emphatically.

"Why ever not? I figured you were already living there," she said.

"Because I want this to be our home," he explained to her, making her heart soar at his sweet declaration of love. "I know I'm not a romantic man, full of many charming words, but I want that tomorrow, when we open this door, it will be the start of our new life together. I want us both to leave our mark on this place, so it belongs to us from the start."

"You are truly the sweetest man I could ever hope to meet!" Sarah exclaimed, joy bubbling up inside of her as she counted

down the hours until they were joined together until death did
they part.

Chapter Four

Sarah's wedding day dawned bright and warm, the air feeling sultry with high humidity. As she stepped out the door in the morning to gather eggs, it felt as if the earth had decided to wrap her in its embrace until George's arms could envelop her later that night.

Her mother had told her that she didn't need to do the chores, seeing how it was her last day at home, but somehow, it only felt fitting that she would do as she normally would in her childhood home one more time before embarking on her new journey as her own woman and a wife.

The wedding was scheduled for two in the afternoon, and by that time, the air had changed to oppressive. Sarah fanned herself incessantly, trying desperately to keep herself cool beneath all the layers of clothing she had put on her body. Her chemise and drawers were stuck to her form, feeling as if they had fused with her skin. She begged her mother to please not pull her stays too tightly, stating dramatically that she wouldn't be able to breathe, and her mother had for once taken pity on her, perhaps realizing that her daughter wasn't exaggerating. However, it was more likely that the physical exertion her mother would use to cinch her in seemed entirely unconscionable in the heat. Whatever the reason, Sarah was grateful for the extra room to expand her lungs and knew that her dress would fit just as well, regardless. Her slip and petticoat were next, followed by the white skirt and bodice she had carefully sewn out of precious silk. She knew her mother and father had spent a small fortune on the material for both her and Ginny's dresses that summer, but they had assured her that they had no need to spend the money on anything else. Her father had sweetly explained that their last gift to her was that she would have a dress as fine as any of the girls in Chicago, or even New York City, especially since she had as much talent as all those big city seamstresses, anyhow. Sarah had hugged him tightly and thanked him profusely for their generosity.

By the time she and her parents had made it to the church, storm clouds had begun to form in the west. They continued to build upon each other throughout the ceremony, as George and Sarah pledged their lives and love to one another, while all their guests fanned themselves in a futile attempt to escape the sweltering heat. Thankfully, however, the storm held off through the ceremony and the party after.

As the sun sank lower in the sky, it was swallowed by the rising clouds, now black with unshed moisture. The women hurried to cover the dishes they had brought, while the men worked hard at breaking down the tables and chairs that were set up for the reception on the side yard of the church. Everyone finished in the nick of time as the wind started to pick up and the clouds began billowing out across the sky.

"You'd best be getting on home!" Sarah's father hollered to George, while giving his hand to his youngest daughter to help her into the buggy.

"You'll have a devil of a time getting there in time!" her father continued as he leaned over and placed a kiss on her cheek.

"Goodbye, Pa!" she exclaimed as George grabbed the reigns and snapped them to start the horses. "Thank you for a beautiful wedding!" she yelled as the buggy jumped before starting down the lane.

George drove the horses hard, and they made record time to their homestead, but the rain had already started to fall. When they pulled up in front of their house, he turned to her and said, "You go on in out of this rain. I'm going to drive the team as close to the barn as I can, and then I will be in after you just as soon as I get them unhitched and settled."

He then jumped out of the buggy and ran around to her side, giving her his hand to assist her descent off the seat. As she stepped down, she reached up and kissed him chastely on his cheek. "Hurry back!" she told him, calling over her shoulder as she ran up the front steps.

George watched her as she hurried through the door, appreciating how the rain had soaked her dress so that it clung to her lithe form. He shook his head out of his reverie, while uttering a soft swear word, and set out to attend to the horses in record time. After unhitching them, he brought them in, and hastily wiped off the excess water on their coats, making sure that they had ample amounts of fresh straw, water, and feed for the night before shutting the barn door firmly behind him. Guilt gnawed at him that he should take more care, so he promised himself that he would do a more thorough job in the morning. For now, though, he could think of nothing more than his new bride awaiting him in the house, wet and cold, longing for him to come in and warm her, and warm her he fully intended to do.

When he came through the door, he shed his boots and looked around the room. Sarah had lit several of the kerosene lamps around the place, but what caught his attention instead was the trail of wet women's clothing he found scattered from where she first left her shoes right by the door, to her dress, then her corset, and so forth, down the hall leading into their bedroom, ending with her stockings in a sopping pile on the rag rug. He looked curiously up and saw her already in their bed, with the covers pulled up tight over her shoulders.

Not sure of her current state of dress, he quickly began to shed his clothes under her watchful stare as the lightning flashed around them. They both felt their cheeks redden, but he was too motivated by desire to truly care that she was staring at him. He held her gaze, feeling his longing bubble up in him as he watched her face change from embarrassment to inquisitiveness to finally wonder as she observed him naked for the first time. When he was finished, he didn't hesitate to lift the quilts up on his side and slide in beside her.

"Hello," he breathed, shocked, but pleased to find her naked, silky legs rubbing up against him. He pulled her to him and was delighted to feel that her whole body was unclothed and waiting for him as she quickly settled into his arms with a satisfied sigh while the thunder cracked overhead.

Sarah had seen naked males before. Growing up in a small farmhouse with both a brother and a father, it was sometimes hard to avoid, especially on bath nights. However, her breath caught in her throat as she realized that George was truly a fine specimen of a man. She had felt herself grow flushed and warm all over with anticipation as she had watched him strip his clothing from his body. Now that he was beside her, she could feel the intense heat radiating from him and couldn't help but to sink further back into him, his arms engulfing her, and she smiled as she felt his hands begin to roam. His hand ran up and down her side, over her thigh up to the side of her breast. Soon he got bolder, reaching out to cup her breast in his hand, and when he then began to gently massage it, Sarah heard herself moan softly. She looked back over her shoulder, taking his lips in hers, and it didn't take long until he was carefully turning her onto her back. She felt his hands begin to wander over her chest and abdomen as he enthusiastically explored her body beneath his careful touch while every few seconds the room exploded in brilliant bursts of light. He took both hands and placed them lightly over each breast, cautiously watching her expression as he ran his thumbs over their crests and felt her reaction.

"Is this all right?" he whispered, somehow feeling in his awe it was the only appropriate way to communicate, to which she couldn't even formulate a coherent response, but rather heard herself offer a quiet whimper. She then reached for him as a sly, almost naughty smile crept over his features.

"Good?" he asked her. Feeling shy, she merely nodded into his neck as he had leaned down to kiss her.

"Sarah, you're so incredibly beautiful!" he breathed out before sinking his inviting mouth against hers once more, gently separating her lips as he slid his tongue inside. She sighed and wrapped her hands tightly around his back, worrying that she had no idea what to expect or how to proceed, and hoping that he did.

36

George eventually had found his way over the top of her, and she clung to him, at times digging her nails into his back as he nibbled softly on the skin directly below her ear. He had been straddling her hips, but as things became more intense, she was surprised to discover he was now between her knees, and she was astonished that her body knew exactly what to do to accommodate him.

"Are you all right?" he inquired quietly, his voice low and husky.

"Yes," she tried to assure him with more confidence than what she felt. "I'm fine."

"Good!" he answered her, but his voice sounded strangled.

"Are you?" she asked him.

"Yes!" he answered her with such enthusiasm that she almost began to laugh. She stopped in a hurry, though, when she realized what came next, instead trying to both brace herself and relax at the same time in an attempt to combine the advice of both her mother and her sister.

George then began to move so agonizingly slowly and with such precision that she was amazed. Her body felt as though it were about to explode, and she had no idea how he was able to move so carefully and with so much control. Her focus returned to what came next as she heard him whisper quietly in her ear, "I will try to do this as slowly and carefully as I can. I don't mean to hurt you, my love, and I want you to tell me if I do."

Her heart felt as though it was overflowing with love for him, and she again nodded, her forehead striking his collarbone as he pressed his hips slightly forward, and she discovered he had been telling the truth. He was so gentle that she only felt a slight burn until he was settled and asked her again if she was all right. After affirming she was indeed fine, he began to move, and she lost all coherent thought for a few minutes as she listened to his quiet sounds of desire; his deeply private moans and sighs that would only be privy to her from this day forward. Surprised, she felt a strange surge of power in that realization. No matter how well anyone else knew him, no one would ever know this part of him as she now did. She decided then that this was the true meaning of two becoming one. Even more than sharing their bodies in this manner, it was the wonderfully intimate sounds of pleasure made only for each other. She rubbed his back gently until he suddenly reared up with a long groan of ecstasy before collapsing fully on top of her. After a few minutes of resting with his head on her chest, he rose slightly and gave her a luminous smile that told her everything she needed to know about his feelings regarding the experience. With a satiated sigh, he rolled over and settled beside her, pulling her to him, before smoothing her hair from her forehead and planting a kiss there.

"Thank you, my darling," he told her as he tightened his arms further around her in a squeeze.

"You're welcome," she answered politely, wondering if that was all there was to it, grateful that he was as gentle and caring as he had been.

"Were you terribly uncomfortable?" he asked her, his concern apparent.

"Not terribly," she answered, unsure of how to tell him that while it hadn't been pleasurable for her in the way it had seemed to be for him, she had enjoyed the feelings of closeness and intimacy from the experience.

"I can say that there's no place I would have rather been than with you," she added shyly, not sure if she was fully conveying her meaning, but hoping he would understand that there was no one else with whom she would have wanted to share this experience, both now and forever.

He reached for her hand and gave it a gentle squeeze. "I'm glad," he replied. "I have wanted this… I have wanted you… for so long. It was as wonderful for me as any of my dreams."

***

The summer days went fast and faded into fall as the couple readied for the harvest and all the other preparations needed before the snow began to fly. Soon, they were cozy in their little house and had settled into a routine of sorts that allowed them to grow closer to one another as they built their new life together.

As Christmas came nearer, Sarah began to feel ill. She was tired all the time, and then, just a few days before the holiday, she became violently ill. George, fearing for her health, went and collected her mother to stay with her while he hunted down the doctor.

Sarah's mother gasped when she took in the sight of her daughter wrapped in the quilts on their big bed, with only her head sticking out. Her cheeks were pale, and she had dark circles surrounding her sunken eyes.

"Oh, my poor dear!" her mother exclaimed as she rushed to her bedside. "What's wrong?"

"I don't know!" Sarah wailed, her fear evident in her voice. "I have been so tired and feeling ill. Then, since yesterday, I can't get out of bed without the room spinning and getting sick."

Suddenly, her mother looked at her daughter with a softening expression as her words sank in.

"Sarah?"

"Yes, Mama?"

"When was your last monthly?"

"Oh!" Sarah exclaimed in surprise.

"I don't know, actually," she admitted. "I don't really keep track of such things. Why?"

"I think that what you have will be cured in time… Another six or seven months, to be exact!" her mother explained thoughtfully.

"What do you mean, Mama?"

"Sarah, I think that you are with child."

Sarah's eyes grew big in her already diminished face as the shock overtook her. "Do you really think so?"

Her mother nodded. "I do," she answered confidently. "Once the doctor arrives, I would be amazed if he said anything different."

"A baby? Really?" Sarah couldn't move past her surprise. Of course, she knew that being a wife would most likely lead to her being a mother, and she and George certainly were not shy about enjoying each other at every opportunity. Somehow, though, she was still amazed that the one had led to the other. In her mind, becoming a mother was more dependent on age than activity, and she didn't feel old enough to have it happen to her yet.

"But what will George say?" she fretted, her hands in her lap.

"I'm sure he will be thrilled!" her mother responded. "Every man wants a home full of children, especially a farmer. I guarantee you that he will be over the moon to hear the news."

Just then, the front door opened and then shut quickly, and the women heard the distinct sounds of the two men stomping their feet and removing their boots and jackets. Sarah heard George tell the doctor that he could hang his outerwear on the empty hook behind the door, and then he burst into the bedroom, his concern written indelibly on his handsome face.

"Here she is, doctor," he said, his voice sounding somewhat panicked.

"All right, George," the doctor soothed. "I will see to her now. Why don't you go sit and wait in the parlor while I examine her?"

Sarah saw the look of fear and dread on her husband's face as he wrestled with himself about if it was okay to leave her or not. She tried to give him what she hoped was a reassuring smile but was grateful when her mother took his elbow and spoke gently to him as he allowed her to lead him from the room.

"So, Mrs. Johnson, your husband told me that you have been feeling a bit under the weather?"

"Yes," she responded softly.

"I see. And how long have you been feeling this way, my dear?"

"I'm not sure, exactly. Perhaps a week or so? But the dizziness and nausea weren't horrible until yesterday."

"All right, then, let's take a look," he soothed, reaching for her wrist and holding his fingers there to find her pulse. Next, he took out his apparatus to listen to her heart.

"So, tell me, please, Mrs. Johnson," he asked her, "Is there any time of day where you feel worse or better?"

"I am worst when I wake up," she answered him.

"I see," he replied. "Is there anything that makes it better?"

"Sleeping seems to help."

"That's good. Is it better or worse when you eat?"

"It can be either," she answered. "Doctor?"

"Yes?"

"My mother thinks that I may be with child. Do you think she is correct?"

"I do, Sarah," he answered, smiling gently at her, his eyes gleaming. "I think that is exactly what's wrong with you."

"Oh!" Sarah exclaimed in surprise.

"But Doctor, we haven't been married for that long," she blurted.

The doctor threw his head back and laughed, "Sarah, my dear, you have most certainly been married long enough. All it takes is once, you know!" he answered her good-naturedly.

"Yes, I know," she mumbled, her cheeks blazing.

"Well, now, let's just see how far along you are, then, shall we?" he asked her, and she nodded back to him in response. "When was your last monthly?"

She answered him with the same response she had given her mother. The doctor shook his head and said reproachfully, "Mrs. Johnson, I must advise you that as a married woman, it would behoove you to keep better track of that detail from here on out."

She simply smiled in response, unsure of how to reply, never before having heard a man speak so frankly about monthlies before.

Finally, she calculated back and said, "I think it was right around that first snowstorm at the end of October or beginning of November... You know the one that caught us all by surprise?"

"I do, indeed. And that would put you right about where I thought you were, which is about two months. It is a little late for your sickness to hit you now, but the good news is that most nausea subsides by the end of the third month, so hopefully you will only have a few more weeks of this before you begin to feel better again. Shall we go get your husband? I know he's very worried. Talked my ear off nonstop on the way over here. Definitely not the norm for a Johnson boy!"

"Yes, please," she answered.

While she waited for her husband to return, she began thinking about what the news would mean to her and to them. She hadn't really thought about babies, other than a rather nebulous knowledge that they would eventually come, but for some reason, she hadn't realized that eventually would be so soon. As she heard the doctor's voice in the parlor, followed by George's deeper one as he responded, she began to work herself into a frenzy about if she were old or responsible enough to care entirely for another whole, helpless human being. By the time George's figure appeared in the doorway, her eyes were filling with tears as she realized it really wasn't that long ago that she had been playing with her rag doll and had left her out in the rain, ruining her.

George rushed to her bedside, unaware of what was going on. The doctor had merely told him he could finally go to her, the older man thinking that the news of their impending family should come from her lips and not his.

"Sarah? Sarah, what is it? Why are you crying? Are you so ill?"

She hiccoughed in response, making him smile in spite of himself, realizing that for as long as he had known her, that was what she did when she cried. She then shook her head.

"No, I'm not so ill," she answered, leaving him even more bewildered.

"Then why are you crying?"

"Because, George, we're going to have a baby!"

Sarah watched as the realization of her words sunk in and then as the pure joy spread across his face.

"Really? That's all? How wonderful! I'm so happy!"

"That's all?" she wailed at him. "Whatever do you mean, 'That's all?' Isn't that enough?"

"I didn't mean it like that, Sarah! I meant thank goodness it's something that will soon be remedied, and at the end of it, we will have our first son!"

"Or daughter…" she added quietly.

"Oh! Yes! Well, of course!" he quickly added. "That would be wonderful, too!"

She nodded and looked away.

"Sarah, what is it, my love? Why do you seem unhappy? I thought this is what we wanted: a house full of children to help us on the farm."

"I don't think…" she whispered and then trailed off.

"I'm sorry, sweetheart, I didn't hear you. What did you say? What don't you think?"

"I don't think I'm ready," she said, looking down at her hands in her lap, fiddling with her fingers.

"Why would you not be ready?" he asked her, his confusion evident in his voice.

"Because, George, I'm not even eighteen yet! I have never told you this, but I once left my rag doll out, only to be ruined in the rain! It wasn't even that many years ago… maybe only seven? And it wasn't so long ago that *I* was only seven!" Sarah's voice was rising in pitch as she grew more panicked. "What am I doing having a baby, George? I'm not old enough! I'm not responsible enough! What am I even doing being married, George?"

He struggled to hide his smile at her anxiety. He reached out his hand and with a finger, he gently lifted her chin, so that he could look in her eyes.

"My darling, of course, you're old and responsible enough! Don't forget that I'm even older and more responsible at almost twenty-one," he told her with a grin. "But not only that, your ma and my ma are just a stone's throw away. Between them and me, you will never be alone or without help."

She shook her head solemnly at him, her eyes wide. He gave an exasperated sigh as he reached for her hands and engulfed them in his large ones.

"Did you hear me, sweetheart? I will never leave you alone!"

"Do you promise me?" she whispered, wanting so much to believe it would all be all right.

He leaned down and placed a soft kiss on her forehead. "I promise you, darling. We will grow old together, surrounded by our sons and daughters. I promise I will never leave you."

Chapter Five

Winter moved to spring and then spring became summer. George watched with pride as both his young wife and his fields sprouted and bloomed with new growth. Sarah was quickly over her nausea, as the doctor had predicted, and was soon resigned to the fact that she was going to become a mother sooner rather than later. Miraculously, as her form expanded, so did her joy with the situation.

George worked hard in the fields and tended to the livestock, and as the days grew longer, he began the exhaustive process of calving and lambing. Many nights, Sarah was in bed, asleep, and his dinner held warm on the corner of the stove when he stumbled in after delivering yet another new addition to their livestock. He had joked with Sarah that he was more than prepared to deliver their baby, as well, after having to assist more cows and sheep than he had ever imagined, to which he received a scowl and grunt in response.

"You don't think I could?" he asked, mirth evident in his tired expression.

"Perhaps if I was going to in fact be delivering a calf or maybe a lamb, I would let you try. But as this is a human baby, I would prefer the doctor do it, if you please!"

He had only crossed his arms and huffed out an exaggerated, "Humph!" in response before they both collapsed in giggles.

They spent many a night snuggled together in their warm bed, with his arms wrapped lovingly around her with his hands resting on her belly, relishing the nudges and kicks his son or daughter bestowed on them. Sarah was so incredibly happy she couldn't believe how perfect her life was.

***

On a warm June morning, Sarah awoke feeling off. She couldn't put her finger on it, but she was aware that she was vaguely uncomfortable, though nothing was painful, and she felt exhausted, yet energetic. George, who had begun to watch her carefully as the time for her confinement drew nearer, became concerned as he observed her pushing the food around her plate at breakfast, rather than eating it.

"Not feeling well today, sweetheart?" he asked her, trying to mask the concern in his voice.

"I'm all right, thank you," she sighed. "I'm just not feeling too hungry. Perhaps it is the heat."

"Hmmm…" he agreed noncommittally.

"I do feel a bit strange today," she offered after a few more minutes of silence.

"How so?" he asked as he lifted another fork full of eggs to his mouth.

"I don't know exactly. I just feel… different somehow."

"Well, you did all of that washing yesterday. Perhaps you just overexerted yourself. Why don't you take it easy and try to stay cool today? Don't work yourself too hard. I'm going to be out at the back cornfield for the day, so you don't need to worry about me coming in for lunch. I'll bring something with me back there, so you can rest."

"All right," she answered, grateful that he was always so conscientious and thoughtful, putting her first.

Together, they did the breakfast dishes, and after Sarah had straightened up around the house a bit, she sat on the settee to settle in and read. Not long after she drifted off to sleep, she awoke to a strange tightening sensation in her belly. She didn't think much of it until it happened again a few minutes later, and then again. The last time, it began to hurt. Realization hit her, but she couldn't think straight about what to do. Despite George's multiple promises that she would not be alone, she remembered that he said he was going to be in the back cornfield for the day. She knew that even if she was feeling fine, there was

46

a real possibility that she could walk out there and never find him among the stalks. Changing course, her next thought was that she would try to walk to George's parents' house down the road, but then realized that she was still in her nightgown. Determined, she started toward the bedroom to change her clothes when she was gripped by another pain, her strongest yet. She whimpered as she slapped her hands against the sides of the hall and bent over, just trying to breathe through the minute-long contraction. When it was over, she straightened again and continued her trek, but hadn't made it very far when she was hit yet again by a contraction that was stronger still.

Sarah tried to swallow her panic and remember that labor, especially the first one, generally took hours. She tried to reassure herself with that in his latest letter, her brother had written to their mother that his new wife's labor had lasted twenty-six hours before their daughter had been born. Her mother had remarked when reading it, in an attempt to calm the panic she saw rising on her own daughter's face, that while long, it certainly was not an unheard of length of time for a first child. When the latest pain subsided, Sarah managed to walk to her wardrobe and pulled down a dress, placing it on the bed in preparation for taking off her nightgown.

As soon as she had lifted her nightgown over her head, however, another pain hit her, and she then noticed that there was a trickle of water running down her legs. Embarrassed, she thought that she was urinating on herself until the line continued and grew into a small puddle at her feet. Then the next pain came, and it knocked her off her feet. She fell to her knees beside the bed, her head resting against the mattress, as she gasped her way through the contraction. She realized then that she would not be going anywhere and instead had better make herself as comfortable as possible.

When she was able, she reached up onto the bed and grabbed her pillow. She had enough wits about her to think about that birthing was messy and she was in no position to make their bed ready, so she figured she would be better off on the floor, where the mess could be mopped up, rather than ruining their mattress and bedding.

She lay down on the braided rag rug in front of the fireplace, her nightgown up around her chest, and chuckled to herself at the irony of how many nights she and George had lain on this exact spot in front of a roaring fire and how one of those times may just have led to her current predicament. Eventually, she lost track of time as her body took over its task.

George had finally pulled out his pocket watch and looked at its face, seeing that the hour was approaching two o'clock. He had been fighting a nagging feeling that he needed to go home for the past few hours but had convinced himself that he was being silly. He had brought his lunch with him, and Sarah had been quietly reading on the settee when he had walked from the barn with his tools and stuck his head in through the door one last time. Wondering why the pull was so strong, he had managed to shake it off for a while, figuring that Sarah knew where he was and that his mother wasn't more than a quarter mile down the road if she needed something. Nevertheless, when he made it to a natural breaking point in his work, he decided that perhaps it would be best to check on his young wife before continuing with other chores around the farm.

When he walked through the front door, it was eerily silent. He couldn't see Sarah anywhere, and his concern grew. Rushing toward their bedroom, he had tried to convince himself that she had merely stepped down the road to visit with his mother and that she was fine, but as he entered the threshold, he heard her whimper softly. He looked down at the floor and saw her laying on the rug, a wet puddle surrounding her, her brow sweaty and her face grimaced in pain. He immediately dropped to his knees in front of her and kissed her forehead.

"I'm so sorry, Sarah! I had no idea that you were in labor! Why didn't you come find me?" he asked, his voice revealing his anguish.

She could only look at him, the exhaustion evident on her features. She didn't want to waste the energy required to explain.

George rose to his feet and hurried to the kitchen. He washed his hands thoroughly and wiped them on the clean towel, and then he grabbed a pot, filling it with water before stoking the stove. As he waited for the pot to boil, he found some scissors and string, so he was prepared to drop them into the tempest in the pan when it was ready. He walked back to their room and stood over her.

"Sweetheart, wouldn't you be more comfortable on the bed?" he gently inquired. Sarah had only shaken her head in response. She was too far along to want to move. When he understood that she was not willing to budge, he kissed her on top of her head before returning to the kitchen and boiling his supplies for several minutes. Heading back down the hall, he grabbed a handful of fresh towels from the linen cupboard.

He knelt beside her and took her hand in his. "How long have you been doing this?"

"I don't know," she whimpered. "I don't even know what time it is. But it started not long after you left."

Again, tormented about why she hadn't come for him then, he pressed on. "Has your bag of waters broken?"

She nodded at him, her eyes big and scared.

"All right. You will be fine, I promise. Do you trust me?"

"Yes," she gasped.

"Good. We will figure this out together."

For the rest of the afternoon, they quietly worked. When it came time for her to push, George was torn between wanting to comfort his wife and cajoling her onward. Sarah was exhausted, and it broke her husband's heart, but he knew through his years of birthing livestock on the farm, that once it was over, she would be out of her discomfort, and he couldn't wait until the child was in their arms.

After a good, solid hour of her struggling and pushing, the baby emerged into the world, kicking and screaming. George had caught the small, writhing bundle in a towel as it broke free from Sarah's body and his broad smile was enough to bolster Sarah's resolve.

"What is it?" she cried, wanting desperately to know if it was a boy or a girl.

"Well, I reckon it is a baby!" he retorted with a wink.

"Oh, you!" Sarah growled as she struggled to push herself up onto her elbows to see the face of the baby in the bundle.

"Sweetheart, just lie back. I'm kidding you. Just give me a second to wipe the baby down, and I'll tell you. I don't know yet, either, honestly."

The small baby's wails increased as George carefully opened the towel in order to rub away any residual moisture on its skin. As soon as he did so, a small stream shot up and got him in the face. He hurriedly shut the towel again and happily declared, "Most definitely, he's a boy!", to which Sarah squealed in delight.

Several hours later, Sarah and her newborn son were both cleaned up and resting quietly, as George lay beside them on the mattress. After helping Sarah clean herself up, he had carefully lifted her exhausted body off the floor and placed her in the bed, and then moved the boy from the middle of the mattress into her arms. He watched with wonder as the small infant rooted against his mother's chest until she understood what he was searching for and was able to accommodate him. Eventually, George had gathered the towels and other soiled linen, removing them to be laundered, and then cleaned the floor before returning to his little family.

"Well, this certainly was not in my plans for the day when I left this morning!" he joked with his wife as she rested her head on his shoulder.

"Nor mine," she responded. "I am sorry that I ruined our rug, though."

George threw his head back and laughed. "No harm done," he assured her. "There are plenty more where that came from, I'm sure. Why my ma could probably whip up another one in a week or so. Just so long as we have another one by the time winter rolls around, I'm perfectly happy." He looked down and winked at Sarah.

"Whoa, there, mister!" she told him. "Let me recover from this one before we get ourselves into trouble with another one!"

"You have to admit he's pretty darn cute! You can't blame a man for seeing him and wanting a whole house full!"

Sarah smiled as she sniffed the top of the baby's head. "What should we call him? Seems a bit premature to be speaking of future babies when we haven't even named this one yet."

"I still like Adam. What do you think?"

"I think Adam will serve him just fine," Sarah agreed.

Sarah recovered well and was soon back up to her normal routine within a few short weeks, learning to juggle both her household chores and an infant son. When George returned from his days in the fields, the first thing he would do was to wash up, kiss his wife, and then take the baby from her arms to settle in with him on the settee. He always told Sarah it was so that she could cook supper in peace, but when she would stand in the threshold of the kitchen and watch the two of them, she saw the truth with her own eyes. Her big, strong, tough farmer husband was completely enamored and smitten with his young son. At night, George was the first to hop out of bed and collect him from his cradle when he was hungry, presenting him to Sarah to feed, and then cradling them both in his arms as they all fell back to sleep together. He was incredibly proud, and every opportunity to show off his boy in town resulted in a beaming smile and shining eyes as everyone complimented the adorable, strapping young lad. Sarah thanked the Lord daily for her handsome, loving husband and her delightful son, wondering how her life could ever get any better than it was.

Chapter Six

When Adam was almost eight months old, Sarah began to experience the telltale exhaustion and nausea that led her to believe she was once again expecting. It hadn't taken George long to put two and two together, and he was bursting his buttons with pride as her belly grew larger all through the early spring.

Sarah found that caring for a toddler while pregnant was no small feat and George would often come home to find her and Adam asleep in each other's arms on the settee, the book she had been reading to him askew on the floor. Every time, she would awake with a start and apologize, while he assured her it was no problem; she needed her rest to take care of their next son.

When Sarah was a little over six months along, she was on her way to the outhouse when her feet hit a patch of ice, and she fell forward, landing hard onto her belly. She had lain where she landed in the ice and snow for several minutes while taking stock of all that was painful, and after deciding that she was all right, she gingerly picked herself up and finished her business. Her left wrist was beginning to throb, so she hurried back into the house to show George and whimpered while he manipulated it back and forth. He determined that it was a bad sprain or perhaps even a small fracture, but he devised a splint for her and a sling, and she sat on the settee for the rest of the evening while he insisted on waiting on her hand and foot.

In the middle of the night, Sarah awoke as she rolled onto her side, her wrist throbbing painfully. As she became more aware, she felt something warm and sticky between her thighs and terror grabbed at her heart. She shook George awake, and with her panic evident, he scrambled to light the lamp on his side of the bed before roughly pulling back the blankets to find that Sarah was surrounded by a puddle of blood. She began to cry, understanding immediately what was happening as the first cramps gripped her. They spent the rest of the night and most of the morning holding each other as her body fought to remove the injured fetus from her womb. When all was finished, and her cramping had subsided, George had bundled up against the cold morning and went to town to fetch the doctor, who confirmed that they had most likely lost their child because of the fall Sarah had suffered the day before. He told George to give her aspirin and keep her as comfortable as possible, quietly assuring him that they could try again as soon as she felt physically and emotionally ready.

George had taken Adam to his parents' house, allowing him and Sarah to spend the day clinging to one another, grieving the loss of their second son. Sarah heaved heavy sobs as she took responsibility for what had happened, lamenting that if she would have only been more careful, the miscarriage would never have happened. George tried desperately to reassure her that it was merely an accident and that they would soon again be expecting another baby, and all would be well. By the time little Adam was returned to them the next morning, both his parents were feeling more settled and optimistic about the future.

True to George's prediction, by late summer, just in time for their second anniversary, Sarah was once again expecting. This time, George hardly let her out of his sight, even escorting her to and from the outhouse when there was ice and snow on the ground, holding her elbow to ensure she didn't slip. Her pregnancy progressed normally, and as the end was nearing, they both relaxed and enjoyed the last little while before their baby came.

May arrived, finding Sarah enormously pregnant and ready to give birth at any moment. George watched her like a hawk and even hired his younger brother, David, as his farmhand so that he was free to come back in from the fields and check on his wife several times a day. This time, her pains started in the middle of the night, however, and their daughter was born in their bed, with the doctor present, rather than the floor.

The baby girl, whom they named Melissa, was small and pale. She had a weak cry, which worried Sarah, but the doctor assured them that all was indeed well, and the small girl just needed a bit more time to get acclimated in the outside world.

Sarah tried desperately to strengthen her little daughter but felt that she was only getting worse as her skin yellowed, and she became weaker. Sarah felt that she was fighting a losing battle but didn't want to admit defeat for George's sake.

He was as enamored of his baby girl as he had been of Adam, and Sarah could read the fear and worry in his eyes every time he held their daughter. Sarah began to feel self-conscious, as she wondered if George thought she wasn't doing enough to help the little girl thrive, and when he would offer suggestions in his own desperation, she would take them as an affront, as if he doubted her mothering skills, making her defensive. The two of them felt the wedge of fear and despair growing between them, but neither knew what to do to fix things.

When Melissa was almost three weeks old, Sarah rose in the morning and found the baby still and cold in her cradle. Her wails woke George, and he rose out of bed to cradle his young wife as grief came pouring out of her. Feeling helpless as she sobbed, "I'm so sorry," over and over again, all he could do was stroke her hair as he held her to him, whispering that everything would be all right, trying to assure her of his love for her.

George settled her in bed and then left to get the doctor. He had removed Melissa's now-still body from the room and shut the door behind him, once again taking Adam to his parents' house on his way into town.

When the doctor and George walked back in, they found Sarah sitting in her rocking chair, clasping the baby to her chest, her tears falling from her cheeks. As the doctor spoke calmly to her, George gently pried her fingers from around the baby girl and took her out the door to the barn. The doctor escorted Sarah back to bed, where he gave her a cocktail of medication to help her sleep, and she woke only to use the outhouse or drink water for three solid days. When she came back to reality, the funeral was planned, so she just showed up, leaning heavily on George's arm, wanting to melt into him to escape the looks of pity from all in attendance. She sat numbly in the first pew, holding tightly to a sleeping Adam, wondering how she could have moved from being so blissfully happy to utterly defeated in just a few short years.

Because George and Sarah were above all else the best of friends, they had already shared every emotion for the majority of their lives, long before they recognized what they had was love. They had told each other everything; nothing was too sad or shameful. This gift was all that allowed them to pull together in their grief rather than drift apart.

They took comfort in each other both emotionally and physically. Most nights they came together in a loving expression of sorrow and perseverance. As they would make love, Sarah was rarely cognizant of the tears that ran down her cheeks while George would gently wipe them away. He felt guilty that he felt such pleasure while she endured so much pain, but she reassured him that she found comfort in being close to him.

Under the circumstances, it had not taken long until Sarah was again with child. This time, Sarah felt no joy, only foreboding. However, when she tried to speak to George about it, he would quickly try to soothe her by saying that despite their bad luck they still were young and had plenty of time for more children. He still spent many nights, however, consoling her as she lay sobbing in his arms, questioning why they struggled so to grow their family.

Meanwhile, she and Ginny had begun to write regularly. Ginny also had struggled to conceive after giving birth to healthy twin girls. In her latest letter, though, she had instead lamented that her husband was being given a promotion overseeing the development and implementation of a spur line the railroad he worked for in Chicago was building from Colorado Springs to a cluster of small coal mining towns in the mountains. They would, of course, be moving to one of the small towns and Ginny was terrified of the changes looming for her family.

How can I even imagine how it will be to move from the big city of Chicago to some tiny mining town in the middle of nowhere? She had complained bitterly to Sarah in her flowing copperplate script.

Nevertheless, because her husband was thrilled with the opportunity, Ginny had packed up their home and prayed for the best. Eventually, she again wrote to Sarah, letting her know they had arrived and were settled, inviting her to come and visit. Sarah had laughed aloud at the prospect, thinking that her late pregnancy body aside, they would never be able to get away from the farm in the summer, and traveling to Colorado in the winter seemed like a miserable proposition. She told George that she was content to stay where she was and could think of no reason why she would ever venture all that way West, even if it was to visit family.

Though things were seemingly fine, Sarah couldn't shake her sense of trepidation. Therefore, she was almost anticipating it when at eight months pregnant, disaster struck, and her baby suddenly stopped moving. At first, she thought nothing of it, but as the day wore on, she began to become more concerned. By the time George had come back from his chores around the homestead and the barn, she knew. One look at her as she told him, "Something's wrong with the baby," had sent him immediately turning around to go for the doctor.

The physician listened for a long time, poking and prodding her belly, but finally he admitted defeat. Their baby was gone. Then, to add insult to injury, there was nothing that could be done until nature took its course. Sarah was once again numb as she faced the reality of laboring with a full-term stillborn infant and felt that she would rather die than face the reality that she knew was coming.

George hung around the house for the next few days, also begrudgingly anticipating the inevitable. When her contractions finally started, there was no joy in their home; only tears coupled with screams of agony and hopelessness. Sarah labored stoically as George hovered near her, helpless, frustrated, and angry.

Sarah couldn't bear to meet his gaze, for no matter how he tried to hide it, or as much as he denied it, his disappointment was palatable. For the first time, she also saw blame in his eyes, and it made her feel all the worse, like a failure as a woman, and even more so as his wife.

The little boy was indeed born still after a long and grueling labor. Sarah sat dumbstruck as she looked at his tiny, perfectly formed body, wondering what in the world had gone wrong. George had refused to look, declining to even acknowledge the child's presence. The doctor quietly asked Sarah for a name for the death certificate, and she realized that they had not even discussed it. She called for her husband, but when he came to the doorway, he glanced away and muttered that the name was of no consequence to him before turning on his heel to march back down the hall. She then heard him slamming pots and pans around the kitchen, the utensils and implements taking the full brunt of his frustration. Sarah had softly told the doctor that she wished for her son to be remembered by the name Robert, and then he quickly wrapped the boy in a blanket to take with him, grateful for enclosing all of the terrible, insidious hostility and grief in the house as he shut the door firmly behind him on his way out.

Later, when George brought her a plate of stew for supper, she whispered, "I'm so sorry," to him as he turned to leave the room.

"I am, too," he said mournfully.

"George, what is wrong with me?" she pleaded to him, her heartbreak apparent. He was simply too angry to feel any empathy for her.

"I don't know," he replied honestly.

"Why is this happening?" she wailed. "Adam was born perfectly healthy and fine."

"I can't talk about this," he told her in exasperation and took another step toward the door.

"Are you sorry you married me?" she called out to him, not wanting the answer, but clinging to the hope in her heart that he could never be that disappointed in her.

Instead, he surprised her when he refused to turn around to face her, his shoulders drooping in defeat, as he answered, "I'm not sure… I think I actually might be."

Silently, he walked out the door as her anguished sobs escaped, having no capacity for forgiveness or understanding of her grief at that moment, as his own angst was too much to bear.

Trying to avoid hearing his wife cry and scream in utter despair in their bedroom, George looked around the home he had built them. He was livid, so incredibly angry, and it was only made worse when he thought back to four years earlier, when he had carried her through the front door, so full of promise and excitement that they finally could start their life together. Hating himself for it, over the last few weeks, his thoughts had begun to wander, and he wondered about what his life would have been like if he had never married her. Would he have chosen her if he had known how much difficulty she would have producing healthy children for them? Though they had Adam, now a sturdy three-and-a-half-year-old, he was hardly enough when George had imagined at least five or six children underfoot. Sarah seemed damaged, and he began to feel as though he had been hoodwinked. George couldn't help but wonder what could have been if only he hadn't been so intent on pursuing her. He even considered that perhaps her sister might have been a better choice when he thought about the way he had imagined his life would go.

When he could no longer stand the sounds of her sobs, he put on his overcoat and headed into town. He needed a stiff drink and knew where he could get it, heading to the local tavern. Adam had been staying with Sarah's parents since the discovery that their latest child had passed, so George stayed out drinking far longer than he should have and was gone all night. When he sobered up enough to realize that he had abandoned his wife in her suffering, his guilt overtook him, and he hurried home, afraid of what he would find there.

When he walked through their bedroom door, he found her peacefully sleeping, though as he approached the bed, he saw the tear stains running over her cheeks. An overwhelming feeling of pity overtook him, so he lifted the quilts to join her, but was shocked to discover that she still clutched the handle of a butcher knife tightly in her hand. His breath caught in his throat as he realized what she had intended to do. Quickly loosening her grip, he ran to the front door and flung the knife out into the yard before shutting and locking the door behind him. He hastened back to their bed and gathered her in his arms. She awoke enough to tell him again, "I'm so sorry," as her tears started once more, before settling into his broad chest, her breaths shuddering with unshed sobs even in her sleep.

George lay beside her for several hours, berating himself for neglecting and forsaking her while engrossed in his own grief, fully realizing what he should do, but not prepared to do it. Unable to face the agony, after all their loss, of having her placed in an institution somewhere that would only make things worse. He made up his mind that her actions had only come from the deep despondency she felt and blamed himself for his abandonment of her in her darkest hour. He vowed then and there to never desert her again, but to also make sure she would never again have a reason to feel like a failure and disappointment to him.

Chapter Seven

Sarah and George continued about their lives, neither of them mentioning the events of that terrible night again. Nevertheless, in holding to his resolution, George refused to touch Sarah in any capacity other than a quick hug or peck on the lips, leaving her to believe he was so disappointed with their life together that he no longer loved or felt attracted to her. Though he still told her that he loved her, his lack of affection, along with his heartbreaking confession that he indeed thought he was sorry he had married her, made her believe that he only stayed out of obligation.

Despite their inner turmoil roiling like a toxic fog, they continued working side by side to grow their farm and raise their son. Adam was, in contrast to the rest of his siblings, healthy and thriving. The child hardly even got a sniffle, which made all of their other losses even harder to fathom.

Sarah had seen the doctor after the loss of their last child, and she had pleaded with him to find what could be wrong with her. He had examined her thoroughly and then tried to reassure her that he could see nothing amiss. He told her to just keep trying, that sometimes people just had a lot of rotten luck. She didn't know how to tell him that it was hard to keep trying when her husband would hardly touch her.

It wasn't just George, either, whom Sarah felt she was disappointing. George's brother, David, had finished school the year before and was courting a young woman named Rebecca. At a Sunday supper with the family, six months after the loss of Robert, David proudly announced that the two were engaged to be married.

"Well, I couldn't be more pleased! I am dying for some more grandchildren, and since Sarah can't seem to do her duty, I will be turning my sights to the two of you!" George's mother proclaimed with ruthless joy.

Already known for her definitive ideas and sharp tongue, Sarah was certain that her mother-in-law had been waiting for the perfect opportunity to strike. She sat stunned as an uncomfortable silence fell over the table, but when she saw the look of pity George's father bestowed upon his son, she couldn't take it anymore, shoving back her chair and running from the room to the front porch, her shoulders heaving in defeat.

The scraping of her husband's chair as he harshly bellowed, "Ma!" was all that broke the silence as he rose to find his wife. The petty woman was not finished, though, as when George opened the front door to join Sarah, she heard her mother-in-law complain bitterly, "Humph! It isn't like I wasn't telling the truth!"

George took her in his arms and truly held her for the first time in she couldn't remember how long as the sobs shook her body. He stroked her hair and murmured to her that it was all right, and that he was sorry she had to hear that, but she knew in her heart that his mother had spoken the truth, and that knowledge made it all the more painful.

The couple stumbled through the next few weeks as summer appeared again. Adam was now four years old and doted on by both of his parents. Since he was older, he had begun to spend a good deal of time with his father out in the fields and caring for the animals, always up with the sun to start their day. Sarah would smile when she would look up from her work in the house or the garden and see her two men going about their chores. Though George was distant with her, he was always warm and loving with the boy and her heart took comfort in that fact that at least he was not disappointed in their son.

Not long after that fateful night with George's parents, however, on an already scorching June morning, Adam did not wake up with his parents. Sarah didn't think much of it as she prepared their breakfast, while George left to take care of the morning chores. It wasn't until the hot meal was on the table before her that Sarah realized that the boy was still in bed.

She walked quickly to his bedroom and opened the door. From there she could clearly see his body's outline under the bedding, obviously still sound asleep. Perplexed, she moved toward him, reaching out to sweep an unruly lock of hair off his forehead before recoiling in shock at the heat radiating up through her fingers. She reached forward again, this time using the whole back of her hand to feel his forehead and cheeks. When it registered that the child was burning up with fever, she ripped the bedding off him and began to remove his pajamas. It was then that she noticed the fine rash covering his body and was immediately filled with dread.

She lay her boy back down and hurried as fast as she could to the front door, flinging it wide open and hollering at the top of her lungs, "George!"

Hearing the urgency in her voice, he dropped everything and ran out of the barn toward the house. He raced down the hall, not even bothering to remove his filthy boots, and stopped at the boy's bedside, worry deeply etched in his features.

"What's the matter with him?" he whispered to Sarah urgently.

"I'm not sure. I think it's measles," she answered back and saw the weight of her words settle in his eyes.

"I'll go get Doc Harrison," he muttered, turning on his heel and walking back out of the front door. Sarah heard the hooves of one of their horses as it galloped past the house a few minutes later.

The doctor confirmed the illness was indeed measles, telling Sarah and George that there was not much to be done other than trying to control his fever and keeping him comfortable until it had run its course. He stated that there were several other cases around town, and that barring no complications, little Adam would be fine in a week or two.

Sarah and George kept a vigil over the boy day and night. Sarah slept beside him, and George made a pallet on the floor, neither of them willing to leave him alone. George left the house only to take care of the livestock, relying on David to run the rest of the farm, and Sarah would leave to cook or do dishes only when George was sitting with their child.

By the time the illness had run its course, George and Sarah were exhausted. On the first night they felt confident in leaving the boy alone in his room to sleep, they had both collapsed on their bed, utterly spent. Neither of them said a word as they each slipped under their covers and closed their eyes, both dead to the world within seconds.

Sarah later awoke snuggled into George, his arm around her. She was surprised, as even in sleep, he usually seemed to want to avoid touching her. However, the real shock came as she awakened further and was more cognizant of her surroundings, feeling his arm pulling her closer to him. She reached her hand up and placed it on his chest, and he let out a soft moan in his sleep. Driven by his reaction, she then began softly stroking his abdomen with her fingers and his grasp tightened around her. After a few minutes, she felt his other arm encircle her, and she smiled softly as his hand closed around her breast, gently kneading it. Unable to stop herself, she swept her leg over his thigh, and then closed her fist around him, gently moving her hand up and down, relishing in his physical response to her ministrations. She tipped her head up and caught his lips in hers, at first massaging them gently, then nipping and sucking on them, her need for him growing. He groaned, and in the moonlit room, she could see he had opened his eyes. Without saying a word, he nudged her onto her back as he rose above her, lowering himself to capture her mouth, his hunger very apparent. Before she knew what was happening, they were clawing at each other's nightclothes, removing them from one another as quickly as they could. He ravaged her body like a starving man, worshipping her all over with his lips, tongue, and hands. When he finally settled between her thighs, they both sighed with relief as his body joined with hers. Together they moved in the moonlight, savoring every sensation as they loved each other completely.

Afterward, when they were satisfied, George held her in his arms, feeling more totally relaxed than he had in he couldn't remember how long. He was therefore surprised when he heard the sound of Sarah sniffling and reached out to push her hair off her forehead before rising to place a single, gentle kiss there.

"What's the matter, sweetheart?" he asked her tenderly.

"I thought you didn't love me anymore," she whispered. "That you didn't want me."

All at once, George was hit by the wave of realization that by trying to save Sarah any more grief, he had, in turn, caused her the worst kind of pain: rejection. Remorseful of what he had done, he pulled her close and stroked her cheek with his thumb.

"I'm so sorry," he answered. "The problem was that I wanted you too much, but I couldn't face the prospect of putting you into a position that would hurt you further."

"What do you mean?" she asked him quietly, rolling over onto her back to watch his face.

"I don't want to get you in the family way ever again, Sarah. It's too much for you, and I don't see it ever ending well. I'm grateful for Adam and am resigned to the fact that he may well be our only living child."

"I'm sorry I can't bear you more children," she apologized, her anguish evident in her voice.

"Honestly, Sarah, it's all right. I had a hard time at first, but then I realized that I was being foolish. I have a healthy son, and so much to be thankful for! I've come to understand that I would rather have you than a whole houseful of some other woman's children. You're the one I adore."

He bent down to kiss her, and that started their love making all over again.

The rest of the summer passed joyfully as Adam recovered and the farm continued to flourish. David was helping George and their father in equal amounts, preparing for his own plot of the family land on which he would build a house when the weather turned colder.

Life for Sarah and George was returning to normal as their fifth anniversary rolled around. Sarah finally accepted that the cruel words George had spoken to her had been in response to his own grief. She had just started feeling assured in his love for her when it was time again to start bringing in the crops.

Chapter Eight

George and David labored hard to complete the harvest before the first frost, while Sarah worked to preserve the bounty of her garden. The days were warm, and the evenings cool, in a perfect Indian Summer.

A few days later, however, a cold wind blew in from the north. George and David began to panic that they were running out of time and worked at a fever pitch to bring everything in before winter arrived. It suddenly seemed entirely possible that a rare October blizzard could take them by surprise that year. Spurred by the thought that a whole season's work could end up rotting under a foot of snow, the men kept up an impossible pace, rising well before sunrise, then only quickly eating a few sandwiches Sarah prepared for lunch, before coming in well after sundown when they had finally finished in the fields and caring for the livestock.

Sarah felt guilty as she watched her husband work himself so hard. She wished that she could have given him a household full of sons by now, not thinking logically that with Adam being their oldest at four, it would have been several more years before any boys they would have had were old and strong enough to be of any real assistance rather than a hindrance.

The crops were almost all in and accounted for, and the majority of the seed was bagged for the winter in preparation for the spring planting, when George came in one night even more exhausted than normal. His eyes were sunken into his face, and his cheeks were flushed. His strong shoulders sagged, and he looked as if he would fall asleep right into his plate of stew. As Sarah observed him, her heart swelled with tenderness.

"George, sweetheart, why don't you go to bed?"

George responded by looking up at the clock on the wall. "No, Sarah, it's hardly seven o'clock yet. I'm just sleepy. I'll try to eat a bit more, and that should perk me right up!"

"How about you instead lay on the settee with Adam, while I clean up the supper dishes?"

"That sounds even better. Come on, now, boy! Let's read a book!"

As George stood, he lost his footing and grabbed forcefully onto the table. Sarah looked up in surprise as the dishes all rattled and the table shook.

"George, what is it?"

"Nothing! I'm fine. Just a mite dizzy is all."

Sarah placed the pot she was carrying on the kitchen counter and walked briskly over to her exhausted husband. She placed her hand on his forehead, causing him to moan slightly at the coolness of her fingers and say, "That feels real nice!"

"George!" Sarah exclaimed, "You're burning up! You need to get to bed this instant."

Sarah abandoned the dishes and supported her big husband with her little frame as they walked down the hall. When they got to their room, he sat weakly on the bed as she worked to undress him, and then got him situated under the covers.

"There, now! Just rest, my darling. I will tell David to handle the last bit of work tomorrow. You should be right as rain in a few days' time. Goodnight and I love you!" she ordered him as she leaned over and kissed his forehead.

He smiled weakly and thanked her. By the time she had closed the curtains and blown out the lamp on his side of the bed, he was already asleep.

The next morning, George, who was usually up and out of bed by the time the rooster started crowing, was still sound asleep when Sarah awoke. She was puzzled for a moment as the sun streamed in and she realized that not only had she slept much later than usual, but she could also feel an unusual amount of heat radiating off George even from the few inches' distance between them in the bed. She propped herself up and saw just how pale her normally big, strong husband looked, his eyelashes gently brushing the bluish-black circles under his eyes. Reaching out her hand to his forehead, she was taken aback by the sheer strength of his fever. He moaned slightly in response, thrashing his head back and forth before settling back into a deep sleep.

Sarah quickly got dressed and went to rouse Adam. While he was putting on his breeches, she asked him to run down the road to his grandparents' house and ask George's father to go for the doctor.

By the time the doctor arrived, George lay shivering under the blankets, his body convulsing almost as if he was having a seizure. Sarah was lying beside him, trying to share her body heat with him and control his shaking. She raised her head as the doctor came in and took charge.

Sarah jumped down from the high bed, straightening her dress, and waited for the doctor to examine the love of her life. After a few moments, he turned to her, his eyes shining with concern.

"Mrs. Johnson, I'm sorry to tell you that George here has caught the influenza that is making the rounds through town. Unfortunately, he seems to have contracted an especially bad case."

"Oh dear!" Sarah exclaimed, trying to think where he might have picked it up.

"Many have come down with it in the last few days. I have a feeling that someone at church had it and spread it around at both the Wednesday evening and Sunday services last week."

"Oh no!"

"Keep him hydrated and let him sleep. It's the best thing for him right now," the doctor informed her. "Give him some aspirin from time to time to keep his fever from getting too high. I will be back by tomorrow to check in on him. Don't hesitate, though, to send the senior Mr. Johnson to fetch me if anything changes."

Sarah spent the rest of the day trying to keep George comfortable and hydrated. She made him tea with honey, broth, and even broke out some of her cherry cordial that she made for special occasions, trying to make drinking more palatable. He

68

would wake up for only a few spoonfuls, too tired to even properly draw from a glass.

Sarah spent much of the night next to her husband, cuddling him in her arms, willing him to get better quickly. Now that things had improved between them, Sarah felt lonely, as well as worried. Adam was once again with George's parents; Sarah was concerned the boy would catch the flu too soon after his bout with measles. Therefore, she had no one to talk to, and only stared into her husband's familiar face slackened with sleep, willing him to wake up.

By the next morning, things had not improved. In fact, to Sarah, it seemed that George was doing worse. His cough had an intense rumble, and he didn't even seem to awaken as his body hacked. When he breathed in, she could hear a series of small squeaks emanating from deep in his lungs that she had never heard before in her life.

The doctor came to check on him around eleven o'clock. He listened for a long time with his stethoscope to George's chest, as the man lay listless in the bed, too weak to even sit up, and his face looked grave as he turned to the man's young wife.

"Sarah, it isn't looking good," he warned her.

"Well, he just got sick..."

"Sarah," he continued, interrupting her. "He has pneumonia."

"Pneumonia?" Sarah asked, the shock evident in her voice. "But how is that even possible? He hasn't even been sick for two whole days yet!"

"I know. But this influenza... It's bad, Sarah. It has been killing people the world over. He was just one of the unlucky ones who got exposed and caught it... George is a young man, though, so I'm hoping he may still pull through. I have to admit that I am worried, however, with as sick as he is. Maybe he was especially run down?"

An alarm sounded in Sarah's head as the words sunk in. "He has been, Doctor. He's been working himself to the bone from sunup to sundown, trying to bring in the crops before the weather gets bad. He's been rising before the sun and coming in long after it has gone to bed for the last three weeks or so."

"Well, there you have it, then. I'm hoping he will be all right if we leave him be and let him sleep. That is the best medicine of all for him."

"All right, Doctor. I'll let him."

"Good girl! I will be back again tomorrow to check on him."

By the next day, not much had changed. Sarah was trying desperately to keep George hydrated, but he just was not interested. She began to feel panicked.

As she went to bed that night, she took an extra-long time to say her prayers, begging God to help George get better. Instead of feeling peace in her heart, though, she felt a strong sense of foreboding and doubt. At some point in the night, however, she awoke to his hand slipping into hers and giving it a weak squeeze. Her heart soared as she thought that maybe a corner had been turned.

The next morning, though, he seemed worse than ever. His skin had begun to look grey and papery in the daylight. His fingernails were dusky, as were his lips. Sarah carefully washed his face and while doing so, stared at his mouth, thinking of all the words he had spoken, secrets he had shared, and kisses he had indulged her with. She couldn't help herself as she bent down and gently placed her mouth on his, savoring the familiar feeling. When she stood back up straight, she leaned over and whispered in his ear, "You promised me you would never leave me! You hear me, George Johnson? You swore you would never leave me!"

But alas, it was not to be. George Johnson would never awaken again, and so instead, their families stood beside her on the windswept hill as she watched the dirt being shoveled over the top of the simple wooden box which now contained the empty shell of the only man she had ever loved.

Chapter Nine

In the first few weeks after George's death, Sarah was numb. The days blurred together, while she spent all of her waking hours crying, regardless of the time of day. Adam was staying with her parents, so Sarah was all alone, waking only to wander aimlessly through her little house, seeing George in every small detail. She would run her hand along a windowsill or a drawer in the pantry and would hiccough a sob, thinking about the love and care they had shared for almost as far back as she could remember.

David came daily to do the chores. The crops were all in, so now it was only the creatures that needed tending. For the first few days, he had knocked on the door when he was finished, but when Sarah would answer with a blank expression and swollen eyes, he knew that she really didn't care enough to hear what he was saying to bother.

Adam came back home ten days after the funeral, and he was also hurting badly. Since it had become apparent that Sarah and George might never have another living child, George had poured all of his love and affection into the body of that one little boy. Adam had followed his father around the farm, trying to help whenever he could, even if it was detrimental to what George ultimately wanted to accomplish. Sarah would often smile when she would see her men walking toward the house, carrying the full milking pail, George bent at an awkward angle, just so that Adam could feel he was assisting to lighten a burden. When they would come into the kitchen, Adam would gleefully declare, "Ma, I brought in the milk!"

George would look up at Sarah and smile, winking as his eyes twinkled, and she realized her sweet husband was content to let their little boy believe he had done the majority of the work himself. It always made her heart skip a beat to see the care and understanding her big farmer husband bestowed on their young son.

Adam tried to help David in George's absence but soon grew tired when his uncle did not exhibit the same appreciation his father had. One day, he returned to the kitchen in tears and ran to his room. Sarah followed swiftly after him, inquiring what was wrong as his little torso shook with sobs.

"I miss Pa!" her little one declared, his anguish apparent.

"I know you do, baby," Sarah answered, gently rubbing his back. "I do, too."

"Uncle David told me today that I wasn't helping none! He yelled at me, telling me to get on back to the house instead of letting me help him finish mucking out the stalls."

Sarah's heart broke thinking about how young David wouldn't know to allow Adam to assist him, no matter how poorly he did, so that the boy could learn. Instead, he just wanted to finish quickly and get back to his fiancée.

"Adam, honey, David isn't much more than a boy himself, sweetheart. I'm sure he didn't want to hurt your feelings. He's just in a hurry to see his girl!"

The boy lifted his little tearstained face and said, "Well, then, he shoulda let me help him! We would have been done that much faster!"

"He doesn't have children yet, Adam. He doesn't see the benefits of a young one helping out and instead just sees you as being underfoot. Try not to take it so personally."

The boy sat and pondered for a long time. Sarah breathed a sigh of relief, happy the situation had seemingly been diffused, when little Adam suddenly sat up and spit out angrily, "I hate Uncle David!"

"Adam Edward!" Sarah reprimanded, shocked by the hatred her little boy was suddenly spouting.

"I do! I do, Ma! He's mean! He don't love me none! In fact, I hate Pa, too! I hate him! Why did he have to go and leave me? Why, Ma, why?"

The small boy then jumped into her arms, sobbing heartily as Sarah gently rubbed his back.

"I know you're angry, Adam. I know you're hurt and missing your pa. But you don't hate him, not really. You're just sad and scared of being alone. You can't face what it means now that he's gone."

Tears were streaming down her face, as well, while she repeated to her son exactly what she was thinking to herself. She understood her boy's frustration, as she also struggled with anger and uncertainty, and it was hard to not interpret it as hate, even with the knowledge and experience she had that came with age.

***

Several weeks after George's passing, Sarah and Adam were invited to George's parents' home for supper. Though George's parents had been extremely helpful with Adam when George had first passed, lately they had become distant and cold. Sarah had chalked it up to their grieving the loss of their oldest child, resolving to give them space and let them work through it themselves. She was therefore elated for Adam's sake when she received the invitation through David for Sunday supper.

Sarah dressed in her Sunday best and Adam wore his, as well. Together, hand in hand, they walked down the dusty lane to knock on the door of George's childhood home. When it opened, Sarah greeted George's father with a quick peck on the cheek, noticing that he seemed a bit aloof, but she didn't think much of it.

The family all gathered at the table as the conversation revolved around the weather, the price of grain from the harvest, some of the happenings in town, and about family members whom Sarah did not know. David's Rebecca was also there, and Sarah tried to smile in solidarity at her on a few occasions, wondering if the girl was as bored as she was, but never got much of a response besides a cool smile in return.

Finally, to her relief, the evening was winding down and dessert was served. Everyone ate their apple pie in relative silence. Sarah was looking forward to finishing up and heading home, as this first official social engagement after her husband's passing had exhausted her far more than she would have ever imagined. But just as she was pushing her plate away in preparation to thank her hosts for the meal, the hammer was dropped.

"Sarah, we need to talk to you about something," George's father began softly.

"All right," she replied, wondering what would be said. She expected to hear something about how George's passing was difficult on all of them, and maybe even an apology about their recent distance, but that she could count on them to be there if she ever needed anything. What came next, however, hit her like a punch to the gut.

"We will be needing the house and land back now," he said, unwilling to look her in the eye.

"I beg your pardon?" she asked, wondering if she had misheard.

"I'm saying, Sarah, that we are taking George's farm back."

"But I don't understand…" She looked around the table and found that no one would meet her gaze.

"Sarah," George's mother broke in, "what we are saying is that now that George is gone, we will be taking back the ownership of his home and land."

"But why?" she questioned, panic rising in her chest, making her feel like she might regurgitate her supper right back on the table in front of her.

"Because, dear, he's no longer alive to care for it."

"But I'm his wife! Surely you wouldn't make me, let alone his son, leave our home? George built that home for us with his own two hands!"

"Well," George's father broke back in, "the way we see it is when George died, the property we gave him reverted back to us. So, we will be gifting it to David instead, and he and Rebecca will live there and work the farm."

"But that is our house! George built it for *us*! Please, you can't take our home!" Her voice rose in panic with each word.

Tears began glistening in Sarah's eyes, but she was too proud to let them fall. Adam, knowing that he may not rise from the table without being excused, but worrying about his mother, sat glued in place, his eyes darting between all of the adults, trying to piece together what was being said in a way he could understand.

"That's just it, Sarah," George's father explained. "It isn't your house or land. Women can't own property."

"But I have Adam! He's George's son! Shouldn't he be allowed to inherit the land owned and worked by his own father?"

"Adam is too young to have ownership over the land, Sarah. You know that," George's mother answered her condescendingly.

"But he's George's son! How am I supposed to support him? What is he supposed to inherit?"

"Sarah, listen here! George is dead! Adam is his only living child, but it will be years until he's old enough to work the land. If it's too much of a hardship for you, then the boy can stay here with us, but we will be taking back the property. Perhaps if your family was larger, if any of your other children would have lived, we might have reconsidered."

"Please! I beg of you! Don't make us leave our home! It's all I have left of him besides Adam," Sarah pleaded, shuddering breaths interrupting every word. "What am I supposed to do now? Where am I supposed to go?"

"I don't know, dear," came the heartless reply from her mother-in-law. "But David and Rebecca want to wed soon and need a place to live. Someone needs to work that land; it only makes sense now that George is gone that David should be the one to live on and own that property. As I said, the boy can live here with us, if that makes things easier for you, but where you go is no longer any concern of ours."

"Please, please, don't do this!" Sarah wailed. "This is not what George would have wanted at all!"

"What George wanted was a successful farm with a houseful of children. That didn't happen. In fact, it was the pain of it all that killed him, I know it!" his mother chastised bitterly. "If you would have been better at doing your wifely duty, he would have had many helpers, instead of killing himself day in and day out."

"So, you think it's *my* fault that George died because we didn't have any more children?" Sarah asked in quiet disbelief.

"I am sure of it. He died of a broken heart."

Sarah was beside herself with grief and pain. Yet, she drew on every ounce of strength she possessed.

"Thank you for supper. Adam and I appreciate it," she said stoically.

"You're welcome, Sarah. Just so you know, we will need you out of the house and off the property within a month's time."

Sarah only nodded in response and reached for Adam's hand. She made it out the door and up the lane before she couldn't contain herself any longer. She cried big, silent tears, praying Adam wouldn't see in the darkness. After they got home, she put her son to bed and walked out into the middle of a field, screaming at the top of her lungs. She shrieked for several minutes, releasing her anger, loneliness, and pain. She bawled until her voice was gone and she fell in a heap on the spent dirt and leftover organic material from the previous growing season. When she could take no more, she picked herself up and walked back into her little home, putting herself to bed, crying even as she slept.

Chapter Ten

Sarah had no other choice but to return to her childhood home, broken and defeated. Not wanting to wait out the entire month stipulated by George's family when they had demanded their land back, she left in just under two weeks. She had almost killed herself in the process, but her stubborn pride refused to let her stay where she wasn't wanted any longer than necessary.

Sarah's parents said very little about the circumstances that brought their daughter back under their roof. It was a small town, and they knew that they would have to continue to live in the same community as the Johnsons, and therefore chose to swallow their anger and disappointment over the treatment of their daughter. They tried to be kind and understanding with Sarah, but after having kept her own home and raising her son, she felt that they were often suffocating her with their constant fussing and attention. She truly began to understand the phrase that one cannot go home again.

Sarah was despondent and angry, unable to find anything that would allow her troubled soul to settle, missing her husband in every sense of the word. She missed the physical love that they shared: his warm caresses and deep, meaningful kisses, when he would be most vulnerable, exposing the rawest of his emotions to her without ever uttering a word. Most of all, though, she missed her best friend. Her confidant since she was eight years old, she had seen him every day. He had also been fun, with a quick laugh, wicked sense of humor, and the tendency to good-naturedly tease her mercilessly. This had not stopped once they were married but was enhanced by the added benefit of his making love to her with wild abandon, and her heart was not yet used to the lonely, gaping hole his death had left.

A month after she had returned home, her father came back from the post office with a letter from her sister. Sarah had written to her and let her know all that had happened, secretly beseeching her sister's love and support to pour out in her response. Taking the letter to her bedroom, she shut the door firmly behind her before she ripped open the envelope and began to read.

My Dearest Sarah,

I cannot believe all that has transpired in such a short amount of time, most notably the incredibly tragic loss of George. I cannot imagine how painful it is to lose not only your soulmate and father of your children, but also your best friend, and even your home! I'm so angry about how his family has treated you that I could just spit! His mother always was a bitter, heartless woman! I assume that by now you and Adam are comfortably settled back with Ma and Pa.

Sarah, I don't have the slightest notion about what to say or how I can help you. My heart is breaking at your incredible loss. I wish that we lived closer so that I could hug you and we could cry together.

Colorado is beyond beautiful. We are finally settled, and the house is large; indeed, it is really far too large for us, but Jacob insisted that we "build to grow". Alas, there are still no more babies on the way for us, though, at least not yet.

Jacob is working incredibly long hours, and there are very few women here. Those who are here are not the sort of women with whom I can cultivate a friendship, so the girls and I are often lonely and find that there is little to occupy our long days until Jacob comes home again. I do so long for female companionship, though, to help break up the monotony of the days, but I don't dare complain to Jacob. He is so all-consumed with his work that I fear he wouldn't even hear me, even if I were somehow brave enough to broach the subject with him.

Oh, how I do wish that you could come for a visit, darling! I'm thinking that the brisk mountain air may do you

That night, as Sarah lie awake, listening to the cold rain pound the window of her childhood bedroom, she began to ponder if it would be possible for her to go and visit Ginny and her family in the spring.

She had the money to travel there: despite their cruel treatment, to their credit, at least George's family had given her a small sum of money from the harvest that was brought in right before he died so that she would have a little something with which to start over. George's father, always the kinder of her husband's parents, had met her on the road from town one day and had informed her that he also had every intention of giving her a small stipend every year to help care for the boy. Sarah wondered if George's mother was aware of his promise, but somehow, she didn't think so, and it delighted her that it was something that the woman didn't know and couldn't control.

Sarah was unsure exactly how much money would be needed to purchase the fare for her and Adam to travel but made up her mind the next time that she went into town, she would make some discreet inquiries at the depot.

Within a few days, Sarah had her answer, and determined that if she scrimped and saved throughout the winter, she would just have enough for them to leave after the spring thaw. Her heart felt lighter when she realized she now had something to look forward to and sent a telegram to her sister to inform her of her plans. A few days later, a reply came back, letting Sarah know that they would welcome her whenever she felt ready to travel.

With Christmas rapidly approaching, Sarah became unrelentingly restless and couldn't sit still. She would sit and take up her knitting for a few minutes, then place it aside, walking instead to the window to look out across the bleak wintery landscape, darkened by the cold rain that fell. After a few more minutes, she would walk to the settee to pick up a book and flip through it until she would soon abandon it, as well.

Her father watched with amused sympathy for his youngest daughter. While it was entertaining to observe her flitting about, he understood how lost she felt, how alone.

"Sarah?" he inquired gently.

"Yes, Pa?" she answered him, turning around from the window to look at him.

"I've been thinking. There's no reason for you to stay here with us until spring. It might do both you and Adam some good to get out to Colorado now instead of waiting."

"But Pa!" she exclaimed, trying to make sense of what he was telling her. "It's cold now! According to Ginny, there's already snow in the mountains near them. Whatever would I do there in the dead of winter that I couldn't do here?"

"Nothing, I supposed, except that a change of scenery may be in order." He paused a minute before continuing, "I am afraid, though, my dear, of how you will handle this first Christmas alone. I know that you miss George terribly because he was not only your husband but also your dearest friend. I have been thinking that there's nothing for you here but your Ma and me, and we certainly aren't going to help take your mind off your loss or having to return to your childhood home. I believe it would be better for you to be somewhere else this first Christmas and I speculate that seeing Ginny in Colorado might just provide the respite you need."

Tears filled Sarah's eyes as she thought about her father's words. She had put Christmas in the back of her mind, as it was just too painful to think about. Now that her father had brought it up, however, memories of Christmases past flooded her consciousness. She saw their first Christmas tree, so proudly cut down at the back of their land, decorated lovingly with the salt dough and paper ornaments she had made. She recalled the Christmas George had come up behind her to steal a cookie as she was removing them from the baking tray to cool. After giving him a stern warning that they were right from the oven, he had taken one anyway, and had yelled in exaggerated pain when the hot dough burned his fingers. He had held them out for her, his bottom lip protruding with the mock injustice of it all. She had blown on them at first, and then begun to suck on them one by one while looking deep into his eyes. Needless to say, with Adam down for his afternoon nap, the rest of the cookie dough sat until much later in the day, when Sarah finally returned to her earlier task.

Her tears spilled over and down her cheeks. "I miss him, Pa," she whispered. "I miss him so much!"

Big sobs wracked her small frame as her father rose from his chair and pulled her to him. He held onto her tightly as he gently patted her head. "I know you do, dearest. I know you do, and it won't get any easier as the festivities draw nearer. I think a change of pace would be helpful with Adam's transition, as well. This Christmas will be difficult for him, too."

Sarah pondered her father's words for a long time. She had been so engulfed in her own misery and grief that she hadn't really even considered Adam's. She hadn't thought about how he would wrestle with his own painful memories, such as how George always read aloud the Christmas story from the Gospel of Luke first thing on Christmas morning, and how after the chores were done, her two men would settle down to play with the new toys and read the new books which Adam had received. She realized that this first Christmas without George was going to affect her son greatly, as well.

George's family had already sent word to Sarah that she and Adam would not be celebrating the holiday with them that year, stating it would simply be too painful for them to have her and

Adam there, reminding them that their beloved son was gone. They had some small gifts for Adam delivered from the mercantile in town, but that was the extent of their willingness to participate in the first Christmas without George. There was no reason in which to stay.

Eventually, Sarah nodded slowly. "I suppose you're right, Pa. Going to Colorado might be just the thing Adam and I need to help us get through. I will wire to Ginny first thing in the morning, and then, if she says it is safe to travel, we will make the arrangements."

Chapter Eleven

Three days later, Sarah looked up as her father burst through the door, bringing with him a strong gust of wind and a few rogue snowflakes that dared to follow him in from the first winter storm of the season. Despite George's earlier panic, in a cruel irony, the weather thus far had been warmer and milder than most other years, so the snow was not yet sticking, but it made for a picturesque view from the windows as it swirled and dove in the wind. In his hand, her father was waving a piece of paper, and as he got closer, Sarah could see it was a telegram.

"This just came in from the mercantile, my dear!" he exclaimed breathlessly, thrusting it toward her.

She took it eagerly from his hand and ripped open the envelope. As she read for a bit, she let out a small squeal of surprise, making both her mother and father look up at her in shock.

"Ginny said that because of Jacob's position with the railroad, he was able to secure the tickets for us to come and see them in Colorado, meaning we do not have to pay the fare! She said all we will be responsible for is the food onboard! She said he has even reserved a berth for the both of us in a Pullman car!" she exclaimed in excitement.

"That's wonderful, dear!" her mother responded with gratitude that there was something exciting for her daughter and grandson to anticipate.

Sarah continued to read. "She says that she wishes we would be there and settled for Christmas, so we will need to leave in five days!"

"So soon?" her mother exclaimed.

"Apparently," she answered, holding the paper limply in her hand.

"Well, then, we don't have much time, do we, dear? Of course, your clothing will be relatively simple, what with you still in mourning. However, the boy… Well, he may be a bit more challenging. With our unusually warm weather, we will have to make sure that his winter clothing from last year still fits him, or we will have to quickly make some up for him. And, of course, we need to prepare some small gifts for you to bring to Ginny, Jacob, and the girls!" Sarah's mother began rattling off her plans aloud.

The next few days were a flurry of activity and fuss. Clothing was washed and pressed, new mittens, hats and scarves were made, and trunks were packed, including gifts wrapped in the carefully saved paper from the packages purchased at the mercantile during the past year. Thankfully, though a little small, Adam's winter coat from the previous winter was deemed "good enough" to make it another few months before he would officially outgrow it. Only a mother or grandmother would notice that the sleeves were a bit too short, and the bottom of the thing hit just a bit too high on his legs. Nevertheless, since the visit was scheduled for only a month long, everyone figured that these issues could be quickly resolved once they returned home, none the worse for the wear.

Early on the sixth morning after she had received Ginny's initial letter, Adam and Sarah stood on the platform, awaiting the big locomotive which would bring them first to Chicago, where they would then change trains before heading west to Colorado Springs. Once there, they would change trains again, heading up a mountainside to the small mining community at the end of the line, where Ginny and her husband had made their home so that he could manage the new spur line.

Sarah had been on a train before to go to her brother's wedding in Chicago, but Adam had never left their small farming town. There had never been a reason to: he was the son of a farmer, and everything they needed could be produced themselves or bought in town with money made from their own property. George had never ventured farther than a twenty-mile radius around his farm in his entire life.

As the hulking, smoke-bellowing, steaming engine slowed to a crawl and finally stopped with a loud hiss, Sarah and her parents kissed each other goodbye before she and Adam quickly scuttled up the steep staircase into one of the cars. They found their spots and waved furiously to Sarah's mother and father on the platform below until the train again hissed loudly, and then began to slowly lurch away from the station. It picked up speed as Sarah and Adam watched the people and the station grow smaller and smaller, until they were nothing but small dots on the horizon before it all disappeared completely from view.

Adam sat high on his knees, peering out the window, watching the world pass by faster than he ever could have imagined. Sarah smiled to herself as she saw his tiny forehead pressed tightly up against the glass, his warm breath fogging up the window in front of his open mouth as he started agog at the scenery before him. She suddenly had an overwhelming need to turn to George and smile at the joy exhibited by their son, but she was once again struck by the immense feeling of loss when she realized that he was not with them.

Sarah was still perplexed by how often she felt that he was right beside her: she swore that she could sometimes feel his warm breath down her neck, but whenever she turned, he was nowhere to be seen, leaving her feeling even more sad and lonely than before. Many times, she could have sworn he was so near that she could touch him, and while it comforted her to feel his presence, it infuriated her that she could not interact with him as she longed to. When alone, she would catch herself conversing with him, as if he would answer her back, and was often genuinely surprised to discover she was merely talking into thin air yet again.

Soon tiring of the same wintery fields and windblown cows, Sarah reached into her bag to pull out her knitting. She was soon lost in her own little world until Adam excitedly poked her, and when she looked up, she saw that the view from their window had changed drastically as they were quickly approaching Chicago. She hurriedly gathered their things, shoving them in her bag, then admonished herself when the ride took another twenty minutes until they pulled into the bustling station.

Sarah had already spoken with Adam about the size of the train station and the city overall. She ordered him to stay directly behind her, holding onto her skirts, as they exited the train, and then hold her hand on the platform as they crossed to the next locomotive to ensure their luggage was transferred before they then went to the hotel dining room across the street. They had arranged to see Sarah's brother, Matthew, and his wife, Ruby, during the few short hours before their next train departed.

Sarah and Adam were already seated when Matthew and Ruby found them, their three children in tow. After the chaos of greeting each other ended, Sarah held out her arms and received her newborn niece into them from Ruby. Sarah had met her older niece and nephew before when they had come to visit the previous Easter, but this was the first time she had beheld the tiny baby, just seven weeks old, and her arms were aching to hold her. All through their meal, Sarah held tightly to little Josephine, rejecting any attempts by her brother or his wife to relieve her of her duties to allow her to eat. Assuring them that she was fine, Sarah was more than willing to give them a break to eat unencumbered. What she didn't voice was that she was in actuality clinging to the babe for dear life, wondering if it would be the last time she would ever hold a newborn again, or at least until Adam was grown and married, if he chose to settle anywhere near her. She knew that her body was too broken for birthing healthy children, even in the unlikely scenario that her broken heart would someday mend to the point that she could entertain the thought of marrying again.

As she held the sweet little girl, Sarah's eyes welled up several times as she thought about the life she thought she would have versus the one that she was living. She recalled in her mind the three small graves close together in the corner of the churchyard reserved especially for children where her infants laid at rest. While brooding, she saw the sympathetic look on her brother's face out of the corner of her eye, but she chose to ignore him, focusing instead on cooing at the baby while drinking in her fill of the newborn's sweet fragrance.

When it was time for her and Adam to return to the station, with hugs of goodbye and promises of meeting again on their return visit home, Sarah reluctantly handed the baby girl back to her mother, telling her parents how incredibly blessed they were. Matthew and Ruby had merely nodded their agreement, devastated for the many losses they knew she was still working through.

The next leg of the train ride was long and boring for Sarah. Still restless, she couldn't seem to get settled enough to relax. She sat quietly and tried to concentrate on her knitting or reading while keeping a watchful eye on Adam during the day as the landscape sped by. At night, though, as she lay rocking gently in her berth, Adam tucked up securely between her and the wall, her mind would replay the scenes of the last few months in her head over and over again while sleep eluded her.

By the time they reached Colorado Springs, Sarah was exhausted. She had deep circles under her eyes, and she was bone weary, but somehow she managed to get them to the hotel for their overnight stay and onto the train the next morning to head up the mountain to Ginny's waiting home.

In the morning when she woke, Sarah had discovered that she was bleeding. She tried to ignore it and instead went about the business of settling them on the train and in their seats, telling herself to simply hang on: soon she would be at her sister's house, and she could finally rest there, where Ginny could help with Adam. She prayed vehemently that she could make it just a few more hours, when all would be well, but alas, it was not to be.

Sarah shifted uncomfortably in her seat as the excruciating cramping overtook her. She bit her lip in a feeble attempt not to cry out in pain, but every once in a while, a soft moan would escape her lips and Adam would turn his concerned face to her. She would gather all her strength and smile at him in a desperate attempt to reassure him. As the train began to climb in elevation, though, she began to feel weaker. She felt the blood pooling around her, making her desperate to ebb the flow, but she had no idea how. Knowing she was losing consciousness, she fought valiantly to stay alert. As the train made its final push toward the station, however, Sarah was only able to grab Adam's arm and gasp, "Go find someone," before she slid to the floor in a heap.

The young boy ran screaming for help, and several passengers, mostly rugged young miners, had come down the aisle to try to be of some assistance. However, when they saw the grisly scene before them, they hurriedly stepped away and relinquished any responsibility to the conductor who was pushing his way through, the boy anxiously pulling on his hand in an attempt to make him hurry.

The conductor took one look at the young woman and knew he was way out of his depth. All he could think to do was to clear the space around her to allow her some dignity and sit with the boy for the last few minutes before the train arrived at the station. As they pulled alongside the platform, the conductor jumped down and grabbed a young porter, asking him to run for the sheriff, saying that there was a "situation" onboard that required his attention. The young man had immediately set off toward the jail, and the conductor went back to sit with the young woman until help arrived.

Chapter Twelve

Ginny and her family were running late getting to the station. Since they did not leave home very often, it was often a chore to get the girls out the door. Her husband, who had come home to escort them, stood impatiently by as he watched his wife try to wrestle their two young daughters into their coats, hats, mittens, and scarves. He had been delayed himself, losing track of time while trying to finish up a ledger, and heard the train whistle a few miles from the station as he was halfway home, so he was especially irritated that they were not ready when he came through the door. By the time they made it back to the station, the platform was empty. Jacob turned to see his wife watching him with questioning eyes, so he said, "Perhaps they missed the connection in the city?"

"Perhaps…" Ginny agreed, but doubt was etched on her features.

"Meanwhile, I had better send a telegram to the station master in Colorado Springs and see if he can tell me if they came through before the connection today," he told her. "Why don't you take the girls and go sit in the lobby while I see what I can dig up?"

Ginny had merely nodded, unsure of what else to do in the situation, but realized that her husband, a railroad employee, would be able to discover much more information about what possibly had happened than she could. So, she took the hands of her small daughters and found a bench on which to wait out of the wind and the cold.

***

Twenty minutes earlier, on the train, the young sheriff asked, "So, John, what seems to be the problem?" as he walked down the aisle toward where the conductor was standing.

"Well, I reckon I'm not rightly sure," the older man responded, his expression slightly perplexed.

"What did you call me over for, then?"

"Because I don't know quite what to make of this," the conductor replied, his hand gesturing toward the floor between two benches.

The sheriff crossed the last few steps to close the gap and looked down at the unconscious young woman surrounded by a pool of blood.

"Oh, Christ almighty!" he declared, the words flying out of his mouth before he even thought to stop them. "What have we here?"

"I don't know, Joe. This here young man came tearin' up the aisle, cryin' about his mama needin' help. When I came back here, this is what I saw."

The sheriff turned, and for the first time saw a young boy sitting across the aisle, his eyes as big as saucers, his face pale and drawn.

"It's going to be all right," Joe assured him, reaching out and tussling the child's brown hair before turning back to the woman.

"First off, we've got to get her out of that small space," he said, thinking out loud. "Let's try to spread her out here in the aisle so that we have some room to work."

He looked up again and noticed a few passengers still milling around, fascinated by what was happening, but trying to give the men some space to work.

"Anyone know who she is?" he asked, glancing around him. Everyone shook their heads, looking to one another for reassurance that the identity of the woman was indeed a mystery.

Joe sighed. Once again, for the millionth time, he wondered how he had ever allowed himself to get wrangled into this job. "Then can anyone tell me if anything happened? Was she traveling with anyone? Did someone or something strike her?"

Again, he was met with headshakes and murmurs that no one saw a thing.

"Really? Not one of you noticed a thing?" he asked again, one eyebrow raised in disbelief, annoyed that he obviously had a very ill or injured woman on his hands and no experience with what to do about it. "Was she traveling with anyone?" he asked again.

An older miner finally spoke up. "No, sir. She wasn't travelin' with no one but the boy there. She was real quiet-like on the trip. Never said a word to no one that I saw. I saw her there, and then I dinn't. Not sure what all happened to her."

Joe scrutinized the man for a few moments and then he turned back to the conductor as the man asked, "What do you think is wrong with her, Joe? Is she hurt?"

Joe shook his head. "No, I don't think so… At least, not anywhere I can see. I don't even know where the blood is coming from. Let's get her up."

On his signal, they each grabbed an arm of the woman and got her to a sitting position. Then, Joe was able to bend down and hoist her over his shoulder. When he felt how light she was, he thought to himself how it had been a long time since he had carried a woman, and how he was much more used to hauling drunken miners than those of the female persuasion. It made sense, though, in that there certainly was not an overabundance of women where they were, in stark contrast to all the men.

"On second thought, let's bring her to the jail and lay her down on one of the cots in a cell. Someone go and find Doc Miller, too," he called back over his shoulder. "He was out of his office on my way down here."

"Oh, and make sure no one forgets the boy!" he added as an afterthought, now thinking that it was even rarer to have to worry about a child in his line of work in that town.

Joe picked his way up the aisle to the exit at the back of the car. He turned back and tried to lean forward to balance the young woman over his shoulder while he used his hands to grab onto the handles on the way down the steep stairs. He prayed silently that he wouldn't slip and fall, dropping the mother in front of her boy and further traumatizing him. When he made it to the platform, there were still a few people milling around, talking in groups or in pairs, wondering what all the commotion was about.

Joe didn't waste any time walking through the small station, bypassing it completely to come out onto the main street, quickly trekking to the jail and straight into an empty cell to deposit the woman on the cot therein. Standing up to stretch his back, he lamented that he hadn't had a good workout like that in a long while; that carrying over one hundred pounds on his back uphill at over fifty-five hundred feet was no small feat. He was still a young man, but he certainly wasn't feeling like it right at that moment.

Joe grabbed the blanket at the end of the bed and spread it over the woman. He had a fire going and the room was warm, but not knowing what exactly was going on, he began to worry about shock and wanted to make sure that she didn't catch a chill. He looked up in time to see the conductor coming in, leading the small boy by the hand before depositing him in the middle of the room.

"Joe, I'm sorry, but I gotta get back…" the man said apologetically. "I gotta make sure everythin' is set with the train."

"That's all right. I understand," replied Joe, forcing himself to smile while thinking that he was at a loss on what to do next. "Just tell me before you leave, did anyone go for Doc Miller?"

"Yeah, I saw Carl runnin' up the street to his office."

"Good!" Joe stated, feeling a bit more confident that things may soon be under control. "Thanks again, man."

"Hey, no problem, Joe. Thanks for showin' up. Not every day I find a woman in a puddle of blood on my train!"

"No, I suppose it isn't," Joe answered him, suddenly distracted by a small moan escaping his charge's lips. "Thank God! Thanks, again."

"Hey!" he added as an afterthought as the conductor was almost at the door. "Make sure that you let someone at the depot know what's going on, would ya?"

"Sure! Have a good evening, Joe!"

"Thanks! You, too."

The door shut, leaving Joe to scrutinize the woman, running his hand through his hair. "Well, damn! If this isn't just a fine predicament!" he said aloud, forgetting again that there was a child in the room.

He nearly jumped out of his skin when he heard a quiet little voice ask, "Mister? Mister, what's wrong with my mama?"

"I don't know, son," Joe answered, not really having had a lot of experience around kids in traumatic situations but figuring that answering honestly would be the best option. "But someone has gone for the doctor, and he should be able to let us know."

As if on cue, the jail door opened, and the doctor walked in.

"Whatcha got for me here, Joe?"

"I'm not exactly sure, Doc. The train got in this afternoon and Carl Smith came to get me after this woman was discovered in a puddle of blood on the floor in one of the cars. I wasn't sure what was wrong… Still not, if the truth be told… I think it may be medical more than criminal, so I sent someone to grab you."

The doctor nodded his understanding and glanced around. "And who might this be?" he asked, looking a bit surprised to see the little boy hovering in the shadows of the falling winter evening.

"I reckon I didn't even ask him his name, Doc. He said she's his mama, and he's traveling with her."

"Well, I would hope he's the woman's child. You didn't ask him anything?"

Joe felt stupid for not thinking to question the boy for any helpful information. Then again, if women were scarce in town, children were even more so, and not having had many opportunities to be around them since he was a child himself, he wasn't even sure how old the boy was, or how well he would be able to communicate with him. He merely shook his head at the doctor, his cheeks reddening a bit that he had overlooked a pretty obvious information source as to what had happened.

"Well, young man, I'm Dr. Miller. Is this woman your mama?"

The boy only nodded, and his eyes large with fright.

"That's good. We are gonna do our best to fix her right up, all right?" the doctor pressed on.

Again, the boy nodded, but his terrified and confused expression was not lessened.

"Do you know your mama's name, son?" the doctor continued.

Another nod.

"Can you tell me?"

"Sarah," he whispered.

"Sarah?"

"Yes, sir."

"That's great, son. Thank you! Now, tell me, is your mama sick?"

The boy shook his head.

"Has this ever happened to Mama before?"

Another shake.

"Do you have a Pa?"

The little boy looked hesitant for a few seconds before he started to nod his head, then thought better of it and began to shake it instead.

"I see. What's your name?"

"Adam."

"Well, it's nice to meet you, Adam. This here is Sheriff Joe and, as I said, I'm Doc Miller. We're gonna take real good care of your mama and you, don't you worry."

"Thank you," the little boy said with as much dignity as he could muster.

"Joe, why don't you take the boy to your desk and let him sit down to scribble on something. I need to examine my patient and I'm pretty certain she would rather not have her son present when I do," the doctor said.

"All right, come on over here," said Joe, holding out his hand, feeling shocked when the boy actually reached for it and took it in his. Leading the boy to his desk, he pulled out some blank paper and a pencil, telling him that he could draw, and was pleased when the boy nodded his head in understanding. He hurried back to the jail cell, curious about what the doctor had discovered.

"You think someone hurt her, Doc?"

"No, I don't think so," the man answered. He then looked over his shoulder to the little boy at the desk. "Adam?"

The boy looked up.

"What's Mama's name again, son?"

"Sarah," he said, glancing up momentarily from his scribbles.

"Thank you," the doctor said, turning back to the woman laying before him.

The doctor began to palpate the woman's stomach and she moaned softly but did not regain consciousness. He listened to her heart, breathing, and felt her pulse, then moving down to her waist, he began to unfasten and pull down her skirts.

"Whoa! Wait! Doc, what are you doing? I can't have some naked woman in my jail!" Joe exclaimed, turning quickly around to face the far wall, shocked at what he was witnessing.

The doctor took off the woman's shoes and pulled down her thick woolen stockings over her legs. Her skirt and petticoat came next, and Joe didn't know where to avert his eyes when he turned back around.

"I've gotta get her out of these bloody clothes, Joe. Blood is liquid and she's gonna get too chilled laying here drenched in it."

The doctor then lifted up her chemise, so that it was laying over her lower abdomen. He next began working on getting her pantalets off before Joe began to object again.

"Really, Doc, is this necessary?" he asked as he looked up at the ceiling. His cheeks were flaming bright red, and he felt like he was going to pass out at any second.

The doctor turned around and started laughing. "What's the matter, there, Joe? Haven't you ever seen a naked woman before?"

"NO!" Joe shouted, with equal parts shock and humiliation.

"Really?" the doctor asked incredulously.

"Yes! Really!" the young man answered, mortified beyond belief.

"But aren't you close to thirty years old?"

"Yeah. So?"

"So… You're almost thirty years old and you haven't ever seen a naked woman?"

"No! I mean, yes, of course! But not like this…" he stammered as his hand flapped weakly back and forth to signify her laying down. "Am I married, Doc?" he continued, his voice cracking slightly at the end of his sentence.

"Well, no, I guess you aren't. But still…" the older man replied, surprised that the man hadn't at least had some intimate experience with the fairer sex.

"Look, I'm not married, nor do I have any sisters. My ma, God rest her soul, was a proper lady. I haven't ever done much more with a girl than kiss and maybe neck a little."

"Well, in that case, I guess I can see why you might be a bit uncomfortable!" the doctor said, trying to save the young sheriff more embarrassment.

"It isn't like there's an overabundance of women here," Joe felt the need to further explain. "Not proper ladies, anyway. Believe me, with my occupation, I have seen plenty of half and fully naked women down at the saloons, but I'm doing my job, so it doesn't really register. Besides, if there's a situation… ahem… a problem… up in one of the rooms, they usually have a blanket around them by the time I get in there. And, believe me, after dealing with some of the men who go to them, I have absolutely no interest in… visiting… any of them when I'm not on the clock."

"That's a good thing. I treat those poor young women and many of the men who utilize their services, too, and I can tell you to stay far, far away from them. Most of the time what they have, you don't want!"

By this time, the doctor had everything off below Sarah's waist and was gently prodding her lower abdomen before he peered quickly between her legs. Then when he seemed satisfied, he pulled the blanket back up over her hips.

"All right, Joe. I'm finished now. You don't have to face the wall anymore," the man chuckled. "But I'm going to need another blanket to spread over her body, as I had to use this one to cover her legs. Her skirts are far too wet to leave on her all night."

"What do you mean, leave her here, half-naked, all night?" Joe asked, his unease with the whole situation evident in his voice. He had no idea what to do with a woman rooming in the jail.

"Joe, she's not well. We can't be moving her. She has lost a lot of blood and she's in shock. She needs a place to stay tonight that is warm."

Just then, the door to the jail flew open as Jacob and Ginny rushed in. Ginny's eyes jumped from the woman on the cot, to the pile of bloody clothing discarded on the floor, then to the little boy at the desk, before settling her gaze on the doctor and Joe. Tears sprang into her eyes and a strangled cry escaped her throat.

"What's going on?" she pleaded. "Please, tell me what is wrong with my sister!"

"She's your sister?" Joe asked.

"Yes! Please, tell me what happened!" she sobbed as she crossed over to her little nephew sitting at the desk.

"Mrs. McAllister, your sister is suffering a miscarriage. I'm sorry to report that it is a fairly late one; I believe her to have been, based on her size, about four and a half to five months pregnant."

"Oh, no!" Ginny moaned.

"I'm afraid that she's not finished yet, and I'm quite worried about her. She's lost a lot of blood."

"What happened?" Ginny's husband, Jacob, broke in, looking directly at Joe.

"When the train pulled in, someone rushed in here to report a problem. When I ran there, I found her passed out in a pool of blood. Her boy here couldn't really tell us much, so I brought her here until Dr. Miller was found so he could examine her in peace."

"The boy said that his father isn't with her?" the doctor said, hoping that perhaps the child had misunderstood the question.

"No," Ginny answered, tears spilling from her eyes. "He died a few months ago."

Joe and the doctor looked at each other in surprise.

"I didn't even know she was pregnant again," Ginny lamented as the tears rolled down her cheeks. "Poor Sarah! I cannot believe that she just lost her husband and now another baby."

"Another baby?" the doctor interjected, trying to gather more information regarding her condition.

"Yes, Doctor. This will be her… let's see…" Ginny counted in her head, "fourth child lost."

"Oh, God," Joe exclaimed, without even realizing he was speaking aloud. "She's so young!"

"Yes, Sheriff, she's only twenty-two. Adam here is her first and only surviving child. Jacob and I brought them out here for the holidays to try to spare them some pain of their first Christmas without George. But I never would have insisted she come if I had known she was expecting again." Ginny put her face in her hands and began to sob. Jacob walked over to her and rubbed her back.

"Do you think it was the travel that did it, Doc?" he inquired.

"Given the report that this is her fourth child lost, I'm apt to say that no, her travel here did nothing to precipitate this. I think that she has a history of difficult pregnancies, and this would have happened at home if she had been there. For some women, their bodies don't tolerate carrying a baby. She's fortunate that she has at least had one. Many women are not even that lucky."

"What do we do for her?" Ginny asked.

"Well, for tonight, until the miscarriage is complete, she needs to stay right where she is. Joe and I will be with her and keep her as comfortable and hydrated as we can. Mrs. McAllister, if you would be so kind as to help me find in her things a clean nightgown, then perhaps we can change her into it so that she will be more comfortable."

"Of course. The teamster should have already delivered her trunk to the house."

"And, also, I would ask you to please take the boy home. This is no place for him. He needs to be safe, warm, and dry, instead of worrying about his mother for the rest of the night."

Jacob broke in, "We will take the boy home and get him settled, as well as go through the trunk. Once Ginny is able to find something suitable for Sarah to wear among her things, I will bring it back down."

When the McAllisters left with Adam in tow, Joe turned to the doctor, his eyes wide and a bit wild with panic.

"Doc, you can't expect me to stay here alone all night with a woman, sick or not!"

"No, of course not. I will stay here, too. She's too unstable for me to consider anything else. However, if there's an emergency in the night to which I must attend, you'll have to be responsible for her until I get back, all right?"

"No! That is not all right! I have no idea on God's green Earth what to do with a woman!"

"Now I see why you aren't married, Joe!" the doctor broke in, hiding his smile as he tried adding some levity to the situation. The withering look the young sheriff gave him in response showed, however, that he was not amused.

"Honestly, Joe, I don't think I will have to step out. But if I do, the most important things are to keep her warm and hydrated. Her body has to take care of this itself. There is nothing more we can do for her, other than support her through it."

"Will she sleep the whole time?" Joe asked, his voice unsteady, unwilling to think about what could happen. He had certainly heard enough stories about women having babies that he knew it could get loud and messy. He wasn't sure about a miscarriage, but he was mentally trying to prepare himself for the possibility that things could quickly change from the quiet calm they were experiencing now to the polar opposite.

"First things first, as soon as Jacob gets back here with the clean nightclothes, we will get her changed. I'm hoping that the jostling and moving her around will wake her, but it may not. She's lost a lot of blood today and the elevation here is high, much higher than she's used to. It isn't a good combination, Joe. In all honesty, between you and me, at this point, I'm simply hoping she makes it through the night."

"What? You mean this could kill her?"

"Hopefully not, but you know as well as I do that Easterners sometimes don't do so well up here, even without essentially going through labor, on top of losing a lot of blood. Rest is the best thing for her. Her body will do what it needs to do, of that I am certain, and I'm hoping she will be awake by the time it happens. I will continue to check her periodically. Meanwhile, make sure you have enough wood in here to keep that fire stoked, and I will need some heated water to try to clean her up a bit. If it gets too bad, I will give her some Laudanum."

Joe nodded quietly and went out to bring in more firewood. He already had a more than sufficient pile in the wood box inside the jail, as well as a tall stack along the back wall outside, but it gave him something to do, and he wanted to get out into the fresh air to clear his head. As he walked in with his last armload, Jacob McAllister opened the front door and met Joe just as he was arriving back inside. He then handed over to Dr. Miller a long, white nightgown, a fluffy red robe, and thick woolen socks, saying only, "From Ginny."

"Thanks, Jacob," the doctor stated, and Sarah's brother-in-law turned abruptly to leave, feeling very out of place in the situation.

100

"Tell Mrs. McAllister that we will bring her sister to her tomorrow morning if all goes as planned, all right?" the doctor asked.

"That's fine. We appreciate it. Thanks for watching over her, Doc and Joe."

"Thanks for taking the boy!" Joe responded, grateful to not have to worry about him, too.

Once the door closed, the doctor turned again to the sheriff.

"You think you're up to helping me getting her cleaned up?" he asked.

"I suppose so..." Joe responded, his voice showing his hesitation.

"Just get me some washrags and a bowl full of that hot water for now. You got any clean towels?"

Joe looked up and scowled at the doctor. "I'm not a savage, Doc. Yes, I have clean towels and even sheets available."

"Well, I wasn't sure, with you being a bachelor and all..." the doctor responded with a teasing grin.

"You know," Joe said, as he set to work fulfilling the doctor's supply list, "we talked about what would happen if you got called out in the night, but what happens if I do? More specifically, what if I have to make an arrest?"

"Well," the older man replied thoughtfully, "I thought about that. It's a Thursday night, so I'm guessing we will just be thankful that it's not Friday or Saturday. If something does happen, then we will maybe have to consider... Well, let's not even think about that, all right?"

"From your mouth to God's ear."

Joe put the water and supplies at the end of the cot. The doctor lifted the blankets and began to carefully wash the dried blood off Sarah's legs. She moaned slightly at the intrusion, but the doctor was just as quick to wipe her dry again with a clean towel that she did little more than stir. Joe went out multiple times to throw out the spent water back between the jail and the privy, only to come in to refill the receptacle with warm water once again. Finally, when the doctor decided that Sarah was clean enough, he asked Joe to please sit down on the bed and hold her up so the older man could pull the blouse off her back. Joe obliged, and he was surprised by how heavy such a small woman felt against him while she was limp. Then, after a few seconds, he was caught even more off-guard as he noticed the warmth of her body radiating through to his, right before he noticed her scent, soft and slightly floral. He chuckled, realizing that this young woman certainly smelled better than most of the guests in his jail whom he had to manhandle. In fact, if he had to admit it, he would say that she felt much better in his arms, too. He got lost in a daydream, thinking about how nice women were to have around. *They are a damned sight more civilized than the rowdy men I have to deal with day in and day out!* he thought. *I could get used to this!*

However, Joe was brought abruptly back to the reality of the situation when the doctor asked him to lift her toward him just a bit more, so that he could get to the laces of her corset more easily in order to loosen them.

"Doc, you're going to take off her… her…. corset, too?"

"Absolutely! Can you imagine being in pain and being trussed up like a chicken? I honestly don't even understand why women wear these things, anyway. I prefer me a woman who looks more natural, don't you?"

"She looks pretty natural to me!" Joe replied, without thinking.

The doctor tried to hide his smile as he replied, "Yeah, well, these things are atrocious, even the pregnancy ones! Help me get it off her so we can put her gown on over her chemise. It's dry now and I think she'll be more comfortable when she wakes up with two strange men around her to learn that she was never completely naked."

"Sounds like a plan to me." Joe exhaled a breath he wasn't even aware he was holding, grateful that she wouldn't be in a position of having been embarrassed, thinking, *Me, too, for that matter.*

Chapter Thirteen

Once they got Sarah settled into her nightgown and her blankets put back over her lithe body, the two men sat down to cups of coffee, facing each other across the desk.

"So, how long do you think this is going to take?" Joe warily asked the doctor.

"I can't really say for sure. Should be at least a few hours yet, but without knowing her history, when she started bleeding or the heaviness of the flow, let alone exactly how far along she is, it's all speculation at this point anyway."

The doctor looked up to see the slightly repulsed expression on the face of the town sheriff in front of him.

"What is it?" he asked.

"Did you really have to talk about the heaviness of flow?"

"Sorry, Joe. Don't mean to make you uncomfortable, but this is all part of God's design. Women bring forth life into our world, and this is just how it goes sometimes. But I get that you're a bit squeamish, I guess, given this isn't your line of work," the doctor said.

Then he thought for a moment before adding, "You know what, though … You've seen a gunshot wound, right?"

"Well, sure. I have seen plenty. Kind of comes along with the territory of being sheriff. You know that."

"Do you get repulsed by the flow of blood out of one of those?"

"No, not really," the younger man answered quizzically, never having really thought about it before. "I mean, I don't like it, but it is just part of the job. It's what happens when someone gets shot."

"Exactly," the doctor said, looking poignantly at Joe over the rim of his coffee cup.

"All right, I guess I see your point," Joe conceded. "It's just blood from gunshot wounds doesn't normally come from *that* general vicinity," he waved his hand down over his crotch and added for emphasis. *"On women."*

The doctor just laughed and shook his head. "Oh, Joe… You have a lot to learn about women if you ever want to get married."

"Well, seeing as how there's about one woman to every five hundred men up here, no exaggeration, I guess I have time to learn," Joe retorted. "But I won't ever get married, anyway," he added as an afterthought.

"Why not?"

"Because… well…" Joe caught himself as he almost let his guard down. "Because! First of all, where would I meet a decent woman here, and where do I ever go where I could meet a decent woman who would want to come here? Not to mention that would only happen if I could speak to a woman to make her acquaintance in the first place, which, after so many years up here, I'm pretty much certain I'm unable to do. So, all added together, I would have to say that makes my prospects for marriage exactly zero."

"Joe, are you saying you're too shy to talk to women?"

Joe looked incredulously at the doctor. "If there were any around here, other than the ladies at the saloon, anyway, I guess you would have to say that I'm too shy."

"But you just said you could talk to the women at the saloon."

"Sure!"

"Why is that?"

"I don't know. I guess it's because when I talk to them, it's usually dealing with something regarding the law: either they're breaking it or one of their patrons are. On top of that, I have no interest in any of them in a romantic sort of way, so I reckon it's more like talking to a sister or cousin or something… I haven't really thought about it."

"Hmm…" the doctor agreed, not really able to argue with Joe's statement. He had summed up being a single man in their town pretty accurately.

All evening long, Joe and the doctor kept a vigil over Sarah, watching her closely to see if there had been any change. Occasionally she would writhe on the mattress in obvious pain, a strangled moan escaping her lips, but other than that, she remained largely unresponsive. The doctor would periodically go to her, feeling her forehead, then her pulse, before gently and carefully lifting the blankets covering her legs, checking her progress, and changing out the soiled bedding under her. He would then turn his head toward Joe and slowly shake his head, letting the younger man know that no progress had yet been made. Every so often he would also place a wetted towel into her mouth in an attempt for her to at least get some hydration, though he knew it was far from ideal.

Around midnight, Joe lifted his head in surprise, shocked to find that he had put it down on his folded arms on his desk and drifted off to sleep. He squinted in the lamplight to see the doctor standing over their young charge who was moaning and moving around in obvious distress. The older man placed a comforting hand on her forehead, gently pushing back the hair that had slipped out of her topknot onto her face, soothing her, "Shh… Sarah, you're doing well, my dear. You're almost through this. Just hang on a bit longer and then you can rest."

"Is she awake?" Joe asked, his voice sounding louder than he meant it to as it cut through the quiet of the jail.

"Yes and no," the doctor replied. "She's aware something is happening, but she's too unresponsive and weak to really comprehend what that something is. She's hovering between consciousness and sleep, but I gave her some laudanum to take the edge off the pain, which certainly accounts for her being drowsy."

Joe sat back in his chair and waited, watching helplessly as the doctor administered to her as much as he could. After about another hour or so, Joe heard the doctor sigh in relief.

"What?" he asked, his voice sounding far away to his tired ears.

"She's passed it. The worst is over. Thank God! I was really beginning to worry that she wouldn't be able to do it."

And with that, the doctor gently lifted Sarah's knees up and whisked away yet another towel he had placed under her to keep the bed clean. Joe could see that he was gently cradling something very small in his hand, studying it.

After a few minutes, he turned and looked up at Joe, saying, "It is a crying shame, really. He seems just perfect. I can't say as though I can find one thing wrong with him to justify why this happened." Frustration was clearly written on his face.

"He?" Joe whispered reverently. "It's a boy? You can tell already?"

"Yes," the doctor added pensively. "Anyone could tell, really. By this stage in pregnancy, the babe is pretty much fully formed. It just needs the remainder of the time to grow."

He turned his attention back to examining the child. "It's a crying shame," he added again. Joe could only nod in response, surprised to feel the lump in his throat.

I'm a grown man. A sheriff, for God's sake! He admonished himself for being so emotional, but all he could think of was how this poor woman would feel being told that she had lost yet another child, the last of her deceased husband's she would ever carry. The fact that it would have been destined to be male seemed to make it all the worse, as he would have most likely grown into a man who would have reminded her of her lost spouse.

Joe placed his head down on the desk and took several deep breaths, trying to clear his head. He heard the back door open and then close quietly, assuming it was the doctor leaving to take a break, but he felt too drained and spent to bother to raise his head to look.

The next thing he knew, Joe awoke to a voice in the stillness. For a second, he was confused, wondering what his mother was doing in his jail, until his brain engaged, realizing what was happening. The window of the jail framed the pink and gold strands of the morning, and Sarah was finally awake and getting agitated. He raised his head off his desk and saw that Dr. Miller was asleep on the cot in his other jail cell, snoring softly. Joe slowly rose and walked over to Sarah, standing beside her, ready to let her know she was safe, and all was well. He looked down at her, thinking about how small and helpless she seemed, lost on the cot, covered by blankets. He felt a twinge of protective pity for her as he studied her face, still slackened with sleep, her right hand curved prettily beside her head on the pillow. He was marveling at her ivory skin, stunning blonde hair, and soft, feminine features, thinking that she was a beautiful woman. It wasn't so much an attraction, but rather more how one thinks a work of art or a sunset is beautiful: pleasant to look at and intriguing to behold. A few seconds later, she moaned again in her sleep, writhing a bit under her covers, causing Joe to instinctually take a step back. He didn't want to appear that he was hovering over her, staring, even though he realized that was exactly what he had been doing.

Joe had not been kidding when he told the doctor that he was too shy, not having had a sweetheart in years, to have had the opportunity to get close enough to study a woman's face very long, without feeling awkward or bashful. He had to admit that he was enjoying looking at her face, so like his, with a nose, mouth, eyes; yet still so different from his own, with her soft, dewy skin and gentler lines.

When her eyes opened for the first time and focused on his, he felt himself involuntarily taking in a sharp inhalation. Her eyes were pools of deep blue, deeper than any blue he had ever seen before, like sapphires. They were the crowning glory of her already beautiful face, even while showing signs of fatigue with deep, dark circles under them, hinting at the physical trauma she had endured. When their eyes locked, Joe was surprised to feel his heart jump into his throat, his appreciation of her turning into a lightning bolt of attraction in an instant. His heart began beating a mile a minute when he saw she was opening her mouth to speak.

"I'm in jail?" she queried, speaking low, her whisper washing over him like a wave while her eyes clouded over with confusion and fear.

"Umm... No," Joe answered, while hearing how highly pitched his voice sounded to his own ears, giving away that he was horribly uncomfortable and out of his depth with this interaction. He took a deep breath and tried again, consciously lowering his voice back to his normal range.

"No... No, ma'am, you aren't in jail, per se... Well, yes, you are... But you aren't... I mean..." Joe's voice trailed off as he realized how ridiculous he sounded. He shook his head slightly, his cheeks blazing with embarrassment.

Nice introduction, you idiot! he chided himself as she studied him with a bemused expression.

"So, am I in jail or am I not?" Sarah asked, her voice a little stronger this time.

"No... No, ma'am, as I was saying, you aren't in jail. You're in the jailhouse because you got sick on the train, and I had to come and get you. We didn't know where Doc Miller was, and the porter who ran for him said his office was locked, so this seemed a better location to bring you than just leaving you on the train until he could get a good look at you."

Suddenly, panic filled Sarah's eyes. "Where's my boy? Where's Adam?"

She started to get up, but Joe gently put his hands on her shoulders and pushed her lightly back down.

"Now, then, ma'am, your boy is just fine. Your sister and her husband have him with them. But you have been very ill, and I don't think I can let you get up until the doctor has a chance to look at you."

"If my sister has my son, why am I here and not at her house?" Sarah demanded, her voice getting a bit shrill.

"Because when I found you on the train, we didn't know yet who you were. Your family was made aware that there had been a commotion on the train from someone at the station and came up here, but by that time, the doctor was examining you and determined that you were too ill to move right then. So, you stayed here last night."

"With you?" she asked incredulously. "Alone?"

"No, ma'am," Joe answered her. "Doc Miller's here, too. He's asleep on the cot in the other cell right now." He stretched out a long finger to point to her what he meant as he spoke, noticing that her eyes followed.

She then turned back to look at him once more. "I got sick on the train?" she asked him, her voice an almost imperceptible whisper.

"Yes."

"What happened? I remember feeling a bit faint."

"Yes, well, you passed out. You were unconscious when I found you."

"I was?"

"Yes, ma'am."

"Well, what happened? Why did I pass out?" she demanded of him.

"You... umm... Well, you... umm... lost a lot of blood..." Joe started to explain before he realized that unless Dr. Miller suddenly awoke, he was going to have to describe very soon what had happened to her and he panicked, realizing that he hardly knew where to begin, let alone what words to use.

Men don't just go around talking to women who are expecting about their delicate condition, he thought, *especially when one of those men would be me*!

He looked over at the sleeping doctor, secretly praying that the man would suddenly rouse and save him from this very unusual situation, but alas, he still slumbered away.

"Yes?" Sarah inquired, wondering what Joe's hang-up was. She sensed that he was very uncomfortable but wasn't sure of the reasoning.

"Well, you see, ma'am, you passed out on the train..."

"Yes, you told me that part already," she gently chided him, hoping he would press on.

Sarah saw a look of helplessness and panic flash across his features for a second until he was able to talk himself down. *Good Lord, I am being a dolt! I'm a sheriff, for crying out loud! I've arrested and shot men; why is this so damn hard? Why is she affecting me like this?* He took a deep breath before continuing with his internal dialog.

That's it... I have to suck it up. I'll tell her what she needs to know, while trying to stick to facts. I can do this.

He took a deep breath and started again, this time sounding much more matter of fact and controlled, albeit speaking the words in rapid succession. "Ma'am, you passed out on the train, and your little boy ran to get help. The conductor came and found you unconscious in a puddle of blood. He wasn't sure what had happened to you, so he sent someone to fetch me. When I saw you there, I figured that I needed to take you somewhere a bit more private and hauled you here, so the doctor could come and examine you."

He took another deep breath, not wanting to deliver the next bit of news, but knew he had to. He had the same pit in his stomach that he had any time he had to let a loved one know that a family member had passed. *This is truly the worst part about being a sheriff*, he thought, *having to deliver such devastating news.*

"Once you were here, ma'am, the doctor came and discovered the source of the bleeding." He paused and cleared his throat. "I'm sorry to say, ma'am, that you lost your unborn child last night."

He stood helplessly by as he watched her face crumple and tears magnify her big, blue eyes. "I was hoping this time would be different," she whispered.

"I'm so sorry, ma'am. I don't know what to say. There was nothing the doctor could do, but he was really worried about you, given the amount of blood you lost and the fact that the elevation's so high here. He didn't want to move you and stress your body further."

110

Sarah nodded slowly, understanding reflected in her face. "Well, then I guess I should thank you…" Sarah began before she looked down at her arms and realized that she was in her nightgown.

"Wait… where is my dress? How did I get changed into this? Did the doctor do this? How did you get my nightgown? Did you do this?" Sarah began rapidly firing the questions at him as he stumbled to find the right words to explain the situation.

"We had to remove your dress. It was wet with blood. Your sister sent us your nightgown. She figured you would be more comfortable in it."

"We?" she asked.

"Yes, the doctor and me."

"You?"

"Well, as I said, the doctor and me together," Joe tried to explain.

"You helped get me undressed?"

"Yes, and cleaned up, too," Joe said, before he thought, then instantly regretted his last words as he heard her indignant gasp.

"You? You saw me… saw me… *indisposed*?" she screeched, her cheeks reddening as her humiliation grew.

Suddenly, something snapped in Joe. He was trying so hard to be patient and kind to this woman, a stranger, and here she was acting as if he had done something unseemly, instead of helping the doctor in her time of need.

"Look, ma'am, don't get so indignant. You were more clothed at any point last night than ninety percent of the female inhabitants of this town on any given day. And believe me when I say I had no interest in buying what little you were selling, either!"

He realized as he said the words how it came across and he cringed slightly as she gasped in shock, immediately wondering what she must think of him, and then a second later, why he would even care?

Just then, he heard Dr. Miller behind him ask, "How's our patient doing over here, Joe?"

"She's fine," he muttered, still angry at her insinuation that he would be so bold and improper as to ogle her in her sickly, weakened state, taking advantage of her at her worst.

"Well, young lady, you had quite a day yesterday and gave us quite a scare last night. I'm glad to see that you have made it through all right. Now, how are you feeling, my dear?"

"Thirsty," she said, "and very tired."

"I can do something about the thirsty part. Joe, hand me a glass of water, would you? The tired part is something that a little rest and recuperation will have to take care of, unfortunately."

"When can I leave here and go to my sister's?" Sarah asked, anxious to get to a place that did not have strangers caring for her. She longed to be in a big feather bed, snuggled warmly underneath a feather tick, instead of stuck in a jail cell on a hard cot with nothing but rough, woolen blankets. In fact, Sarah noticed the whole place smelled. It wasn't pungent, but there was definitely a hint of something manly and unwashed embedded deep within the wooden walls, like how she presumed a bunkhouse would smell, where a bunch of grimy men would live together for weeks on end, none of them caring about hygiene because there were no womenfolk around to make them.

"Let's first take a look at you and see what we can see, all right?" the doctor asked her, reaching out to take her pulse.

Sarah looked over at Joe and asked, "Does *he* have to be here for this?"

I have already given him enough of a peep show, Sarah thought. She wasn't willing to have this man, who wasn't even medically trained, standing around looking at her when she wasn't decent. It was bad enough that a strange doctor was doing it, but at least he was a doctor! She wasn't even really sure what the other man did and why he was there as her foggy brain tried to piece together the past twenty-four hours.

"No, he doesn't, if you're comfortable with just me here. Why don't you get started on wrangling us up some breakfast, Joe?"

Joe stiffly nodded and went into another room, shoving the door closed behind him. *The nerve of that woman!* He huffed angrily. *Here I found her, carried her limp body up the hill, and stayed with her all night, but she's acting like I'm a lecher! For Christ's sake, I'm a lawman, not some pervert!*

Joe continued to seethe as he banged pans around making pancakes and eggs, the noise and force combating some of his aggression. He had never been so insulted in all his life! This woman had made him feel indecorous and uncouth! *Why, I have never been anything but a gentleman to women!* he fumed.

Before he knew it, he had plated breakfast for all three of them and put it on a tray before going back to his office, and depositing everything on his desk. By that time, the doctor was finished with Sarah, and when Joe looked up, he heard her sniffle helplessly and saw her red-rimmed eyes.

Oh, Lord. Why did she have to start crying! he thought to himself in disgust, realizing that his anger at her was now turning to pity, but he didn't want to feel sorry for this rude woman.

He carried her plate to her and held it out for her to take, saying somewhat snidely, "Ladies first."

Sarah took the plate and wondered for what felt like the hundredth time what was wrong with this man. "Thank you," she responded hesitantly.

"No problem," was his cool reply.

Joe handed off the next plate to the doctor before sitting down at his desk to eat his portion. He was caught a little off guard when he heard Sarah exclaim, "I'm not sure if it's because I'm so famished, but I think these are the best pancakes I have ever eaten!"

"Glad you like them," he said flatly in return, confused about how almost everything out of this woman's mouth sounded like a back-handed insult.

"Joe's the best pancake maker in town!" the doctor declared as he happily stabbed another bite before shoving it into his mouth. When he was done chewing, he continued, "He always makes them for the whole town for the Fourth of July breakfast. It's a given!"

When they were done eating, Joe took the dishes and returned to his small kitchen before freshening up a bit. By that point, he had been in his clothes for more than twenty-four hours and was feeling rather grubby. He put on a fresh shirt, brushed his teeth, combed his hair, and washed his face, contemplating for an instant if he wanted to shave or not, but decided he was too tired to mess with it right then and would do it later.

He walked back into the jail just in time to see Sarah's sister and brother-in-law walk into the room, Ginny holding Adam by the hand.

"Mama!" the young boy cried, running to his mother and flinging himself into her arms. "Are you all right? I was so scared!"

"Yes, baby, I'm fine!" Sarah said brightly, with much more conviction than she felt, and Joe had to admit that he admired the way she tried to remain cheerful for her child.

"So, Doc, can we bring her home yet?" Jacob McAllister asked.

"If she's feeling up to it, then she can certainly go back to your place. However, she is under strict orders to stay in bed and rest as much as possible for the next few days, to eat well, and drink lots of fluids. Got that?" Dr. Miller asked, looking at everyone, including Joe, making him wonder how he had gotten included in this woman's aftercare instructions. He had no input at all about what she would or wouldn't do.

"And Joe… I need you to go to the livery and get a buggy. She shouldn't be walking, so you'll have to drive her home."

"Me?" he responded in shock, once again not thinking about how he would come off.

"Mr. and Mrs. McAllister and the children all walked here and should go on ahead and prepare for her arrival, if you don't mind?" he added, turning back toward them.

"Sure," Joe mumbled, ready to escape the whole situation as soon as possible. He threw his coat on over his clothes and

114

walked out the door, shoving his hands in his pockets as he strode down the street.

When Joe returned to the jail, Sarah was dressed and sitting limply on the bed. When the doctor gave the all-clear, Joe went to offer his arm to help her up, but she waved him off and opted for the arm of the doctor instead. When she stood, the room began to spin, making her wobble, so Joe found himself rushing to her other side to help hold her steady. She took a few deep breaths and shook her head before beginning to walk. With every step, she felt like the floor was tilting and that at any second she was going to find herself sprawled out over the wooden slats, but she clung tightly to Dr. Miller's arm, dragging herself out to the street and the waiting buggy. She faltered a bit when she was trying to climb into the carriage as though she was too weak to make it, even with the doctor's support, and so Joe reached up instinctively to push her read end. She gasped in horror that he would be so bold on a public street, but it accomplished the goal, and she was able to sit. She clung to the underside of the seat with both hands, willing herself to stay upright, but as soon as Joe climbed in on the other side and the buggy began moving, she started to slump down further and further, like she was melting. Joe quickly moved the reins from both hands to his left and reached his right arm around her shoulders in order to pull her closer in an attempt to give her something to lean on so she wouldn't topple out of the seat. He was surprised when she snuggled deeper into him, then he realized that she was asleep. The short trek from the jail to the buggy had exhausted her to the point of collapse.

The McAllisters lived further up the hill, a bit above the small town. They were heading up the walk as Joe had pulled up in front of their home and he noted Ginny's surprised look when she saw how intimately he was holding her sister.

"She's asleep," he whispered over Sarah's head to her family, and they nodded their understanding. Jacob opened their front door and Ginny went in, followed by Adam and their two girls. Then he walked down to the buggy as Joe was gently shaking Sarah awake. When she opened her eyes, they widened in surprise.

"You fell asleep," Joe quickly informed her, and she nodded her understanding.

"Thank you for taking me here. I will see myself in now," Sarah said, as she tried to stand.

"Now, just hold on a second!" Joe told her, gently pushing her back down on the seat. He threw the reins at Jacob, who tied them around the porch railing to hold the horse. Joe managed to make it around to Sarah's side of the buggy just as she attempted to stand again and tumbled out into his arms, Joe barely managing to catch her before she would have hit the ground.

"Pardon me!" she gasped when she straightened up and felt how tightly his arms were wrapped around her.

"I will just be getting inside now!" she told him resolutely, before trying to take a step, only to begin to crumple yet again.

Suddenly, she felt one of Joe's arms around her back while the other reached down under her legs as he swung her up. "What are you doing?" she huffed in surprise.

"I'm making sure you make it into the house all right," he told her determinedly, his face grim.

"I am perfectly capable of walking myself" She insisted, trying unsuccessfully to block the mental images of the last time a man had carried her like that, while struggling to wriggle her way free, but he held fast to her.

"We can discuss that another time!" he told her firmly, as he continued to carry her up the front steps and through the door.

Once in the foyer, he looked to Ginny and asked, "Where do you want me to put her down?"

Sarah, once again overcome with how exhausted and weak she felt, thought to herself that he made her sound like a sack of flour.

"Follow me," Ginny ordered, as she began to climb the staircase. She stopped at the third door on the left, holding it open for him as he walked through, and waited for her to lift back the quilts before dumping Sarah rather unceremoniously onto the mattress and stepping back.

"All right?" he asked Ginny, who nodded her head.

"We're good now, Joe. Thank you for all you have done!"

"Well, I'll be off, then!" he said, looking at both women. "I hope you feel better," he told Sarah with a small tip of his head, before turning around and walking out the door.

Driving back to the livery, Joe wrestled with himself, but he couldn't put what he was feeling into words. All he knew was that Sarah was intriguing and infuriating all at once. He still couldn't believe that she had alluded to the fact that she thought him so depraved that he would take advantage of a poor, sick woman, but nor could he forget the warm and electrifying feeling he got in his chest when she had first opened her eyes to lock them on his. He pulled up out front of the stable and handed the reins off to an employee, and then shaking his head, tried to knock himself out of his reverie. He hadn't been this distracted by a woman in years. But the craziest thing of all was he never thought he would be again.

Chapter Fourteen

Sarah spent the next few days sleeping most of the time. She had never been so exhausted in her life and didn't know if it was the medical event she had endured, or if the stress and sadness of the past few months had all finally come to a head, but she could hardly keep her eyes open. Every now and again she would awaken enough to hear others' voices in her semiconscious state: Ginny's, Jacob's, and the children, and she was aware that Adam was brought into her room a few times a day, but even that was not a strong enough pull to rouse her completely.

Dr. Miller came several times to check on her, ensuring that her bleeding had stopped and check that she was not getting an infection that could indicate her body had not successfully expelled everything during her miscarriage. Nothing seemed to be amiss that he could find, so he continued to answer Ginny's concerned questions with a wait and see attitude, reminding her gently of the ordeals her sister had recently endured.

As she continued drifting in and out of sleep in the days following her affliction, she continued to hear the screaming and laughter of her young nieces and son, the low rumble of her brother-in-law's voice, and the lighter, softer vocalizations of her sister, so familiar to her from their years of growing up together. She got to where she could also pick out the voice of the doctor when he was let in to visit and stood in the foyer as he discarded his heavy winter outerwear. But as the days all rolled into each other, there was another voice that sometimes added to the fray, puzzling her. It was low and pleasant, with a deep resonance, and whenever she heard it, she would feel strangely safe. Though she couldn't pick out any particular words, when that certain voice traveled up the stairs and into her ears, she would snuggle back down in her covers and fall immediately back to sleep. It felt like nothing could ever go wrong in her universe again as long as that voice was in the house. She was reminded of how she had felt as a child at night in her bed when her father and mother would speak in the parlor.

In the days leading up to Christmas, Sarah was beginning to feel strong enough to join her family in the parlor and dining room for short stints, but still spent the majority of the time resting in her room. She was frustrated that she continued to be so exhausted, but everyone else tried to soothe her, saying that it was not only because of her miscarriage, but also the emotional turmoil and pain of losing her husband, and then, as a final blow, the last child she would ever conceive with him. No one spoke it aloud, but it seemed as though depression might be the last and most difficult obstacle in her recovery to overcome.

Christmas Eve dawned cold and bright, filling Sarah's room with so much light from the snow-covered ground, she was at first thinking she was at home on the farm in the summer. She stretched her arm over to what would be George's side of the bed but found it cold and empty. Then she remembered. Everything came flooding back with crystal clarity, and the tears flowed freely as she allowed herself to truly cry for him since the funeral.

By midday, she was completely cried out but felt well enough to get properly dressed and go downstairs for a while, lured by the promise that Adam and her nieces would be decorating the fine spruce that Jacob had brought in.

"Jacob?" Sarah asked in amazement. "Did you cut down that big tree?"

He chuckled lightly before answering. "No, Sarah, it was a friend. You know me. I'm a city boy. I hardly even knew what side of an axe to swing when we got here. Thankfully, I can do a bit more now, but I am still far from what anyone would bother to call a woodsman!"

"Well, it's lovely!" Sarah said.

"George would have loved it," she added in a whisper, the longing in her voice very apparent, as her eyes brimmed with fresh tears. Ginny looked up, concern ever-present in her eyes.

"How are you holding up?" she asked quietly, bracing herself for the answer. She had heard Sarah's sobs earlier that morning when she tried to bring her a breakfast tray and had decided it was better to leave her alone than to disturb her just then.

"I'm all right, I suppose," Sarah told her, but her shaking voice didn't sound very convincing. "I knew that this would be the hardest period for a long time. You know George… He always loved Christmas best of all."

"That he did!" Ginny concurred. Turning to Jacob, she continued, "Did we ever tell you about the year that George broke into the church and stole all of the gifts under the Christmas tree?"

"No! What?" Jacob exclaimed, aghast, leaning slightly toward his wife, knowing that this story was going to be too good to miss.

"It's true! How old was he again, Sarah?"

"Seventeen," she answered softly, her eyes sparkling with more unshed tears.

"That's right. We were seventeen. The thing is George didn't steal the gifts to be bad. He just loved the spirit of Christmas so much. He wanted to be the one to give the children their gifts and not the boring old Peabodys, who were the committee chairs and always handed out the gifts at the church Christmas party, which was happening the next afternoon. So, on the day of the party, while everyone was wailing and lamenting over the lost gifts for all the parish's children, in strolls George, with a big red sack on his back, a red coat and red pants on his body, with a bed pillow tied under it with rope. He had tried to make a beard of white wool on a paper backing, but that hadn't worked out so well. Everyone knew who it was, but they were so shocked to see him like that and happy to have the presents back that no one said a thing. He sat down and handed out presents to everyone and when it came to Sarah's turn…" Ginny stopped to take a deep breath, her own eyes filling with tears at the memory, "he took her onto his lap and asked

120

her quietly if she had been a good girl that year." She glanced at her sister, who nodded her encouragement.

"Then, he proceeded to produce a beautifully wrapped package which held the silver brush, comb, and mirror set that Sarah still uses," Ginny continued. "It was most certainly not the gift that the committee had chosen for her; that was some old boring book, but we didn't know that at the time. Everyone gasped when she opened it in front of him. It is such a beautiful set. He must have saved up all year to buy it for her." Ginny tied up the story nicely, conveniently failing to mention to her husband how jealous she was at the time, angry that George was paying such attention to her little sister.

"Two, actually," Sarah added, tears streaming down her face. "He saved up for two years."

Sarah recalled how thrilled she had been with getting to be so near him, feeling his warm breath on her neck and reveling in his manly scent as she sat on his lap, opening the beautiful things she had received. She hadn't known then that they were from him. But still, her delight was so great that she had instinctively flung her arms around his neck. He had taken advantage of that moment to whisper in her ear, "Thank you for being my best friend."

At the time, she hadn't known that there was so much more he wanted to tell her. It wasn't until years later, while lying in bed with her in his arms and enjoying the afterglow of their passionate lovemaking, that he had expressed to her his strong feelings about that night so long ago. He revealed that he had wanted to ask her to be his wife, even back then, but knew they were both too young.

"You had no idea how much I wanted to beg you to be mine that night," he had explained tenderly. "I wanted you so much."

Sarah was snapped back to reality when Ginny continued, "The best thing about it was that he started a tradition. Every year, he would dress up in that same old Father Christmas outfit and hand out gifts, at least until I left. Did he continue to do that, Sarah?" As she spoke, she recalled for the first time in a long time all the small details of life at home that she had given up when she had married Jacob and left town, realizing how much she had missed them.

"Yes," Sarah said softly. "It was always his favorite time of year."

"I wonder who will do it this year?" Ginny asked wistfully, without thinking.

"I don't know," Sarah answered sadly, "but it's a big part of the reason why I had to go. No one will ever look right in that suit again."

"Sarah sewed George a suit two Christmases later for him to wear. You know that she's a very talented seamstress, right?"

"Oh yes! I remember your wedding dress very fondly, my dear," Jacob concurred as he pulled his wife closer to him with an arm around her waist.

Later, after dinner was finished and the children were tucked in their beds, Sarah lay awake, running through the memories in her head, like a moving picture, of all the Christmases she spent with George. As painful as it was, she didn't want the images to stop, as it made her feel closer to him somehow, like he was there with her, just beyond her reach. Eventually, she fell asleep, only to awaken to the shrieks of three very excited children when they saw what was awaiting them in their socks hanging over the fireplace and packages under the tree.

Sarah wasn't sure how, but when she made it downstairs, she saw that all the packages from George's parents, as well as her own, for Adam had been found and placed under the tree. His stocking contained the same thing as the McAllister girls', with two sticks of peppermint candy, ten pennies, and an orange. When Sarah looked up at Ginny, her thanks shining in her eyes, her sister had merely nodded her head toward Jacob, letting Sarah know that he had been the one to ensure that Adam's stocking was not empty. But the most amazing gift was the sled that was leaning against the wall with her son's name on it. It was a beautiful thing with shining golden wood and metal

122

runners. Adam could hardly contain his excitement, begging his mother for a chance to try it out. She laughingly told him that he maybe could on another day, but today was for family and fellowship, all the while having no idea where the gift had come from. When she met Jacob's eyes again, he shook his head silently letting her know that he had nothing to do with that surprise.

At two o'clock, there came a rap at the door, and Ginny went to open it. On the porch stood Dr. Miller, and behind him, Joe. She ushered them in as they stomped their boots and shook their heads and shoulders to remove any lingering snow before walking further into the house.

Joe glanced over at Sarah, observing her for several seconds without her noticing. He was pleased to see that the color was coming back to her cheeks, and it seemed as though her strength was returning. She did not stand to greet the guests, but her smile was warm and welcoming.

"Merry Christmas!" the doctor jubilantly exclaimed, handing Jacob a bottle of whiskey. "Kentucky's finest, young man!"

"Thank you, Doc! We will certainly have to break into this and give it a try!"

Joe moved forward, and Sarah saw for the first time that he held something in his hands as he passed it off to Ginny.

"Plum pudding. My mother's special recipe. It just doesn't feel like Christmas without it."

"Thank you, Joe! I'm sure that we will all enjoy it!"

Everyone sat and talked, Jacob and the doctor nursing their whiskeys, watching the children play.

"You sure you won't join us, Joe?" Jacob had asked several times, but the man continued to refuse.

"No, thank you. I'm on duty today, just like any other, and I need to keep my wits about me. But you two enjoy!"

Sarah was lulled back into a hazy state of half-slumbering, listening to the drone of the voices around her. Sitting up with a start, it suddenly dawned on her that the voice she had been hearing but couldn't place for the past several days had been Joe's. She was shocked when she realized he had been coming to Jacob and Ginny's house so often, but eventually rationalized that both he and the doctor appeared to be good friends with her brother-in-law, so perhaps he came often to visit with him.

When it came time for Christmas dinner, Sarah found herself sitting across from Joe and next to Adam. As the meal went on, she would glance up occasionally to find Joe was studying her. She had at first blushed, then looked down at her plate again, but after catching him staring for the fourth time, she began to worry. She started to feel self-conscious, thinking that perhaps she had something amiss. Glancing down at the front of her black gown, she checked to see if she had spilled something on it. Finding nothing, she then ran her tongue along her teeth in fear that something might be lodged in them. He knew that she had discovered he was looking at her and gave her a half-smile, then quickly glanced down at his own plate.

As the meal went on, the group somehow settled on speaking about Christmases long ago from their childhoods, reminiscing about special toys and dear people. Joe had remained especially quiet, appearing to be content simply listening to the memories of the others, rather than contributing his own. But later, he finally joined in.

"I know snow feels like Christmas to everyone else, but I have never gotten used to these cold Colorado winters."

"Why is that, Joe?" Ginny asked.

"Because in California, winters are nothing like here. At least in the part of California where I grew up."

The table was silent as everyone's eyes focused on Joe.

"You know, it just dawned on me… In all the time we have known you now, I don't think I ever knew you were from California, Joe. Were you actually born there?" Ginny asked.

"Yes, ma'am, born and raised."

"I guess I just always figured you were a Southern boy, why with how polite you always are," Ginny stated.

"Well, my ma and pa were Southern, that much is true. But shortly after my pa married my ma, he decided he didn't like the direction that things were taking in Tennessee, so he figured they should perhaps instead try their luck out West. They packed up the wagon a year after their wedding, dreaming of seeing if the Forty-Niners had happened to leave any gold laying around, and headed to California. My ma was expecting my oldest brother on the way there, and he was actually born somewhere along in Nevada territory, or so I recall. My pa felt really bad when he heard that the war he had feared had finally broken out, but my ma refused to let him go back and fight. He lost three brothers in the war, but he gained four more sons out of the whole thing, so I guess it all evened out."

"I have never met anyone who was born in California and then went east!" Ginny declared. "Why, I thought California was the land of milk and honey. Why ever did you leave?"

Joe cleared his throat and simply stated, "Anyone ready for some plum pudding?"

Sarah had been struggling to stay awake after the heavy dinner, so she was embarrassed when, after she had tried the first bite of Joe's dessert, she exclaimed, "Hey! This is really good!"

She looked up to see Joe holding her gaze before he gave her a curt, "Thank you."

"Joe, you are a wonder!" Jacob said. "Making all of the rest of us men look bad. You're a woodsman, a toy maker, and a chef, not to mention the sheriff. How are the rest of us supposed to compete?"

"Speak for yourself, Jacob. You have a pretty little wife already. How about the likes of me?" Dr. Miller added. "There isn't one woman in town who pays attention to any of the rest of us bachelors the minute Joe saunters by: they all swoon after him. We don't stand a chance."

"Wait…" Sarah exclaimed, shaking her fuzzy head, "*you're* the sheriff?"

Joe looked at her with a puzzled look on his face. "Yes! Of course! That's why I was at the jail with Dr. Miller the other night. Why did you think I was there?"

"I guess… I guess I just didn't even think about it," Sarah stammered, wondering to herself why she didn't put two and two together, before trying to explain away her embarrassment. "I was so ill…"

No wonder he had been there all along, helping to take care of me. It was his jail!

"Surely, you didn't think he was a prisoner!" Ginny gently teased her.

"No, I honestly didn't even think about it. He certainly doesn't look the way I would have thought a sheriff would look!"

"And how would that be, exactly?" Joe countered, wondering where this conversation would go.

"Well, for one thing, you're so young! I thought sheriffs were all older men. That's certainly how they are at home!" Sarah declared, pleased to see Ginny nodding in agreement.

"Mining in the West isn't exactly an old man's game," Jacob interjected.

"And you're so quiet! I always thought that sheriffs were loud, with big, deep, manly voices," Sarah continued.

"So… I don't sound manly?" Joe asked, not trying to hide his amusement. He was enjoying making Sarah squirm.

"Oh! I didn't mean it like that!" Sarah declared.

"Go on," he prodded her, interested to hear more about her preconceived notions regarding how lawmen were supposed to be.

"I thought that sheriffs carried big guns out West, and rode horses, wearing chaps and big hats."

"You haven't seen me in the summer," Joe countered dryly.

"And I certainly didn't think that sheriffs liked to cook!"

"Well, a man has to eat somehow, hasn't he?" Joe's eyes were beginning to twinkle, but Sarah was too discombobulated to notice.

Finally, Joe let her off the hook by no longer goading her responses. He figured she had been through enough in the last little while that it made sense that she wasn't particularly in tune to what was happening around her; at this point, she was still most likely in survival mode. But he was surprisingly saddened that he had been seemingly too insignificant to have made even a small impression on her.

Sarah, feeling very foolish and still very weary, tried to gather her wits about her to see if she could salvage a shred of courtesy in the situation. She had seen how Joe's face had fallen just a bit when she questioned him about if he was indeed the sheriff and chastened herself for not realizing sooner what his role was. But then she struggled with her conscience, wondering why she felt the need to apologize for something that she was too sick to worry about before. She decided then that she would give a bit of his arrogance back to him.

"So, how does one so young get to be sheriff in a town like this? Surely, there were more qualified and experienced candidates than you?"

"That's where you would be right, Mrs. Johnson, was it? There was someone more experienced and qualified than me."

"And so, how did you end up with such a prestigious position then, Mister…" Suddenly, Sarah fell silent. She realized that she didn't even know the man's last name.

"It's McIntyre, and the last guy died," Joe answered her unabashedly.

"Oh!" Sarah exclaimed, shocked that he would be so blunt.

"But don't let him fool you, Mrs. Johnson. Joe here is the best we've got!" Dr. Miller defended his friend. "It was during the miners' riots a few years ago. Things got a little out of hand, and Sheriff Williams was killed by some drunk miners who were causing a ruckus. Shot clean through the heart, actually," the man stated, adding details that only a medical clinician would deem necessary.

"Anyway, Joe here had a way of talking so that everyone listened. He helped defuse the situation on all sides and got people negotiating again. When it came time to nominate some new candidates for the position, Joe's name was thrown into the hat, and that was that. It was pretty much a unanimous vote."

"And I don't think I ever got around to thanking you properly, Dr. Miller, for that nomination," Joe added wryly.

"If he wouldn't have, I most certainly would have," interjected Jacob. "We had pretty much just opened the rail line, and then all hell broke loose! You managed to get those tempers settled down and got people back to work."

"Really?" Sarah asked incredulously, wondering how this quiet, socially awkward man could have had that much influence to single-handedly resolve a full strike.

"Thanks for your confidence," he answered her hotly.

Turning to the others, he added, "Being the middle of five boys taught me the fine art of negotiation with the added benefit of fisticuffs if need be. And on that note, it is getting late, and I need to do some final rounds before I head back. Holidays always seem to bring out the worst in these fellows, with thoughts of home fueling their desire for drink and women. Thank you and have a goodnight, Jacob, Mrs. McAllister, Doc. Hope you continue to feel better, Mrs. Johnson."

He put on his hat, gloves, scarf, and overcoat, and as he opened the door and stepped into the inky darkness, said "Merry Christmas!"

As the doctor soon followed suit and Jacob and Ginny began to clean up, Sarah stood to help, but seeing her condition was still precarious, her sister sent her to bed. After getting Adam settled for the night, she stared at the ceiling for several hours as she contemplated what to do next. She had never felt so aimless and alone in her life.

Chapter Fifteen

Sarah continued to improve after the holidays but was still loath to step out of the house. The frigid Colorado winter was upon them, with the wind cutting through her like a knife. As she grew a bit stronger every day, she would spend more time in the parlor with Ginny, silently working on needlepoint or sewing. Her sister knew that Sarah was still struggling with all the immense losses she had endured and so she tried hard not to press her into interacting more than necessary, figuring that she would come out of her shell when she was ready. Adam and his cousins played well together, spending many hours building blocks, coloring, playing in the snow and even, much to the little boy's chagrin, playing with dollies. But he was occupied, and as the days passed, he would question Sarah less and less about his father and what had happened to him. It seemed to her that he was adjusting much better to the loss of George than she was, and it made her both pleased that he was not suffering as intensely, and strangely jealous that he had the benefit of youthful exuberance to help him through.

One Saturday morning in mid-January, Sarah awoke to a much quieter than normal house. She quickly washed, dressed, and carefully picked her way down the stairs, feeling that something was amiss. When she found Ginny in the parlor, she let out a huff in relief as she joined her sister on the sofa.

"Good morning! I was getting worried when it was so quiet in here!"

"The sun is shining, so Jacob and Joe took the children sledding. That's why it's so peaceful."

"Joe went with Jacob and the children?"

"Yes."

"Does Joe have children?" Sarah asked, surprised, and then wondered why she cared.

"No, not that I know of," Ginny answered her. "I mean, with men, who can really tell, but no, he has no children of which I'm aware."

"But… that makes no sense! If he has no children, then why would he go?"

"Probably to see how his sled turned out."

"His sled?"

"Of course! You know: the one he made Adam for Christmas. He probably wants to see how it performs," Ginny flippantly explained.

"He *made* that sled?" Sarah was flabbergasted.

"Sure! Didn't you hear Doc Miller that night? Joe makes toys."

"But we had just barely arrived! How in the world did he get it ready on time?"

"I really don't know. I only know that he brought it over here on Christmas morning for Adam before you awoke, saying something about not being sure if we'd had a chance to plan anything for him since you were so sick. I didn't think much of it at the time, but Joe is always doing nice things for the people in town. They all love him."

"Really?" Sarah asked incredulously. "Joe?"

"Yes, Sarah. Joe is one of a kind."

"I don't know how to respond to that," Sarah said. "What's his story, anyway?"

"You know about as much as I do. He was born and raised in California, I guess, and then something brought him here. He became sheriff, and the rest… well, the rest is history. He's a pretty quiet man. He holds things close to his vest."

Sarah didn't know what to think. When the two men and the children came back, stomping off the snow and hanging up their gear, Sarah had studied Joe until he had glanced up, catching her in the act. She looked away quickly as she felt a blush rush over her cheeks.

130

When the kids trooped into the kitchen with the promise made by Ginny of hot cocoa, Sarah moved over to Joe and quietly said, "Thank you."

"For?" he inquired.

"For making the sled for Adam. It wasn't necessary, but it is appreciated. I would have thanked you sooner, but I thought it was a gift from Jacob and Ginny."

"It was no trouble, ma'am. I just didn't want the little guy thinking Santa Claus had forgotten about him on account of your being so ill. How are you feeling now, anyway?"

He had turned to face her by this point, and she felt as if he was trying to gauge her health by staring intently into her eyes but was instead reading her soul. She shuddered a little under his scrutiny, noticing that his exceptional hazel eyes had a very kind look to them.

"I'm better, thank you. Still weak, but I am improving every day. I hope to be well enough to travel back home soon. It already is much later than I had originally planned to do so."

Joe felt his heart skip a beat, and then sink a bit in his chest. He abruptly realized that he didn't want her to leave, but just as quickly admonished himself for being stupid. Women were a sore subject with him, so he had pretty much given up the thought of ever finding one who wasn't attached or crazy, and he wasn't about to change his opinion now.

He gave her a small smile, before answering, "Well, then, ma'am, I hope you're well enough to travel safely soon."

Sarah watched as he picked up his Stetson and placed it back on his head, wondering why she felt a pang of disappointment that he seemed happy to let her go. She didn't know him, and so far, her encounters with him had left her feeling inadequate and defensive.

All through the rest of January, while Sarah continued to recuperate, Jacob and Joe took the kids out sledding any chance they got. By the final weekend of the month, after Adam had been unceasingly begging her, she finally relented and decided that she would see what all the fuss was about. She dressed warmly and walked out the door with the pack, but felt Joe scrutinize her as she came outside.

"Ma'am, are you going to be warm enough?"

"Yes, we have winter where I come from, too, Sheriff," she answered hotly.

He gave her an exasperated look. "I realize that, ma'am. But the wind coming off the snow in those mountains can be brutal here, and you have been under the weather, not to mention the elevation. In fact, I'm not sure you're up to the challenge yet," he smirked at her.

"You worry about yourself, Mr. McIntyre, and I will worry about me."

"Suit yourself, ma'am."

About halfway up the hill, Sarah realized that Joe had been right. The wind was blowing fiercely in her face, and it cut her to the bone, even through all her layers. Battling against the steep rise in elevation and the force of the wind pushing her backward, she fought with every fiber of her being to hang on and keep going, if nothing more than to simply prove Joe McIntyre wrong. He would look back at her every so often, his concern showing on his face, but when she caught him watching her, he would shrug and quickly turn away. When she made it to the top of the hill, she stood and panted, trying hard not to fall over, feeling her lungs rapidly expanding and retracting within the constraints of her firm corset. However, when Joe looked over to her, she smiled sweetly all the while telling herself she would be damned to let him know that his concerns had been warranted.

After watching the little ones go for a few runs, Sarah was so cold she was numb. She stomped her feet demurely under her long skirts and had her hands parked securely under her armpits. Joe continued to glance at her, knowing that she was freezing. When he had finally asked if she was cold, she replied stoically that she was fine. He studied her, and then shook his head, obviously wondering why she was so stubborn, which infuriated her all the more. By the time Jacob, Joe, and the children were done, the consequence of her stubborn pride was that Sarah was

132

so stiff from the cold that she could hardly walk. Joe silently offered his arm to her, which she snubbed at first, but soon realized that despite her smug determination, without his assistance, she would fall onto her backside and likely stay there. They walked quietly behind the excited children and Jacob, both only staring straight ahead.

When they got to the house, Ginny opened the door to the excited brood and told them that there was hot chocolate available for all. She observed her sister walking gingerly in the door with the sheriff but said nothing, instead watching the scene before her play out.

"I'm afraid that she got mighty cold out there, Mrs. McAllister. I'm sorry we kept her out so long."

"I'm just fine!" Sarah snapped, but Ginny could see her sister was shivering and her lips had a bluish tinge.

Ginny looked up and caught Joe's eye before responding. "Well, Sarah, you can be just fine over here, in the chair by the fire, wrapped in the quilt, drinking some hot cocoa."

Joe followed Ginny back into the kitchen and after the children were served their hot drinks and cookies, worked up the nerve to ask her, "When are Sarah and Adam heading home?"

Ginny smiled to herself before turning around. Joe tried to have a tough exterior, but she knew it was just an act. Inside he had a heart of gold.

"Only because," Joe began to quickly explain when he saw her smile, "I think she needs a better pair of boots if she will be here much longer."

"I don't know, Joe. I guess you'll have to ask her that question, because it depends on her. In all honesty, between you and me, she doesn't really have a whole lot to go back to. Her in-laws took back the house her husband built them, and so she's living with my folks. She has no money, no home, not one thing left to her name but the clothes on her back and that little boy. I truly don't know what she's going to do."

Ginny's sad expression tugged at Joe even more. Though he knew only a small smattering of what Sarah had been through, he understood how tough she actually was.

No wonder she seems so defensive and closed off; she has been abandoned and hurt by those who should have cared the most, he thought.

With that, he decided immediately that he would like to get to know her better, despite his earlier misgivings. He picked up Sarah's cup of cocoa to take to her along with his but stopped as he got halfway across the parlor. He glanced over his shoulder toward Ginny and shrugged in Sarah's direction. The young widow was sound asleep, wrapped tightly in the blankets. Joe put down the cups he was carrying on a side table and went to her, gently scooping her up to follow Ginny up the stairs to the guest bedroom. Joe gently placed her on the bed before spreading the quilt up over the top of her. He watched transfixed as she snuggled down deeper into her pillow, then followed Ginny out the door.

When they had retreated down the stairs back into the parlor, Joe said earnestly to Ginny, "Mrs. McAllister, you have to talk to your sister! She exhausted herself after just a few hours of sledding in the hills. There is no way she can travel halfway back across the country right now! I really hope that you won't let her do something foolish by leaving before she's ready. Heck, if her life back home is as bleak as you made it sound, then perhaps she shouldn't head back at all."

Before giving her a chance to respond, he thanked her prior to doffing his hat as he headed back into the windy afternoon, leaving Ginny to ponder his words. She couldn't deny that she had selfishly enjoyed having her sister and nephew with her, especially where her friends were few, and she was certainly in no hurry for them to leave. Indeed, she thought long into the evening about how she could break through Sarah's stubborn nature and get her to see that perhaps staying in their little town might truly be the best option for her. By the time she crawled into her bed that night, snuggling up against Jacob in an attempt to stave off the cold night air, she had come up with the plan.

Now all she needed was her husband's, Joe's and Dr. Miller's help.

Chapter Sixteen

A few days later, Sarah was sitting in the parlor, working on a needlepoint with Ginny when there came a knock at the door. Ginny quickly rose, trying hard to ignore her sister's questioning gaze. When she opened it, Joe walked in and stomped the remaining snow off his boots. He was holding a bag in his hands, and he seemed a bit sheepish as he removed his hat.

"Good afternoon, ladies," he started, clearing his throat before continuing. "Mrs. McAllister, I was wondering if you might be willing to help a bachelor out? You see, I have these clothes," he continued, holding up the bag.

"You see, I have these clothes that need mending, and though I can do it, as you can imagine, I'm not too elegant with a needle and thread. I was wondering if you would mind helping me?"

"Well, of course, Joe," Ginny smiled graciously at him, "I would be happy to. However, Sarah here is truly the magician with a needle and thread. She's an amazing seamstress and is much faster than me."

Sarah looked at both of them, wondering what was going on. They seemed like they were conspiring over something, though she couldn't put her finger on what it could be. It seemed a reasonable enough request that a bachelor would bring his things to a woman to be fixed. What she wasn't so certain about was whether or not there was a seamstress in town who would be a better option than the wife of his friend.

"Would you mind, then, Mrs. Johnson, please?"

"Of course, I would be happy to help, Sheriff, but surely the town seamstress would do a better job than I would."

"No, ma'am," he answered quickly. "There is no seamstress in town anymore after the slump and strike. That family moved on. Your sister is the only woman who I know well enough to ask such a personal favor."

"Oh!"

Ginny saw the opening for which she was waiting. "Sarah, would you mind desperately, please? You're so much faster than I am. I have so much going on with the children's needs, as well. Spring is coming, and they have outgrown everything. It will take me long enough just seeing to their clothing."

Sarah turned to Joe. "So, how soon do you need it, then?"

"As soon as possible, ma'am. My job can get pretty physical at times, and I tend to wear my clothes out quickly."

"Well, let me see what you have in there, then, shall we? That will give me a better idea of the time frame I will need to help you."

"All right."

Sarah opened the bag and began to pull out the clothing in varying levels of disrepair. Soon, she had divided out two piles: one for shirts and one for pants. Sarah shook her head in disbelief as she looked over the shirts. Those in the best condition were missing buttons or had ripped pockets. One shirt had several missing buttons and a pocket that was nearly ripped clean off. She held it up and looked at him, one eyebrow raised in question.

"What?" Joe asked her.

"What on earth did you do to this poor shirt?" she questioned him, her mouth turning up at the corners.

"That one? Well, let me think… I think that was when I had to break up a fight at one of the saloons a few weeks ago. As I went to grab Old John White, he whipped around and grabbed my shirt, lifting me off the ground before throwing me over a table."

"What? Oh, my goodness!" Sarah gasped.

"Yeah, it's a pretty physical job sometimes."

"Were you hurt?" she asked him. He studied her and wondered if he had indeed detected a hint of concern in her voice and expression.

"Sure," he replied with a shrug. "Something fierce. But I still had to arrest him for disorderly conduct, so after a few seconds of collecting myself, I stood on the table and jumped on his back, beating him down from behind until I could subdue him."

"Oh, my!" Sarah exclaimed.

Next, she pulled a pair of pants from their pile and held them up, her eyebrows knit together. "And these?"

"Oh! Those I stepped on the hem and ripped it out when I put them on in a hurry after I heard gunshots at three a.m. a few months ago. I damn near fell on my face! Oh! Pardon me, ladies. I didn't mean to curse."

"No matter. I probably would have, too, if that had happened to me. Was everything all right?"

"Sure! Just some dumb, young, drunk yahoos living it up too much after a night of women, whiskey, and cards."

Joe looked up and saw the blush rising on Sarah's cheeks, serving as a quick reminder that life, and women, were very different out here than from whence she came.

The next pair of pants she held up was a pair of Levi Strauss jeans with both knees ripped out. "And these?" she inquired with a smirk, wondering what would make a grown man blow the knees out of his denim.

"Those were the pair I was wearing when I got dragged down Main Street after someone tried to rob the bank a while back. I grabbed onto his horse, but he pushed me off, so I held onto his leg and the stirrup until I could pull him off, but I got dragged down the street in the process."

Sarah studied them a bit more in depth and saw that they were shredded on the shins, as well. "I'm not sure I could do anything to save these," she told him sadly.

"That's all right. Just do what you can, and I will be most grateful," he assured her.

He shot Ginny a sly smile before pulling on his hat and walking out the door without another word.

So far, so good, he thought. Their plan had been put into motion.

Chapter Seventeen

Sarah went to work fixing all of Joe's mending and afterward, washed and pressed everything before carefully bundling it to take to him. Three days after he had dropped it off, she walked down to the jail and tentatively knocked on the door.

"Come in!" she heard Joe call. She cautiously turned the doorknob and pushed it into the room where she saw Joe at his desk, head down, writing on a piece of paper.

"Hello," she called out softly, causing his head to jerk up.

"Oh!" he exclaimed, taken aback to see her standing in front of him.

"Come on in!" he told her while he rose out of his seat.

"Thank you," she answered politely.

Both stood awkwardly in the center of the room, neither of them saying anything until they both began to speak at once.

"What can I do for you…"

"I brought you your…"

Joe recovered fastest. "Please," he said, "ladies first."

"Thank you," she responded. "I was saying that I have brought you your things."

"Already? Wow! You *are* fast!"

"Thank you," Sarah mumbled, embarrassed and not sure what to say in response. "Anyway, they are finished."

"What do I owe you?"

"Nothing."

"Sarah, what do I owe you?"

"Nothing, Joe. Please, just consider it repayment for the help and kindness you have shown Adam and me since we arrived."

"Sarah," he began, trying to maintain his patience. "You did work for me. Please, let me know how much I can pay you for your time and effort."

Sarah began to bristle. "I told you, it was nothing. Please, just accept my thank you for all you did to take care of me when we first arrived, and for Adam's Christmas sled, as well as helping Jacob take the children outside. I will not take a penny from you!"

"Are you always this stubborn, Sarah?"

"Are you?"

Frustrated, Joe sighed, "You truly are the most exasperating woman I have ever met!" he exclaimed.

"Why?" she demanded, eyes flashing. "Because I won't accept your charity? I know what you're doing, Joe. Ginny must have told you my tale of woe. I don't need anyone's pity!"

"Dammit, woman, I'm not pitying you! I had a need for someone to fix my clothes, and you did it. I'm paying you for a service, fair and square. Just like if…" He stopped short when he realized what he was about to say. He was going to say that he would pay her for her service just like he would any other working girl but realized what the connotation would be.

"Just like what?"

He had to think fast. "Just like if you were working in town as a seamstress."

"Well, I'm not!"

"Why not?"

"Because I'm not!"

"But why not? This town needs one, and you're obviously fast and," he added, looking at the pile he had taken from her and placed on his desk, "thorough."

"Because I don't live here!"

"But why can't you live here?"

"Because I need to go home!"

"Why, Sarah? Why do you need to go home? Ginny told me that there's nothing left there for you. She said that your in-laws took your home back and that you're forced to live with your folks. Why do you need to go back to that?"

"Because…" she said softly, willing herself not to cry.

"Why, Sarah? Truly, I want to know. What is waiting for you at home?" he asked her softly.

"You wouldn't understand," she whispered to him, while her eyes involuntarily teared up.

"You're right about that. I don't understand. There's nothing for you or Adam there."

"My husband is there!" she declared angrily.

"He passed away, didn't he?"

"Yes. But… that's where…." she broke off and sniffled. "I told you that you wouldn't understand."

"Is it because you feel like you have to be close to his grave?" he asked so quietly she could barely hear him.

She wouldn't look at him or answer, instead continuing to stare at the far wall. He reached out and gently took her chin in his hand, turning her face to look at him. When she looked up into his eyes, he continued. "Is it?"

She glanced away again, her eyes brimming with tears.

"Sarah, talk to me. Is it?"

She slowly nodded her head.

"Sarah, he's gone. I'm sorry, but your husband is dead. You can't go home simply to care for his grave. You're a young woman yet. I can't imagine he would want you to move home and stay with your folks, living the rest of your days as a widow, only so you can tend his grave. Stay here. Open a dress shop. Build a life for you and Adam that your husband would be proud of."

"You know nothing about my husband!" she spat out, a blush rising to her cheeks, her bosom rising and falling rapidly with her emotion. He couldn't help it; he looked down quickly at her chest, admiring the way her creamy skin was moving in and out with each breath. He caught himself and looked up, just in time to meet her eyes and then he felt his own cheeks redden. She had caught him.

Sarah couldn't believe the audacity of this man before her. He infuriated her. First, he had a very thinly veiled attempt at giving her charity, and then he claimed to know what was best for her and her son's lives, and even more offensive, he dared to look down to admire her chest! But what frightened her was the tingle of excitement she felt when she realized what he had done, and that incensed her all the more.

Joe could see the fire flashing in her eyes. He hadn't meant to hurt her. He had only wanted to try to help. And, he admitted to himself, keep her there because she intrigued him. Nonetheless, he knew he had to tread carefully.

"You're right, Sarah. I didn't know your husband. However, I know you and I can imagine that he must have loved your spunk and fire very much, not to mention that I know that little boy, and any man who fathered and raised him was a good one."

He took a deep breath and continued. "I also know that you can't live for the past. You have to look forward and move on."

And I should listen to my own advice, he thought wryly.

His last sentence piqued Sarah's interest. With the sorrowful tone of his last words, she wondered if he spoke from experience.

"Joe, did you lose a wife?"

He was quiet for a few seconds before answering, his mind spinning on how to answer her. "Yes," he finally replied.

"Oh! I'm so sorry!" Sarah declared, suddenly feeling bad for assuming he didn't understand her pain. "When?"

"A while ago now," he answered.

"Where?"

"Back home in California."

"Is that why you came here?" she asked him.

"You could say that."

Joe knew he should tell her the truth. He could see in her eyes the pity she had for him and the commiseration she felt for what she thought was a shared experience. But he couldn't tell her. He hadn't told anyone what had driven him away from California, and it was easier to let her think that his Caroline had died, rather than to have to relive the truth of what happened. To speak it aloud was to make him feel like it was happening all over again, and his heart still couldn't take the pain. He quickly decided to steer the conversation back to safer ground.

"Please, Sarah," he practically begged her, "let me pay you for your time and effort."

"So, we are back to this, then, are we, Joe? I said no! Please, just consider it a gift from one friend to another."

With that, Sarah briskly walked across the floor and opened the door, exiting before he had time to react. Frustrated, hurt, and angry, he turned his attention to the bundle on his desk and untied it, and was immediately hit with the scent of freshly laundered clothing. As it had been washed by her, it smelled familiar, back to when she had been so ill, and he had helped Dr. Miller remove her garments. He pulled up a shirt to inspect it. All the buttons were sewn on tightly, and the pocket had been resewn with tiny, neat stitches. The shirt looked as if it had just come from the mercantile and he pressed the fabric up to his face and inhaled. The crisp, starched cotton and the feminine aroma made him think of home and his mother, the longing to go back and see her overwhelming him. But not only had she passed away years before, to go back would mean he would have to see Caroline and he wasn't strong enough to do that.

Over the next few days, men kept coming by Ginny's house, asking if Sarah would be willing to do a bit of mending for them. Joe had started it, but soon it seemed that every man in town wanted Sarah to fix something, and after a few weeks, Sarah had grown quite a nest egg as she collected payment for the endless stream of repairs that seemed to come through the door.

The miners would come in, dirty and timid, their hats twisting in their hands as they asked her if she would be so kind as to repair the rips and loose buttons on their clothing. But when the prostitutes came to the door, asking if she would mind helping them with their mending, Ginny drew the line.

"Sarah, perhaps it is time for you to think about opening a shop in town? We need a good seamstress, as you can see, and I think that if you're going to be sewing for everyone, you might be better served with a bigger space and a place where people can come and go more freely than traipsing in and out of my house."

"Ginny, that's ridiculous! Why ever would you suggest that? You *know* that I'm going home! I've saved enough money for Adam's and my tickets, so I'll be leaving in another week or so. I've already overstayed my welcome, and for that, I apologize. But I'm better now, and I have the means to travel, so now it is time to go."

"Sarah, please don't leave. I'm enjoying having you here in town, and your services are desperately needed, as you can easily see. I'm not demanding you stay, of course. I'm merely suggesting that perhaps it's time for you to put down roots here."

Sarah, however, would not be budged. She asked Jacob to please buy her and Adam's tickets and, after procrastinating as long as he could, he finally arranged the passage for his sister-in-law and her son, but he refused to take any money.

"If I have one perk at all for living all the way out here in this godforsaken town, it is that I'm able to arrange for my family to travel the rails at no cost," he had told her after she tried to shove some money into his hand.

Chapter Eighteen

The day before Sarah and Adam were due to leave, Ginny had invited Joe and Dr. Miller to her home for dinner as a sort of goodbye celebration. In the early afternoon, however, Sarah had been doing her last-minute packing when there was a knock at the door, and Ginny called out from the kitchen, asking her to answer it.

Standing on the porch was an uncomfortable looking Joe. Without greeting her, he held out two fishing poles and blurted, "Since you're leaving tomorrow, I was wondering if I might take the boy fishing one more time?"

Sarah knew that Adam had enjoyed fishing with Jacob and Joe very much in the past few weeks since the weather had warmed, but Joe had never taken the boy alone. Before she could answer, though, Adam, having heard the invitation, was down the stairs in a flash, begging his mother to let him go.

"How long were you planning to fish?" she asked Joe.

"I don't know. Just an hour or two."

On a whim, Sarah quickly calculated an estimate of the amount of work left prior to the departure of their train in the morning before deciding that she could spare a few hours to allow her boy one more outing in the Colorado wilderness. She went into the kitchen to speak to Ginny, then grabbed a shawl, and they all set out toward a small creek a bit further from town.

She sat on a downed tree, watching her boy and the sheriff down by the water. Her memories pulled her back to the fishing hole she shared with George so many years before. Her breath hitched in her throat a bit when it dawned on her that he should have been the one who was patiently showing her son how to bait a hook and drop it into the water. She smiled with gratitude, though, when she thought about Joe's willingness to spend his free time with a child with whom he had no connection.

Eventually, Joe came up and sat down beside her, both of them watching Adam bobbing his pole up and down, waiting for a bite in the cool afternoon breeze.

"Thank you for doing this with him, Joe. With his father gone, I hadn't even begun to think of all the things he won't be taught. It means the world that you would be so kind."

"It is no problem, ma'am. He's a good boy."

Even though things had become much more relaxed between Sarah and Joe, he still called her ma'am more often than not.

"Thank you."

They were silent again for several more minutes when Joe turned to look at her. His heart skipped a beat as he took in her delicate profile. As much as he hated to admit it, he did not want her to go home.

"Please don't leave," he whispered, surprised as the words exited his mouth.

"I'm sorry?" Sarah asked him, having heard what he said, but unsure of whether or not to believe her ears.

He cleared his throat. "I said, 'Please don't leave.'"

She immediately turned to him, her face an open question.

"Please, Sarah, don't go home."

"I beg your pardon?"

"I don't know why, but I feel your place is here. I don't think you should go home. I don't want you to leave."

"Joe…"

"Listen, Sarah, we need you here. We want you here. Please stay. Don't go home and fade away. This town could use you."

"To do what, Joe?"

"What we talked about before: we need a seamstress."

"And where would I live?"

"Come on," he said, standing up and holding his hand out to her. "I have an idea."

Sarah rose when she grabbed his hand, and as he closed his fingers around hers, she was shocked at the wave of desire that washed over her. She had not touched a man's hand this intimately since George had passed. She had forgotten how comforting it was to feel her tiny, delicate, soft fingers engulfed in the large, work-hardened palm of a man who labored: it was the ultimate reminder that a man and woman were designed to work together to build a life. Her mind instantly became awash in a flood of memories of all the times she had noticed how exactly opposite George's beloved hands were to hers, but how wonderfully perfect they had been. She saw them helping her up the hill from their fishing hole, or up and down from their wagon or carriage. He would open jars with an easy laugh after he had watched her struggle before gracing her with a look of amusement mixed with pity while removing the offending object from her inept fingers. She saw his loving hands wrapped tenderly around their son as an infant; the boy dwarfed by their sheer size. Her cheeks grew warm and rosy as she recalled how his rough hands had traversed over her soft curves so lovingly in their bed and how he could draw from her a desire so strong that she couldn't wait to slake it by taking him inside of her.

Sarah glanced up to see Joe watching her from above, a curious look in his eyes. She knew he was wondering what she was thinking about, and it galled her to have him think that her blush had anything to do with him. She met his gaze and cleared her throat.

"I'm intrigued," she told him.

Joe called for Adam, and they all walked into town. Two doors away from the jail, Joe stopped abruptly.

"Here," he told her, pointing.

"Here what?" she asked, confused.

"Here's where you could set up shop. It's empty. It isn't too large but isn't small. It's right on Main Street, but not too close to the saloons. It even has living quarters on the second floor. Best of all, you would be close to me here at the jail!"

Sarah looked at him peculiarly at his last sentence as Joe quickly tried to backtrack.

"I mean, I can keep an eye on you better if you're closer to me."

"Keep an eye on me? Is that what you just said?"

"Well, yes, but… but I didn't mean it like that! Come on! I just meant that this town can be rough."

Sarah interrupted him.

"Oh, I see. Just because I'm a woman, I'm incapable of taking care of myself?"

"Yes," Joe said, without thinking and he felt his breath catch as he saw the look of fire in her eyes.

"Wait! No! I didn't mean that you couldn't take care of yourself! I simply meant that as a single woman with a young child, I would feel better, as the town sheriff, to have you where I can make sure you aren't going to be bothered by some of these ruffians here in town! That's it! I swear!" he quickly tried to explain.

Sarah took a deep breath and let it out, deciding to let the conversation slide for now. She walked up to the window, cupping her hands around her eyes in order to better see inside. She immediately saw that Joe was right: the room was small but large enough for her purposes, and she began envisioning where she would put her machine and how she could curtain off a little partition for people to try on her creations.

"Well, it does look promising, Joe. I wish I could go inside and take a look around."

"That can be arranged!" he exclaimed smugly, holding out the key and stepping toward the door. He was about to slide it into the lock when he thought better of it and handed it to her.

"After you," he said.

Sarah opened the door and looked around. The place was dusty, immediately confirming desertion. She continued to the back of the store and looked out, seeing a small yard with an outhouse. Coming back inside, she found the stairs and climbed up, discovering a large, open floor plan with a small kitchen nook, complete with a cookstove and a sink with a pump. It wasn't any larger than the downstairs, but for just her and Adam, it would do.

148

She nodded her head with determination. "Well, Joe, this could work!"

"Great! So, you will stay, then?"

"It isn't that easy," Sarah said sadly.

"Why not?"

"Because…" she began before she trailed off. Then, she decided that there was no use pussyfooting around. "I don't have much money, Joe. I just don't have the funds necessary to rent this place and run a shop or set up a home. My machine isn't here, either. My only option is to go home and live with my folks."

"But, Sarah, I know it could be worked out. I could help you! Or maybe Jacob and Ginny, or even Doc Miller? Or perhaps the bank could loan you some money to get established?"

"Joe McIntyre, I do not accept charity, nor will I go into debt. I appreciate what you're trying to do for me, but truly, I am not your responsibility. Adam and I will be going home in the morning."

With that, she pressed the key back into his palm, gently closing his fingers over it, before taking Adam by his little hand and hurrying out the door.

Joe walked to the wall, slamming his closed fist into it, before putting his forehead on it. He was so incredibly frustrated! Never before had he felt so riled. He was a take-charge sort of man, but he had never met a woman as infuriatingly stubborn as Sarah.

Why can't she see that I'm only trying to help her? I want to help her, but she won't even allow me to try.

He took a few cleansing breaths before standing straight up. He couldn't explain it: this pull he felt to her. She made him so incredibly exasperated, but yet … he felt all mixed up inside because he also couldn't deny his strongly growing attraction to her. She was beautiful, smart, poised, talented, but she was also determined, passionate, and very proud; exactly the kind of woman he never knew he needed… until now. He had always known that he never wanted a mousey, delicate wife, but after what had happened to him in California, he had vowed he never wanted a wife at all. That was until Sarah Johnson had walked into his life.

At dinner later that night, everyone was unusually quiet. Joe felt the tension in the room, pressing down on them all like a wet blanket, and it was all he could do not to stand and shout at Sarah, "You incredibly stubborn woman! Will you just look around at all these people who want you to stay? I'm begging you to stay… I think I might be falling in love with you!" However, his stubborn pride was no better than hers, and so the evening passed with distant pleasantries until everyone called it a night.

Early the next morning, Sarah and Adam were all ready for Jacob to take them to the station. Ginny, unwilling to let her sister go, cried as she clung to her, begging her not to leave her all alone again in the Wild West. Sarah had removed her arms gently from around her shoulders and promised that she would be back for a visit just as soon as she could afford it.

At the station, Sarah was surprised to see Joe milling around.

"Waiting for someone?" she asked him, surprising herself that she hoped his answer would be yes, he was indeed waiting for her.

"Yes and no. Payroll for one of the mines is due in on the train. I always have to meet it to ensure it gets to the right place."

"Oh," Sarah said, trying to hide the disappointment in her voice.

Oh, come on, you idiot! Joe chided himself. *You know you want to say something more. Anything that would make it clear that you're not ready for her to walk out of your life.* However, because of his lingering self-doubt, he was afraid that even if he dared to open his mouth to speak of his burgeoning feelings, nothing but a squeak would come out.

"Well, then, I guess it was just Providence that Adam is able to say goodbye to you here, then."

150

Joe looked down at the little boy in his traveling clothes, and he thought the child looked uncomfortable and distressed, his mind choosing instead to remember how happy and relaxed he had looked wearing his every-day breeches and shirt as they fished together.

When Sarah nudged her son gently, he turned to Joe and said, "Thank you, Sheriff, for showing me around and taking me fishing and sledding."

Joe was shocked to feel a lump rising in his throat.

Goddammit! He blustered internally. *I barely know this kid. What the hell is wrong with me?*

He cleared his throat before he spoke, which caught Sarah's attention. She knew that he seemed to like the few children in town, but in that moment, it struck her that he seemed to have a special affinity for her son.

"Any time, Adam. I enjoyed it as much as you did. Did you bring your sled with you?"

Adam shook his head, his expression sad. "No, sir. Mama wouldn't let me. She said there's no place to use it at home… I guess she's right. It's as flat as a pancake there, but I was thinking of hooking up Grandpa's big dog, Rufous, to it and having him pull me like they do way up north! But Mama says it has to stay here until next time."

Joe looked at Sarah and leaned in closer to her. "So, you're planning on coming back, then, are you?" he inquired a little huskily.

Sarah felt a shiver of desire run down her spine. *Stop it!* she chided herself.

"That's my plan," she told him, hoping that she sounded more aloof and distant than she felt.

Just then, the ground began rumbling and the train whistle blew as smoke from the engine was seen coming up the hill before the locomotive itself. Joe knew he had to meet the engineer and the guards with the payroll, so it was time for him to leave, but he didn't want to. He took a deep breath and swallowed his nerves as he reached for Sarah's hand, bringing it to his lips while holding his eyes locked on hers the entire time.

"Until we meet again, then," he said.

Sarah couldn't help the blush rising in her cheeks as she responded, "Until we meet again, Sheriff."

Joe took off running down the platform but couldn't help but turn to look at her one more time. It was in that moment that he understood he was a goner and couldn't wait until their paths crossed again.

Chapter Nineteen

As soon as the train pulled away from the station, Sarah realized her mistake. Her eyes welled with tears when she realized that leaving this place was the last thing she wanted to do, and she fought hard with herself to not stand up and scream to the conductor to stop the train. In the end, however, once again, her stubborn pride won out.

By the time she had made it all the way to Illinois, she was despondent. She had realized in Colorado Springs when she changed trains that it was her arrogance propelling her home. Her refusal to accept the charity of friends had made this her own fault. By the time they had hit Nebraska, she had realized she had nothing to go back home to but her painful memories. In Missouri, Adam had begun to cry that he missed his aunt, uncle, cousins, and even Sheriff Joe. When Sarah had tried to instead get him excited about going home, he had only cried harder, saying that he missed his pa.

Sarah's father met them when the train pulled in at their station. He took one look at his youngest daughter and quickly embraced her, making soothing sounds while petting her hair as her tears rolled down her face.

He had no idea what to say to her; he had been shocked when he got her telegram stating that she was returning. Secretly, he had been thrilled for her when she had left, hoping that Colorado would give her a new lease on life. He knew that they would miss her terribly, but he felt strongly that she needed to escape the painful memories of her life with George, rather than facing them every day.

He knew she was still in mourning. It had hardly been six months since George's body had been laid to rest, and yet he continued racking his brain for any local eligible young men whom she may want to court once her mourning period was over, but so far, he could think of no one.

Anyone remotely close to her age was either already married or would never be. Those who were older and single often had a brood of children they would expect her to raise, and her father wondered if any man in that situation would truly love his daughter or would merely want someone to care for his family. Even worse, though, were the men who had been unable to find respectable women to be suitable wives because of odd personalities, problems with drinking, gambling, or they hit women.

Her prospects were even further limited because of the issue she seemed to have with carrying and delivering healthy children. As much as it killed him to admit it, he knew that most men around their parts would not take kindly to a woman who could not produce strong laborers for their farm. He knew that George's parents had certainly held her difficulties against her, even going as far as blaming her issues for the loss of their son, which really galled him. Nonetheless, her father understood that realistically most men would feel she was damaged, leaving the very real possibility that his beloved daughter, at only twenty-two years old, would be alone for the rest of her life.

If he had been honest with himself, he would have admitted that he had valiantly hoped that with such a shortage of eligible women out West, Sarah would have met a man in Colorado who was willing to overlook her being unable to bear any more children and love her anyway. He wished that she could have found for herself a miner or a railroad man, for whom her inability to produce children wouldn't be such a detriment.

After all, she is still a beautiful girl and has many homemaking talents. Without a homestead to manage, more children in that environment would be a burden to a working man. It would mean more mouths to feed with the money he had to earn rather than food he could produce, he had rationalized with himself several times while she was gone.

Inevitably, though, his thoughts eventually went in a different direction. *Perhaps Adam would be detrimental to her*

154

prospects there, though. Maybe a man wouldn't want to work to support another man's son.

Now she was home, his determined young daughter with her small son, and he was distraught. He didn't know what to do for her. He was also angry with himself that he hadn't insisted that she finish her schooling. If he had known then what he knew now, he never would have allowed her to marry George before she had her certificate of completion in hand. Now, she was stuck with no property, no income, no husband, and no way that he could see that she could make money to support herself and her child. She certainly couldn't teach or become a nurse without proof of a completed education, and their town already had several dress shops.

His heart ached when he realized that his favorite child was seemingly condemned to live with them until they died, due in large part to his leniency. Even more disturbing, he had no idea where she would go when that day came. God willing, Adam would grow to be a strong and healthy man before his grandfather and grandmother left this earth and would be willing to take his mother in with him and his family.

That is as long as his future wife would allow it, he mused.

As he drove the buggy home in relative silence, Sarah's father was surprised with the ferocity of anger hitting him out of nowhere that George had died and left his daughter in such a predicament. Logically he knew that the man hadn't done anything wrong and that his demise wasn't preventable, but his heart told him that if George had only fought harder or loved her more, he would have found the strength to stay with her. Stronger than any other emotion, however, was the rage he felt at the man's parents for their total disregard for the well-being of their son's widow and their grandchild.

A less logical man would go home and get his gun, he thought, before taking several deep breaths in an attempt to calm himself before Sarah noticed something was troubling him.

"So," he said after the hatred and disgust he had been feeling dissipated slightly, "how was the trip?"

"I didn't end up in a puddle of blood at the end of it, so it was good, thanks. Long, but uneventful. Adam did better this way, knowing what to expect."

Sarah's father just nodded his head, and they continued to plod along for several minutes more.

"What is your plan now, Sarah?"

"I don't know, Pa," she answered, glancing nervously at the small boy between them.

He nodded again, understanding her consternation. Therefore, her next sentence surprised him, breaking through his thoughts. "First thing I want to do is go see George."

"I beg your pardon?" he probed her, startled.

"I mean I want to visit his grave. I have some things I feel I want to discuss with him, and I don't know… I feel closer to him when I'm there, somehow."

"Well, I'm sure that can be arranged," he appeased her.

By the time they pulled up to the house, it was getting late. While her father took care of the team in the barn, Sarah's mother put supper on the table. After a quiet dinner, during which poor little Adam was nearly dropping into his plate in utter exhaustion, Sarah had excused herself to put both of them to bed.

"But of course, dear," her mother had answered her when she had asked to leave the table. "There's no reason for you to stay up. Sleep, and we will catch up tomorrow."

After the dishes were done, Sarah's mother joined her father on the sofa.

"How is she?"

"Not well. You can see for yourself how pale and thin she still is."

"Yes, I saw. Her clothes are nearly hanging off of her."

They sat in silence together for a few minutes in the dim light.

"Has she said what she intends to do?"

"No, all she said was that she wanted to go and see George. She said she had a lot to discuss with him."

"Poor dear."

True to her word, the next morning, Sarah was up with the sun. She quickly dressed, grabbed a blanket, and an apple before walking to George's gravesite. She noted that it had been well maintained and figured it was his mother who had done it. As angry as she was with the woman, she was grateful to see that George's plot had not been neglected.

She lay her blanket down on top of the small mound of dirt that hadn't yet been covered in grass since his grave had been dug in the late fall. Falling to her knees, she touched the gravestone, despising the cold stone beneath her hand. As the tears slid from her nose and onto the blanket below, she whispered, "I miss you!"

She was unsure of how long she stayed in that position, feeling the last vestiges of his spirit near her. At some point, she realized that she had lain down on the blanket as sobs wracked her body. When she felt she had no tears left in her, she rolled over and looked up at the sky.

"George, I miss you terribly. I wish you would come back to me," she whimpered.

She took a centering breath before continuing. "Colorado was nice. It was good to get away… Your parents, I'm sorry to say, though not surprisingly, haven't been the kindest. I stayed with Ginny and Jacob and the girls. It is beautiful country out there. Oh! How I wish you could have seen it! You would have loved the mountains and the big, open sky!"

She lay quietly again, watching the clouds race by overhead.

After a while, she began to speak, her voice sounding small and forlorn. "I lost another baby. On the train, if you can imagine that. I was so close to Ginny and Jacob's home, but I didn't make it in time. I knew that it would most likely happen. But George… Oh, George! I was so hoping that this time would be different! That somehow, God would let me keep that last part of you because He took you Home and away from me. But alas, God didn't care too much about that, I guess." She sniffled. "It was another little boy. I didn't even bother to give him a name…"

Sarah sobbed for a few minutes before collecting herself again.

"Adam is getting so big! He's growing and changing every day. In Colorado, there was a man… a man named Joe, a sheriff, actually, who took Adam under his wing. He's the one who found me on the train and took me to the jail when the doctor couldn't be found. Can you imagine, me spending the night in jail?" she chuckled slightly.

"Anyway, Jacob and Joe took the children sledding on several occasions, and once the weather warmed enough, he took Adam fishing. But it was so hard, George. I always thought you would be the one to teach our son to fish. I always pictured you taking him to our fishing hole when he was old enough. Part of me wanted to tell Joe that he couldn't take him: that it was your job to teach our son how to fish because it still doesn't feel real that you're gone."

She paused and took a deep breath before continuing. "I thought you would be the one to teach him to be a man." More tears rolled out of her eyes and down the sides of her face, as she rose up on her knees, her anguish finally boiling over.

"But you left me, George Johnson! YOU LEFT ME!" she screamed at the top of her lungs. "You left me here all alone with this little boy who I have no idea how to raise into a man. I'm so incredibly angry that you are gone! Why did you leave me? Was it because I couldn't give you more babies? Was your mother right? Why, George? Why? What am I going to do now? Why did you have to leave me all alone?"

Sarah wasn't sure how long she stayed, crying, pleading, and talking beside her husband's grave. Though she knew his spirit was not there, there was no other place where she felt more of a connection. He had been her best friend for the majority of her life, and she honestly didn't know how to go on from there. She missed her lover, her partner, but most of all, her best friend. She missed talking with him, his joking and cajoling, the way he flirted with her by teasing her. She was a young woman, and she couldn't face the idea that she would be alone indefinitely, but she had no desire to find someone else.

She had told anyone who asked that she came home to be near George again, even if it was only where he was buried. However, if she had been truthful with herself, she would have admitted how scared she was for noticing Joe as a man, rather than just a random person, and it made her feel guilty.

Before she and Adam had left to come home, she found herself wanting Joe's attention, and she enjoyed when he touched her, even if it was simply to take her arm on the slippery wooden sidewalk. She hadn't realized just how much she was missing physical contact until Joe had given her some. It was in those moments that she recognized that she and George had engaged in an active and fulfilling physical relationship, but she was now facing the probability of a lifetime of never being loved like that again at only twenty-two years old. Feeling Joe's warm, solid, masculine body beside hers as they walked, or having him take her hand to help her down the steps, had made her acutely aware of how much she missed the attentions of a man, and it horrified her because she had decided that she had no intention of ever loving anyone again after George. Even more distressing to her, though, was that she had begun to hope that perhaps Joe enjoyed touching her, too, based on how often he seemed to do so. She then felt shamefully wanton, especially with her husband having only been buried less than half a year before.

Wracked with guilt, Sarah worked hard to persuade herself that she was grasping for anything to make her feel better. She told herself to be logical: that Joe wasn't attracted to her but was only being polite. Given his treatment of her, well-mannered, yet aloof, and sometimes even seemingly annoyed by her stubborn nature, it wasn't hard to convince herself that he wasn't interested, but instead of dissuading her guilt, it only served to make her feel all the lonelier and more abandoned.

The most upsetting of all, however, was how Sarah perceived herself as a failure as a woman.

Surely, she convinced herself, *no man would ever want me for a wife once he learned of my inability to provide him with the fruits of a union with me.*

This summation was not helped by George's mother's accusations that Sarah's inadequacies were responsible for her son's lack of will to live. Her constant barbs and obvious disappointment hadn't allowed Sarah to shake the belief that George's disillusionment with her and their life together had frustrated him, and that any other man would eventually feel the same.

She was unfulfilled in her need to be loved and had the same physical urges and desires as before, but it angered her that she could do nothing about them as a respectable widowed woman, while realizing it was not the same for a man. *If a man only wants his needs slacked,* she thought, *he could certainly find an unseemly woman to do so without the burden of having to take her on as his wife, and no one would think any worse of him.*

The more she ruminated it over, it seemed as if God were punishing her for some unknown transgression by longing to be wanted but having nothing to offer.

Coming home to George's memory was her only solace. She figured that she would not be tempted to look to anyone else in the shadow of her husband's grave, which would, in turn, provide her heart protection from being hurt again, as any man she was interested in would surely reject her when he learned of her difficulties. At home, she could raise her son with the help of his grandfathers, and whenever she felt lonely, she determined she would be content to sit and talk with George at his final resting place. She figured that eventually, she would even grow accustomed to going without feeling loved and sharing physical intimacy, deciding instead to be grateful for the love and desire she and her husband had shared.

Chapter Twenty

The weeks went by with Sarah helping her mother around the house, sewing a new spring wardrobe for Adam, and spending time at George's burial plot. She had been going at least every other day since she had been home and had not run into anyone else while doing it, but one warm afternoon, that all changed.

Sarah had been laying on her back, face to the sun, eyes closed, talking to George's memory about how fast Adam was growing and changing, when she opened her eyes at the sound of an "Ahem!"

When she could focus, she saw George's parents standing above her, both staring down at her. His father looked slightly amused, a kindly smile on his lips. However, his mother's expression was as dark as thunder, as though Sarah had violated some sacred ordinance of which she was not aware.

The young woman scrambled to her feet, straightening her hair and dress before saying, "Good afternoon," as politely and with as much dignity as she could muster.

"Good afternoon, Sarah," George's mother responded, her voice as cold as her demeanor. "What, may I ask, are you doing laying on George's grave?"

"I'm speaking with him," she responded quietly.

"I beg your pardon?"

"I miss him terribly, so I come here and speak with him whenever I can. Somehow I feel closer to him here than I do anywhere else."

"Well, I would like to ask that you no longer come here and lay all over his grave like a common harlot!"

"Cheryl!" Even George's father was shocked by his wife's statement and tried to intervene.

"It's disgraceful, Donald!"

She turned back to Sarah. "I would like you to note that you're preventing grass from growing over his grave. All around us, the grass is greening up nicely and spreading to the newly dug plots. I had been wondering why George's grave was looking so shoddy, but now I know why."

Sarah ducked her head in both anger and embarrassment. George belonged to her as much as he belonged to his mother. Just as it said in the Bible, he had left his mother and father to build a life and home with her, his wife, but his mother had always refused to acknowledge it. If Sarah hadn't had been so emotionally fragile, she might have drawn on some of the spunk she still possessed deep down inside and confronted the woman, but because of earlier dealings with her, she knew that it would make little difference.

"So, you have obviously been home for quite a while," George's mother continued.

"Yes, ma'am," Sarah replied.

"Yet you have not brought the boy to see us?"

By now, Sarah was seething with anger. The woman would not even acknowledge her grandson by name. "No, ma'am, I haven't brought *Adam* to see you," she said, deliberately emphasizing Adam's name.

"Why's that?"

Sarah knew that she had two ways she could handle this. She could lie and say that she had been too busy, but that was an obviously hollow fabrication, or she could just say as she felt. As she pondered which way to go, she felt a stirring in the wind around her and could have sworn she had heard George's loving voice caressing her ear, saying, "Let'er have it, baby!"

She took a deep breath and calmly stated, "Because quite frankly, based on your treatment of us, I figured that you were not interested in seeing us."

She looked up and held George's mother's gaze with hers and was pleased to see that the woman eventually caved, and her eyes darted to the side.

George's father was quick to jump in to try to rectify the uncomfortable situation. "But, Sarah, of course, we would love to see Adam! He's George's son!"

Having recovered, George's mother gathered her wits about her and asked Sarah to bring the boy by the next afternoon. After reluctantly agreeing, Sarah gathered her blanket and belongings to head for home, excusing herself as quickly as possible.

The next morning brought much anxiety to Sarah's family home. Sarah was distraught with panic as she tried to decide what Adam should wear while running through proper etiquette with him over and over again to ensure that he would act appropriately and not give her former in-laws any more fodder in their hatred of her. Sarah's parents were anxiously watching their daughter as she fretted about impressing people who, in their minds, did not deserve to be impressed.

Sarah's father had hitched up the team to the buggy, so it was ready for her twenty minutes before two, giving her enough time to make it to her in-laws precisely when expected and not a minute before or after. As Sarah and Adam exited the house, her father helped the young boy into the buggy seat, and then moved to assist Sarah.

"You look lovely, Sarah. Truly striking!"

"Thank you, Pa! Although I am so incredibly sick of black!"

He placed his loving hand on her cheek before speaking. "Remember, my dear, you have done nothing wrong. Hold your head high in knowing that your husband chose to love you. You are the mother of his son, their grandchild. You deserve respect, and if you don't get it, you have no reason to stay."

"Thank you, Pa."

"You're welcome."

Sarah felt a renewed sense of fortitude when she arrived at her in-law's home. Her father-in-law met her, taking the horse and buggy to the barn after helping her and Adam down. She wanted desperately to wait for him on the porch, but instead squared her shoulders and marched up the front steps. After knocking on the door, it was opened momentarily by George's mother. They were shown inside to the sitting room, where they all sat in silence, unsmiling and extremely uncomfortable.

George's father soon came in, sitting in a chair. His mother then beckoned Adam to come stand in front of her. The boy reluctantly went, glancing over his shoulder to Sarah, who gave him a small nod and a reassuring smile in return. After several moments of looking him over, George's mother's eyes teared up and she turned to her husband.

"Well, as I live and breathe, this boy is the spitting image of our George."

Sarah, unsure of how to respond, said nothing, while his father agreed.

"Sarah, don't you think Adam is just like George?"

"The resemblance is certainly there," she responded. Then, in an act of rebelliousness, she tipped her chin and added saucily, "But there is also a good deal of me in him, as well."

"Well, I don't see it!" his mother responded.

"I guarantee that Adam is a combination of the two of us and the love we shared," Sarah continued, unwilling to have her place in George's life diminished by this cruel and calculating woman.

Sarah was unsure what the ultimate purpose of this meeting was supposed to be. She found it surprising that they wanted to see them at all since his family had cared nothing about their whereabouts until discovering that she and her son had been home for over a month. They hadn't shown any interest in them until they ran into her, so Sarah was wary of their motivation, spending the whole evening waiting for the real reason they were invited to visit to be revealed.

Whatever the intentions were, however, they were not discovered that night. Despite all of the discomfort, it warmed Sarah's heart to see how George's father had taken to Adam, telling him stories of George as a child. While they ate supper, however, the food felt and tasted like sawdust in her mouth as she thought bitterly, *I'm surprised they are willing to share their precious food with us.*

As Sarah and Adam were getting ready to leave, she politely thanked George's mother for her hospitality, slightly shuddering when she received an icy, "You're welcome," in response, for as cold as his mother was, she had simultaneously remembered the warm caresses and heated kisses she had shared with this woman's son. It was unfathomable to think that her beloved George could have come from such a hard, unfeeling person.

In the yard, when she took George's father's hand as he helped her into the buggy, she felt him press something into her palm. Surprised, she looked up at him as he blushed slightly, while answering her unspoken question, "For the boy."

She nodded her understanding and settled into the seat before taking the reins. Once they were underway, she opened her hand, seeing the twenty dollars George's father had given her. As her eyes welled up, it was then that she realized that all the caring and warmth she had shared with George had obviously come from this man.

For the next few weeks, the invitations continued until it became understood that Sarah and Adam were expected at the Johnson farm every Sunday after church. While Sarah never felt comfortable with her in-laws, her son grew more attached to his grandparents, so she was willing to suffer the insults, insinuations, and scorn in order to bring her child happiness.

Chapter Twenty-One

One sunny Saturday morning, when the sun was hot, and the breeze was warm, Sarah's father came from town bearing a letter from Ginny. As Sarah ripped into the envelope and pulled out the sheets contained therein, she swore she could smell the fresh Colorado air and the scent of pine, bringing her a smile. What the letter contained, however, was far from refreshing.

Ginny wrote to her sister that after several years of trying, she was pregnant again. However, it was not an easy pregnancy, especially with the girls underfoot. She begged Sarah to please consider returning to Colorado to help her, as she had no one else on whom she could rely, and Dr. Miller was encouraging her to stay off her feet as much as possible. Then, at the very bottom of the letter, there was a postscript that said simply, "Joe sends his regards to you and Adam."

That afternoon, she weighed the pluses and minuses of returning to Colorado while Adam was fishing with George's father. In the end, she made a list of the pros and cons, which ended up being even. She continued her contemplation all afternoon through Adam's coming back home, supper, and then bedtime, until she finally conceded that Colorado would never have George and the memories surrounding him and their lives there. As she lay in her bed, she wondered if there would ever be anything strong enough to allow her the freedom to permanently cut the ties of home.

Sunday morning dawned warm and bright. Sarah and Adam went to church, and then, because it was such a nice day, headed out on foot for the mile-long walk to George's family's farm in the midafternoon. For some reason, Sarah was feeling exceptionally apprehensive about this visit, though she had no reason to be, but something unseen had her on edge.

From the moment she walked into the house, she felt an underlying tension. Something was not right, and she wanted desperately to take Adam's hand and head right back out the door. George's mother was even icier than normal, while even his father was aloof and standoffish. Thankfully, dinner was soon served.

About halfway through the meal, the other shoe Sarah felt like she had been waiting for was dropped.

"Sarah, who is Joe?" George's mother asked after a long stretch of silence.

"I beg your pardon?"

"You heard me! Who is Joe?"

A look of confusion came over Sarah's face for a minute as she tried to understand how her in-laws at home would know about the sheriff in Colorado. George's father took her lack of immediate response, however, as an admission of guilt for some unknown offense.

"See?" he said, turning to his wife. "I told you that there was something going on."

"I'm sorry?" Sarah was still perplexed.

"How dare you!" George's mother spat out.

"How dare I what?"

"How dare you take up with another man so soon after George's passing! Have you no respect for the man who fathered your children and lies cold and still in his grave?"

"I don't understand..." Sarah tried again.

"Oh, you understand, all right," George's father added.

"How do you know about Joe?" Sarah's thoughts were still not coming together.

"Adam, of course!"

With this, Sarah turned to look at her small son sitting frozen in fear and confusion, with his fork midway to his mouth.

What did he tell him yesterday? Sarah thought wildly in a panic.

"Oh, yes. Adam told me all about how this Joe character was so happy to teach my grandson to fish. Apparently, you accompanied him on many excursions, as well. Did you happen to tell the man you were courting in Colorado that my son hadn't been six feet under the cold ground for even two months before you began gallivanting around, entertaining other men?"

"But…" Sarah tried to interrupt.

"There are no 'buts', Sarah," George's mother interjected. "You are a loose woman of low moral character. I have always thought that there was something off about you, but I had no idea that you would stoop to something this low. Couldn't even wait until my George was cold in the grave, could you, until you tried to entice and trick yet another man into thinking you would make a decent wife."

"I'm sorry! If you would just let me explain…" Sarah tried again.

"There is nothing to explain. You, Sarah, are nothing but a hussy! I knew it when you and George first started courting. Don't you think for a second that I didn't know what you were getting up to with my son, and God only knows who else, down by the fishing hole! In fact, quite frankly I was surprised you weren't already expecting on your wedding day! Of course, now I know it was only because children do not come easily to you, or it would have been the case, of that I am certain! Children don't come easily to loose women who enjoy the company of many men. You tricked my poor boy into marrying you and now…" George's mother ended with a sob.

Sarah sat too stunned to think, but after a few minutes of trying to make heads or tails of what was going on, she felt another stirring in her soul that she could swear came directly from George, letting her know that she should fight their allegations. Suddenly, her temper boiled over.

Sarah took a deep breath and said, "With all due respect, how dare you say such horrible things about me? How dare you insinuate that I'm loose and immoral? I loved your son with every fiber of my being, and I feel his loss deeply every second of every day. Not only was he my husband, but he was also my *only* lover and my best friend."

She let out a shuddering sigh before continuing, trying her damnedest to keep from crying. "Joe, if you must know, is the

168

sheriff in the town where my sister lives. He's a good friend of my sister and her husband. I fell ill on the way to Colorado, and he helped me get safely to my sister's house." Sarah knew she had to tread carefully, that she would rather die than admit to them that she had lost another baby.

She pushed on, "While I was recovering, Joe helped Ginny's husband take the children on excursions. Ginny and Jacob have twin girls, and the men took the children to allow me to rest and get better. In the dead of winter, they took the children sledding, but as the weather warmed, they turned to fishing!" Sarah knew she wasn't being completely honest about how the fishing trips had been often only Joe and Adam, sometimes with her in tow.

"Adam reported seeing you in his bed! In your nightclothes!" George's father spat out in disgust.

Sarah turned her shocked gaze to Adam. Of course, she hadn't thought about how her four-year-old son would perceive things when he had come with his aunt and uncle to collect her the morning after her ordeal. All he knew was that his ma and pa had shared a bed in their nightclothes, so of course, he didn't understand the finer details of the situation.

"No! Please, let me explain!" Sarah got out as soon as she had recovered her wits about her, but she was quickly interrupted.

"There's no explanation that we are willing to listen to, Sarah!"

"But…"

"We will hear nothing more from you! We have decided that we are taking our son's son to live with us here. You are in no way a fit mother. As we have already stated and made abundantly clear, you are a loose woman and are obviously incapable of raising Adam in a respectable manner. If you wish to be a harlot, that is completely up to you. But the boy will be staying here with us, brought up in a real Christian household."

"You can't do that! He's my child!" Sarah cried out.

"Oh, we can, and we will. We have already spoken to the town magistrate this morning before services and have started the process of deeming you unfit and removing Adam from your care."

"But you simply can't prove anything! My sister and her husband will attest to my innocence in your accusations! I stayed the night in the jail…" she began to explain and then realized how much worse it made the situation sound. She hurried on before they could use that against her.

"I spent the night at the jailhouse because when I was taken ill off the train, the doctor couldn't be found straight away. The sheriff, Joe, took me to the jailhouse until the doctor arrived. They were both there with me all night!" Sarah then realized that what she just said could be construed as even worse than they originally thought. "You can't take Adam from me! I have done nothing wrong!"

"Sarah, you don't even have an income. That alone makes us fitter to raise Adam than you," George's father added quietly.

"I have no income because you kicked me off my farm! Of course, I have no way to earn an income!" she shouted.

"No, dear," George's mother jumped in. "We kicked you off *our* farm."

With that, Sarah rose from the table, desperately trying to hold onto her last shred of composure. She lifted her boy off his chair and placed his feet on the floor, taking his hand in hers. "Adam and I thank you for our meal. We will be leaving now!"

Sarah and Adam walked out of the house, quickly returning to her parents' home. As she crashed through the door, her father looked up from his paper, pipe in hand, startled at the sudden commotion in the room.

"What happened?" he asked, jumping immediately to his feet.

"Oh, Pa!" Sarah sobbed. "They're accusing me of taking up with the sheriff in Colorado only because he was kind to Adam and me, taking us fishing. They're threatening to have Adam removed from my care and placed with them, as they have deemed me a loose and immoral woman without the means to provide for him! They have started the process with the magistrate already!"

Her father shook his head in disgust. "Now listen, Sarah. This is not to be taken lightly. The magistrate and the Johnsons are good friends. He will do their bidding, I'm sure. Go pack some things for you and Adam while I hitch up the team. I'm driving you three towns over as soon as you're ready, and you're going back to your sister's home in Colorado until this all blows over. Quick, now! We don't have much time for me to get you there and be back by morning, so hurry!"

Sarah did as she was bid, along with her mother's help. When it came to her own clothing, she reached for her black garments, pausing only when her mother mentioned that she might not be returning until after her mourning period was over. With that reminder, she grabbed her other dresses and stuffed them into a trunk, along with some towels and sheets thrown in hastily by her mother at the last moment. Her father then carried the trunk to the buggy, with Sarah following him with her bag and Adam, who was looking scared and lost. Her mother quickly hugged her and kissed her cheek, before doing the same to Adam.

True to his word, her father dropped them three towns over at a little before eleven o'clock that night. Because he didn't want to chance running into anyone they knew, he had used back roads, taking the better part of six hours to get there. Once they arrived, he had quickly secured Sarah and Adam's tickets and a hotel room. He hugged her to him and kissed her cheek, telling her, "Go, Sarah, and make a new life for yourself. We love you, but there's nothing left for you here but heartache and pain."

Sarah sniffed as the tears rolled down her cheeks. "Just please promise me that you will take care of George's grave. Please, Pa!"

"Of course, my dear. We will make sure he is never forgotten."

"Thank you!"

Sarah and Adam went to their room in the hotel, and Sarah watched from the window overlooking the street below as her father's buggy departed for home. She felt like she was watching the last vestiges of her old life slipping away, not knowing if she would ever see him again. She knew she would not be able to return home for many years, until Adam was, or almost was an adult, if she ever would at all.

Chapter Twenty-Two

The trip to Colorado was just as long and arduous as it had been before, though the weather was beautiful, and the scenery divine. It was now early summer, and the landscape was alive with lush greens enhanced by explosions of colorful wildflowers.

Finally, the train pulled into the station and Sarah woke her sleeping son, slumped beside her, to prepare to exit. As she stepped off onto the platform, it dawned on her that she had not let her sister know she was coming and hoped that her father had thought to send a telegram in advance.

As Sarah waited for the porter to collect her trunk, she heard, "Mrs. Johnson?"

Turning in the direction of the voice, Sarah was pleased to see Joe coming toward her, his long strides quickly bridging the gap between them, with a mixture of confusion and shock on his face. When he made it to her, he grabbed her hand and lifted it, surprised that he had to fight himself from bringing her fingers up to his lips.

"What are you doing here?" he asked her in amazement, having already reconciled himself to the fact that he would most likely never see her again. "I thought you had gone home to stay?"

As soon as he asked the question, he saw the tears building in her eyes. She only shook her head in response, letting him know she was not prepared to speak with him about it. Instead, he gave her a few moments to recover by turning his attention to the small boy at her side.

"Hey, there, Adam! I hope you're ready to hit that creek again. Those fish are calling your name!"

"Yes, sir," the small boy responded shyly.

"What are you doing at the depot, Sheriff?" Sarah asked after she had gathered her wits about her.

"Payroll," he answered. "In fact, I had better get to it. I will see you around town, I guess."

Sarah nodded politely and watched as Joe jogged off down the platform to the armed guards who had been hired to transport the money to town.

Sarah caught the attention of the porter, asking him to please help her find transportation to her sister's house and soon she was on the front porch of Ginny and Jacob's home. She rapped on the door three times in quick succession and was soon greeted by her sister's surprised squeal of delight.

"Sarah! What on earth? What are you doing here?"

"Did Pa not send a telegram?" Sarah asked as she stepped over the threshold, motioning to the teamster who had collected her things to take them inside.

"No! I haven't heard anything from anyone since I sent my last letter!"

With that, Sarah looked down and saw her sister's already expanding waist, and she quickly hugged her.

"I'm here to help you!" she declared stoutly.

"Well, that's wonderful! I'm so glad! But why didn't you tell me you were coming?"

"There wasn't time, Ginny."

"Is everything all right?"

"It will be. I mean, it should be now, yes," Sarah answered her cryptically.

"I don't understand…" Ginny said, trailing off as Sarah jerked her head toward the little boy standing beside her, letting her know that now was not the time to discuss such matters.

Later that evening, after supper, when the children were in bed, Sarah filled in Ginny and Jacob about what had happened, and why she had left in such haste. They were thrilled that she had come to them but were unhappy about the circumstances which had brought her. It was decided that Sarah and Adam would stay at the house with them so that Ginny could rest and hopefully birth a healthy baby. Sarah was concerned about how she would pay for herself and her son, but Jacob insisted that he was glad to pay her, as he would have to pay anyone else to assist with the tasks needed for Ginny's convalescence. Ginny was approximately four months pregnant, having discovered she was expecting not long after Sarah had returned home.

The next little while passed quickly, with the children needing a lot of care and catching the housework up from when Ginny had been placed on bedrest. Jacob had done his best when he had taken over, but it had proven to be too much on top of his job.

A few weeks after Sarah arrived, a letter came from home. Her father apologized for not sending a telegram ahead of time to Ginny and Jacob to let them know Sarah was coming, but that it hadn't dawned on him to do so when he dropped her off, and he didn't dare send one from their town. In fact, he had written that the reason the letter had taken so long was that he had posted it from another nearby town so that no one would have any idea where Sarah and her son had gone. He stated that he and their mother had merely told people that Sarah had left in the night, taking the boy with her, and they had no idea where they had gone. He knew that it didn't sound good for her reputation, but he wanted to throw the magistrate off because, as he was afraid of, the man had determined that Adam would be better off in the care of George's parents than with his mother.

Sarah read the letter, tears springing to her eyes, the reality of what had transpired hitting her: she really could never go home again. Ginny had also cried when she read the letter, understanding the pain her sister was in. While she was happy to have her with them, she knew how difficult it was for Sarah to leave the only place she had ever considered home and the place where her husband was buried.

However, life went on, and one Friday night, Jacob asked Sarah if she would mind cooking the next evening for Joe and Dr. Miller, as well as the normal brood, so that they could get together.

Saturday morning dawned bright and warm, and Sarah was surprised when Joe knocked on the door at eight o'clock. He stood on the front porch, fishing poles in hand and asked if Adam would be up to helping him catch their supper that night.

The little boy, having just finished his breakfast in the kitchen, was out in the entryway, hat in hand, before Sarah had the chance to turn around and call for him. She smiled as Joe ruffled her little boy's hair and handed him the basket they would use to carry their fish. When she asked if they needed any food for lunch, Joe assured her that he had already packed enough for the two of them.

Several hours later brought in a very happy little boy, a relaxed-looking man, and a pile of fish in the basket. When Sarah took it from Adam, his excitement flowed into her, and she was instantly transported back to when she would come home from her fishing hole with the same bounty.

"I will go home and freshen up, and then I will be back to help you clean and cook that fish," Joe told her.

"That's all right, Sheriff. I have lots of experience cleaning and cooking fish," she answered.

He cocked his head to the side and looked at her before responding, "Well, nonetheless, I'll be back shortly. I'm sure no matter how well you say you can cook fish that you don't have anything on me and my recipe!" And with that, he turned on his heel and walked out of the kitchen.

Sarah put Adam down to rest and got to work scaling and cleaning the plethora of fish. She had just about finished and was preparing to peel and boil some potatoes when Joe came back. She greeted him at the front door, and they walked together into the kitchen.

Joe looked stunned when he saw the pile of fish she had already prepared, and he turned to her.

"I said I would clean all of these! Why didn't you wait for me?"

"Mr. McIntyre, honestly, this is not a big deal. I've cooked fish for many, many years. My husband and I both loved to fish and spent many years together, poles in hand, getting to know and love each other."

"Well, regardless, you could have waited for me."

Sarah could have kept arguing, but she realized that it wasn't worth it. Instead, she looked down at his hand for the first time and noticed he was carrying a jar of amber liquid. "What's that?" she asked, intrigued.

"That, Sarah, is beer."

"Beer?"

"Yes, beer! Brought over from one of the finest Colorado breweries we have. I bought it from the saloon closest to the jail."

Sarah was quite taken aback. George was not a drinker. He would very occasionally go into town to sit and talk with other farmers in the area over a shot of whiskey or a glass of beer, but she could count on one hand the times he had done it, and never at home or in front of her. In fact, the only way she could tell that he had imbibed when he came home was that she could smell it on his breath, and he seemed to be a bit friskier than usual.

Sarah knew, though, that alcohol and mining towns out West went hand and hand. Saloons had long been touted as the local gathering point for miners and railroad men to go let off steam after their shifts. What surprised her, however, was that Joe, the sheriff in town, would imbibe. It struck her as odd that the lawman would indulge in such an activity, especially when that activity led to the majority of the issues he had to deal with in his profession.

Joe watched Sarah and could see that the wheels were turning in her head as she processed and speculated about what he was going to do with the contents in the jar. Finally, it dawned on him that she thought he intended to drink it and quickly clarified, "It's for the fish."

"Oh?"

"Yes! Nothing beats beer battered fish. Have you ever tried it?"

"No, I can't say that I have."

"Well, then, prepare to be impressed!" he told her as he reached around her for a bowl to pour the beer into for making the batter.

Sarah watched as he worked, dipping the fish, then placing it into the sizzling oil in a skillet on the cookstove. After a while, her mouth began watering, and she told him, "They look amazing!"

"Yeah, these are all right," he told her, looking over his shoulder at her. "But nothing beats the fish at home!"

Sarah saw her opportunity to delve deeper into his background and asked, "Sheriff, why did you leave California?"

"Oh!" he responded, taken aback. "Just needed a change is all."

"And please call me Joe," he added hastily.

"Did you not like it there? I have heard it is beautiful!"

"No, I liked it just fine. I just… I just needed to get away."

"From what?"

"Look, Sarah, I don't really want to talk about it!" Joe stated gruffly, letting her know in no uncertain terms that he was unwilling to divulge anything further, but Sarah wasn't ready to give up so easily.

"Come on, Joe. You know all about me and my past. Don't I deserve to know something about yours?"

"No," he stated plainly. "I can't help it if you go around telling people your personal business. I don't need to tell you mine!"

Sarah recoiled as if she had been slapped. Joe saw her expression and realized that once again, he had come across as too gruff, too insensitive. In all truth, he knew that she did deserve, as his friend, to know at least a little more about him, but it was just too painful to talk about. He had opened himself up before and had paid dearly for it, so he had learned to keep to himself.

Sarah turned around and left the kitchen without another word, heading into the dining room to set the table. When she did come into the kitchen, she wouldn't even look at him, leaving Joe wanting to kick himself for being so bad-tempered, but he didn't know how to begin to tell her his story.

Dinner was a quiet affair, with Joe and Sarah not contributing much to the conversation. Ginny had come down to the table, but she, Dr. Miller and Jacob eventually ran out of things to say as they felt the tensions running high between their other two companions.

Finally, Dr. Miller couldn't stand it anymore. Sarah was a beautiful woman, and even though he was almost fifteen years her senior, he had to admit that he found her intriguing and beguiling. Out of respect for his friend, Dr. Miller had kept his feelings in check to allow the younger man the opportunity to make his move, but as it seemed like the two of them couldn't get along for more than even a few minutes, he decided it was time to pull out his charm and take his chance with Sarah. Though he knew she was still mourning her husband's death, he figured that there would be no harm in laying down a foundation upon which he hoped to build once the timing was right.

"So, Sarah, have you thought any more about opening a dress shop in town?" he asked to break the ice.

"Uh, no!" Sarah exclaimed in surprise, suddenly dragged from her reverie.

"Well, I think you should!" Dr. Miller responded, giving her his most charismatic smile.

"Well, there's Ginny and the children to look after," Sarah explained.

"Not only that," she added, "I don't have a machine here."

"Ah, but that is something that can be easily remedied, my dear." He smiled at her again.

Joe watched the conversation unfold before him and couldn't understand why he felt like clobbering his closest friend. He was angry that the doctor was so shamelessly flirting with Sarah, but he kept arguing with himself that he shouldn't care because he was not interested in her. He couldn't deny, however, that he was secretly glad that Sarah seemed mostly perplexed about the doctor's advances, and he chuckled smugly to himself, until he noticed that Sarah was watching him, her confusion apparent.

Great! Now she must think I'm crazy, too! he inwardly groaned.

The awkward supper finally came to an end, and Sarah was grateful when the men said goodnight. She was exhausted and spent from the day of trying to figure out what made Joe tick and why she even cared. He annoyed her–they bickered constantly, he treated her like a child, and most of all, she was still in mourning. He had no redeeming qualities that she could see that would attract her to him, other than his rugged good looks and how he took a shine to Adam, but those certainly did not make up for his gruff and surly personality. She was so perplexed how someone with such a kind heart could be such a rude, pretentious bastard!

***

A few days later, a knock came at the door, and Sarah rushed to open it before the sound woke up Adam and her two nieces, along with Ginny, who were all down for an afternoon nap. When Sarah swung open the portal, she was surprised to see a nervous-looking Joe on the front porch. She cocked her head to the side, wondering why he would be coming to the house when it was obvious Jacob would still be at work at the station.

"Yes?" she inquired a bit more archly than she meant to.

"Uh… Good afternoon, Sarah. I… uh… have something to deliver to you…" he answered, silently cursing himself that she always made him so flustered that more often than not he sounded like a bumbling idiot.

"All right," Sarah answered, still puzzled.

Then she noticed his outstretched hand, in which he was holding an envelope. She took it and thanked him, but her face displayed her confusion about why he would feel the need to hand-deliver a letter when it was well-known that Jacob passed by the small postal outpost in the mercantile every day on his way home from work.

Sarah began to shut the door, thinking that his errand was through. She was in the middle of preparing supper and was anxious to return to the kitchen, so she was surprised when Joe stuck his foot out and caught the door before it shut in his face.

"That's not all!" he told her, as his frustration was coming out in his voice.

He looked up and saw her eyes questioning him, and he continued. "I have something in the wagon over there that I need to deliver."

Sarah watched him as he moved effortlessly down the walk and out to the parked wagon, not even realizing that she was enjoying the view of his departing backside. When he got to the wagon, she moved her eyes from his denim-clad bottom and thighs and onto the vehicle. She gasped as he moved a blanket to reveal a beautiful, gleaming sewing machine under it.

Sarah clapped her hands together in delight and exclaimed with joy. She watched with shining eyes as he lifted the thing out of the wagon box and carried it up to the front porch. She ran ahead to fling open the door and stood in the entryway as he maneuvered the big, awkward piece of equipment into the house.

"Where do you want it?" he panted slightly with exertion.

Sarah didn't even know how to respond she was so overcome with joy and shock. Finally, after waiting for a few moments, he stated, "If you don't let me know soon, I swear I'll just put it where I think it should go!"

She smiled and responded, "I'm debating about if I want it down here or in my room. Ginny has one in her room, but that's most inconvenient when I wish to sew something late into the evening or while the children are playing down here. Why don't we leave it down here and if Ginny wants it somewhere else, she can let me know?"

Once he had moved it to where she had asked he watched her as she admired the thing, her face alive with pure delight. His eyes followed as she ran her hand over the body of the machine, lovingly caressing it.

She turned to him, and her voice thick with emotion. "Joe, wherever did you get this?"

"Don't get too excited, Sarah!" he exclaimed. "It isn't new or anything. It was the machine that was left in the seamstress's shop when she left. She told me that they didn't have any room for it in their wagon, and as it was her extra machine, she intended to leave it for me to give to someone I felt could use it the most. I think you certainly fit that bill, so I took it apart, cleaned and greased it up, and brought it over here to you."

He seemed surprised when tears started sliding down her face, and he panicked about what he could have possibly done wrong.

Maybe I wasn't supposed to tell her it wasn't new? Women had always flustered him, but now more than ever.

"What?" he demanded, his frustration with not knowing why she was crying making the word come out harsher than he intended.

"You shouldn't have!"

"Why?" he asked more gently. "Don't you like it?

"I love it," she answered him, her voice cracking slightly through her tears.

"Then why are you crying?"

"Because other than the house that my late husband built for me, this is the most tender, sweetest gift I have ever received. How can I ever thank you?"

Joe blushed deeply scarlet, unsure of what to say next. Finally, he blurted out the first thing that came into his mind.

"I fully intend for you to use this thing to make something of yourself!"

He groaned inwardly about what he had just said and how it had come off as a disappointed father figure rather than as a concerned friend.

She looked a little taken aback, but then nodded her head, "I intend to! Thank you, Joe!"

He turned to leave, but as his hand touched the doorknob, he turned back to her and said, "You be sure to let everyone know I got you a machine, all right?" He then stepped through the door and closed it firmly behind him.

As he drove back to the livery, he chastised himself the entire way.

What an idiot I am! I only wanted to make sure that people knew she was now set up for business, not to boast that I did something for her. Surely, she knows that, right? Certainly, she understands that I'm not looking for any compliments or praise!

He discovered that he had spoken the last few sentences out loud to the horse, and what was worse was that he actually paused in between them as if the horse would answer!

"Joe McIntyre," he said aloud, despite his realization just moments before, "you need to stop letting that woman get under your skin!"

Chapter Twenty-Three

The last few months of Ginny's pregnancy went smoothly, despite the fear both she and Sarah felt. Sarah hovered over her sister like a mother hen, insisting that she rest, eat well, and stay off her feet as much as possible. She kept her sister's household running while doing some sewing on the side, but soon the amount of sewing was growing to the point that it was almost a full-time job.

Joe mentioned to her during a visit to get more clothes repaired that the shop next to the jail was still vacant in hopes of convincing her to be closer to him, though he would have never admitted why. The look she shot him, however, let him clearly know that she was not interested in revisiting that discussion again.

The weather was beginning to get chilly at night and there was just a faint hint of the slightest color shifts in the aspen leaves when Ginny went into labor. She worked hard into the night, Sarah at her side, and Dr. Miller popping in from time to time to check on her progress. It was nearly dawn when Ginny gave the final push that welcomed her son into the world, with Sarah beside her as tears streamed down her face.

Sarah was terrified to look at the boy, for fear he was as ill as her children had been, but though he was a bit skinny and small, he looked healthy enough. His cry started off weak but grew in intensity until Jacob burst into the room, having heard his son's mewling through the door. His eyes sparkled and his hands twitched as Sarah reluctantly handed over the warm little bundle she had just cleaned up. She watched the father and son regard each other for a few moments, wistfully remembering how her own husband had been with his two children who had been born alive. It dawned on her that she had not grieved George as much lately. In fact, she had been so busy, she had hardly thought about him in the craziness of the past few months and when she had, her memories had brought her more joy than sadness.

Jacob and Dr. Miller left the room so that Sarah could get Ginny cleaned up. Afterward, Sarah held the baby and evaluated him critically, seeing if she could detect any similarities with either of her full-term babies who had passed. She couldn't see anything, other than what she had already noted: he was a little small and had what she thought was a weaker than normal cry. She, of course, did not mention any of this to her sister, though. She instead made a mental note to mention her concerns to Dr. Miller when she got an opportunity.

Later in the day, Joe came over with Dr. Miller when he came back to check on his patients. Sarah had been in the kitchen, busy with dinner preparations, when she walked into the sitting room and stopped short at the sight of the big, burly sheriff holding the very tiny babe in his arms. He was alone in the room and was studying the boy's face, with one finger wrapped in the child's hand. He wasn't talking to the boy, but his eyes were smiling, and Sarah was loath to disturb their private moment. She tried to back silently out of the room, a little discombobulated over what the picture before her had done to her emotions, seeing in her mind George holding their son and daughter in much the same manner, his face full of wonder, and it made her heart hurt. In her daze of painful memories, she bumped into a side table, causing it to hit the wall with a resounding thump.

Joe looked up and found her across the room, a wry smile moving over his lips. He cleared his throat self-consciously and said, "Good afternoon, Sarah."

"Hello, Joe. Enjoying yourself?"

Looking a little sheepish, he answered her while shrugging his shoulders, "I always marvel at just how small they really are when they're first born."

She nodded in agreement.

"Do you have a lot of experience with babies, then?" she asked him.

"No, not really. Just some cousins and a few nieces and nephews. I have helped deliver a few here in town when Doc needs a hand."

"Oh! No children of your own, then?" She was surprisingly shocked when she realized that she still didn't know that much about him.

"No," he answered her shortly.

Sarah misinterpreted his answer. "You don't want children, then?"

He looked up and his eyes met hers before falling back down to look at the baby's sleeping face. "I never said that," he responded softly, as he unconsciously touched the boy's cheek gently with the tip of his finger.

"Just never had the opportunity, then?" she asked him innocently.

He did not answer her. Instead, he shifted the baby in his arms and looked away. After a few moments of his staring at the far wall, he finally replied, "Something like that," in a tone that let her know that it was clearly not a subject on which he wanted to elaborate.

"Well, I hope that someday you have the opportunity, because from what I have seen, you're a natural with children."

"Thanks, but I don't see that happening. So, I will instead continue to enjoy other people's," he replied.

"And they enjoy you, too, Joe. I have been meaning to thank you for your attentiveness to Adam. It has made this transition much easier."

Joe searched out her eyes and waited for her to raise her gaze to meet his. "It's my pleasure, Sarah, truly. With the work I do, I have to say it is nice to see the innocence of children. It reminds me of the good in people that lies beneath."

Sarah nodded in response before Jacob came back in from the outhouse and Joe handed his son back to him.

Over the next week, Sarah grew more concerned that she was seeing some similar symptoms in Ginny and Jacob's little boy that she had seen in her Melissa. The boy was lethargic and didn't seem to be thriving, not to mention the very yellow tone of his skin. The doctor would come by every day and check on them and didn't seem overly concerned, but one day, she cornered him on his way out.

"Dr. Miller?" she called softly as he was putting on his overcoat in preparation to face the evening chill.

He turned and smiled at the young woman before him, still enchanted by her.

"Yes, Sarah?"

"I… um… I'm just concerned," she stammered, not looking up at him.

"About?"

"About Joshua."

"What about him?" the doctor asked, alarm creeping into his tone.

"I'm troubled," she said, dropping her voice almost to a whisper, "that he's not thriving, much like my Melissa before she passed."

"I see," the doctor replied. "Honestly, Sarah, I'm a bit troubled, too. However, I don't think that we need to worry too much… yet. I'm checking on him every day. If this continues, or he worsens, though, I may try something radical which could possibly require your help."

"Oh?"

"Yes, it's a procedure my old medical school professor back home has written to me about," he continued. "He gave an infant who was failing to thrive something called a blood transfusion. It worked, and the baby did much better and is, as far as I know, still alive and well."

"Where do I fit into this, then?"

"Well, in the case of the infant in the hospital, the blood that was used was his father's, but I have wondered if perhaps blood from the mother would be better, since she carried the infant the whole time. However, I'm not comfortable taking blood from Ginny so soon after she delivered; it was a long labor and she's tired, not to mention that she lost more blood than I'm comfortable with. But you're your sister's next of kin, so I can only deduce that you would be the next best person after his mother to give him what he needs."

"You want my blood?" Sarah squeaked.

"Yes, Sarah," the doctor laughed. "It isn't as bad as it seems, I promise. I just stick a small needle in your arm attached to some rubber tubing, collecting it in a beaker to then give it to the boy through a needle in his arm. But I'm hoping I won't need to."

"All right," Sarah said resolutely. "If that's what's needed, then I'll do it."

"Thank you!" The doctor gave her his most charming smile.

For the next few days, everyone watched the baby. He seemed to be getting worse and the doctor decided it was time to try what he had read about from his trusted instructor. Two days before the procedure, he spoke again with Sarah, explaining in greater detail exactly what would happen. However, when he arrived at the house the next afternoon, he said that he had sent a telegram to his instructor who had advised him that he had done the procedure a few more times and that the infants in question seemed to actually do better with their fathers' blood, rather than their mothers', so he would not be needing Sarah's help in that respect anymore. Instead, she watched the blood drain from Jacob's face when the doctor changed his focus to him.

However, as if by some miracle, on the morning of the procedure, the baby seemed to have rallied, so Dr. Miller went back to employing his "wait and see" approach, and by the end of the week, Baby Joshua was markedly better. All in all, everyone felt as though they had dodged a bullet and were grateful. Four weeks later, everyone breathed a final sigh of relief. Though still somewhat weak, the boy had begun to gain weight and his color continued to improve.

Dr. Miller still came every day, and as the boy did better, he had begun to spend more time talking with Sarah. One afternoon, he arrived at the peaceful scene of Sarah rocking her young nephew as his mother slept. She looked up at him when he came through the door and she smiled, though he thought he could detect sadness behind her gently curved lips.

"How's our young patient doing today, Sarah?" he asked softly.

"He's still doing well, Dr. Miller," she responded.

Nodding, he put his bag down on the armchair and brought out his stethoscope to listen to little Joshua's heart. After he had checked the rest of his vital signs, he declared the boy healthy and stable, as he stood upright again after having been bent over the baby and Sarah in the chair. When he looked into her eyes, however, he could see the raw pain that haunted them.

"Everything all right, Sarah?" he asked gently, not wanting to intrude, but wondering what was troubling her. "You don't need to fret over the baby. He's perfectly healthy! In fact, I don't think I need to come and see him every day anymore," he declared victoriously, hoping that if she was simply worried, the news of his clean bill of health would relax her a bit.

She had merely nodded, as the tears spilled over her cheeks, eventually uttering, "That's good."

"Sarah?" he asked softly, his voice gentle and soft due to his concern. "What is it?"

"I've just been thinking," she answered him.

"About?"

"About if your procedure would have saved my baby girl," she said quietly.

"I don't know, my dear," he said as he sat on the settee to the right of her chair. "Possibly? I can't say. My instructor has had some limited success with it, but even he isn't sure why or how it works, and it hasn't saved everyone. But little Joshua was so ill, I figured it was worth trying if we ran out of other options."

She nodded her understanding as he stood and retrieved his handkerchief from his pocket and handed it to her.

"It wouldn't have helped with your last child, though, Sarah, I'm sorry to say. The babies have to be born alive in order for it to work, obviously."

Sarah nodded mechanically. He stood from the settee and placed a warm hand on her shoulder. "I had best be getting on my way. I will be back every other day for the next few weeks, if you wouldn't mind passing along the information to your sister and Jacob."

"All right. Thank you, Dr. Miller," she told him, trying to smile as he gathered his things and showed himself out the door.

Joe often came during the same time period to take the other children on outings to give Sarah a break, sometimes with Jacob, sometimes without. As much as he tried to deny it, he had begun to get jealous regarding the time spent between Dr. Miller and Sarah, often finding excuses to stay after returning the children home if the doctor was still there. He told himself that it was for no other reason than to maintain Sarah's reputation, because he knew she was still in mourning and therefore shouldn't be spending time alone with a man who was making his intentions so obvious. For her part, Sarah seemed quite oblivious to the whole thing. Dr. Miller, however, began to get irritated that Joe was always underfoot when he was trying to get to know Sarah better. The tension between the two friends definitely was building.

Chapter Twenty-Four

All through the fall, things were status quo. The baby was thriving, but the doctor still came almost every day, and while he would examine the boy fairly quickly, he would stay behind and take coffee with Sarah in the sitting room. He was never forward, but he found that he enjoyed conversing with her as the days passed and they got to know each other better. She was easy to talk to, as well as beautiful to behold, and he found himself looking forward to seeing her, rushing through his other appointments in order to have as much time as possible with her, but he tried very hard not to make his feelings apparent. As the days got colder, however, he began to more seriously entertain the idea that she would indeed make him a good wife and partner.

Joe, for his part, had decided to stop interfering, concluding that he was only interested in her because his friend was, and reminded himself that he was resolved to be a bachelor the rest of his days. He continued to try to convince himself that he wanted nothing to do with women, that they only caused heartache and grief, while working hard to plaster on what he hoped was an encouraging smile any time he would see the two of them together, ignoring the twinges in his heart.

When the first week of October came, Sarah became sad and withdrawn, recalling how much had happened in her life in just one short year. She found herself remembering George more as the anniversary of his death loomed closer and reflecting on all that she had lost, despite her earlier best efforts to stay busy and focused on her new life.

He had started to come to her in dreams for the first time in a long time about a month before the anniversary of his death. She had awoken in the middle of the night from a dream so vivid, she was sure that he was right beside her in bed. When she was cognizant enough to realize that he was not, she had cried big, hot tears of sorrow, gasping and gulping for air, cursing her mind for taking her back all the way to the pain she had felt when he had first passed. This continued to happen for several nights in a row before she allowed herself the indulgence of going to her trunk and pulling out a shirt of his, bringing it with her into bed, where she held it against her face. At first, it had been comforting, but as the nights wore on, she realized that the last lingering scent of him was deteriorating to the point that it would no longer be there, and she had quickly packed it away again before all traces of him were gone from the garment.

A week before the anniversary, Ginny had gently asked if she intended to come out of mourning. Sarah had seemed surprised and shocked by the prospect, having fully expected to mourn the traditional two-year period. Ginny went on to carefully point out that in the West, things were not always done in the same way as back East, and that as a young woman with a small child, no one would begrudge her if she decided she was ready to fully come back into society, such as it was, in their small rural town.

It also became clearer to Sarah what Dr. Miller's intentions were as the year since her husband's passing drew to a close. While she liked the man very much as a friend, she began to fret because she did not feel ready to court, let alone entertain marriage to him, or any other man, for that matter. Though he was kind, and certainly could provide for her and Adam, she knew she didn't love him, and furthermore wasn't sure she ever could. Surprisingly, it was not the large age difference between them that bothered her, but rather how even though she enjoyed him, she frankly felt that he was draining to be around. For some reason, she simply couldn't relax and be herself with him, like she had been able to do with George. In an attempt at objectivity, however, she chastised herself for being unfair to expect the same level of ease with the doctor that she had enjoyed with George, whom she had known for her entire life.

Eventually, Sarah admitted to herself that she found comfort and protection in the shrouds of black because it kept her from having to make any decisions regarding how she felt about moving forward in her life and was therefore not in any hurry to discard them for that purpose alone.

However, with the gently consistent promptings of her sister, Sarah finally relented and decided that she would go into half-mourning, switching from black to gray clothing, and allowed the doctor to take her out to supper one evening soon after. Despite her trepidations, she tried to convince herself she owed it to her son to investigate if there was any chance that love could eventually develop, and while it had been a pleasant enough evening, she still had to admit that she found him rather intense. Feeling as though she had to be on her best behavior around him, it seemed more like she was eating with one of her father's friends than a potential love interest.

Throughout the night, Dr. Miller had dropped several not-so-subtle hints about finally being ready to settle down and having enough of an established practice to provide well for a family, though he never came out and asked to court her, or for her hand. In fact, he was so devoid of romanticism that Sarah felt as though he was presenting a business proposition instead of a potential relationship, focusing only on extolling how he could take care of her and Adam, and not how he felt about her. In spite of this, and because of her now-constant worries about making ends meet, she found herself seriously considering if being taken care of was enough incentive that she would be able to at least entertain a proposition from him if one came.

Tempted by the promise of economic stability, as she listened to him, Sarah tried to convince herself that since she had already experienced the love of her life, all that she required now was to be reasonably content. Try as she might, though, her main concern, other than her constant worry that any man would see her as a burden when he discovered she couldn't bear him healthy children, was that even though she liked Dr. Miller, she did not love him. No matter what her mind was trying to persuade her of, her heart, because she had experienced love, was not ready to entertain thoughts of marrying again, even if it was only to obtain security for her and her boy.

Later that night, she dreamt about George. They were back at their fishing hole, and she was talking to him about why she felt it would be impossible to ever marry again, despite her economic worries. She knew she should have felt awkward, but surprisingly she was entirely at ease deliberating the situation with him. He listened attentively as she worked through the pros and cons of entertaining the doctor's advances. After being silent for a long time, staring out across their pond, he eventually told her, "Sarah, you're a young woman. I love you dearly, but you can't be alone for the rest of your life. I do want you to remarry. But not right now, and not the doctor; he's not the right choice."

Sarah had opened her mouth to ask him why he felt that way but had awoken before he had responded. Laying in her bed, the room translucent with the silvery light of the early morning dawn, she wondered why George objected specifically to Dr. Miller.

She felt compelled in that moment to look at Adam sleeping peacefully beside her, and felt her eyes fill with tears. He looked so much like George, even sleeping in the same position as his father had–on his back, one arm thrown across his forehead. She knew that whatever she decided would affect her son, as well, and that made her decision even harder.

Over the next few days, she continued to ponder her dream and tried to pinpoint exactly why George would have told her that the doctor was not the right choice. If he was worried about their well-being, marrying Dr. Miller seemed like it would be a viable solution. He was kind, financially stable, and seemed to like Adam well enough. Her problems with carrying children to term didn't seem to deter him, either, making her wonder if he had accepted her difficulties and didn't care, or if he thought as a doctor, he could somehow change the outcome.

Sarah couldn't deny, however, that despite all Dr. Miller's good points, it still wasn't enough for her. Even without George's objections, whatever they were, she still couldn't refute that deep down she wanted more. She didn't want to merely be taken care of: she wanted to love and be loved, or nothing at all. However, she then began thinking about all the mail-order brides she had heard of throughout her life and tried to convince herself that perhaps love would eventually come if she just took a chance. Those women married men they had never even met and made the best of their situations, so she couldn't understand her own ongoing hesitancy about marrying the perfectly kind and polite town doctor.

One afternoon, a few days after her dream, she walked into town to visit the mercantile to pick up something for Ginny. Still soul-searching, she didn't notice that someone was addressing her until she felt a gentle hand on her shoulder. She turned in shock and saw that it was Joe.

"Lost in thought?" he asked her, a twinkle gleaming in his eye.

"You could say that," she answered with a shrug.

"So, I guess that's why you didn't answer my good morning, then?"

"I'm sorry. To be honest, I didn't hear you."

"I'll say it again, then. Good morning, Sarah!"

She blushed while responding, "Good morning!"

Joe began to feel warmth spreading in his chest as he watched her cheeks garner an enchantingly rosy hue. "So, what brings you to town on such a fine morning?"

"I'm running an errand for Ginny."

"I see," he told her. "Where are you headed? I would be happy to accompany you."

She smiled gently at him, "I'm just going to the mercantile, Joe. Certainly, there's no need for you to accompany me. I'm sure that you're busy with work."

"I'm heading that way, anyway," he lied. In truth, he had been walking the other direction.

"All right, then. I can't stop you."

They walked together in silence until his curiosity got the best of him.

"How are things? I don't see you as much as I used to."

"Things are well."

"That's good."

Neither spoke for several more steps.

"I have been waiting for the snow to fall so that Jacob and I can take the youngsters sledding."

"That would be nice. I know Adam is looking forward to it," she affirmed.

After a few more steps, he looked sideways at her and took a deep breath. "Almost a year since you arrived here," he mentioned quietly, wanting instead to ask her how she was holding up after the anniversary of the date of her husband's demise, but was unsure of how to ask it without sounding too personal.

"Indeed," she affirmed absently.

"Well, it was quite an entrance you made into our little town," he added. "Made my heart race!"

He cringed when he realized what he had just admitted. "I meant with all of the blood and you not being conscious and all..."

God, I'm a hopeless idiot! He admonished himself. *No wonder she's interested in Doc. He at least can speak with her like an intelligent adult!*

Sarah turned her head and studied him with a quizzical expression. She felt like he was trying to connect with her, but always seemed to come up short when he spoke, much like a teenage boy. Even though George had staked his claim on her early, it hadn't meant that other boys didn't try to win her favor when he wasn't around. Joe reminded her of their awkward, knobby-kneed, voice cracking attempts to speak with her, and she felt the same mix of amusement and pity for him that she had for them.

Sarah decided good-naturedly that she would throw Joe a bone and put him out of his communication misery. "I don't think I ever thanked you properly for that day. I'm sure that it was a scary experience to discover a strange woman unconscious in a puddle of blood."

He nodded. They kept walking until he looked over to her and exclaimed, "Hey! You aren't wearing all black! You look nice!"

She glanced down and saw her grey dress, surprised that he would notice such a small change. "Thank you," she told him politely.

"So, how is life at the McAlister's?" he asked her, trying desperately to keep the conversation going.

"Good. Great! Joshua is growing, and the girls are doing well. Ginny's getting stronger every day and I wonder if I'm beginning to step on her toes a bit," she bit her lip. She had been feeling that she had overstayed her welcome in the last few weeks, and that even though she would never say anything, Ginny was ready to get her home and family back.

"Well, my offer still stands, Sarah. The seamstress storefront is still available, and I know you'll have plenty of business."

She just shook her head. "Thanks, Joe, but nothing has changed. I still don't have the money to rent the place, nor will I accept charity."

"Fine. How about a trade, then?"

"A trade?"

Joe nodded. "Yes, a trade. I could use some help with the jail upkeep. I need someone to do the laundry, clean, and make meals when I have a prisoner. It won't be any different from what you were doing for Ginny and Jacob, yet you'll be able to stay in your own place. We don't often have prisoners, so it won't take very much of your time, and will still allow you to make your living sewing."

They had made it to the steps in front of the mercantile, so he turned to face her, his excitement palatable. "Sarah, please promise me that you'll at least consider it. You said you can't go home, and you're feeling like a burden with Ginny and Jacob.

Please take me up on my offer so that you can establish a life here.”

Her thoughts went through her mind with lightning speed before she nodded her agreement. “All right, I will!” she exclaimed, leaving him speechless and giddy with excitement.

Chapter Twenty-Five

Sarah made the move with the help of Jacob, Dr. Miller, and Joe the following Saturday. The men hauled the few belongings she had and helped her set up a bedstead and other items she would need for her and Adam to get settled. Joe hadn't told anyone that he had bought several pieces of furniture he knew she would need, but had instead informed her that unbeknownst to him, the items had been left by the previous tenants in the attic at the top of the building and were therefore available for her use.

As the afternoon turned to evening, Jacob had long since returned home, while Dr. Miller, who had planned to stay as long as Joe, was eventually called out to see to an injured miner who had almost chopped off his foot with a pickax.

Sarah glanced up from her unpacking and noticed the darkening sky. Looking toward Joe, she asked, "Are you hungry?"

"I guess. I can wait until we are finished, though. I'll eat once I get home."

"Well, Adam and I have to eat, so it's the least I can do to feed you supper as well."

"You don't have to do that!"

"I know. There aren't any prisoners," she deadpanned, her eyes twinkling mischievously at him. "I want to, though. No reason for us both to cook supper separately when we both need to eat. It won't be anything fancy; just cheese sandwiches and eggs."

"Sounds just fine," he answered, his stomach growling.

It was all so domestic as he sat at the small table in the upstairs apartment, watching her cook while Adam sat on the floor, playing with his tin soldiers, and he was surprised by how at ease he felt.

Truth be told, he had not had a meal alone with a young woman since he had left California years before. There were not really any available women in town for such activities. The ones who lived there were all either married to miners or railroad men or were otherwise working girls.

The only thing that made him slightly uncomfortable was that Sarah had seated him at the head of the small table and it made him feel fraudulent, as if he was pretending to be something he wasn't. He felt that as a guest in her home, he should sit on the side, but she had directed him where to sit and he hadn't wanted to argue. The meal was fairly quiet, as everyone was exhausted, and Joe couldn't think of much to say. Adam and his mother spoke occasionally and at one point, Joe closed his eyes, envisioning what it must have been like for them when Sarah's husband was still alive. Then, he drifted for a bit, seeing again in his mind the wife and children he thought he would have, and he had to give his head a small shake in order to escape the scene running wild through his thoughts. He had promised himself unrelentingly through the years that there was no point in rehashing the events that had broken his heart and had forever changed him.

Sarah caught him daydreaming and asked, "Joe? Are you all right? You look like you're falling asleep."

He opened his eyes and smiled weakly at her. "I *am* pretty exhausted."

"If you're finished, you don't have to stay. I know you have worked hard all day, and it is Saturday, so you will also have your hands full later tonight at the saloons."

"You're right. Thank you," he told her gratefully as he pushed back his chair.

She walked with him down the stairs to the front of the shop. As he stood before the door, his hand on the knob, he turned back to Sarah and said, "I'm only a few feet away. Don't hesitate to ask me for any help with anything you need."

"All right," she responded. "Thank you!"

"And Sarah?"

200

"Yes?"

"Make sure you lock this door behind me when I leave," he ordered gruffly.

"Yes, Father!" she quipped back.

"I'm only trying to protect you and Adam, Sarah. You're staying in town now and you need to be cautious," he bristled, a hint of annoyance in his voice.

"I understand, Joe, but I'm not a child. I'm well aware that I need to lock my front door at night!"

"Fine, then," he huffed. "I will just bid you goodnight, then."

"Goodnight, Joe. Thank you for all of your help today!" she told him and shut the door behind him. She listened for his footsteps down the wooden sidewalk but didn't hear anything until after she turned the lock. Then, as she heard him start to walk away, it dawned on her that he had been waiting there to ensure that she did what he had advised her to do, and she rolled her eyes in irritation.

As the evening grew later, Sarah lay in her bed, listening to the sounds of a bustling frontier town rising up from the street level and reverberating off the walls. Though she was utterly exhausted, she couldn't sleep as she listened to very obviously drunk men shuffle up and down the street, talking, laughing, and even singing loudly. At one point, she heard Joe's big, booming voice telling everyone to calm down and head home before he had to shut everything down, and it made her feel somewhat safer knowing that he was close. Only then had she settled down into her feather tick and fallen into a deeper sleep than she would have thought possible in a strange place.

Around two in the morning, however, something jolted her out of bed. She awoke, sweaty and frightened, wondering what the sound was that had dragged her from sleep until she heard it again: gunshots.

She fell back down on the mattress and took Adam into her arms, cowering and praying that none of the bullets would strike them through either the glass windowpanes or the wooden walls.

A few seconds later, she heard Joe's voice ring out over the street, "Hey! McCurdy! What the hell are you doing, man? It's two o'clock in the morning and you're shooting your gun up at the sky?"

She could then hear the low rumbling of someone answering back. Joe obviously was not pleased with the answer he received because she heard him snap, "I've warned you before, McCurdy! Give me your gun and then go home and sleep it off, or I'll take you in for disorderly conduct."

Then, all was quiet.

After her heart had stopped feeling as though it was going to beat right out of her chest, she managed to relax enough to allow sleep to once again overtake her weary body.

Chapter Twenty-Six

Over the next few months, Sarah would see Joe often. However, since she had moved from her sister's home, Dr. Miller hadn't had a reason to see her as much as before, and Joe couldn't have been happier about the situation. He knew that the doctor was still interested but was now without a legitimate reason to call on her, especially while she was still in half mourning.

Joe, on the other hand, living just down the street from Sarah, would often stop by the shop during the day and chat with her, helping her with whatever needed to be done maintenance-wise and inquiring about her safety. However, he never went to her rooms above the shop again after that first night for anything other than repairs.

Meanwhile, Sarah was getting annoyed with him, feeling like he was checking up on her, keeping an eye on her, and under his thumb. She was mostly irritated with herself, though, when she realized that she enjoyed having a man around again to help her and keep her company.

Her business, as predicted by both her sister and Joe, was booming. Every man from miles around brought her in more work than she could do in a day, every day. Not only had a seamstress been unavailable for a long while, but the majority of the jobs also held by the menfolk in town were extremely physical ones, and this, coupled with the fact that the seamstress was a beautiful woman, had made her services extremely popular.

As the days rolled on, she found that more men were lingering longer after they would drop off or pick up their orders, trying to make conversation with her, making her nervous with their obvious and sometimes painful attempts at flirtation, but she didn't know how to politely tell them to leave, and they were not taking her subtle hints.

This continued until one afternoon, during an unusual lull, she stepped outside and swept the sidewalk in front of her door as Joe came out of the jail, coffee cup in hand, his face raised to the sky.

"Enjoying the sunshine?" she asked him, not really wanting to talk to him, but not wanting to appear rude, either.

He glanced over at her and smiled. "Yes. I have to say that I'm looking forward to spring."

"Me, too."

She continued sweeping for a while before he spoke again. "How's business?"

"Good! A little too good, actually…"

"What do you mean by that? How can business be too good?"

"I swear I'm beginning to think some of the men are purposefully ripping their clothes for an excuse to come by. Once they're here, they seem to want to stay for a long time, trying to talk with me. I try to tell them politely that I'm busy, but they don't seem to care. Sometimes, I'm trying to sew while I have two or three different men attempting to carry on conversations with me!"

"Ah! Well, you know what they say: in spring, a young man's fancy turns to love."

"I beg your pardon?"

"I mean, Sarah, that you're a woman and they're men and so… well… they find you… intriguing."

"Why me?"

Careful, Joe. Don't reveal too much, he warned himself.

"Because you're unattached as much as anything. It's a rarity to have a young, unattached woman around these parts. You just need to get firmer with them! That's what they're used to hearing."

"What do you mean?" Sarah asked, looking for clarification.

"What are you doing Saturday night?"

"The same as always. Nothing special. Working until five o'clock, then cooking supper for Adam and me, cleaning up, and then going to bed until I'm awoken once again in the wee hours by drunkards on the street."

"Sounds identical to my life," Joe added dryly. "Anyway, do you think Jacob and Ginny would mind keeping Adam overnight? I have someplace I'd like you to see."

"I can ask them, I guess."

"Great! I'll come and get you around eight on Saturday night, if that's all right with you?"

"Fine."

By Saturday night, Sarah was extremely confused. She had no idea where Joe wanted to take her, but as he requested, Adam was with his aunt and uncle, and she was ready when he knocked on her door precisely at eight.

"You all set?" he asked her.

"I am. Just let me get my shawl," she answered, before stepping out on the uneven planks of the sidewalk.

Without another word, he offered her his arm to help her negotiate the walkway in the dark. He stopped suddenly in front of a saloon, and he opened the door. "After you," he said.

"Joe! What are you thinking? I'm not going into a saloon! Have you lost your mind?"

"Just trust me!"

"Joe, I've never been in a saloon in my entire life!"

He sighed with exasperation. "Sarah, we're not going for the saloon. I want you to see something."

She followed him in after that, to a dark, cavernous room full of small, round, wooden tables, and filled with smoke. Sarah could see the bar on the left side of the room, and somewhere in the back, she could hear the piano playing. Her eyes adjusted to the darkness, and she saw that men were in every seat and sidled up to the bar, as well. Card games were going on all around when one of the men at the first table looked up and saw Joe. "Hey, Sheriff! We're just havin' some fun, blowin' off a little steam. Don't arrest us!"

"Settle down, Thompson! I'm not here for any of you guys. Keep it civil and we'll have no problems." The man nodded. "Meanwhile, I'm looking for Mama D. Have you seen her?"

"Not for a while, no," the man answered, obviously wanting to stop talking and get back to his hand.

Joe clapped him on the shoulder and said, "Thanks for the help, Thompson!"

Joe stood upright again and looked around. Sarah did the same until she noticed several women, dressed in what appeared to be less than underclothing, sitting on the laps of various men. Others were leaning on the support posts and bar, and most of them were drinking and smoking, acting as if they were having the time of their lives. Eventually, Joe's gaze came to rest on an older woman leaning over the railing of the second story.

"There she is!" he exclaimed happily.

He began to move forward through the crowd before motioning for Sarah, who had been hanging back, to follow. They went up the stairs and he stopped in front of the woman for whom he had been looking.

"Hello, Dorothy!" he bellowed as he walked up to her.

"Well, good evenin', Sheriff," the woman drawled. "To what do we owe the pleasure of your presence tonight? None of these here young men are causin' any trouble… yet."

"That's good! I'm not here for that, Dorothy. I just wanted to introduce you to Mrs. Johnson, the new seamstress in town."

"Oh, yes! I've seen your shop! Welcome!"

"Thank you, ma'am," Sarah answered politely, feeling uncomfortable under the stare of a woman who made it a habit to appraise other women for their attractiveness to men.

"You sure are a pretty little thing!" Dorothy said. "If you ever get tired of sewin' for a livin', I can set you up real nice, sweetheart!"

"Ummm…" Sarah exclaimed, shocked.

Just then, something on the floor below caught Dorothy's eye and she was down the stairs like a shot.

"Watch and learn," Joe leaned down and whispered close to Sarah's ear, making her shiver slightly in anticipation or his close proximity; she wasn't sure which.

Dorothy marched over to a man with a young woman on his knee. She stopped in front of him before saying, "Daniel! Are you takin' liberties with one of my girls which you ain't payin' for?"

"No, ma'am!" the young man in question quickly answered.

"Then, why, pray tell, did I see you with your hand down Annie's corset, fondlin' her breast?"

"Ah, come on, Mama D," interjected one of the other young men at the table. "He's just having a little sample of the merchandise before deciding if he wants to buy!"

Dorothy turned her steely gaze to the man who had just spoken. "Was I talkin' to you, Andrew?"

The man sat up straighter and answered hastily, "No, ma'am!"

She turned back to the first man. "All right, now. You've had your sample, it's time to put your money where your hand's been, son, or you might not have a hand to use next time, ya hear?"

"But Mama D, I'm in the middle of a hand!" Daniel whined.

Dorothy leaned over and took his cards, laying them out on the table for all the other players to see. "You ain't got nothin' but shit cards, anyway, honey. You was goin' to have to fold. Either you pay to take your liberties with my girls, or you keep your filthy paws off 'em. Got it?"

All the men around the table threw their cards down in disgust as Daniel rose up out of his seat and allowed Annie to walk him up the stairs, past where Joe and Sarah were standing, and into a room.

Joe turned to Sarah, ignoring the look of utter shock on her face. "Let's go!" he ordered.

He walked down the stairs and stopped by Mama D on the way out. "Thanks, Dorothy. I'll be swinging back by in a little while on my rounds to make sure everything's good for the night."

When they got outside, Joe turned to her and said, "That, Sarah, is how you handle miners!"

"Who was that?" Sarah cried in complete confusion over what had just transpired.

"That," Joe told her, "is Dorothy, or Mama D, as everyone calls her. Best madam in all of Colorado. No one messes with her girls!"

"What's a madam?" Sarah asked him.

"Oh!" Joe exclaimed in surprise. "You mean you don't know?"

Sarah just shook her head.

Great! He thought. *I can barely talk to this woman about everyday topics, and now I have to explain to her the inner workings of a cathouse. Just my luck!*

"I forgot you aren't from the West," he began. "A madam is a woman who is…uh… like the business manager… for women who are… um... Women who sell… Wait… No… Entertain… No… That's not right, either."

Sarah watched in amusement as Joe stumbled over his words, getting redder by the minute. By this time, she had a pretty good idea about what he was trying to say, and she decided to put him out of his misery.

"You mean she's the business manager for women who work as ladies of the night?"

"Exactly!" he breathed out, relieved that she had rescued him from his deep humiliation. "She's in charge of keeping the women safe, making sure they have what they need, that sort of thing."

"Oh," Sarah answered.

"But I wanted you to meet her so you could see how she handles these men. This is the West, Sarah. Men out here are used to being treated more like how Dorothy does it than how a polite, reserved woman from Illinois would. You can be a lot less polite and much more direct than you think you can here. Everyone's used to it."

"I could never speak to a man like that!" she exclaimed, flabbergasted.

"You may find you have to, Sarah. As you have seen, these men aren't good at taking subtle hints."

They continued down the street in silence for a while, Joe feeling how tense Sarah was.

"Hey," he said softly. "Let me take you over to the restaurant for a piece of pie and some coffee before they close."

Sarah didn't say anything but nodded her head in agreement.

When they were seated, he noticed that she still seemed a bit out of sorts.

"You doing all right there, Sarah?" he asked, concerned about her.

"I'm fine," she responded.

"Good!"

After several more minutes of silence, he decided she wasn't telling him the truth.

"Sarah, what's wrong?"

She looked up at Joe, with tears in her eyes. "That could be me!" she exclaimed.

"Who?"

"Any one of those girls!"

"Why do you say that?"

"Because I'm widowed and penniless. I never finished school! If I didn't know how to sew, that could have been me!"

"But it isn't," he said quietly.

"But it could have been," she insisted.

He studied her face for a few seconds before he acquiesced. "All right. You're right. It could have been you *if* you didn't know how to sew. But thankfully, you do, and you do it very well!"

"Thank you," she responded softly.

"Sarah, listen to me. Those girls… Those girls have had it rough. You said you haven't finished your education? Most of these girls never even got to go to school! They can't read, they can't write. Many of them were beaten and abused as children and kicked out as soon as they were old enough to fend for themselves. To be frank, Dorothy has been more of a mother to most of those girls than those who gave them life. She treats them well. She feeds them, clothes them, gives them shelter, and support. They form a ragtag family of sorts."

"Isn't it illegal?" Sarah asked.

"No," he replied. "But even if it were, I would turn a blind eye."

"What? You're the sheriff! Why would you do that?" Then a thought struck her, making her feel almost panicked, causing her to sound nearly hysterical. "Unless you go there yourself! Joe, do you go there yourself? Is that why you know so much about these women?"

"No! I do *not* go there, at least not in the capacity which you're thinking," he answered her emphatically, as he felt his face flush. "But, Sarah, I ask you… what are they really doing wrong? They've got to support themselves somehow! The men are glad to pay for their services and it keeps them calmer, too. All these girls are doing is taking financial advantage of the weakness of men. If they weren't allowed to do it, there would be a lot more crime all around. The girls would have to resort to stealing to survive and the men… Well, the men would be more… aggressive. As far as I can figure it, from a legal standpoint, it is a win-win!"

"So, the woman who brought that man upstairs… She was taking him there to have… relations… with him?"

"Yes! They sure weren't going to play poker!" Joe replied, causing Sarah to smile in spite of herself.

Sarah and Joe continued talking for a long while, until he noticed that the restaurant was empty, and it seemed as if everyone else had gone home. He got up and looked around, walking to the front desk, where he was told, "Oh, it's okay,

210

Sheriff. Mr. Scrougin knew that you'd just close up behind you! Have a goodnight!"

"What about the bill?"

"Don't worry about that! Mr. Scrougin said to tell you that since you were enjoying yourself for once, that was enough payment for him. It's on the house!"

Joe walked back to the table where Sarah was still waiting for him. "Well, I guess there are some advantages in being a lawman after all!" he joked as he explained what happened.

He threw some coins on the table before helping her up and together they walked out the door, Joe making sure that he pulled it shut tightly behind them. In the lobby of the hotel, the large clock struck eleven, surprising them both. "Wow! I had no idea it was so late!" Sarah remarked as he held the door for her.

"Me, either," he answered, truly amazed. Time had flown by.

He walked her to her front door and took her hand, raising it up before bidding her goodnight. She walked inside and closed the door, taking off her shawl and hanging it on a hook on the wall. It wasn't until she turned the lock that she heard his footsteps as he moved away. She shook her head in a combination of humor and annoyance.

Sarah was lonely as she got into her bed. She still missed George the most at bedtime. It was the time of day where they could fully relax, talk, snuggle, or even make love to one another. She came to think of it as "their" time and was still surprised by the wave of grief that would sometimes rear up and hit her as she crawled between her sheets. Adam helped to temper some of that loneliness, she discovered that night. She realized that having him in the room with her, listening to his breathing, lessened the solitude she felt.

She lay in her bed, watching the shadows dance across the walls and listened to the sounds of the street below. Joe's voice rang out a few times, calling out when a miner was a little too rowdy. Thinking back to their evening, she was shocked when she realized that they had sat and talked for over two hours together. It struck her that not once did she struggle for topics of conversation, nor did she feel like she would be taking an exam afterward, as she often did whenever she spent time with Dr. Miller. She hadn't been as comfortable talking with a man since George had been alive.

***

The night was calmer than most Saturday nights and Joe was thankful for that, as he was distracted. Sitting on the front porch until the saloons were mostly empty, he ruminated over the evening. He concluded that he had not been so at ease in years. In all honesty, he had never thought that he would ever be able to speak with a woman like Sarah for such a long time and not stick his foot in his mouth or make an ass out of himself. After everything he had been through, his confidence regarding women was shattered, and he had figured that he was simply physically and emotionally incapable of conversing with them, at least for any extended length of time. For so long, he had felt so rejected, so unlovable, that he had forgotten how it felt to be relaxed and not have to think about every word before it left his mouth. It scared him that he had let his guard down. He never thought he would be able to do that again.

Chapter Twenty-Seven

Joe stood and rapped on Sarah's front door very early one morning. He felt guilty for perhaps waking her, but he had something very important to tell her. She came down the stairs and opened the door, her hair loosely flowing over her shoulders, her robe drawn tight around her, and her face dewy with sleep.

"Good morning, Joe!" she said with a yawn. "What brings you out on such an early morning?"

He dove right in. "Sarah, there's a guest in the jail."

"All right," Sarah responded, unsure of why he sounded so dire. There had been plenty of guests at the jail before now. Most of them Joe had arrested in various forms of drunkenness, and they had stayed there overnight into the next day, until they had sobered up enough that they could slink away back home.

"Sarah, listen to me, he's a bad guy," Joe continued. "I don't want you interacting with him, all right?"

"What'd he do?"

"Don't concern yourself with that now. Just go in there and give him his food, but don't talk to him. Please?"

Sarah had never seen Joe quite so concerned before. While it was always apparent that he had a deeply vested interest in the welfare of the town and genuinely cared for all of those who lived there, he generally seemed more like a kindly older brother than a stalwart lawman. Therefore, when he sounded so grave and troubled, she immediately took notice.

"I won't," she acquiesced, sensing this was not the time to antagonize him.

"Good! Thank you! I want you in and out, that's it! I'm going to have to be down at the station sending telegrams for most of the morning in order to arrange for his transfer. This guy is going down the hill, thank goodness! Oh! And leave Adam at home, too. He will be safer here for the few minutes you're in the jail."

"I will, Joe! I promise I'll be fine!"

Sarah dressed and cooked, preparing a basket of food for Joe's prisoner. When she walked into the jail, she shut the door firmly behind her and continued further in. Her eyes took a second to adjust to the comparative darkness in the room from the bright sunshine outside when she heard from one of the cells, "My, my, my! What have we here? Don't tell me that you're the sheriff's pretty little wife, now, are you?"

Sarah said nothing, instead walking to the cell to hand the prisoner's breakfast to him through the bars. As he reached for each item, he let his hand linger on hers too long, caressing her. Feeling violated, she looked up and met his eyes in a silent challenge, which widened in surprise as he licked his lips lasciviously.

"Mmm, mmm… I can see why the sheriff likes to keep a hot little number like you hidden! He don't want to share, I reckon. Too bad, too, 'cause I bet you're a mighty fine tastin' morsel!"

Sarah turned without a word and stepped away from the cell to begin cleaning up. She straightened the papers on Joe's desk and swept the floor while the prisoner ate. Sensing his eyes on her the whole time, he was making her feel extremely uncomfortable. Earlier, she had thought she would wait until the man was done eating, so that she could take his plate and utensils with her, but she began to rethink her plan. She quickly rationalized, however, that she was already there and dealing with him, and would really rather not come back, so she waited in silence on the far side of the room until he was finished.

The prisoner signaled he was done by passing his cup through the bars for her to take. However, as she reached for it, he let go of the tin mug, and as it hit the floor, he grabbed her wrist with his other hand, pulling her in closer. He then ran his tongue up her palm, his eyes closed in ecstasy. "Just as I thought: you're as sweet as sugar."

When she attempted to pull away, he would not let her go. Trying desperately to obey Joe's wishes of not speaking to this man, Sarah pleaded silently with her eyes for him to release her. Even without Joe's warnings, Sarah didn't trust this man and knew the less she reacted, the better off she would be. Finally, though, when his grip had begun to tighten even more, she cried, "Please let go of me! You're hurting me!"

"Good!" growled the man. "All you whores are the same and deserved to be hurt!" he added with disgust.

"I'm not a whore!" Sarah retorted hotly.

"All you women is whores!"

"I'm not!"

The man still wouldn't release her. "That sheriff is crazy to let his hot little wife out of his sight! You never know when you might come across the likes of me!" he cackled.

"Please," Sarah whimpered, "just let me go!"

"Oh, sweet thing, I'm just gettin' started!" the man chided as he pulled Sarah even closer into the bars and grabbed her blouse with his free hand, ripping it. He then jammed his hand down her corset and grabbed her breast- hard! He twisted her nipple and she gasped in pain. "Please! Stop!" she cried out.

Just then, the door opened, and Joe stepped through. "Joe!" Sarah shrieked, both panic and relief evident in her voice, while her face reflected how thankful she was to see him. Even though the bars were between them, Sarah was sure that this man would not have stopped without molesting her further.

"What the hell is going on?" Joe bellowed, crossing quickly across the floor. He stopped short when he saw where the prisoner's hand was, and then his eyes locked with Sarah's.

"I suggest you unhand her right now, Brown! You're in enough trouble as it is!"

In response, the man twisted Sarah's nipple again, causing her to whimper in pain.

"Brown," Joe countered calmly, "don't make this worse for yourself."

"How can it get any worse, Sheriff? I'm gonna hang for what I done. Can't hang me twice!" he cackled, amused at his own joke. "I might as well go out doin' what I like!"

"Brown, so help me God. This woman isn't a whore. She's a respectable woman. A mother!"

"I know, Sheriff. She's your hot little wife! Oh, she may act all demure, but I know just by lookin' at her that she's a lioness between those sheets, ain't she? Where you take her, Sheriff? How often?"

Sarah's eyes were imploring Joe to do something; anything.

"She's not my wife," Joe countered.

Leering openly at Sarah's exposed bosom, the man continued, "Oh! Even better! How's about you and I share, then, Sheriff? I bet that between the two of us, we could give her an experience she would never forget!"

Sarah then heard the cock of a gun and looked to her side. Joe had managed to keep the prisoner talking long enough to get up beside Sarah and had reached through the bars, grabbing his collar. He had the end of the gun resting on the man's temple as he murmured, "Just give me a reason, Brown. One good reason!"

At that, the prisoner released his grip on Sarah and tried to step back into the cell, but Joe kept hold of him. "You would do well to leave this and any other woman alone, Brown."

Joe turned to Sarah. "Leave!" he ordered in a way that for once brokered no argument from her. With a small sob, she bent down and grabbed the basket, while she held her blouse together as best she could with her other hand, before running out the door and back to her dwelling.

"You have no idea how much I want to put a bullet in your head right now!" Joe hissed at the man.

"Why? She ain't nothin' but a lyin', cheatin' whore!"

"No! She isn't! Stop talking about her like that!" Joe roared as he pressed the gun a little harder into Brown's head.

"All right, Sheriff. Anythin' you say. Tell me, just how long you been in love with her?"

Joe started to deny it, but then figured he didn't owe this man any explanations before he turned around and walked out.

216

He marched to Sarah's door and knocked gently. She came and opened it, her eyes red and watery.

"Come in," she whispered, shutting the door behind him.

"You all right?" he inquired gently, his voice revealing his concern.

"Yes," Sarah responded stoically.

Joe was shocked then by the wave of anger, not relief, that washed over him. "I *told* you not to interact with him!" he yelled, causing her to jump.

"I didn't!" she hollered back.

"You must have!"

"Joe, I didn't!" she argued. "I swear all I did was give him his breakfast and straighten up while he ate. I didn't say a word to him the whole entire time. But when I went back to collect his dishes, he grabbed my arm and pulled me in. I couldn't get away!"

"I never should have had you come in there this morning, especially when I was gone. But I never thought you would be stupid enough to go up to him, Sarah!" he cried in frustration.

"Well, how else was I supposed to get his food to him, Joe?"

"I don't know!" Joe replied, feeling so angry with himself for endangering her that he wanted to punch something–a wall perhaps. Instead, he took several deep breaths to calm himself.

"How badly did he hurt you?" Joe asked softly.

"I'll be all right," she replied.

"Do you want me to go get Doc?"

"No! Please! I'll be fine!"

They stood opposite each other, each staring the other down. Their chests were heaving with adrenaline and anger. Joe, much to Sarah's surprise, broke first.

"I'm so sorry, Sarah!" he said dejectedly. "I knew he was dangerous, and I let you go in there anyway. I'm sorry he violated you. I'll never forgive myself."

When Joe looked up, Sarah had begun to cry silently. He felt so helpless. All he could think to do was open his arms to embrace her. He did, and she collapsed immediately against him, sobs now choking her supple body.

"I was so scared!" she wept.

"Shhh!" he soothed her, stroking her hair while holding her tight. "You're safe now. I'm leaving this afternoon to get that bastard transferred and you will never have to see him again!"

She sniffled and nodded her head against his chest. He continued to hold her and that's when it hit him: he was completely, utterly, madly in love with this woman.

Chapter Twenty-Eight

Joe thought about his predicament the whole way down to Colorado Springs and then to the state penitentiary in Canon City. The prisoner was relentless in trying to get him to talk about Sarah, harassing him about how much he had enjoyed molesting her, and then when Joe wouldn't respond, taunting him with barbs about how no woman like her would ever love a man like him.

Once Joe had handed the man over, he was free to think through the events of the last twenty-four hours and how best to handle his new realization. What bothered him the most was that he agreed with the criminal: no woman like Sarah would ever want him. He was sure of it. By the time the train had rolled back into town two days later, he had decided that he would hide his feelings from her at all costs. She couldn't help it if he had foolishly fallen for her, and he didn't want to make things awkward between them.

***

Back home, Sarah was left wondering what exactly had gone on in the middle of the night. She hadn't heard anything unusual. It had been a typical Wednesday night when the miners seemed to all be home and in bed by midnight in order to get up for their early morning shifts. She still had no idea who the prisoner was or how he ended up in Joe's jail.

Late the next afternoon, Mama D was in front of the jail, looking into the locked and deserted building. When she couldn't find Joe, she decided to pay a visit to the town's new seamstress.

"Good afternoon, Sarah, was it?" Mama D asked after she had come into the room.

"Yes, ma'am," Sarah answered her politely. "How are you doing today?"

"Oh, dearie, ma'am is my mama. Please, call me Mama D."

"All right, Mama D. What can I help you with today?"

"Have you seen Joe?"

"No, not since this morning. He left on the train to transport a prisoner to the penitentiary."

"I see. Any idea when he might be comin' back?"

"I'm sorry, I don't. I know that the jail is right next to me, but we don't see as much of each other as one might think," Sarah explained. "Can I help you with something? Or can I leave a message for him?"

"I just wanted to come by and thank him for all of his help the other night."

"Oh!" Sarah answered, her curiosity now extremely piqued.

"I know it was a tragic situation and I'm just so grateful that he's supportive of my girls and me. Some lawmen love to harass those who do what we do, but Joe… Joe's a good guy. Treats us with a lot of respect."

"Joe is very dedicated!" Sarah responded.

"That he is!"

"Well," Mama D said, standing up from the stool she had sat upon, "you've got a real nice place here! I would tell you that me and my girls will frequent your establishment, but as you can imagine, the demand for dresses ain't that high for us," she laughed. "We've all got our Sunday best and that's it! Now, if you start handlin' corsets and stockin's, we'll talk!"

"I understand," Sarah said methodically, praying she was able to hide how shocked she was with how open the woman was about what she did for a living.

Mama D scrutinized her for a second before heading toward the door. "You know, Sarah, you've got great potential. I wasn't kiddin' when I said that I could make a place for you!"

"Uh… Thank you!" Sarah answered her. "I think I'm good where I am right now,"

"Yeah, Joe's got you set up real nice in here."

"Oh, no!" Sarah felt compelled to explain, so that the woman didn't get the wrong idea. "Joe doesn't have me set up anywhere. He just knew that there was a vacancy here and convinced me I should go into business.”

“I see,” replied Mama D. “So, the fact that you don’t pay any rent to anyone doesn’t seem a bit odd to you?”

“I work at the jail in exchange for rent. I help Joe with the cooking and cleaning when he has an inmate.”

Mama D was silent for a few seconds, wryly thinking that Joe had done just fine with cooking and maintaining the jail before Sarah had arrived. She recalled when she had overheard him talking to Clayton Sweeney, the owner of the building, the first time Sarah came to town, and discovered that Joe was preparing to pay a pretty penny in rent on Sarah’s shop, far more than what someone would have earned by helping out with the upkeep of the jail. In negotiating a price, Joe had even offered to pay the man six months’ rent in advance. Later, after the conversation had ended, she asked him then what he was thinking.

Annoyed that he had been overheard and then questioned, Joe had answered angrily, “She has no other place to go, Dorothy!”

“That’s all well and good, Sheriff, but one of these days you’re gonna realize that you can’t save the world!”

“I don’t want to save the world, Mama D. I just want to give people a helping hand when I can.”

“Uh-huh!” she had answered, shaking her head. “I know you, Joe McIntyre. You would give the shirt off your back and your last dime to anyone who needed it. You’ve got a heart that is way too big to be a lawman! What I don’t understand is how it is that you don’t have a woman!”

“It’s something I would rather not discuss.”

“Oh! You ain’t one of those,” she whispered, “men who ain’t interested in ladies, now are you, Joe? I mean it makes sense: after all these years, you’ve never come and visited any of my girls, even though I’ve told you that you can have whatever you like on the house. No wife, none of my girls… It gets a person to wonderin’ there, Joe!”

"No, Mama D, I am *not* 'one of those' types of men. I just… Well, I just…"

"You haven't found the right one yet?"

"That's right."

"So, is that why you're settin' up that little lady in the shop? She strike your fancy?"

Joe just glared at her, giving her no response.

"Well, does she?"

"No! I just feel that a young widow ought to have a way to support herself and her child. To be honest, she and I butt heads constantly. But her little boy is a good kid and she's had it rough, so I figure that I can do what I can to help them out."

"You know what they say, Joe. Opposites attract. All that buttin' heads could really just be pent up sexual tension! Maybe you need to just get a leg over and see?"

"Dorothy!" he shouted. "Good grief! The woman's a recent widow!"

"All the more reason! She's probably lonely, missin' her man. It's a perfect opportunity!"

"Mama D, I will not continue this conversation with you! You know I can arrest you for solicitation, don't you?"

"Joe, sweetheart, I ain't solicitin' anythin'. I'm just a normal, everyday citizen sittin' here in the saloon, conversin' with my sheriff!" She gave him a cocky grin. "But I will say that you're droppin' an awful lot of money on some woman who you say is just a friend!"

"And she is!"

"Sure, honey! You keep on tellin' yourself that!"

Mama D had meant what she said. She knew men. She had entertained them, but also cared for the women who did. One thing she had learned is that men never parted with their money more readily than when they were infatuated with a woman. Most men would pay for the company of one of her girls, but it was the fools who fell in love with them whom she pitied. They hung around, spending their money like water, buying them pretty trinkets, drinks, clothing, and more. Her girls were smart, too. They knew how to work these poor saps until they had milked every last penny out of them. The only true love her chickadees had was that of money. In fact, she had only lost one girl who had married a miner in the almost twenty years she had been doing this. The young woman had been an impressionable little thing, brought up in a good Christian household, and she had never felt right about whoring. The man had promised her the world: a house, a buggy, a fur coat, pretty dresses, and best of all in her mind, respectability. They had married as soon as possible, and last Dorothy had heard, they were happy together somewhere in Nevada, with a household full of brats.

Based on the conversation with her it was clear to Mama D that still Sarah had no clue that Joe had painstakingly paid her rent every month for over a year, even when she had gone home. She also saw how he looked at her whenever he thought no one was looking. To Mama's trained eye, however, it was obvious that he adored her. Whenever he had been in the saloon full of her scantily clothed girls she had watched him, but he had never even glanced at any of them. However, he couldn't keep his eyes off Sarah whenever she was around.

"Joe's a good man!"

"I know he is," Sarah answered. She was quiet for a few minutes and then asked, "Miss Dorothy, do you know his story?"

"Oh, please, honey! Truly! No one has called me Miss in years. It is either simply Dorothy or Mama D."

"All right, then. Dorothy, do you know much about Joe's background?"

"I don't," Mama D answered, though truthfully, she knew more than she let on. Joe, on a few occasions after Sarah had gone home, had been so depressed that he had actually sat and nursed a whiskey in the bar, something he never did, so she had joined him and was able to glean more information than ever before about the young sheriff. Even after that, though, all she knew for sure was that someone at some point had hurt him deeply, shaking him to his core, making him give up on love and focus instead on merely avoiding women.

"He comes from California," Sarah said.

"Aye, that's what he says."

"I wonder why?"

"I don't know. Perhaps he was just needin' a change."

"I suppose you're right. That's honestly what brought me here."

"'Tis what brought almost all of us here, sweetheart!"

Both women were quiet while they each ruminated over their own experiences that had brought them to this tiny gold mining town, clinging to a mountainside in the wilds of Colorado. It seemed to Sarah that Mama D was right. The town seemed like a mishmash of people who had come because it was the last stop on the rail line. There was work, shelter, water, alcohol, and food; everything a person needed to survive in their attempts to escape their past lives.

Dorothy stood up. "Well, tell Joe that I'm lookin' for him when he returns, please, if you happen to see him before I do."

"I'm sure that I won't, but I will tell him, just the same. Have a good evening, Dorothy!"

***

The train was taking an agonizingly long time to chug its way up the hill and seemed even more so because Joe was tired and anxious. He kept telling himself that he simply wanted to get home in an attempt to convince himself that Sarah wasn't the first and only person he wanted to see. She had been injured and he knew she had been violated, making him desperate to ensure that she wasn't too distraught over the whole situation. He realized that he probably should have taken the time to tell her what had happened before he left town, but in all honesty, he was only thinking at the time that he wanted to transport the prisoner as far away as possible because she was there, and he wanted to keep her safe.

To keep from rehashing everything that had happened, Joe allowed himself to entertain the fantasy that Sarah would be waiting on the platform, with arms open, thanking him for saving her and declaring her love for him. Despite knowing it would never happen, the indulgence of it running repeatedly in his head helped to pass the last lagging minutes.

He knew she wouldn't be there, as he hadn't even told her when he was coming back. For that matter, he didn't remember if he had told her where he was going, either. He still couldn't help but wish, however, that she would somehow instinctively know.

After mulling things over for the entire journey down the mountain and back, Joe realized that Sarah couldn't be pining over him when he hadn't really even allowed her to get to know him. The one evening they had spent together going to the saloon and then the restaurant at the hotel had been the first and only time he had let his guard down, and it had happened so subtly that he hadn't comprehended that it had occurred until he got home. Only then had he realized he had spoken so freely, leaving him to wonder when the last time was he had felt comfortable enough to really open himself up to another person, especially a female. Then he had immediately panicked, unable to remember how much he had actually shared with her.

Though he knew that she wouldn't be there, he was still disappointed when the train puffed to a stop, and he exited onto the platform devoid of her. He dropped by and spoke with Jacob for a few minutes and greeted other residents politely, but while he made a good show of paying attention and engaging in conversation, his focus was determinedly elsewhere.

Walking up the street to the jail, he surprised himself when he couldn't go in; the call to go to her was too strong. It was early evening as he stood in the front of her shop's door and knocked. He listened to her footfalls as they came down each step and he could time exactly how long it would take her to get to the door. When she pulled it open, she looked apprehensive, which broke his heart, as her sense of security had obviously been shaken. She smiled, however, and stepped aside, letting him in.

"Good evening, Joe."

"Good evening, Sarah. Forgive the intrusion, but I just got back, and I wanted to come and check on you to make sure that you're all right."

"I'm doing fine," she answered.

"Good!" he breathed out, glad that she didn't seem upset with him. "Do you have a moment? Now that things have calmed down a bit, I would like to speak with you."

"Sure, Joe, but I'm cooking supper. Won't you come upstairs with Adam and me so that I can continue without burning it?"

"Oh!" he exclaimed. Of course, she was cooking supper; it was that time of day. He could smell it, and once he acknowledged it, his mouth began to water. "That's all right, Sarah. I can come back another time."

"Don't be silly, Joe! You're here now!"

So, he followed her up the stairs and he sat at the table while he watched her move around the cookstove and counter. Unsure of if it was his hunger or the domesticity, including Adam's playing on the floor with a train, the food smelled incredible. It felt so familiar that as he shut his eyes, he saw his brothers, father, and mother as if it were yesterday. It was the first time he allowed himself the luxury of relaxing in he wasn't sure how many days.

Sarah turned to Joe and saw him sitting in the chair, his eyes closed, with a gentle smile playing upon his lips. Feeling something stir inside of her, for just a moment, it felt like she was home again with Adam and George, back on their little farm, insulated from all the harm in the world. She had to admit that it felt good to have a man in her kitchen again. It made it feel like a family, no matter how briefly, and that she mattered to someone. Quickly checking herself, she remembered that it was Joe sitting at her table, not George, but was then surprised that it didn't feel wrong. In fact, it felt right, as if he was supposed to be there with them.

"Joe?"

"Uh-huh?" he asked her, almost about to nod off.

"Would you care to stay for supper with us? It is nothing special, just potato soup and some fresh baked bread. But perhaps you're tired from your trip?"

"I wouldn't want to impose," he heard himself answer all the while, willing her to persist.

"It's no imposition! It certainly isn't a hearty meal, one that a man would need, perhaps. However, it is hot and fresh, and what's more, you don't need to cook it!"

He glanced up at her and saw that she was earnest. She really looked as though she wanted him to stay. There was something about her, perhaps in her voice, mannerism, or her eyes, that told him she was lonely but would always be entirely too proud to admit it.

"All right," he relented.

The food was served, and Joe was once again given the head of the table, as if he belonged to them. It felt good to feel like he was presiding over a family, as though he had an important role in their health and safety, not wanting to acknowledge that in reality he had no say whatsoever about either of them.

The conversation at dinner was stunted and it seemed that neither of them wanted to discuss what happened at the jail, especially in front of Adam. But as he rose to clear his place and to prepare to leave, Sarah reached out her hand and laid it gently on his forearm. "You don't have to leave. In fact, I have something I want to discuss with you. Just let me put Adam to bed and I will be right back."

He nodded dumbly and listened as Sarah helped her son wash his hands and face, change into his nightclothes, read a Bible verse, and then say his prayers. When that was all finished, she leaned over him and kissed his forehead, telling him, "Goodnight, Adam! I love you!"

"I love you, too, Mama!" he replied sleepily.

She was about to get up off the mattress they shared and walk back to the table when he asked, "Mama, is Sheriff Joe staying here with us tonight? Will he be here in the morning?"

Sarah glanced nervously over her shoulder and caught Joe's eye. "No, sweetheart! You know that Sheriff Joe lives at the jail. We just asked him to stay to supper because he has been traveling all day and Mama didn't want him to have to cook for himself when I was already cooking."

"Oh!" Adam sounded sad when he replied. "Because I liked having a pa at the table again!"

Sarah's heart broke into a million pieces. How could she ever explain the concept of friendship to him when the only men who had ever been in his home before the sheriff had been either his father or male relatives?

"I know, darling. I know it is hard not having your pa around anymore. He loved you very much, as do I. Now, close your eyes, darling, and try to sleep. I will be right here when you wake up."

Sarah began to clean up and prepared to wash the dishes while she waited for Adam to drift off. She was surprised when she felt Joe slide up next to her and grab a towel.

"You wash, and I'll dry?" he asked her.

"You don't have to do that!" Sarah protested.

"I know I don't have to, Sarah. I want to. You cooked, you shouldn't have to clean up, as well."

"But I do it every night."

"Maybe so, but not on my watch."

They worked in companionable silence, and when the dishes were finished, he had taken the dishrag and wiped down the table while she had gone to make sure Adam was asleep.

Joe felt inexplicably drawn to them. He crept up beside Sarah and looked at her son's tiny face, slackened with sleep, sticking out from the quilts. A wave of tenderness for the boy overtook him and he turned to her to quietly say, "He's a good boy!"

"Thank you!" she whispered back to him.

Sarah made some tea and they sat down at the table before Sarah said, "So!"

"So, what?" Joe asked her.

"What happened here in the last few days?"

Joe felt at a loss on how to start or what to say. The whole situation had become a blur between his exhaustion, grief, and worry, though he knew he finally owed her an explanation.

He took a deep breath before speaking. "Sarah, that prisoner was a really terrible person. I should have never left you alone with him."

"I know he's a horrible person, but what did he do? I mean besides what he did to me, that is."

Joe dropped his head closer to her and whispered, "He raped and killed one of Mama D's girls."

"What?" Sarah roared. "And you let me be alone in that jail with him?"

"Shhh!" he shushed her when he saw Adam stir out of the corner of his eye.

"He was behind bars then, Sarah! I didn't think you would be stupid enough to go up to the cell!" he whispered angrily.

"As I told you, Joe, how else was I supposed to get his food to him?" she shot back at him.

He stared at her for a minute, before he backed down. "I don't know, Sarah. That's my point. I didn't think it through, and I'm so sorry that my negligence led to your… molestation."

"I'm all right," she assured him. "You couldn't have known he would do that."

"Well, regardless, I'm sorry that he offended your honor."

"Oh, he thought I was honorable enough," she told him. "He kept saying that I was your wife!"

"I heard that. I'm sorry."

"It's fine, Joe. It just isn't every day that I'm called a whore and a wife in the same breath. So, when did all of this happen?"

"In the overnight before yesterday morning."

"And what happened, exactly?"

"Mama D heard what sounded like a struggle coming from Jane's room. The door was barred from the inside, so she couldn't get in, even using her master key. She sent one of the Jones boys down to get me and between the two of us, we were able to break through. What we found on the other side was not pleasant, to say the least."

Sarah's curiosity was piqued but she didn't dare ask him what he had seen.

"So, I arrested him and brought him to the jail before going back to deal with Jane. Thankfully, Mama D had sent someone for the undertaker and so that was soon taken care of."

"Mama D came here looking for you yesterday afternoon."

"I'm not surprised."

"She didn't say anything about one of her girls being murdered!"

"I suspect she didn't want to say anything before the investigation was completed. When I took Brown to the penitentiary, I discovered he had a criminal record as long as my arm and this was not the first time he has been accused of killing a woman. This time, though, I intend to make the charges stick."

"Why didn't they before?"

Joe merely gaped at her.

"Joe! Don't look at me like that! How should I know?"

"Fine. They didn't stick because the other women were whores."

"But so was Jane!"

"Sure, she was, but in my town, she was also a citizen and deserved the same rights and privileges as any other adult female. Sadly, many other towns don't feel the same way."

"Oh!" Sarah said. What more could she say? She knew from her own experience that women were already without enough rights and privileges, even without being named a harlot, too.

"Did Mama D say what she wanted?"

"No, not really. Just that she needed to talk to you about something and wanted to know if I knew where you had gone and when you would be back."

"All right," Joe sighed, thinking that he would have to pay a visit to the saloon when he left Sarah's, when all he really wanted to do was crawl into his bed and sleep. He was running on a couple of days' deficit, and he could feel his body breaking down.

Sarah was quiet for a few minutes, watching him. He was exhausted, she could tell. He had the same look about him that George would get when he was bringing in the crops: glassy eyes that could hardly stay open once he stopped long enough to sit down, the drooping of his shoulders as if it was just too much effort to keep them level, a pale face and big dark circles under his eyes. A rush of pity came over her and the worry that she felt surprised her. She felt compelled to put him in bed, as she would have done with George, while tucking him under the blankets and watching as he would finally succumb to sleep. Reminding herself repeatedly that Joe was not her responsibility, Sarah understood that it would be impossible for her to care for him as she would have liked to. Instead, she knew she should encourage him to go see Mama D so that he could get it over with and retire for the night that much sooner, but for some reason, she felt that she was not quite ready for him to go yet.

"Joe, how did Jane die?" Sarah asked quietly, wondering if he would tell her.

"Sarah, it wasn't pretty. I can't talk about details, as he has not yet been sentenced, but I will tell you that it was not a painless or struggle-free way to pass, and she didn't deserve it."

Sarah nodded her understanding. "Of course," she told him.

He sighed, thinking that it would be nice to be able to unload some of his burden onto her. When he thought about marriage, he didn't think about the conjugal benefits much anymore; he thought instead about having one person he could trust. He envisioned himself tucked away in bed with his wife after a long day, sharing his stressors with her. Even if he couldn't give details, which given the sensitive nature of his job, he would officially be unable to do a good deal of the time, it would still be nice to come home to something ordinary and good. He never dreamed of the things he would learn and see about humanity by being the sheriff and he didn't want to ruminate alone about it anymore. He wanted the normalcy and comfort that a wife and maybe even a child or two would bring him the minute he walked through the door.

"I'd better be going and check in with Dorothy before turning in," Joe told Sarah as he pushed himself back from the table and stood, knowing if he didn't do so, he would never want to leave. "Thank you so much for feeding me. I'm entirely too tired to have done it myself."

"I figured," Sarah said softly.

When they got to the front door, they stood facing one another awkwardly as he pulled on his coat, hat, and gloves. Joe fought his urge to bend forward and lightly touch his lips to hers. All he wanted in the world at that moment was to kiss her, but he didn't dare.

He cleared his throat. "Well, goodnight, Sarah, and thank you again for supper."

"Of course, Joe. Anytime!"

"And I really am sorry about what happened at the jail yesterday."

"Can we just not talk about it anymore, please?" she pleaded, and he nodded in response.

"All right, if that is what you want."

"It is!"

Then, he didn't know what made him do it, but he leaned forward and gently kissed her cheek, shocking even himself. Sarah immediately put her hand up to her face and he worried that he had gone too far, but she had merely opened the door with her other hand and bid him goodnight.

Sarah lay awake in her bed for many hours that night, thinking about the kiss. She and George had grown up together and had gotten closer and closer through the years before they officially became a couple. Before the day when he had kissed her for the first time, he had never even touched her, except to lend a hand if the steep bank to the pond was wet and slippery or the Christmas he had pulled her onto his lap. There had been no slow ramp up to that kiss. It was sudden and had seemingly come out of the blue. Sarah realized then that she had never before experienced the thrill of wondering what a small kiss on the cheek meant, and if it would grow into something more. She and George had gone from nothing to fiery with that single event on the edge of the pond, which had left them both longing for more. A lot more, if she was honest with herself. She then realized that even though she wouldn't change a thing about her relationship with George, she had missed out on the act of courtship.

Chapter Twenty-Nine

Working the next morning, Sarah heard a commotion outside. Curious, she got up from her machine, telling Adam to stay back before opening the door, and was shocked by what she saw.

Coming up the street was a group of men and women, led at the front by Mama D, her girls, and to her surprise, Joe. She watched in astonishment as the crowd passed by her, before stepping outside onto the sidewalk. When they halted in front of the church, Sarah's curiosity was piqued. She told Adam to go up to their rooms above the store and then locked the door behind her, walking quickly to join the mob standing in a semi-circle in front of the church's portico.

Mama D made a big production of pounding on the door and then stepped back down to the dirt below. After a short wait, the door cautiously opened, and the pastor came out to stand on the porch, addressing them all.

"Good morning, my fellow citizens. What can I do for you on this fine day?"

Mama D took a step closer. "Pastor, we want to know why you're refusin' to bury our Jane!"

Sarah watched as the pastor shot a quick look at Joe, but Joe's face remained passive and unmoved.

"You know why, Ms. Weber."

"Please call me Mama D or Dorothy, but never Ms. Weber," she answered hotly.

"All right, then, Dorothy. You know that I cannot bury that young woman here and give her a good Christian funeral! She was…" the pastor paused and glanced around him before continuing, "a whore!"

"So?" Mama D shot back, totally undeterred.

"So? It isn't godly!" the pastor retorted.

"But with all due respect, Pastor, Jesus Himself administered to the whores, did He not?"

"Yes, but… well… they were repentant!"

"Perhaps the woman who washed his feet with her tears and dried them with her hair, but what of the others?"

"Others?"

"Yes, when He said that the tax collectors and prostitutes would go to heaven ahead of the chief priests and elders who did not accept John the Baptist's tellin' of the Parable of the Two Brothers!"

"But that was different!"

"How so?" challenged Mama D. "There was not one word uttered in those verses that stated the prostitutes had to be repentant before they would go ahead of the others."

"No," replied the pastor weakly, "but it was implied…"

"By whom?"

"By Jesus Christ, of course! If they were listening to what John the Baptist was teaching them, then they would have known he was preaching about the need to repent in order to be saved!"

"Merely a technicality!" Mama D fired back with an absent wave of her hand, undeterred.

"I cannot in good conscience allow that… *harlot*… to be buried in my churchyard!" the pastor responded passionately.

"Then you give us no choice: we will have to do it ourselves!" Mama D retorted. "Come on, boys! Let's get to diggin'!"

"Wait!" the pastor cried. "Sheriff, you cannot allow this! You have to do something!"

Everyone turned to Joe, who appeared to be contemplating. Finally, he spoke.

"The way I see it, Pastor, you haven't got much of a choice. The church and the churchyard belong to the people of this town and Jane was one of them."

"But Joe!" the pastor protested weakly, the uncertainty of losing a presumed ally growing. "You cannot possibly think it is Christian to allow such a sinner a plot on our hallowed church grounds?"

Joe was silent for a few seconds before responding. "What I think, Pastor, is that it's not Christian to prevent her from being buried. Ours is not to judge, but we will certainly be judged on how we treat others, even those who are deceased."

"Joe!" the pastor started again.

"Pastor, with all due respect, this young woman died a horrible death because of what she did to make a living. I don't think we need to add insult to injury by making judgments about what sins make someone worthy to be buried here or not. Because as I figure it, all sins are equal in the eyes of God." Joe took a breath and continued. "Therefore, I see no harm in laying this poor girl to rest here, because God loved her as much as any of the rest of us. None of us are without sin, and all are in need of repentance. Now, if you can't do it in good conscience, then we will. Boys, go dig the hole and we will meet back here in an hour for the service."

The pastor closed his mouth, and the crowd began to cheer. Once again, Joe had been the voice of reason and settled a contentious situation. Sarah gazed at him with admiration, wondering for the millionth time what his backstory was. He was such an odd mix of cantankerous and kind that he perplexed her.

Once the mob had dispersed, Sarah began walking back to the shop when she felt someone come up beside her. She turned to see whom it was and smiled as she saw Joe.

"Hi!" he told her, returning her smile with a lopsided grin of his own.

"Hello!" she responded.

They walked in silence for another few steps when Sarah stopped abruptly and turned to him. "You were really amazing back there! How did you do it?"

"I'm not that amazing, Sarah. I had fair warning to prepare. The pastor's unwillingness to bury Jane had been what Mama D had come to you looking for me about. I thought about the situation most of the night and how best to handle it. I wanted her to try, but I had already decided on the argument I would use if her protests fell on deaf ears."

"You were so calm, yet had so much authority. I see now how you managed to negotiate the end to the strike and why they made you sheriff. You have such a level head on your shoulders. Does anything rattle you?"

"Oh, plenty!" he responded. "But with four brothers, one learns quickly how to be the calm and rational one! Saves a lot of black eyes and swollen knuckles." he smirked at her.

"Well, regardless, it was very impressive!"

"Thank you!" he said, his cheeks reddening slightly at the compliment. "I'm off to get my Bible before I go back for the service. Will you be coming?"

"No, I can't. I left Adam alone in the store, so I must get back. I was already gone longer than I should have been."

"That's a shame!" he answered as he took off jogging back toward the jail.

"You won't even know I'm missing," she responded, meaning that he would be too busy to notice who was present or not.

Oh, believe me, he thought. *I will absolutely notice you aren't there!*

Instead, though, he merely waved goodbye and continued on his way.

Chapter Thirty

Winter once again turned into spring and Dr. Miller began to pursue Sarah, this time with more intensity. He started to make it a habit to stop by and chat with her in the afternoons on his way back to his office after rounds. These conversations often led to him asking her to dinner, and eventually, he even invited her to his home where he cooked for her.

She liked him well enough. He was a kind, intelligent man, and she grew to enjoy spending time with him once she learned to relax around him. She finally realized that he liked to be the smartest one in the room and that he didn't necessarily want or need her to keep up a conversation with him. Deeply interested in politics, religion, and philosophy, he just wanted to talk to and bounce his ideas off someone else. Once she let go and didn't try so hard to think of intelligent responses to keep up her side of the conversation, she found what he had to say intriguing and thought-provoking.

He was a good-looking man, too, with his sandy blonde hair and grey eyes. Though Sarah was almost half his age, with him actually being closer in age to her father, he did have a very nice physique, as one of his many interests was physical fitness. He reminded her of George in that regard, and the similarity made her feel a bit more attraction for him than she might otherwise have.

The only problems were that she couldn't shake what George had told her in her dream that he was not the right one for her, as well as the fact that he did not seem to enjoy Adam.

It wasn't specifically Adam. He was polite and nice enough to him. The doctor simply didn't seem to have an affinity for children. She at first hadn't thought much about it, but as his invitations kept coming, she noticed that he always inquired if Ginny and Jacob would take her son, regardless of what he had planned. She had asked them a few times in the beginning but had felt guilty, knowing they were often tired and overwhelmed with their own three young children.

Once Sarah had realized what was going on, she had initially assumed that he had wanted to get to know her better before including Adam, but after several months and multiple encounters, Dr. Miller had still not seemed keen to have the boy join them. So, she had then invited him to her home for dinner a few times in an attempt to force him to interact more with her son in case his discomfort stemmed from something as simple as being unfamiliar with children, but while he was there, he had seemed tense and distracted.

Joe also came often to visit. He still felt incredibly guilty about what had happened to Sarah at the jail, and he kept telling himself he was just checking on her to ensure that she did not suffer any residual trauma from the experience with the handsy prisoner. Sarah would have never admitted it, but she found his visits to be much more enjoyable and relaxing than Dr. Miller's, mostly because Joe seemed as content to spend time with her son as he did with her. It was during one of his visits that her concern about Dr. Miller not wanting to spend time with Adam had eventually come out, so Joe had immediately volunteered to watch the boy.

Despite his growing jealousy regarding the intensifying relationship between Sarah and Dr. Miller, Joe continued to logically reassure himself that since he wasn't interested in a relationship with her, or anyone else for that matter, Sarah's entering into a relationship with his best friend would be the next best thing. Helping the two of them seemed the easiest way he could think of to keep her in his life, and more importantly, still spend time with Adam.

Joe had already come to grips with the fact that he would never have any children of his own, and that was truly what made him saddest about the path his life had taken, especially when he honestly enjoyed spending time with Adam. Joe loved to show him how to do things, and thought it was adorable when

Adam tried to emulate so much of what he did. It was simply incomprehensible to him that his friend didn't feel the same way.

When Joe's curiosity had finally gotten the better of him, he had asked the doctor about it, and Dr. Miller had responded that while he thought Sarah was amazing, he really wasn't interested in raising another man's child. His answer made no sense to Joe: Sarah's husband was dead. Though Adam's paternity was different, if given a chance, Joe figured that with as happy and eager as the boy was to have a father figure in his life, the fact that he was not a biological offspring would quickly become irrelevant to all.

So, every weekend, when Dr. Miller would come to collect Sarah, Joe would already be there. As the weather warmed, he also began taking Adam fishing on Saturdays, and if they caught something, he would prepare it for their supper. It got to the point where Sarah felt like she was being shooed from her own home on her date nights, and as she descended the stairs, she would always look back and see Joe at the cookstove, laughing and talking with Adam. She would always then get a small, inexplicable pang in her heart, which she, after evaluating it on several occasions, eventually concluded must be because it reminded her of George interacting with their son and how happy she had felt seeing them palling around together. Even so, Sarah was still plagued by a nagging feeling that her conclusion was not entirely correct.

After trying hard to reconcile her doubt with the fact that her husband hadn't interacted with Adam much inside the house- his domain had primarily been outside- Sarah finally accepted the painful realization, despite the sense that she was being disloyal to the memory of her husband, that George hadn't related to Adam in the same way Joe seemed to. More than simply a difference in settings, Joe seemed to truly enjoy being with her son in a way even his father hadn't been able to, almost as if he considered the small boy to be a friend and equal.

Feeling guilty, Sarah quickly chastised herself that it wasn't fair to make a comparison, as George had died when Adam was so young, and now he was no longer a toddler. Still, something told her that Adam and Joe's relationship was different; deeper than even the one the child had enjoyed with his father.

Many nights, Sarah would walk up the stairs and find Adam asleep in the bed, Joe beside him on top of the covers, snoring softly, a book that he had been reading to the boy dangling from his hand. It killed her to have to rouse him, and if she would have had a different place to sleep for herself, it wouldn't have started tongues wagging, and the fact that it was a weekend evening, meaning Joe had to work, she would have just let them be. As it stood, she would walk up to the bed and reach out to gently touch Joe's shoulder, shaking him ever so carefully. Those nights were the nights he loved the best, when he awoke to her over him, so near that he could feel his arms twitching to reach out and take her into them. Knowing it wasn't appropriate, though, he would merely apologize and leave as quickly as possible.

As time went on, however, Joe got angry with himself, thinking that he ought to cut his losses, as he was becoming too attached to the kid and his mother. Logically, he knew he needed to retreat before he got hurt again but when he tried, he found he just couldn't stay away.

Joe would sometimes invite Sarah along for outings with him and Adam, but she rarely could go, because he would take him during the day while she was working. Every once in a while, though, Joe would have an especially calm Saturday night and would take Adam out to do something after church. As Sunday was her day of rest, Sarah would pack a picnic lunch, and they would hike in the hills or find a good place to fish. After they would finish eating, she would stretch out in the sun on an old quilt and Joe would long to lie next to her, but he would instead sit on the edge, resigning to watch her when she closed her eyes, tipping her face heavenward to drink in the sunshine.

Joe was contented enough with how things stood until one Sunday afternoon in July, when he thought he was going to ignite, and not only because the day was blistering hot. Sarah had come with him and Adam to their favorite fishing hole and spread out her blanket to lay on. She quickly got too warm in the searing heat, so without a word, she sat up and opened the buttons on her blouse down to just above her corset, exposing her creamy white upper chest. When that wasn't sufficient enough, she then walked to the creek and wet herself down, inadvertently causing her clothing to cling tightly to her lithe frame. Joe's body instantly reacted, extremely and violently, when he turned and saw her. He hadn't felt a rush of excitement like that since he had been an adolescent. It was so strong, he thought he would lose himself right there. He closed his eyes and counted to ten, thought about the worst experiences he had as sheriff, and even tried to recall why he had gone off women in the first place, but none of it had helped. Terrified she would look at him and see the storm happening within, he quickly walked away downstream along the creek's edge, and looked out over the vista for a long time until his heartrate steadied, and his body cooperated.

He had never before been tempted to take Mama D up on her invitation to utilize the services of one of her girls, but with how he felt in that moment, he was ashamed to admit even to himself that he entertained the idea for more than a few seconds. It was only after he realized it would be pointless, as he would just fantasize he was with Sarah anyway, that he had eventually talked himself down, admonishing himself for being so foolish. By the time they had made it back to the jail to return the fishing gear, however, he still felt jittery and not entirely in control of his faculties, so he asked her if he could stay home for the evening instead of watching Adam when she went out to dinner with Dr. Miller.

Sarah was concerned, studying him with the trained eye of a wife and mother. Self-conscious, he felt as though he was radiating heat, and he was sure she could feel it, too. Noticing that he appeared flushed and feverish, she was worried that he had gotten too overheated. She had then started fussing over him, even stepping close enough to place a smooth, cool hand on his forehead to check for fever. Feeling as though they were breathing the same air, he heard a soft moan of pleasure escape him. Mortified, he had shifted his gaze, and then immediately noticed her blouse was still open over her chest. He felt himself stare down as if he was controlled entirely by someone else. When he realized what he had done, however, he whipped his eyes back up to her face and was relieved to see that she hadn't caught him.

Next thing he knew, she had left and come back to the jail with soup and bread, and after he ate, she tucked him under his covers and gently touched his forehead again.

"I hope you feel better!" she told him. "I'm right next door if you need me!"

"Thank you," he mumbled, humiliated because all that was wrong with him was that he was a young, virile adult male in the vicinity of a beautiful, nurturing, and kind woman.

A little while later, when Dr. Miller came by to collect Sarah, he was visibly frustrated that they would not be able to be alone now that Joe was unavailable to watch Adam. Sarah tried to explain that Adam could join them or that she could make them supper at her home, but at his refusal, her worst suspicions were realized that Dr. Miller was just not interested in having children around.

Knowing what she had to do, Sarah then told him that while she cared for and enjoyed him, her son would always come first in her life, and if he couldn't understand that, then they would have to stop spending so much time together.

She wasn't even sure what else to call what they had been doing. He had never asked formally to court her, and indeed, she was still not one hundred percent sure he was romantically interested in her. He had never tried to hold her hand or kiss her: he was just verbally intimate with her, discussing things with ease the way one would speak with a spouse.

Dr. Miller at first tried to object, but then realized that Sarah was correct in that she should not be willing to put aside her son for a relationship with him. His plan had been to marry her and send the boy to a boarding school back East as soon as he was old enough, but it was abundantly clear to him in that moment that when the time came, she would have been unwilling to do so.

Dr. Miller didn't have anything against the boy personally, or even children, and in all honesty, he was looking forward to keeping her belly full of his own offspring. Even with knowing that she had difficulty carrying pregnancies, he was arrogant enough to believe that his being a physician, coupled with her young age, would be enough to prevent history from repeating itself. His objection to Adam was that he was a tie to her former husband. He didn't want to be reminded that she had been married before and had loved and belonged to another. He wanted to have a nice, easy family without any complications, even fooling himself into thinking that Sarah would be thrilled for the opportunity to send her son to an elite and expensive school. As he did feel slightly guilty about not wanting the boy around, he had already in his mind committed to a plan where he would pay for Adam's schooling to become whatever he wanted to be, including a doctor. He didn't want the child there, but he still wanted to be seen as his benefactor, so he could further win Sarah's affections by being considered the boy's champion.

They parted ways and Sarah came back up the stairs to where Adam sat on the floor, lining up his tin soldiers. She had expected to cry a few tears, but to her surprise, she only felt relief. Thinking back to the dream when George had told her Dr. Miller was not the man for her, it suddenly made more sense.

"Thank you, George," she whispered quietly to herself as she watched her beloved only living child play.

Chapter Thirty-One

For the next few weeks, Sarah saw very little of both men. Dr. Miller was still nursing his disappointment, and with that came his avoidance of Sarah, so Joe had no excuse to be around as much. He had made up his mind after the day at the fishing hole that for his own sanity, he needed to keep his distance and was determined to do so, even though the news of Dr. Miller's backing off his pursuit of her had taken him by surprise. Any temporary joy in that news, however, was tempered by the fact that he no longer had an excuse to see her or Adam nearly as much.

Life returned to a tedious normalcy for Sarah and her son until one Saturday evening in the late summer, after Adam had spent a hot, lonely day in the apartment above his mother's shop while she worked. He had surprised her by bursting into tears when it was time for her to tuck him into bed.

"Adam, sweetheart, what's the matter?" she gently coaxed him.

"Mama, I miss Pa!"

"I know you do, darling. I do, too."

"I miss how he used to take me sledding and fishing," he wailed as he flung himself into her arms. Meanwhile, Sarah's heart had frozen.

"Adam," she said gently to him, "it's been Joe who has done those things for you, not your father."

She was met by a blank stare.

She tried again. "Adam, your father was the one who took you around the farm. You would help him in the fields and milk the cow. Do you remember?"

The boy shook his head.

"Your father loved you so much!" Sarah whispered, her voice breaking. She recalled how much George had adored their boy, and it broke her heart that Adam could no longer remember him. She then clutched him to her and tried to jog his memory for any recollection he may have had, but to no avail.

As she sat quietly crying over their loss yet again, Adam broke into her thoughts. "Mama? If Joe is the one who has done all those things with me, then why can't he be my pa?"

"Because he isn't your pa!" Sarah said sharply, angry with herself about the whole situation.

"But why isn't he? He treats me like a pa should! He takes me places and shows me things."

"Adam, it isn't that simple…" she started.

He broke in, "But why not, Ma? I want him to be my pa!"

"Sheriff Joe is not my husband. We are only friends. But even if we were married, he still would not be your father!"

"Please, Ma!" the boy cried quietly.

Taking a deep breath trying to calm her nerves, she said, "I'm sorry, Adam, but that is not going to happen."

"Why not, Ma?"

Patiently, she began to explain. "Because we would have to get married first, Adam, and even if we did that, it wouldn't change the fact that I was married before and you are that man's child. That man, your father, loved you so incredibly much."

"But he isn't here anymore, and I want a pa. Why can't you and Sheriff Joe just get married?"

"Well, I guess mostly because Joe doesn't love me, dear heart," she answered. "People need to be in love when they get married."

"You're nice, though! I bet he would learn to love you, Mama!" her boy tried again.

"Sweetheart, I don't see that happening. We're good friends and we need to be grateful for that, all right? Now, it is time for you to close your eyes and go to sleep. I love you, Adam!"

The little boy nodded, still a bit teary eyed. He mumbled, "I love you, too, Mama!" as he rolled over to go to sleep.

A few evenings later, Sarah brought food over for Joe and his prisoner. He took it from her and thanked her, but she hung around after, which she normally didn't do, and it concerned Joe.

"Everything all right, Sarah?" he asked her.

"Yes, it's fine. I was just… I was just hoping that I could talk to you about something?"

His heart skipped a beat. He had no idea what was coming, but his imagination was running wild. He nodded. "Sure. Here or…?" He pointed over his shoulder to the living quarters behind the closed door.

"In there, please," she answered, feeling self-conscious.

When they got into the room that served as the kitchen and Joe's bedroom, he turned to her, apprehension written all over his face.

"Sarah, what's wrong? Is everything okay?"

"Yes," she confirmed, but she was not sure of where to start.

He watched her carefully as she picked apart what she wanted to tell him so that it would come out right.

"Joe, Adam is upset that he doesn't get to see you as much anymore," she blurted.

"Oh," he replied.

"That's it? Oh? My little boy thinks the world of you and all you can say is 'Oh'?"

"I'm sorry," Joe answered.

"I don't know what you expect me to do about it," he added in bewilderment.

"I don't know!" Sarah said, feeling her hackles rise. "But seeing how when I spoke with him the other night, it became clear that the only memories he thinks he has of his father are in actuality things that he has done with you, I thought you should know that you mean a lot to him!" Sarah, despite her best efforts, began to cry.

"Oh, dear!" Joe stated. He didn't speak for a long time, as he was truly bemused. It had never been his intention to replace the boy's father. He had just been trying to be nice, and now had no idea about what to do or say to fix it.

Sarah sniffled, wiped her eyes, then squared her shoulders. "Anyway, I was just going to ask if you could please stop by and see him sometime, because he is obviously missing you a lot. I can see now, though, that his feelings are not reciprocated, so never mind."

"Sarah…" he started, his chest constricting with pain for her and her little boy. That was not at all what he had meant to convey to her.

"No!" Sarah interrupted him, her anger boiling just below the surface, and held up her hand. "It's all right, Joe! Just forget I said anything. He'll be okay. We both will. This is my fault: I'm the one who let him get too close to you. I'm sorry!"

He was going to try to speak again, to tell her that he loved Adam and really enjoyed spending time with him, but Sarah turned on her heel and brushed past him. Joe stood for a few seconds in bewilderment before he followed her back into the jail as she stormed out the door. The convict sitting in a cell who had witnessed the whole thing said, "What'd you do there, Sheriff? She seemed mighty steamed!"

Joe just shook his head. "I don't really know," he muttered, still perplexed about what he could have said differently and how to fix it.

Chapter Thirty-Two

As summer turned to fall, Sarah began to slip into a deep depression. By the time the month had changed from October to November, she was utterly despairing in the pain of the anniversary of George's death looming near, compounded by the fact that she felt completely isolated. After the events at the end of the summer with both the doctor and Joe, she didn't socialize with anyone other than Ginny and Jacob occasionally, but even those meetings were awkward, as since Sarah had told them what had happened with both men, they never entertained them all at the same time anymore. Sarah and Ginny were also both constantly occupied, Sarah with her alterations shop, and her sister with the children.

The only saving grace was that the shop was doing well. Sarah was making enough money that she could pay an outright rent to Joe, even though he insisted that she didn't need to do so. She persisted, stating that she didn't want to be beholden to him for anything and after pestering him nonstop, he had finally broken down and told her a sum much lower than what the actual cost was, and she had begun to pay it.

Despite their rift, Sarah continued to bring food, do laundry, and clean the jail. Joe tried to get her to stop once she started to pay the rent, but when she had heard the amount he was charging her, she figured he had to have been grossly undercharging. Every month, they argued back and forth about the situation, neither of them ever acknowledging that in reality they were both just looking for reasons to speak to each other.

Because of her seclusion, Sarah felt George's loss more acutely that year than ever before. She figured it was merely because she was truly alone without much support for the first time since his death. There were many nights she would finally allow herself the luxury of crying herself to sleep after Adam was already slumbering.

Then the anniversary of when she lost her last baby came, and it only seemed to add insult to injury. It was as if her mind had previously numbed her from the full impact of the pain in order for her to survive it, but on that particular day, it was as if the dam had finally broken, and her heart was drowning in sorrow. In her lowest moment, she was convinced that she would die lonely and alone; that her life would be monotonously miserable with no one to love her ever again.

Then, in the third week of January, something happened that changed everything.

Joe still always met the train for the payroll of the mining operations in town. He had done it since he had taken the position and it had never been a problem, so he had unwittingly become somewhat complacent, having gotten used to that when there were no labor disputes, and only the occasional drunken fight or property issues, the job of sheriff in his sleepy town was generally not a particularly dangerous one. In fact, it was his confidence and trust that things were quiet that would end up being his downfall.

Four men who worked in one of the mines discovered that there was no variation with how the payroll came in, noting that it always arrived on the Wednesday midday train of alternating weeks. Soon, after boasting for several months about how they could make so much more money stealing the funds and heading north than they ever could working their daily shifts, they had begun to scheme.

Eventually, one of the men went down the hill to Colorado Springs to watch for the transfer of the money to the train there and then quickly sent off a three-word telegram before jumping on the train himself: "All is well." Then, he sat back and tried to act natural until the train pulled into the alpine station.

Joe was waiting on the platform, as usual, talking with Jacob as the train pulled in. Strictly from habit, he quickly scanned around him, but didn't notice anything amiss. He then met the armed guards, and the payroll was transferred into his care. Bidding farewell to Jacob, he began walking up the hill toward the mine's main office, where the money would be kept in the safe until it was to be counted out and distributed on Friday. He carried his gun in the holster on his hip while holding the bag of currency in his non-draw hand, but he didn't see anything out of the ordinary from what he had observed week in and week out for several years, so his thoughts began to wander.

He still hadn't talked to Sarah about their conversation a few months back. Though they were polite with one another when they were forced by circumstances to interact, there was a cavernous distance between them, and he didn't know how to begin to build a bridge. At first, he had been prideful. He told himself he hadn't done or said anything wrong. Eventually, though, as his anger dissipated, he began to feel guilty that he hadn't sounded more caring and supportive. Kicking himself, he knew that his anxiety in most social interactions with women, especially when they were emotionally charged, was once again to blame. He was also annoyed that Sarah still didn't know him well enough by now to understand that he always managed to stick his foot in his mouth. Surely, she should have understood that his inability to respond appropriately had only stemmed from the shock and dismay that Adam was so confused, not because he didn't care.

However, *I don't know what you expect me to do about it*, repeated over and over in his mind. He had never meant it to come out as it had, as if he were heartless. He merely didn't know what he could do to help. Every time he had closed his eyes since he had uttered those fateful words, he would again see the look of shock that quickly turned to devastation on Sarah's face.

A few times he had even woken himself up, screaming, "No! Sarah, come back!" while caught in a dream where his subconscious tried to fix what he had been unable to do on his own. In fact, only a few days before, he must have dreamed it all again because in the morning when he had gone to check on the prisoner he was holding for a drunken fight the night before, the man had complained bitterly about his being awoken by all the yelling.

Joe suddenly snapped back to attention when he felt as if he was being followed, and began to look around, yet nothing seemed to be awry. Thinking he was only being paranoid, he still slowly moved his free hand around to his front, ready to draw his gun at a moment's notice, but because everyone came at him from behind and at his flanks, he didn't even know it was coming until it was too late.

Suddenly, he was surrounded on three sides, and someone else was sauntering up to him from the front. He felt his heart race, and he began to panic, wondering how he could get out of there with the payroll in hand.

"Good afternoon, Sheriff!" the man who came to a stop directly in front of him stated. "How are you on this fine day?"

Joe recognized him as one of the fairly new miners in town. He wasn't sure how long he had been there, but he had never had an issue with him before. Joe was sure now, though, that was all going to abruptly change.

"Good day, gentlemen," Joe answered, trying to sound nonchalant and keep the fear out of his voice. "What can I do for you?"

"Well, Sheriff, here's the thing. We know you've got the payroll right there in your hand and we are fixing to lighten your load a bit," the apparent ringleader said with a grin.

"I do have the payroll right here, boys, but you will only be taking it over my dead body."

Suddenly, the leader cocked his pistol. "That can be arranged!" he growled.

Joe had known for a long time this was always a possibility. In fact, after he had been nominated and voted into the position, he had dreaded this part of the job more than anything else. As much as he didn't want to die, though, he wasn't about to simply hand over all the money in that bag.

"Jackson!" the leader called. The man on Joe's right side answered him quickly.

"I want you to take the good sheriff's gun there right quick."

Joe fought every urge he had to draw and fire. He knew logically that being surrounded on all four sides meant he had no chance, but his desire to go down in a blaze of glory if he was going to go out was high. Instead, he put his hand up as far as he could and let the man disarm him.

By this time, some people had begun to gather on the street, and it was making the gang jumpy and reckless. The leader spoke again.

"Morrison, when I count to three, I want you to take that bag of money. You got that?" The man, the one who looked the youngest of all of them, nodded nervously.

"Great!" the leader said, sounding pleased. "Jackson, take the bullets out of the gun and then throw it over there." He shrugged his shoulder to demonstrate the direction in which he expected the weapon to go. Joe heard it hit something but didn't dare to look up at what it was.

Eventually, the money changed hands and Joe felt physically ill. He had never felt like such a failure in his life. Employed by the town to protect its citizenry, he had not only lost the largest employer a lot of money, but he also had put everyone on Main Street at risk.

Breathing a sigh of relief when the men took the money and proceeded to gloat, Joe thought he was out of the woods; that they would merely be on their way. They had horses from the livery tied up, waiting for them, in order to make a quick getaway. Figuring that he would give them a head start, he decided he would try to hunt them down later to retrieve what he could.

However, as the men started walking away and Joe was beginning to feel that things would end as well as possible given the situation, at least in regard to no one getting hurt, the leader inexplicably turned back around and pointed his gun right at Joe's chest. Joe looked up and met his cold gaze, knowing in that instant he was a dead man. Quickly saying a little prayer, he closed his eyes, surprised that in that instant that people hadn't been kidding: the images of his life flashed quickly before him. He heard the shot and instinctively turned a little to the right. Then, all he felt was searing pain as he hit the ground.

Sarah had been sewing, her head down, when she was aware of a commotion in the street directly in front of her shop. She glanced up only for a second when she heard something thump against the front of her building before going back to work, not thinking much about it, but then she heard a shot ring out and looked up just in time to see a man crumple. Something familiar about him made her jump up, run to the door, and fling it open. She heard herself screaming Joe's name, but it didn't sound like her; it was as if she were listening to herself in a moving picture of sorts.

Getting to Joe's side felt like it took hours, but in reality, it only took a few seconds. Sarah collapsed to her knees beside him, tears streaming down her face. His eyes and jaw were clenched in pain; his breathing rapid and shallow as the blood poured out of his wound and down his chest. When he heard her helpless sobs, he struggled to open his eyes for a second before he breathed out, "Sarah!"

"Joe! Joe, what happened? Where are you shot?"

"Sarah, you shouldn't be here!" he rasped, his words taking every ounce of strength he possessed to get out. "Get back inside!"

"Joe! You're hurt!"

By this time, a crowd had begun to form around them. The snow and dirt around Joe was turning into a sickly sludge of bloodied mud. Someone threw Sarah a handkerchief and after briefly wondering just how clean it was, she realized it was better than nothing and pressed it against the wound to try to help stem the flow, while screaming for someone to go and find Dr. Miller.

Joe groaned and tried to roll away from the pressure she was applying, but she wouldn't let him go. In that moment, he realized that she was now sitting on her bottom in the middle of the bloody street, his head in her lap, her legs spread to either side of him. And then he passed out.

Sarah had no concept of just how long she sat there, cradling Joe's head in her lap, begging God not to take him, but it seemed to take forever for Dr. Miller to get there. He had come quickly, but in Sarah's mind, it hadn't been nearly fast enough. She refused to let go or move, even when Dr. Miller asked her, so he decided to not waste precious time arguing and instead began to examine Joe as best he could around her. When he was satisfied he had determined the source of the bleeding, he turned to a group of men and said, "All right, boys. Help me get him outta the street."

The men surrounded them, and Sarah panicked, gripping the sheriff tightly, knowing it was his only chance, but still not wanting to let him go.

"Come on, Sarah!" Dr. Miller said gently. "This is the only way to save him. You have to let us take him inside somewhere where I can work on him."

She only stared blankly back at him.

"Sarah!" he coaxed. "Let's take him inside."

She nodded in a daze, pushing herself back, before scrambling to her feet. The men then reached down, and each lifted a limb, causing Joe to moan even in his unconscious state. Without saying a word, they carried Joe into the jail and Sarah went with them. When they got him back to his quarters, she hurriedly pushed in front of them to pull down his quilts and set out towels to protect his mattress.

The other men left after they were sure that Joe was settled, but Sarah still stood beside him, her eyes dry and wide, her expression wrought with shock.

"I can take it from here," Dr. Miller dismissed her gently, but she only shook her head at him.

Then it dawned on him. She had watched her husband die, so this must be a very traumatic experience for her. Then he decided if he couldn't make her leave, perhaps she could assist him. It wasn't going to be an easy job to clean and sew up his friend alone.

"Sarah, if you insist on staying, I do need some help with getting him put back together. How are you with blood?"

"I'll be fine," she heard herself answer him.

"Good!" he said.

"I need you to go to my office and bring me my bag. It is on my desk. On your way through, please put some water on to boil. Check and see, too, if Joe has a bottle of spirits hidden in here somewhere, though with this being a jail, I doubt it, so on the way back from my office, stop by the saloon and grab a bottle of whiskey. Tell Mr. Potter at the bar that I will reimburse him later."

In an instant, the doctor went from friend to medical professional and was all business. Sarah nodded to him and walked to the kitchen area to start the first task on her list and once the pot was on the stove, she left.

Finding Dr. Miller's bag was not difficult, and she was soon on her way to the saloon. She was hurrying as fast as she could, but it still didn't feel like she was moving quickly enough, so she grabbed her skirts in her free hand and began to run.

She crashed noisily through the saloon doors, making everyone's heads pop up in surprise. Mama D was sitting at the bar, talking with Mr. Potter when Sarah rushed up and pleaded for the bottle of whiskey. When Mama D heard that it was Joe who had been shot, she paled and gasped. She thought of Joe almost like a son. He was fiercely protective of her and her girls, and she owed him a lot for his support and protection throughout the years.

"Is he gonna be all right?" she asked Sarah, her eyes wide.

"I don't know yet," the girl whispered back to her, defeat showing in her shoulders. "Hopefully Dr. Miller can fix him up."

"Well, if anyone can, it's Doc!" Mr. Potter affirmed as he placed the bottle on the counter. "You tell him that this bottle is on the house. I would do anything to help Joe!"

"Thank you!" Sarah gushed as she grabbed the bottle and ran.

"That girl right there was on a mission!" Mr. Potter exclaimed as he turned back to Mama D.

Yeah... A mission of love, she thought to herself.

Chapter Thirty-Three

By the time Sarah made it back to the jail, the water was boiling. Dr. Miller handed her some tools and asked her to boil them for five minutes. Then, he asked her for a glass of the whiskey. She only stared at him, until it dawned on him that perhaps she thought he would drink it. He began to chuckle and explained, "It's to sterilize the smaller materials we can't boil, Sarah!"

She was antsy, waiting for the tools to finish sterilizing. Joe was still unconscious, and she couldn't help but watch him, fear clutching her heart. Lost in her own thoughts, she didn't hear that Dr. Miller was talking to her until he tried again.

"Sarah? I asked if you needed to go and get Adam and take him to Jacob and Ginny?"

Not wanting to explain that she was struggling with the pain of her losses, she quickly lied in response, stating, "Oh, no! Thankfully, as I was so busy today, I asked them to keep him overnight last night, so I could catch up."

She looked down at Joe, so helpless, whispering to herself as an afterthought, "It all seems so trivial now, though."

In that moment, the idea that she was mourning the loss of someone already gone seemed to pale in comparison to the trauma of possibly losing someone else dear to her.

"Well, that's a relief, anyway," he answered distractedly. "All right, let's do this. We need to get that shirt off him first. It's gonna be terrible because there's dried blood sticking it to the wound. I need you to unbutton it first and then I will lift him, so you can pull it off. I already cut up the sleeves, so it shouldn't be hard."

With shaking hands, she began the slow process of removing each button from its hole. She was so stressed that she was going to hurt him that she moved more and more slowly. Finally, she pulled apart the two pieces of fabric. The one side came away without an issue, but the side with the wound was a different story. She worked her fingers all around the material that was adhered to his skin in a circle, and then she would move in a little closer while trying not to notice the fresh blood trickling over her fingers as she disturbed the injured tissue. Eventually, she reached the point where she could no longer be gentle and knew that the time for the inevitable had come.

"Just pull it quick," Dr. Miller advised as he looked into her troubled eyes.

Taking a deep cleansing breath, she did, and Joe moaned pitifully.

"Good. Now, let me sit in front of him and he can slump over me while you do the same thing to his back."

Joe grunted as Dr. Miller shifted positions and supported the man's large, slumped body against his. Sarah quickly repeated the process and was relieved for a few seconds that she was done hurting him further until Dr. Miller told her, "Good! Now, take that bowl of hot water with the flannel strip in it and wash around the wound."

Sarah carefully ran the cloth around the bruised and damaged skin, avoiding the unavoidable for as long as she could. Once the dried blood surrounding the wound had all been washed away, she had no choice but to quickly run the cloth as lightly as she could over it.

Joe reacted by twitching and mumbling something. Sarah looked up at Dr. Miller and he glanced back at her, eyebrows raised, wondering if she could make out what he said. She shook her head at him and went back to work. Once the wound was clean, Dr. Miller told her to take the whiskey bottle and to pour some into the wound, keeping the bottle raised so that the lip didn't touch his flesh.

As the amber liquid ran down, Joe reared up for a second before collapsing back onto Dr. Miller's form. Now with the wound clean, the doctor looked at the man's shoulder and said with relief, "Good! It was a clean shot. At least I don't have to go digging!"

Dr. Miller then laid Joe back down and asked Sarah to please do the same to his front. He watched as she carefully cleaned the man, still wishing that things could be different or that he would get over his aversion to marrying a woman who had a living reminder of the fact that she had been married before. She was everything he could dream of in a wife: calm, caring, careful.

Based on how she's doing right now, he thought, *she would possibly even make a good nurse.*

When she had washed him and poured the whiskey onto his front, to which Joe had rolled his head back and forth in response, she watched as Dr. Miller carefully removed his needle and the suturing material from the glass of whiskey they were soaking in. After leaving them to dry on a towel for a few minutes, he then began to sew as Sarah watched, completely fascinated.

"It looks exactly the same as what I do!"

"It is, essentially," he agreed. "I just stitch skin instead of material."

When Dr. Miller was done with Joe's front, he rolled him carefully onto his right side and asked Sarah to sit beside him and hold his arms, so he wouldn't roll onto his back. Right before he began to sew the posterior wound, he looked up and saw Sarah gazing at Joe with such tenderness it shocked him. Then, when the needle went into Joe's skin and the man had moaned and tried to fight, Dr. Miller watched as Sarah, after transferring his two large wrists into one of her small hands, took her other one and gently swept back the hair falling across his forehead. In that moment, it became clear to Dr. Miller that Sarah never had been particularly interested in him. She was instead obviously taken with his friend, but it seemed that neither she nor Joe were aware of it.

The doctor shook his head to clear his thoughts, instead forcing himself to focus on the task at hand. He carefully stitched Joe shut and when he was finished, he told Sarah that she could let go. Dr. Miller then stood and stretched his back, looking down at her, noting that she hadn't moved from Joe's side. He asked her if she would mind staying with him for a little while so that he could go back to his office to restock his bag and clean up the blood on his clothing. Sarah's gaze didn't leave Joe's face as she answered, "Of course!"

She continued to stare at Joe, willing him to awaken. He was extremely pale, and his eyes seemed sunken in. Sometimes squirming around in his discomfort, when she would reach out and touch him, he would be immediately soothed, making her heart melt.

In the late afternoon, Dr. Miller came back and told Sarah that he had run into Jacob and asked him to send a wire to the surrounding towns about four armed and dangerous criminals and if he and Ginny would be willing to care for Adam another night, as he knew Sarah was worn out with both worry and fear. She thanked him politely and asked if he was hungry.

"I could eat a bite and Joe will need something when he awakens. The biggest battle now is to keep him from getting an infection. I'm hoping that because it was a clean shot and I didn't have to go digging in there, he will be okay. The injury would have been much greater if they had used a shotgun. He's wouldn't have survived it at that range. He's lucky enough to have survived this."

"I wondered how he managed," Sarah murmured quietly.

"I don't know. I have been thinking about it. I'm hypothesizing that he turned slightly to the right at the last second, lowering his left shoulder so it wasn't straight on. If he hadn't have done that, I'm thinking it would have been a clean shot straight through his heart and there would have been nothing I could have done."

"Well, all's well that ends well, I guess," Sarah answered, trying to ignore the prickly feeling behind her eyes.

Sarah excused herself and moved across the living quarters to the stove, where she began to cook a simple potato soup and a loaf of fast-rising bread. The smell soon permeated the air and Dr. Miller enjoyed watching her glide across the floor as she worked. After a while, he looked down to check on Joe and saw his eyelids flutter slightly. He leaned down close to him and said quietly, "You're one lucky son of a bitch, Joe. In more ways than one!"

Joe's eyes opened for a second and he looked back at his friend, his eyes full of fog from the laudanum he had received for pain, and a hint of fear. Dr. Miller touched his shoulder and said to him, "Joe, you will be all right, especially with that sweet little woman caring for you. Almost makes me want to go out and get myself shot!" he joked, but Joe was too out of it to laugh.

When the food was ready, Sarah brought a bowl to Dr. Miller and a few slices of bread, smeared thickly with butter she had churned for Joe earlier in the week and cheese slices. The food was simple but warm and filling.

"Won't you join me?" Dr. Miller asked her.

"No, thank you," she answered absent-mindedly, looking at Joe, her worry written on her features.

"He's going to be all right, Sarah," Dr. Miller soothed. "At least as long as infection doesn't set in."

Sarah looked up and caught his eyes. She nodded slightly in response.

"He's going to need someone to look after him, though."

"I can do it," she answered automatically.

"Sarah, you have your shop and Adam. How could you possibly provide him with the care he needs?" He didn't mean to, but he felt jealous about how quickly she was willing to give up everything else in order to care for Joe.

"I have saved some money. I can close the shop for a few days, and I can ask if Ginny will keep Adam for me."

Dr. Miller nodded. "You can't stay here at night, though," he told her, worried about her reputation, but mostly troubled by the thought of her spending time with Joe in close quarters in the quiet overnight hours with no one to disturb them. He knew Joe was unwell now, but he would need care long after he began to regain consciousness.

262

Sarah didn't answer, but only stared back at him, a slight tip of her chin signaling her defiance to his statement. She was going to argue that Joe was in no position to do anything but lie in his bed and sleep, and that anyone who would assume otherwise was either trying to stir up drama or was just plain stupid. But then she looked around and realized that there was no proper place for her to sleep in his quarters and she wasn't comfortable sleeping out in the front room by herself on one of the cots in the jail cells, so she tentatively agreed.

"I will stay here with him in the jail for the next few nights and then you can be here during the day when I do my rounds," he told her matter-of-factly. "However, if something happens in the night where I'm needed, he may need someone to stay with him. I will ask Mama D if she would be willing to be on call at night.

Sarah nodded her agreement. Mama D was a matronly woman in her late forties, and she wouldn't care about any gossip about impropriety with her staying with Joe. It was also no secret that she loved him like a son. It seemed like the best solution and the only one that would work to care for Joe, stem any rumors, and allow Sarah to care for Adam, as well.

In the evening, Dr. Miller left to go to the saloon to talk to some of the men there about what should be done regarding an interim town sheriff while Joe was recovering. There were a few men in town whom Joe would deputize every now and again when there was the threat of something unpleasant taking place, like the whisperings of another strike, but most of those men were miners who spent their days underground. Several men sat and argued back and forth with continuing earnestness as the whiskey they were drinking took a greater hold on their rational thinking. Finally, Dr. Miller, who had imbibed in very little alcohol for fear that Joe would need him further during the night, suggested that the issue be brought to a town meeting the following morning in the church before he retreated to the jailhouse.

While Dr. Miller was gone, Sarah sat in the chair beside Joe and watched as his chest rose and fell in a steady rhythm. Every now and then, he would take an especially long pause between breaths and her heart would clench in fear that he would not take another one. On one such occasion, she stretched her hand out and placed it on his chest, searching for the reassuring beat of his heart. She left her hand there far longer than what would be considered appropriate as she felt the warmth radiating off his body and the supple skin stretched over his well-defined muscles. She leaned in to take a closer look at him, glancing first at the hair on his chest that surrounded her fingers. Her gaze then traveled to his face, slackened with sleep, giving him an almost childlike appearance. His lips were full and perfectly shaped, and deep red in color. She noticed for the first time that he had a small spattering of very light freckles across his nose and cheekbones, making her think that he must have been an adorable child. His dark, sooty eyelashes were thick and long, just brushing the top of his cheeks, and his dark hair was once again spilling over his forehead, so she gently brushed it back with her fingers, garnering a soft moan from him in response.

Joe was uncertain of where he was. He had been drifting in and out of consciousness all afternoon. The pain in his shoulder had dulled considerably compared to what it had been before, but it still throbbed. He was glad that it had subsided because earlier it felt as if someone had shoved a red-hot poker through his skin. Confused, he wondered which of his brothers had injured him so badly and for what infraction.

Joe and his brothers were a spirited bunch, for sure. Five boys, all about two years apart in age, but generally none of them were particularly calculated in their revenge. Instead, they tended to be a hot-tempered lot and they would go at each other for any perceived slight, rolling around and throwing punches, but never using implements to inflict permanent damage. Therefore, he began to wonder if instead he had been in an accident. He felt what he thought was his mother's presence in the room when her hand came over his forehead to push his hair

264

back. She never could stand when her boys' hair fell in their faces. She may have been the mother of five sons, but she did her best to keep them looking neat and orderly. He had tried to ask her what had happened when he felt her hand, but he couldn't find the strength to get the words out.

Sarah saw that it looked as though Joe was trying to say something to her, as his eyes opened slightly and his lips parted, but nothing came out.

"Shhhh... Don't try to talk. You need to rest. Just relax and trust that Dr. Miller and I have everything under control."

That seemed to work, as he sighed softly and sank further down into the pillows, seeking comfort in the familiar. He wasn't aware of how long he was asleep but awoke again when Dr. Miller came back to check on him.

"Water..." he gasped, opening his eyes and locking his gaze on Sarah's.

Sarah turned to the doctor and asked him, "Is that all right?"

"Yes! It's fine! Please, by all means, keep him drinking. The last thing he needs is to get dehydrated."

Sarah filled a tin cup with water and brought it to Joe's lips. His eyes were already closed as he struggled to sit up. Sarah, sensing his trouble, wrapped one arm around his back, while holding the cup to his mouth with the other. He took a few swallows, before realizing his cheek was pillowed up against her breast.

"Hmmm... You feel nice!" he mumbled, shocking her.

"Shh, Joe! Hush!" she responded, her cheeks reddening, especially when she saw that Dr. Miller was watching them with an amused expression on his face.

"Sarah, he's not in his right mind right now because of the laudanum," he explained quietly.

"All right, thank you," she said, trying to maintain some dignity in the situation.

When she went to lie him back down, he pleaded, "No! Please! I want you to hold me, Caroline! Please! Please don't go!"

Sarah glanced up at Dr. Miller, and he merely raised his shoulders in question.

"Is Caroline his mother?" Sarah asked in a whisper.

"No," answered the doctor. He didn't know much about Caroline, but he knew that whoever she was, she was the main reason why Joe had left California and headed east. He knew that he had loved her, but he had never shared any more than that. Any time the doctor had tried to ask him for more details, Joe had merely told him he didn't want to talk about it and clammed up tightly.

"Caroline!" Joe whimpered sadly, while he thrashed around on his bed as if he was trying to get up and go after her, breaking Sarah's heart.

"Joe," she said softly, brushing his hair back off his face, "it's all right. I'm not going to leave you while you're ill. I will stay right here."

She felt bad for tricking him, because she was not Caroline, but in his laudanum-induced fog, it didn't seem to matter much. What was most important was that Joe felt reassured so that he would settle down and rest.

The next day passed in much the same way. Sarah had finally gone back home in the wee hours of the morning after Dr. Miller woke her up in the chair she was sitting in. As she dressed for bed, she couldn't keep her thoughts from wondering if Joe was going to survive the ordeal and her breath hitched in her chest. He was the closest thing to a friend she had there, even with the distance between them over the past few months. Despite everything, he would still go out of his way to stop by and check on her almost every day, even if it was merely to pop his head in and inquire as to her welfare.

She slept fitfully for only a few hours before giving up and lying in bed, staring at the ceiling until the eastern sky began to brighten with a rosy glow. Sighing, she realized that she was too worried and anxious to sleep, so she donned her dress and walked to the jail.

266

Dr. Miller was asleep in one of the jail cells but roused when Sarah came in. He looked at her worried expression and answered her question without her uttering a word.

"Yes, he made it through the night," he told her simply.

"Good!"

Sarah went into Joe's living quarters and saw that he had wrapped himself tightly in his blankets and appeared to be shivering. She reached her hand out and felt his forehead, gasping in surprise.

"Richard!" she cried out.

Dr. Miller came hurrying in, pulling up his suspenders as he rounded the corner. "What is it?" he asked, his voice thick with sleep and his concern evident.

"Feel him!" Sarah exclaimed, fear gripping her heart.

"He's running a fever," the doctor said, opening his bag. "Here… Please mix this in with liquid and we will have to force it down his throat.

Sarah came back into the room with a cup full of cold tea, laced generously with sugar in hopes to make whatever Joe was about to ingest more palatable. The doctor took the cup from her and mixed in a white powder, stirring it well before shaking Joe gently on his good shoulder.

"Come on, Joe. Time to drink some medicine," he said brightly, but Joe hardly reacted.

"Sarah, I'm going to have to lift him and you're going to have to get as much of this into his mouth as you can."

She nodded solemnly at him as he sat down on the bed beside Joe and lifted him up, supporting his bulk against him. Sarah then took the cup and held it to his lips, but all Joe did was moan and turn his head.

"I have to get a spoon," she stated, rising from the chair beside the bed and finding the implement she wanted. Then, she patiently spooned the cup's contents through Joe's lips, going painstakingly slow so that he took in as much as possible.

"Good!" said Dr. Miller, satisfied. "Now, we need to cool him off. Go get some lukewarm water and a cloth. I'll need you to help me wipe him down."

Sarah went and gathered everything, feeling as hopeless as she did when George had been deathly ill. She wished that she could simply will away his suffering and make him whole again. By the time she returned to the mattress where Joe lay, Dr. Miller had already stripped him down to his drawers and ripped back the bedding. Joe lay as helpless as a small child, curling up instinctively as he shivered and shook with fever.

"Now, just start to wipe him down as best you can," Dr. Miller instructed her. "I need to run out to the privy, but I'll be back soon."

Sarah nodded and focused her attention on Joe's needs. He was laying on his uninjured side in the fetal position as she wrung out the cloth and began to run it gently up his arm. He moaned pathetically, trying to move away from her, but she gripped his wrist and spoke firmly to him as she did with Adam.

"Joe! Joe, you must lie still! Do not try to avoid me! We are doing this for your own good!"

Something in her voice must have struck a chord with him, because he stopped fighting her. She tried to speak gently to him as she worked, not really talking about anything of importance, but trying to distract them both from the task at hand and eventually, when she tugged gently on his arm and bid him to roll onto his back, he did as she asked so she could rub down his torso.

"There!" Sarah said brightly, trying to hide the fact that she was highly impressed by the man laying before her. The afternoon before, she had been too overwrought with fear and shock to really appreciate Joe's physical form, but as she ran the cloth in her hands over the peaks and valleys of his abdomen, she couldn't deny that he was magnificent.

"Good mornin'!" Sarah heard a voice ring out from the front of the jail, and she turned to see Mama D walking into Joe's abode.

268

"Good morning," Sarah answered, suddenly feeling very guilty that she was caught enjoying Joe's physique as much as she was, though given Mama D's profession, she figured that she wouldn't be shocked.

"How's our patient?" Mama D asked quietly, leaning over Joe and giving him a motherly smile.

"He's very ill this morning. Sometime between when I left late last night and came back early this morning, he spiked a fever."

"And where was Doc Miller durin' those hours?" Mama D questioned, her annoyance plain that the man she loved like a son was suffering.

"I'm not sure. He was asleep in a cell when I came in this morning."

"Figures!" Mama D answered, shaking her head. "I swear, if you want anythin' done right, you have to have a woman do it. Men are too selfish. We would stay awake until we collapsed from exhaustion to ensure that our loved ones were safe, but men? They feel tired, so they sleep!"

Sarah smiled at the woman. She seemed so gruff on the outside, but when one spoke with her, they could hear immediately that she had a huge heart. "Mama, do you have any children?"

Mama D's face took on a faraway look and she was quiet for a while before answering.

"Aye, I did. A long, long time ago. I married young and we were brought here from Ireland to follow my husband's big dreams. I was just a young lass, not more than fifteen, when we came over and eventually made our way West. I was pregnant not long after we were married. The babe died within two weeks of being born. Never did find out what happened. It wasn't more than six months later that my husband succumbed. He had spent his life in the coal mines, since he was old enough to swing a pickaxe, and his lungs were bad. He caught a bad bout of the flu and that was that…" she said sadly. "Next thing I knew, I was a workin' girl, just so that I had a place to stay and somethin' to eat."

"I lost my husband to the flu, too," Sarah said, feeling an odd kinship with this woman who was so unlike her, yet not.

"I know. I talked to Jacob when you first came," Mama answered.

"Jacob comes to see you?" Sarah asked, surprised.

"Aye!" Mama D said, not quite comprehending Sarah's horror at the possibility that her sister's husband was visiting whores.

"But…" Sarah said. "But… What about his wife?"

"Oh! Well, honey, I can tell you that many a man comes to see us and wants nothin' more than a drink and some good conversation. Jacob is one of those. He's got no interest in touchin'. He just likes to look a little bit," she reported.

"Oh," Sarah said, suddenly feeling sad. She hadn't thought that Jacob would frequent the establishment. He seemed like the most upstanding man in town, after maybe the pastor. It caused her distress to think that her illusion of her brother-in-law had been somewhat tarnished. However, something else bothered her even more.

"What about Joe?" she asked, her voice almost as low as a whisper.

"What about Joe?" Mama D probed.

"Well, does Joe…" she began, trying to get an answer to what she didn't want to know, but felt she had to ask. "Does Joe…"

Suddenly, it dawned on Mama D what she was asking. "You mean, does Joe come in to touch, or just look?"

"Yes!" Sarah answered, relieved that she didn't have to spell it out.

"Oh, honey! Joe doesn't come in to do either. He walks around like a cock watchin' over his hens. He takes his role as protector very seriously, like a big brother."

"So, he has never…"

"Nope. Never! And believe you me, we have all tried to bed this man."

Sarah was shocked beyond words. She had never heard anyone speak so candidly about sex. However, she figured that Mama D, with her many years in the business, no longer saw sex as something of which to be ashamed. It had allowed her to live the life she wanted to lead; indeed, the only one she could have, given her tragic tale.

"The man is so uptight. It would do him a world of good to let loose and kick up his heels a little bit. But every time I offer, he just thanks me and changes the subject. I have even offered services to him for free as a thank you for all he has done for me and my girls, but he still won't take me up on my proposition. Many of the girls, Chelsea and Elizabeth, especially, would love to give Joe a good romp. I mean, look at that body! He's a very attractive man, isn't he?"

"I…" Sarah began, unsure of how to respond. She hadn't thought about other women in town fancying Joe, but it made sense. He was dutiful, handy, hardworking, kind, even if a little gruff, and certainly not a bad looking man. The thought of him bedding some other woman made Sarah's heart hurt, however, even though she had tried a million times to convince herself that they were just friends.

The two women sat together in silence, watching Joe's chest rise and fall.

"He's sure breathing hard!" Sarah remarked.

"Aye! I reckon it's the fever."

"Probably," Sarah agreed.

After a few more minutes, Sarah touched Joe's face and felt that once again, his temperature was rising. Dr. Miller was out on his rounds, but he had left some medicine for Sarah to give Joe if he needed it before his return. Sarah quickly mixed it and tried to spoon it into Joe's mouth, but he would not cooperate. He kept thrashing his head back and forth and trying to swat her hand away. Finally, after he had spilled the contents of the spoon for the fifth time, Sarah lost her patience.

"Joe McIntyre! You open your mouth this instant!" she raged at him.

He continued to fight her, exasperating her even further. "Oh! Joe McIntyre, you are single-handedly the most stubborn man I have ever met! Will you please just take the damn medicine?"

Something in her voice snapped Joe out of his delirium just long enough that he opened his eyes and looked at her. He smiled sloppily as if he'd had too much to drink, before he opened his mouth and took all the contents in the cup at once without another word. When he had drained all the liquid, he said, "Are you happy now, Caroline? You're adorable when you're mad!" before laying back down to sleep again.

Sarah looked to Mama D in surprise. "Who's this Caroline?" she asked her, confusion on her face.

Mama D knew exactly who Caroline was and why she haunted Joe's most suppressed dreams, but she wasn't about to break his confidences, so she merely shrugged.

"You don't know?" Sarah pressed her.

Mama D still didn't respond, thinking that if she kept her mouth shut, it would be the best for everyone. Joe had never shared much personal information at all about himself or his life, especially from before he had left California. For some unknown reason, though, one night Joe had let his guard down and confided in Mama D. It was right after Sarah had left to go back home and he was not pleased. He had been intent on reconciling his sorrows with a bottle of whiskey to assist him, and while he had been pounding back the shots, he told Mama D that it was better this way, as he was incapable of a relationship, anyhow, before he had eventually gotten intoxicated enough to spill his story.

Over the next three days, Joe's fever raged, making him incredibly difficult to nurse. It took both Sarah and Dr. Miller or Mama D to keep him from thrashing about and rising out of bed, risking damage to his injury. Sometimes, he would yell incoherent things about being glad his life was ending because he could never trust anyone again. Other times, he was contrite and gentle, especially with Sarah, who he thought was Caroline, professing his undying love for her and apologizing for ever doubting her love for him. Everyone was bemused by his undulating cycle of behavior, but Joe was completely incognizant of it.

Finally, in the early pre-dawn of the fifth morning since being shot, Joe awoke to both Mama D and Sarah asleep in his quarters. Mama D was sacked out on his small settee while Sarah sat in a chair next to his bed, her body draped over the mattress, just even with his hip.

He listened to the quiet breathing of his two companions and wondered why they were there and what had happened. The last thing he remembered was being surrounded by the gang of men who were trying to steal the payroll for the mine. Then, when he tried to shift slightly in an attempt to sit up higher, the pain in his shoulder hit him full-bore, like a white-hot poker being driven into his skin, and he gasped.

Sarah sat up at the sound and squinted into the blackness, trying to see what was going on, but it was too dark to discern anything out of the ordinary. However, her well-trained mother's ear caught the difference in the way Joe was breathing, so she took a chance and whispered, "Joe?"

"Yeah?" he answered, his voice sounding raspy with dehydration and non-use.

"Are you all right?" she asked him softly, her concern apparent.

"What the hell happened?" he whispered into the inky abyss.

"You were shot in the shoulder. You've been incredibly ill. We were afraid we would lose you, Joe!" Sarah's voice caught.

"Still here!" he laughed sheepishly.

"Good!" Sarah whispered resolutely. "Now, what can I get for you?"

"I'm really thirsty!" he said, feeling like his whisper was a yell in the quiet stillness of the late night.

"I have some water here. Would that be sufficient?"

"Please!"

Sarah grabbed the cup from the small table beside Joe's bed and then sat down beside him, taking his head in her arm to raise him up. His head rested against her soft breast, and he inhaled her fragrance until he remembered that he was in fact supposed to be drinking. He wrapped his lips around the edge of the tin vessel and took a small draw, swallowing some sips of water before his breathing became labored with the exertion of it all.

"Enough!" he told her weakly when he felt as though he might pass out if he continued to drink. Sarah gently laid him back down on his mattress and he closed his eyes, panting slightly at the energy he had expended.

"What happened? Where am I? Why are you here?" Joe rattled off questions as fast as he could, his voice thready and weak.

"You're in your quarters. You got shot. Do you remember?"

"Not really," Joe told her.

"Well, you got shot in the street, right outside my shop!" Sarah reported to him, and as she rehashed it all, her voice became louder and shriller with each word, her distress clear. "When I got out there, I found you bleeding in the street. Thankfully, Dr. Miller was located, and we got you moved in here. He and I fixed you up as best we could, but you still ran a fever." When Sarah finished, she unwittingly swiped the back of her hand across her eyes to wipe away her tears of frustration and fear.

"Gave us quite the scare, there, Joe!" Mama D interjected from her position on the settee.

"I'm so sorry," he said quietly.

"It's all right. We're just glad you lived!"

"Sarah's right, you know. Everyone in town has been pullin' for you!" Mama D added.

"Are you hungry, Joe?" Sarah asked him.

"No… No, not really. Mostly, I just… Um… I just need to use the privy."

"Oh!" Sarah exclaimed, not even thinking of that.

Joe tried to sit up but groaned in agony before settling back down on the pillows. "How's this going to work?" he growled in his frustration.

"I'll help you, Joe," Mama D told him. "You haven't got anythin' I haven't seen before, dearie!"

"But Mama! Do you really think he's up to walking all the way out to the privy?" Sarah asked her, surprised. "It's also freezing out there!"

"You're right!" Mama D answered after a few seconds of pondering. "Where's your pot?"

"Huh?" Joe asked her.

"You know… Your pot! The pot you use to do your business in the middle of the night."

"Oh!" Joe exclaimed, a bit shocked. "I don't use one of those. Normally the walk to the privy isn't a big issue."

"Well, you're gonna have to use somethin' like that tonight, because we can't risk you slippin' and fallin'. Or catchin' your death. But Doc isn't here, so you're stuck with us ladies to assist you. Have you got a large pot or bowl we can use?"

Joe glanced nervously at Sarah. His desire for privacy, away from their prying eyes, more specifically Sarah's, was definitely not boding well for him. For some reason, Mama D's helping him and seeing him exposed didn't bother him, but he felt mortified at the thought of Sarah witnessing the process.

"I guess I do. I have the big metal bowl I use to make pancake batter for the picnic breakfast every year. But really? That's just disgusting!" he said, shuddering slightly at the thought of reusing kitchen equipment after it had been used as a privy.

"Oh, Joe!" Mama D said with a laugh. "It can be washed and then sanitized with boilin' water, for goodness sakes!"

By this time, Joe was feeling all the more anxious to relieve himself. His eyes had adjusted enough in the dim moonlight shining through the window that he could make out Sarah's and Mama D's forms.

Finally, out of necessity, he acquiesced.

"It's in the back of that cupboard there," Joe said, pointing a finger weakly to demonstrate where he was looking.

"Sarah?" Mama D asked. "Would you please be so kind as to go and dig that out while I help Joe stand?"

Mama D's solution sounded good when Sarah realized that she did not have the same amount of bulk as the older woman, and so therefore, Joe would be better serviced by Mama D's support than her own.

"Sure," she replied, heading toward the small kitchen area.

"There are matches on the stove," Joe whispered, his fatigue almost overwhelming him. "And you can light the lantern on the windowsill if you need to."

Sarah lit the lamp and found what she had been looking for, before heading back across the room with brisk steps. When she arrived at the bedside, she could already see that Mama D had everything under control, so she placed the bowl on the floor and waited patiently to see how else she could help.

Mama D, even with her bulk and strength, could not raise Joe by herself. She tried, but Joe had merely fallen back on the pillows, a grunt of pain escaping his lips.

"Come on, Sarah!" Mama D told her. "I be needin' you to help me steady him, please!"

Sarah moved over to Joe's other side, the one with his injury, and tried to find a good place on which to grab. She finally gently rested her hand back behind his bent elbow and pulled as Mama D lifted on his other side. Joe, embarrassed to be so helpless and dependent on two women, tried desperately to control his pain, but still whimpered a bit as he left his reclining position until he was on his feet. He was red in the face, perspiring immensely, and his breath was coming in rapid bursts. Both Sarah and Mama D held him steady as he gulped huge breaths of air into his lungs. Finally, when he was to the point where he could speak again, he stood a little straighter.

"I'm good!" he panted.

"All right, then," said Mama D. "Just whip it out there and let's get this over with."

Sarah and Joe both blushed deep red, and Sarah could not meet his eyes. He kept looking down at the bowl on the floor, as if he stared at it long enough, it would suddenly change into the outdoor privy, with a door, before his eyes. Finally, he reached down and loosened his drawers enough to free himself to urinate, but as he stood there, between two women, he was too self-conscious to go.

Sarah turned away from him, looking at the far wall, surprised that her own curiosity was making her want to take a peek at Joe's goods. She didn't know why the compulsion was strong to see just what he possessed, but she would not allow herself even a glance, as she knew they were both uncomfortable enough already.

Joe cleared his throat and tried to calm down, but try as he might, he could not relax enough to start the task at hand. He closed his eyes, breathing deeply, while trying to forget that he was in his quarters alone with two women, one of which he found extremely attractive, and the other, a mother figure.

Finally, Mama D looked at him. "Joe, what's the problem?

"Umm… This… This is a bit difficult with you both here!" he stammered.

"Why's that?" Mama D asked. "You think we haven't ever seen what you've got before? Come on, Joe! You know what I do for a livin' and Sarah… Well, Sarah's been married and has a son. Neither of us is exactly a stranger to a man's penis. I promise you; you haven't got anythin' that's any different from any other man!"

Joe glanced sideways at Sarah, his face the color of brick. She didn't know what to do or say, so she merely nodded her agreement with Mama D, but still couldn't look him in the eye.

"She's right," she eventually said to encourage him, while looking up at the ceiling.

Joe was able to eventually talk himself down and completed his biological need, though he was conscious of every move and sound that any of them made. When they finally got him settled back in the bed, he was exhausted, his face drawn and grey, but he smiled weakly at Sarah as Mama D had taken the bowl and slipped out the back to empty its contents.

"Thank you," he said quietly as it was still just the two of them.

"It's fine, Joe!" Sarah told him, wanting to smooth over any embarrassment he was feeling. "I wish that you could have gone out to the privy."

"It's all right. Just a bit… awkward!"

"I know," she soothed. "But it's done now, at least until the next time."

Sarah tucked the quilts around him tenderly, then asked him, "How are you feeling, Joe? How's your pain?"

"I hurt!" he said, his face still grimacing a bit from the jostling and exertion of the past little while.

"Would you like some more laudanum?

"I guess a little wouldn't hurt."

"No, you need to rest. That's the best way for you to heal!"

Sarah dosed his next portion of medicine and helped him sit up enough to drink it. Once he was done, she tucked the blankets back up around him and without even thinking, just out of habit from tucking in her son every night, she bent low and placed a kiss on his forehead, realizing what she had done as she rose up.

She blushed furiously and sputtered a quiet apology, mortified that she had done something so intimately personal.

"It's fine, Sarah!" Sensing her embarrassment, he tried to reassure her. "It was actually kind of nice. No one has kissed me since…" He trailed off as his eyes closed and Sarah was unsure if he had fallen asleep or just didn't want to finish his sentence. She sat quietly beside him and listened as his breath became slower and more relaxed.

Mama D came back into the room. "There!" she said with determination after she had emptied the makeshift chamber pot and washed it out at the water pump outside. "'Tis snowin' again!" she added with disgust.

278

Sarah said nothing in response, so Mama D came closer and saw her watching Joe intently. "Everythin' all right?" she asked her.

"Yes. He was hurting, so I gave him his next dose of laudanum."

"Just as well. We maybe can grab a few more hours of sleep ourselves," the older woman added.

Sarah awoke later to Joe's strangled moans of despair. Mama D was not in the room, so Sarah figured she had stepped out to go across the street to check on things. At first, she thought he was in discomfort, but his facial expression was one of anguish and not pain. He was moving his legs and flopping his head back and forth on the pillow, tears streaming down his cheeks, his voice sounding tormented.

"No! Please, no! Caroline! Please, don't do this to me! I love you! I want you! Please…" Joe began to sob, deep wracking cries that seemed to shake his whole body, yet he was not awake. When Sarah tried to wake him, he turned to her, eyes opened, but he was clearly not seeing her.

"Joe!" Sarah said sharply, trying to get him to realize that he was dreaming, but instead, Joe reached up with both arms and pulled her down to him with surprising strength, his lips finding hers and delivering a fervent kiss, which left her breathless. She tried to pull away, but he only held onto her tighter, and when she gasped in surprise, his tongue slid in beside hers, deepening their kiss to the point that Sarah relaxed helplessly against him, all conscious thought relinquished, until she was horrified when she heard herself give a little moan.

Joe's hand was entangled in her hair, which had slid out of its topknot during the night while Sarah had slept in the chair beside his bed. She told herself that she needed to pull away. Joe was not in his right mind, but it had been so long since she had been loved by anyone that her desire was bubbling up to a fever pitch and she had to fight herself from climbing up in his bed to sidle up beside him.

His lips were warm and gentle, and Sarah could feel the fire he was igniting within her. Her knees were weak, her pulse was rapid, and she felt his caresses down through her core. As the kiss continued, one of Joe's hands moved from her face to cup her warm breast in his palm and he began to knead it ever so gently, and Sarah felt her body react even stronger than before as her hand encircled the back of his neck and she gently fingered the hair there. This time, it was Joe who moaned, long and deeply, mumbling something against her lips.

Sarah reluctantly pulled back to ensure that she was not hurting him and asked him, "What did you say?'

"Don't leave me!" he muttered, making her heart swell.

"Make love to me, Caroline!" he begged, his desperation and longing coming through more clearly than the words did. "Please? I want you so much!"

That broke the spell and Sarah pushed herself off him in an instant. She moved so abruptly that he whimpered in response. "Please! Please, Caroline! Don't do this to me! I love you! Please choose me!" he beseeched whomever he thought he was with in that moment.

"Hush, Joe!" Sarah scolded. She hadn't meant to sound so harsh, but she was angry for allowing herself to be sucked in, and at him, for wanting someone who wasn't her.

Her heart was still racing as the tingling of desire continued to rush through her torso and out through her limbs. For the first time in a long time, she was reminded of how it felt to desire someone. Her body was craving a man's touch, feeling as though it was screaming for caresses, kisses, and the feeling of a man loving her again. Her frustration surfaced in a wave of lust at the same moment she realized for what had to be the millionth time that she would never again feel that closeness with a man.

Joe, who hadn't really even been awake in the first place, rolled back over and fell into a deeper sleep, leaving Sarah to sit in the chair, crying silently. Once again, her longing for George struck her full force, but this time, instead of the usual sadness that he wasn't there with her, the strongest emotion she felt was

280

anger. In that instant, she blamed him for all the loneliness and longing she felt, cursing the fact that he had abandoned her at a young age, holding him responsible for the fact that her young, healthy body was giving her desires that would not be fulfilled.

As she sat in the chair and brooded, she seriously considered Mama D's earlier invitation that if she ever wanted to be one of her girls and work as a lady of the night, she would always have a place for her. She was disappointed in herself when she realized her need for physical contact with a man was so great in that moment that she would have seriously considered the offer if it hadn't been for her son. As she calmed back down and began to think rationally again, however, she was grateful that though Lord knew George didn't provide for them in his passing, at least she did thankfully know how to sew, because if she didn't, being a working girl would have been her only option. Only then, could she think logically about the men who frequented Mama D's establishment and how most of them were extremely unattractive and certainly wouldn't make her feel like Joe had.

It was then she understood that it wasn't sex that she missed, but intimacy. Not only did she want to be attracted to a man, but she also longed for a man to desire her, to love and want her: not just her body, but her whole being. Remembering just how sated and safe she felt laying in George's arms and the feelings of affection and contentment she experienced in the afterglow of their lovemaking, she realized then that making love was not to merely have sex. It was clear, though, that whoever tormented Joe so much in his dreams had affected him more than he would ever admit in normal circumstances.

Sarah eventually fell back into a restless sleep and the next time Joe opened his eyes, Dr. Miller was standing over him, examining him as silently as possible as to not wake anyone.

"How are you doing?" Dr. Miller whispered to Joe when he saw the man was awake.

"I'm a bit rough," Joe admitted hoarsely. "I feel like I have run for miles and have had no water!"

"That's the fever," the doctor whispered. "You've given us quite a scare!"

Sarah shifted in her sleep, a small moan escaping her lips. Both men turned to look at her, her face relaxed with slumber, her long eyelashes brushing the tops of the dark circles eclipsing the delicate skin under her eyes. Her red lips were set in a sort of pout and the hair that had escaped her bun was spilling out over her shoulders. However, what Joe noticed were the dried tear marks down her cheeks.

"Has she been crying?" he asked quietly, more to himself than to Dr. Miller.

The doctor looked more closely at her face and answered, "It looks that way, yes."

"I wonder why?"

"I would assume because, as I said, you have given us all quite a scare for the last few days!"

"But why would she fall asleep crying?" Joe asked, perplexed.

"I don't know. But remember, her husband died. Perhaps seeing you so ill reminded her of that. I'm sure it was very traumatic. She's a very young woman and by all accounts from Jacob and Ginny, she loved him very much."

Dr. Miller shoved a thermometer into Joe's mouth and neither man said anything as they waited for the mercury to rise. When he was satisfied it had been enough time, the doctor removed the glass tube and held it up to the window through which the morning light shone.

"Still got a fever, Joe, though it is better. Let's see that shoulder!"

The men struggled with removing the bandage, and the doctor, though concerned, was pleased with what he saw. The skin around the bullet wound was still red and hot to the touch, but the surface area had shrunk and the wound itself was no longer weeping with infection.

"I have said it once and I will say it again, Joe: you're one lucky bastard!"

Joe didn't pick up on the way Dr. Miller looked longingly at Sarah as he said the words, as the man thought, *If only she didn't have a child! Or, even if the boy was old enough that she wouldn't mind sending him away, so we only had to raise children of our own!*

Alas, it was not to be, and he couldn't dwell on it anymore. He shook his head slightly before re-bandaging Joe's wound and then headed out the door again for the morning appointments at his clinic.

Mama D was snoring quietly on the sofa, but Sarah was breathing slowly and deeply. Joe allowed himself to openly stare at her and he had to admit, he liked what he saw. Her features were delicate, and her face looked even younger than her years when the tension she carried from her past struggles was relaxed with sleep. As he watched her, he admired her incredible likeness to Adam and smiled, but while she slumbered, it was hard for him to fathom that she was in fact Adam's mother, as she looked young enough to easily pass for his older sister.

Despite his determination to never love again, sometimes, even before this incident, he had missed what having a good woman by his side would mean in his life. As he lay in the still, quiet morning, however, he began to really think about his legacy in a way he never had before this near-death experience. For the most part, he thought he had been content living a life of solitude, quite resolved to spending his life alone, especially if it meant sparing him further heartbreak. He was beginning to realize now, however, that it was nice to have someone care.

Mama D was like a mother to him. She always babied and kept an eye on him as any good mother would. If he was looking peaked or run down, she would tell him he needed more rest. If he lost weight, she would tell him he needed to eat better. He appreciated that she was there to help in his recovery and had, knowing her, expected nothing less.

Having Sarah care for him, on the other hand, was different entirely. He couldn't define in words what felt so dissimilar, nevertheless his life felt less lonely to have her there. While

Mama made his being incapacitated more comfortable, there was something about Sarah that made him want to fight to get better. He wanted to prove to her that he could do it: that he could rise from the ashes to become again someone on whom she could rely. He didn't want to remain weakened and sickly, dependent on her, but rather wanted to make her feel secure and safe in knowing that once he was well, he could instead take care of her.

Sarah felt that someone was staring at her and opened her eyes to find Joe studying her.

"Good morning!" she whispered, after glancing at the settee and seeing that Mama D was sound asleep upon it.

"Good morning!" he murmured back, the beginnings of a small smile playing at the corners of his lips.

"How are you feeling?" she asked him, concern once again written all over her face.

"All right. A bit better, thank you! Just so very tired."

"I'm sure!" Sarah said. "Your body has had a lot of healing to do."

Sarah stood and reached out her hand to place on his forehead. "May I?" she asked before she actually touched him.

"Please!" he said, sighing as he felt her cold fingers on his smooth skin.

"You're still warm!" she gently chastised, as if he had some control over the situation.

"I know," he replied. "Doc checked me earlier and he said I'm still running a slight fever, but that it's better."

"Well, that's obvious because you're more coherent. Last night, you were nowhere near aware of what you were doing!" she added, her cheeks blushing, making him immediately worry about what he had said or done. He was mortified that he had somehow let it slip that he desired her.

"Really?" he asked, feigning surprise.

"Yes!"

They were quiet for a moment, studying one another, until he finally broke the silence.

"Sarah, you should go home and rest. You look exhausted."

284

"I do?"

"Yes! Please don't let yourself get run down on my account. You have Adam to care for."

"I know. But he's fine with Ginny and Jacob. Joe, this town loves you. Everyone is willing to pitch in. In fact, I got the Sumpter's oldest girl to take on my workload for the next few weeks so that I can help you."

"That isn't necessary!" Joe protested, worrying about how she would make ends meet with no income.

"Don't worry. She's paying me a percentage of her wages. It won't be much, but it will be enough. In fact, given how busy I have become, I think I may want to hire her on to help me in the shop with the more tedious jobs, anyway."

"That sounds like a good idea," he answered.

They were silent again for a few minutes, but Sarah's mind ruminated over and over again the question she was dying to ask him. He could tell that she was deep in thought but had no idea what she was thinking. Finally, she just came out with it.

"Joe, who's Caroline?" she asked quietly.

"Oh!" he answered, surprised. He hadn't expected that question at all, nor was he prepared to reopen that wound, so he tried to play it off as no big deal.

"Just someone I knew in California," he answered with what he hoped was nonchalance. "Why?"

"You have just been mentioning her a lot the last few days," Sarah explained. "Was she someone special?"

Joe's eyes clouded over, looking stormy. His features became sullen and dark. "I don't want to talk about it," he answered, sounding like a petulant child.

"Oh! All right," Sarah said brightly, backtracking, seeing that the subject was making him restless. She certainly hadn't meant to cause him any further distress. "I'm sorry.

"It's fine," he answered her. "It was a long time ago. Water under the bridge and someone who is insignificant now."

"It's fine… Just forget I asked." She paused. "I'm going to go home to clean up a little bit. I'll be back shortly to get you your breakfast. Mama's here if you need anything." Before he could answer, she was on her feet and out the door.

Chapter Thirty-Four

Joe couldn't go back to sleep. His shoulder was hurting, and he was, surprisingly, lonely. Not only had Sarah gone home, but Mama D was still sleeping soundly, snoring deeply, and Doc Miller had already come and gone. Joe was not one to sit idle. In fact, having nothing to do but rest drove him batty. He had been that way since he could remember, always begging his mother to let him get out of bed, even go to school, when he was very sick, but she would never yield. He vividly recollected reclining on his pillow in his bed, his brother's empty space beside him, his arms crossed, glaring at his mother every time she came in.

"Oh, sweetie," she said, her face full of pity. "You are bored and sullen now, but I promise you, when you're an adult, you will long for a time when you can just lie in bed and rest!"

He had never believed her then, and he still didn't now. He had to be incredibly ill or injured to stay put for an hour, let alone an entire day. Mining had suited him. He was always moving, expending his extra energy. When he had instead been voted the town's new sheriff, it had taken some adjustment to what Joe considered to be a life of leisure consisting of mostly sitting behind a desk. After a while, however, he had gone stir-crazy and figured he might as well spend as much time as possible patrolling their little hamlet. That decision ended up serving him well in two ways: first, it had kept him out of the jail where he felt that the four walls were closing in on him, but more importantly, he was also letting his presence be known while getting to know the people in the community and building a rapport with them.

Joe always figured that he had just inherited his father's wanderlust. His pa was constantly in motion, looking to make improvements at home when he wasn't working himself to the bone at the mine. When his parents had moved West, all that had changed was the backdrop. As an adult, Joe had decided his ma was as close to a saint as a woman could get, putting up with his pa's enthusiasm for a life that dragged her from pillar to post throughout the majority of their marriage. She was always a good sport, though, long-suffering in her bearing and raising of five boys, hoping that eventually, God would see fit to bless her with a girl. Though she never got her daughter, even in the middle of the Sierra Nevadas, she was a lady, and so she instead made sure that she raised proper Southern gentlemen.

The only time he ever saw her cry about her lack of femininity and stability was when her porcelain figurine, given to her by her mother on her wedding day, had broken into a million pieces when the family had moved yet again. Joe's two younger brothers had been wrestling in the wagon, and one of them, neither of them would ever admit whom, accidentally kicked the box that contained it to the ground. The whole family had heard the shattering sound and when his pa had finally pushed his way through the gaggle of stunned boys to open the crate, all that was left were the misshapen shards of what had been their mother's most beloved treasure.

Joe never forgot his mother running to the box and dropping to her knees, tears running down her face as she ran her hands through the wreckage, oblivious to the cuts she was getting. His pa had silently handed her a dustpan and the willow branch broom, and she wordlessly swept the debris of the last scrap of femininity she had in her home. When she had again stood, Joe recalled his father held her in his arms for a long time, while no one else moved, or said a word.

"I'm so sorry, love. We will get you a new one," he had offered when he finally felt it was time to speak.

His mother had squared her shoulders and wiped her eyes. "Well, nothing to be done about it now, is there?" she said. "No use crying over spilled milk. Thankfully, I have all of you here, whole and healthy, keeping every one of you God saw fit to give me. Many a woman is not so lucky, so I guess I don't have much to complain about, seeing how He gave me five such strapping young lads."

With that, the incident was never brought up again. His pa had never been able to procure another figurine for his ma, or perhaps she had told him to forget it. Joe never knew the reason, but with five active boys, she might have decided it was better to not become attached to breakable things. All he knew was his ma was a good Christian woman and she loved her family fiercely.

Sometime later, Mama D groaned slightly as she stretched and then sat up. Joe watched in amusement as he saw the middle-aged woman uncurl herself from the settee, mumbling about being too old to sleep in such a fashion. When she looked up and saw Joe, she smiled brightly, despite her morning aches and pains.

"There he is!" she exclaimed happily. "I was wonderin' if we would ever see those pretty hazel eyes again!"

"You and me both!" Joe answered wryly.

"How are you feelin'?"

"A bit rough."

"I'll bet!" Mama D said with a laugh. "Ain't no one ever told you not to get in front of a bullet, Sheriff?"

"Yes, but I didn't listen, apparently," Joe quipped back, enjoying the easy exchange with the woman whom he had come to love like a mother.

"Do you need anythin'?"

"No, thank you. I'm good right now. Doc was here earlier and checked me out. Sarah left about an hour ago to freshen up. I think she said something about bringing some food, too. Good thing, because I could eat a horse!"

"That girl's been here the whole time," Mama D told him, watching his face closely for his reaction.

"I know," he said quietly, trying not to give away too much. He had tried hard to hold her gaze, but eventually, he looked away. Mama D's scrutiny was too intense for him, and he had to tell her what was on his mind.

"She asked me about Caroline," he admitted.

"And?"

"And, what? I didn't tell her anything," he answered haughtily.

"Joe…" Mama D said with a warning tone in her voice. "You've gotta tell her!"

He didn't say anything for a long time before he answered. "I know. But I don't even know how to bring it up to her."

"You can start by just tellin' her the truth."

"And what if she laughs at me or thinks I'm pathetic?"

"Joe, you just got shot in the shoulder and have been lyin' here in a stupor for the last four days, fever ragin', mumblin' all sorts of outlandish things. If she was gonna laugh, son, I guarantee you that she would have done so already."

He nodded at her, hoping that she was right. "I… Mama, I can't… I just…"

"Well, one day soon you may want to. Believe me, Joe, Sarah is a pretty, smart, and kind woman in a minin' town full of men. 'Tis pretty surprisin' honestly that someone hasn't snatched her up already! I think your only savin' grace is that she's sweet on you, though she's as stubborn as you are and would never admit it, even to herself. But eventually… Eventually, someone's gonna realize what a treasure she is, and you'll have been too late."

"I'll think about it!" Joe said, a sulk evident in his voice.

"Good!"

Just then, the door to Joe's quarters opened slowly, drawing Joe's and Mama D's attention, stopping their conversation in its tracks.

"Oh!" Sarah exclaimed as she looked around. "You're both awake! Wonderful! I have some biscuits and butter with strawberry preserves and bacon. Sorry. I know it's a hodgepodge, but I didn't have much, what with my being here so much these past few days, and I didn't want to take any more time away by running to the mercantile and cooking something more elaborate."

Joe noticed right away that she had changed her dress, as well as combed, re-braided, and reset her hair into a new

290

topknot. She looked lovely and refreshed, leaving him feeling like a troll laying in his own filth from four days of sweat, pain, and blood. Suddenly, he was self-conscious of his half-naked state, and when he ran his fingers through his hair out of nerves, he felt how the strands were now standing in clumps around his head. He rubbed his face and felt four days' worth of stubble, noticing for the first time that he was itching something fierce and was dying for a shave. His arms and legs were even still dusty from where he had fallen in the street, and he still had dried blood around on different parts of his body. When he looked up again from discovering his own filthiness, he saw two women looking back at him and he felt bashful.

"Ummm…" he said, "I really need to wash up."

"All right," said Mama D. "We can get you some water boilin'."

"Mama D?" Sarah asked.

"Aye?"

"Will he be strong enough to get in and out of the washtub? Won't he have to use both his arms?"

"Aye, he would have to. That's why we are gonna give him a bed bath."

Both Sarah and Joe's eyes simultaneously opened wide with shock and Mama D had to hold back a burst of laughter.

"You should see your faces!" she chuckled.

"Mama D," Sarah said quietly, "that's not really appropriate, is it? I mean…"

"It is perfectly appropriate for medical purposes, Sarah. We're both here, so that should stem any gossip before it starts."

"I'm not worried about that," she started again. "It's just not… proper!"

"Sarah, you have been married before and had a son with a man, yes?"

"Well, yes. Of course!"

"So, there's no reason to act so pious and coy. As I said the other night, Joe hasn't got anythin' we ain't seen before… lots of times before, right?"

Sarah nodded uncertainly.

"Oh, dear Lord, child. Please don't tell me that your poor, deceased husband was one of those who would only make love in the dark with the sheet pulled up!"

Sarah flushed a deep red, not believing that she was having this conversation. "No!" she answered stiffly.

"So, you have seen a man naked before, have you not?"

"Yes…"

"Let me just tell you, I know most men are extremely proud of their appendages, but…no offense, Joe… take it from me: when you have seen one, you have seen them all! All that changes are the faces and body shapes!"

"Mama D!" Joe interjected, his tone somewhere between amused and utterly humiliated.

"'Tis true, lad. Quit worryin' about somethin' you've got no control over. We are here to help you and help you we will do. You're being ridiculous if you let modesty get in the way of your needs. Now, Sarah, please put that water on!"

By the time the water boiled, Mama D had gotten Joe out of his drawers and pulled the sheet up over his body. He looked so helpless and forlorn as Sarah carried the basin over to his bed that she thought he more resembled a child than a man. Despite his pale face, his cheeks were blazing red, embarrassed once again about not being able to properly care for himself and what that led to.

Sarah had made up her mind that she would attack this task in a detached fashion and together, she and Mama D cleaned off the mud and dried blood that still served as reminders of Joe's recent experience. Mama D thankfully did the scrubbing as Sarah ran back and forth to dump the dirty water and return with new. Eventually, when the rest of him was clean, Mama D handed him the cloth and said, "I think you know what to do, Joe. Can you manage?"

"Yes, ma'am," he mumbled. He lifted the sheet and washed himself before handing the rag back to Mama D, who then handed it to Sarah, saying. "I think we're done here."

"Hey!" Joe exclaimed, "I need a shave desperately!"

"Do we look like barbers, Joe?" Mama D asked him testily.

"No," he answered. "But I need one just the same, and I sure as hell can't do it!" He looked helpless as he gestured to the arm near his wound in a sling to keep it still.

"Well, it has been years since I have had anythin' to do with that particular groomin' habit of a man, so I would cut you to shreds I'm afraid," she answered him. "How about you, Sarah? Have you got any experience shavin' a man?"

A look of sadness passed quickly over Sarah's face. She recalled the times she had cut George's hair and given him a shave. It was always an incredibly intimate time between the two of them as he watched her concentrate on her task, his affection for her boiling over as he felt her tender hands as they lovingly worked. When he couldn't contain himself anymore, he would run his hands over her body, and most of the time the intimacy they shared with that particular task ended with them together naked in their bed.

"Yes," she said quietly. "I can do it, if Joe trusts me."

"Well, as far as I see it, if he wants a shave, he's gonna have to trust you!"

Sarah looked at Joe. "Are you all right with this? Do you trust me to shave you?"

"Sure, if you don't cut me!" he said with a lazy grin.

"I will do my best," Sarah answered. "But honestly, I can make no guarantees. I used to shave my husband every once in a while, but that was a long time ago now…"

Joe saw the sadness clouding her features again and felt the need to say something to make her feel better. "I'm sure it's not something you forget," he told her quietly.

"No, I suppose it's not," she agreed.

Sarah found his shaving kit and began to sharpen his straight edge on the leather strap. Back and forth she traveled until she was sure it was sharp enough, and then she laid it to the side to grab his cup and brush. He laughed as the brush tickled his nose, making Sarah smile. "George used to complain I tickled him, too."

Mama D watched Joe and Sarah as unobtrusively as possible. She observed the emotion flowing between them as Sarah carefully ran the razor across his sensitive skin, while he completely relinquished his fear that she would injure him. She saw how tenderly Sarah touched him and how his eyes followed her every move. It was so incredibly clear to anyone who would have observed them that they were very much drawn to each other, even though neither of them would have ever admitted it.

Sarah felt his eyes on her the entire time, burning through her as she cautiously scraped away the growth of his four days in limbo. She felt an overwhelming sensation of fondness swelling each time she touched his warm skin, close enough to inhale the scent of him, feeling him swallowing hard every once in a while, not knowing he was trying to clear the lump in his throat that had formed with being touched so intimately again for the first time in years. Though she was transported back to the closeness she shared with George while doing this same task, she was surprised when she realized that the longing she was feeling wasn't for him, but for Joe.

Sarah set the razor to the side and grabbed the clean towel. Despite not having done the task for several years and Joe's face being an unfamiliar one, she had not cut him. Quite proud of herself, she raised the towel to wipe away any residual soap but stopped short as she touched around his mouth, her head spinning. Her eyes were drawn to his lips, and she felt herself instinctively bend down for a kiss, as was her habit with her husband before him, but caught herself at the last second when she heard Mama D sneeze in the corner. She quickly backed away, apologizing, and Joe exhaled deeply as he felt, more than saw, her departure, not realizing he had been holding his breath in anticipation.

Sarah, still flustered, took the shaving kit out to the pump as she drew in great deep gulps of frigid air, trying to clear her head. Meanwhile, inside, Mama D looked sternly at Joe.

294

"You *have* to tell her about Caroline!"

"I know!" he sighed, resigned.

"I mean as soon as possible!"

"I will!" he told her testily.

"Joe, I'm not kiddin'! You should see the way you two look at each other. If every man stared at a woman as you gaze at her, I would be out of business."

"I think I love her. But I'm scared."

"Don't be! She loves you, too! I can tell by the way she cares for you."

Joe took a deep, cleansing breath. "All right, Mama. I will. I promise. As soon as the time is right, I will tell Sarah about Caroline."

"Good!" she managed to say just as Sarah came back into the room. Her cheeks were pink from the cold, and she seemed more composed and less distracted. "There!" she said with finality. "All done!"

"Good! Thank you, Sarah! I would have cut him to bits! Now, if you will excuse me, I need to get back to my girls and see if I have a business left! I will see the two of you later this evenin'!"

Joe looked at Sarah, trying to gather his courage. "Sarah…" he began, but then the door opened and in walked the pastor, Jacob, and the mine owner. He shot her a helpless glance, but she already was taking her leave, excusing herself to depart and leaving him in the hands of his friends.

Chapter Thirty-Five

Over the next few days, Joe's determination to let Sarah know about his past began to falter. As he continued to improve, his visitations with other people began to increase and Sarah felt that she wasn't needed as much, so she began to stay away more during the day when he had others with whom to visit.

Dr. Miller stayed at the jail at night for several days, leaving a sign on his office door, letting everyone know where he could be found, but soon, even he felt comfortable enough to leave Joe alone overnight and Joe found himself bored, frustrated, and restless as his solitude increased, but his activity level remained restricted.

Sarah still cooked for him, often just running in with his meals, trying to be as unobtrusive as possible while he had visitors. She was back at work and Adam had returned home to her, so she never stayed long.

Adam began to ask to see Joe. Sarah realized that the episode with his friend had frightened her boy considerably and finally worked up the nerve to ask Joe if he was up to a young visitor. He had agreed and soon Adam was spending every afternoon with him, playing checkers, talking, and a few times, reading a book while the boy lay beside him on the bed.

It was one such evening when Sarah came in with Joe's supper after a long day. Adam was late coming back, frustrating Sarah, as she hoped that her boy wasn't being a burden. As she walked from her store to the jail, she was planning the talking-to she was going to give him about remembering to pay attention to the time and coming home when he was bid.

She marched through the door, ready to bluster, but stopped short when she saw Adam and Joe, laying together on the bed, with *One Hundred and One Arabian Nights* sprawled open on the quilt, and both of them sound asleep. Adam's head was resting on good Joe's shoulder and Joe had his head resting on top of Adam's. She stood and observed them for a long time, not wanting to wake either of them, frustrated that she didn't have a choice.

Sarah walked to the edge of the bed and tried to maneuver under Adam so that she could grab him without disturbing Joe, but when she moved, Joe's eyes opened, and once he focused in on her face, he smiled.

"Hi," he whispered.

"Hi," she said back to him. "Sorry about Adam. I will get him out of the way for you!"

She went again to try to lift the boy, but Joe placed his warm hand on her forearm. "He's fine, Sarah. No rush. Why don't you sit here with us until he wakes?"

"If you're sure?" Sarah asked, uncertain.

"I'm positive," he answered. "To be honest, this feels kind of nice. My younger brother James used to do this all the time. He was six years younger than me, so he loved it when I would read to him, but he could never stay awake for more than a couple of pages."

Sarah studied him for a long moment. "What?" he asked her.

"Nothing. It's just in that all of the years I have known you, I think this is the first time I have ever heard the name of one of your brothers!"

"No!" Joe argued quietly. "That can't be!"

"It is! You have never talked to me about your life before you came here."

Here's my chance, he thought. *Lord give me the strength to get through it!*

"Well, what do you want to know?"

What she really wanted to know was who Caroline was and why he seemed so infatuated with her that he would call for her any time he was semi-conscious, but he had made it abundantly clear that he did not care to discuss that information with her, so she tried a different approach.

"You said that you have brothers. What are their names?"

"The baby is James, like I said. Then Johnathan, then me. Jeremiah is the oldest," he told her.

"That's only four of you. I thought you told me a long time ago you had five boys in your family."

Joe took in a deep breath. "We do," he said flatly.

"Then who's missing?"

"That would be Joshua. He's the one right above me. I don't talk about him much."

"Oh, like Ginny and Jacob's boy!" Sarah exclaimed, noticing the animosity in his voice. "Didn't you get along?"

"We did… when we were younger. Then things changed," he told her vaguely, his eyes clouding over while his expression told Sarah that he wasn't going to divulge much more.

"So, tell me about your mother and father, then!" she said brightly, trying to navigate the conversation to a safer topic.

"My parents came from Tennessee. My pa was a miner there and he married my ma the day she turned sixteen. He had loved her since he had first laid eyes on her when she was twelve and had pursued her ever since. Her mother and father were not pleased, seeing how he was a Catholic and she was a Baptist, but they finally relented when they saw how much he adored her."

"That's sweet!"

"They lived there until my pa started feeling like things were getting unsafe. He was hearing rumblings about the coming war and didn't want to leave his bride to go and fight for a cause he didn't believe in. All he wanted to do was work, not fight. So, he sold everything they had to buy some oxen and a wagon, and then they left to come to California, where they had heard the streets were paved with gold.

"The journey was tough on my ma. As I think I told you before, she was expecting Jeremiah, the oldest, on the trip and my pa had to deliver him with the help of some of the women in the wagon train somewhere in Nevada Territory. It was tough, and she lost a lot of blood, but she made it. She stayed in the back of the wagon with Jeremiah, bouncing all around as they crossed the Sierra Nevadas, until my pa settled at a mine in

298

Placerville. From there, they followed the call of the newest placers or mines until they finally settled in Nevada City."

"I see," Sarah replied, not really following what he was describing, having never been there.

"It's so beautiful there. The mountains are high; almost as high as the Rockies, or so it seems. They are heavily forested with both pine and deciduous trees. The weather is beautiful most of the year, though depending on the elevation, winters can be tough. But it was a great place for five little boys to grow up."

"Did you go to school?" Sarah asked.

"Off and on, sure. My ma also taught us whenever we moved to a new place if there wasn't a school already set up, which was often. She taught us to read, write, and do arithmetic. She was often one of very few wives. There were women around, but most of them… Well, most of them were more along the lines of Mama D and her girls than respectable ladies. But my ma was a saint and treated everyone kindly, so she always had a lot of women from every walk of life wanting to associate with her."

Joe inhaled deeply before continuing. "Which served us all well when she got sick."

"I'm sorry your mother got sick."

"She had cancer, the doctor said. But I tell you, there wasn't a woman in town, whether it was the preacher's wife or the girls in the saloons, who didn't make sure that there was always warm food on our table, clean clothes on our backs, and that our house was spotless.

"By the time she died, most of us boys were grown, working with my pa in the mines, but James was still home, trying to learn. I'm sad to say he was not blessed with getting as good an education as we were because Ma was so sick for a few years before she passed. But he's amazing with his hands and can fix anything, so he can always get a good job fixing equipment at any mine he wants."

"And your brothers?" Sarah carefully inquired. "Are any of them married?"

Joe was silent for a few moments, thinking about how he wanted to approach this. Finally, he nodded. "Yes, a few of them are," he answered. "It's hard there, though, with a shortage of eligible women."

"Which ones of them are?" she ventured, testing how comfortable he was now about sharing personal information with her.

"Jeremiah married a sweet Mexican girl from down in the valley. He met her on a supply trip to Sacramento and he was a goner. Her father owns a ranch there and he has given up mining for good."

"And Jonathan?"

"Yes, he's also married. He actually advertised for a wife in a newspaper back East, and surprisingly, he got very lucky. She's a nice girl with an adventuresome spirit, obviously, and she keeps him in line."

"Either of them have any children?"

"Yes, Jeremiah has several, and Jonathan just has two."

"And what about James?" she asked, pushing just a little further.

"No, he's not married. He's still enjoying the bachelor life. He drinks too much and plays too much poker sometimes, but he's happy and content living with Pa, and it keeps them both from getting too lonely."

"And Joshua?" she finally inquired, knowing that he might not want to talk about the brother he already had expressed he disliked.

Joe didn't speak for a long time, wondering how to broach the uncomfortable subject. Eventually, he looked up and caught her eye. "Yes, he's married, too," he murmured quietly.

"Her name is Caroline," he added, almost as an afterthought.

Sarah was so shocked she didn't know what to say. She couldn't believe that the woman who seemed to torment Joe so much was actually his brother's wife! Everything she thought about him being a decent man seemed to fly out of her head all

300

at once, as she gaped at him, wondering how in the world he could justify longing for someone who was already taken by his own flesh and blood.

"I see the look on your face, Sarah," Joe said softly. "It isn't what you think…"

"No?" she asked, her confusion great.

"No!" he countered firmly. "Not at all."

"Well, that's good, I suppose, because it would be an awful thing indeed if you desired your own brother's wife!"

"I know that," he retorted hotly, but then didn't elaborate.

He saw the way her eyebrows raised in question before she asked, "Do you?"

"Yes, I know because my brother desired my fiancée."

"I'm sorry?" Sarah stuttered, her thoughts trying to shift in a direction she hadn't thought to go.

"Caroline was my fiancée."

"What?" Sarah cried.

"She was my fiancée," he repeated. "I had asked her to marry me right before Ma died. She agreed."

When Sarah didn't say anything, he continued. "We were going to get married quickly, hoping that Ma could see it. But a few days before the wedding, I caught them," he finished.

"Caught them?" Sarah asked, confused.

"Yes," he told her flatly. "I caught them in my bed. Our bed. In the home we were going to share after the wedding. It wasn't much, but it was a little cabin in the woods, not far from the mine, and we would have been on our own."

"Oh, Joe!" Sarah exclaimed sadly.

Her pity bolstered something in him to explain further. "She thought I had gone to work that morning, but I had in fact gone to see my friend who was making her ring for me. When I came back to the house, I heard something, and when I glanced at the bed, there they were… frozen in place in a very…" he paused and cleared his throat before continuing, "compromising… position."

"I…" Sarah began but couldn't continue for a long time. Finally, when she spoke, it was in utter disbelief. "I'm sorry, Joe! I don't even know what to say!"

"Yeah… That was pretty much how I felt, too," he told her with a wry smile.

Getting caught up in the story, she asked, "What did you do?"

"I turned around and walked out," he answered. "I don't know for how long I wandered, not able to do anything else. But when I came home, she was on the front step, waiting for me. She cried and apologized but explained she had thought all along that Joshua 'had been a better prospect.' So, she explained that she had wanted to break off the engagement with me in order to marry him for a long time, but that because she had felt sorry for me, she didn't know how."

"Oh, my Lord!" Sarah said, her heart breaking for the man before her. She couldn't believe that someone would actually think that Joe didn't have potential.

"I found out some time later from my brother Jonathan that it had been going on for quite some time and she actually was already pregnant with his child."

"What?" Sarah cried, horrified.

"Oh, yes! Here I had tried so hard to treat her like a lady, only to find out that she had been kicking up her heels with my brother for at least a month before that day," he grimaced in shame and humiliation. "I could have raised my nephew thinking he was mine for God knows how long if I hadn't discovered them."

"I can't believe that she was that deceitful. I'm so sorry! How did you meet her?"

"Her father was one of the superintendents at the mine. He tended to oversee my shift and we became quite close. It was just Caroline and her father. Her mother had passed when she was five, so her father had packed up his two daughters—Caroline had a younger sister who died of cholera on the way to California—and moved West.

"She was his pride and joy," Joe continued. "She was beautiful and intelligent- everything that a man could ever hope to find in a woman, especially in a place where the pickings were slim. You should have seen her, Sarah... she was simply gorgeous. Long red hair, pretty, green eyed, and so tiny and petite, it seemed like she would break in two if you hugged her too hard. But her father kept a tight hold on her and it was only because I was her father's favorite employee that I had an edge."

Joe glanced up and caught Sarah's eyes. She smiled grimly at him, unable to find the words to describe the disgust and anger she felt that someone had treated him so poorly. Finally, she took a breath. "Joe, I don't know what I could even say in an attempt to make you feel better about what happened. But I have to know: is your brother really that much more successful than you?"

"No," he answered. "Not in the mine, at least. But he's a gambler. He has always been good at cards and cleans up pretty well. Consequently, he had more money to flash around than I did, because I scrimped and saved. I had always wanted a nice little house for myself, and maybe, someday even a wife and family."

"Did you... Did you ever find out what attracted her to Joshua and away from you?"

"Oh, yes. It was the money, for sure. I later found out that he had been buying her things with his winnings; jewelry, clothing, hats... You name it. I thought that she loved me, but unfortunately, all she really wanted was the person with the deepest pockets."

"But what about love?" Sarah asked. "Didn't she love you? Did she love Joshua?"

Joe wouldn't look up at her for the longest time and Sarah thought she had pushed him too far, so he surprised her when he answered quietly.

"I really thought she did love me. But seeing what she was doing with him... Well, let's just say that it was abundantly clear that she loved him more."

"Why do you say that?"

"Because she never did those things with me," he answered quietly. His cheeks were flushed with anger or embarrassment; she couldn't tell which.

Sarah nodded her understanding. "Did you ever… try?" she asked him, wondering if he would still be willing to answer.

"No, not really."

"Oh."

"I mean, of course, I would kiss her goodnight. Chaste, respectful kisses. We shared more intimate kisses once I asked her to marry me, but never anything even remotely close to what I caught them doing. But I never would have asked that of her, either."

"What made your brother ask her, then?"

"That's just it. I don't know if he did. I think that she simply believed she loved him more."

Joe looked utterly dejected, and it broke Sarah's heart to see his expression so miserable and sad. She clasped his hand in hers.

"He always was the one who won. In everything. He has always been just a little bit faster, smarter, and better looking than me. I guess I shouldn't have been surprised that the love of my life would think the same thing. To be honest, I don't blame her. Why would she want me when she could have him?"

"Joe…"

"It's all right, though. Truly, it's fine. So, I left California and came here. I couldn't bear to be around them, and I knew that if I stayed, I would either kill him or beg her to come back to me, and I wasn't willing to do either. So, I went as far away from them as I could and still do what I knew. My ma had passed, and Pa wasn't much of a family man. He worked hard and provided well for us, but he spent so much time underground that it was my ma who raised us and made us a family. He understood, though, that I needed to make my own way in the world."

"Does your father know what happened?"

"I don't know. I never told him the full story. I just told him that Caroline and I broke it off and he said that I needed to get far away from there. I didn't tell him everything, because, crazily enough, even after what they did to me, I still didn't want to ruin her reputation, not to mention, he was still my brother. The easiest, safest thing to do for everyone involved was for me to leave town."

"Oh, Joe! I'm so sorry!"

"I don't want your pity!" Joe answered her harshly. "That's why I make it a habit not to tell anyone. I feel bad enough already. I don't need people feeling sorry for me, too. I have a good life here and have made many good friends. I decided a long time ago that I'm obviously not the marrying kind and made my peace with it. Then, when I got voted in as sheriff, it became very clear why I wasn't supposed to marry. As you can see, this is a tough job, and it is expecting a lot to put a woman through this."

"Not all women are like Caroline," Sarah stated quietly.

"I know. But I'm glad that it happened before I got this job. After watching everything you have gone through after your husband's death, I'm happy that I don't have to worry about leaving a widow and children behind should the next bullet have better aim! Everything happens for a reason."

Sarah felt her blood beginning to boil by that point. She knew Joe was hurt and that she shouldn't press him, but she couldn't contain her anger at his last statement.

"I'm glad that you have reconciled the reasoning behind your tragedy, but what is the reason behind mine?"

"What?" he asked her, slightly taken aback by the sudden ferocity in her voice.

"Please! Tell me! What is the reason why I became a widow at twenty-two years old? Please explain the rationale behind why I was left all alone with a small child and kicked out of my house and off my land. Because I'm a woman, I had no rights to either of them, so my only option was to come out West and accept charity from my sister, her husband, and even you!"

"Me?"

"Yes, *you*, Joe McIntyre! Don't pretend that you don't know what I'm talking about! I *know* that you told every man in town to bring me their clothing to repair before I went home! I also know that you have been paying a much higher rent on this building every month than the amount you told me!"

Joe blushed, while looking down at his hands in his lap.

"I was only trying to help!" he countered.

"I know. But honestly, I don't believe that everything happens for a reason, because I can't think of one good reason that my husband died and left me all alone to fend for myself and our child!"

Tears were running down Sarah's face and Joe felt awful. He had never meant to insinuate that there was anything positive in her situation. In fact, as far as he could tell, she felt her life had essentially ended the day her husband died. She was making a good show of trying to survive, but he could tell that it had been a huge drain on her to be left in the position she was, and he had no explanation why she should have to struggle so much at such a young age.

"Sarah, I'm sorry. I only meant in my situation things happened for a reason. I never intended to make it seem like I feel the same way about every situation."

Sarah nodded and sniffed. "I'm sorry, too. I'm sorry that I snapped at you. I just… I just… still get so lonely without my husband. His death has absolutely been a struggle for me, not only financially, but also having to raise Adam on my own. But I feel like I am finally making some progress on both fronts and things are normalizing a bit. I still don't like it, but I have done it. Being lonely, though? That's something that I can't fix on my own."

"I'm sorry you're lonely," Joe whispered. He wondered again if … maybe… Then he thought better of it. Women equaled heartbreak and there was no use upsetting the proverbial apple cart. Things were settled. He was happy with his life, he loved his job, his community, and his friends. He told himself that it made no sense to add a bunch of unnecessary drama or pain into his life only because he felt sorry for her and could commiserate with her loneliness.

"It's all right," Sarah said, suddenly straightening up in her chair and wiping her eyes. "I have Adam to raise, and I hope that eventually he will even give me a grandchild or two. I guess there are worse things than living on my own for the rest of my life. At least I can say that I have been in love. I may die alone, but at least I wasn't a spinster!"

Joe once again felt completely clueless on what to say in response that would be at all comforting. He had always felt awkward around women, as if he were emotionally stunted, even before the debacle with Joshua and Caroline. He hadn't been kidding when he told Sarah that Joshua was better than him in everything. Joe was smart. Joshua was smarter. Joe was quick. Joshua was quicker. Joe was shy. Joshua was engaging and outgoing. When he was honest with himself, he could see immediately why someone like Caroline would be more attracted to Joshua than to him. What galled him was that his brother had been so disrespectful and hurtful when he pursued the one woman he knew Joe loved.

Joe's mother had lived about another two months after the whole fiasco. She had tried to talk to Joshua and explain why what he had done was wrong, but he refused to see it. Meanwhile, in the weeks following the discovery of his fiancée and brother, Joe contemplated leaving. His mother had understood his need to go as much as his father had later, but knowing she was dying, she had written a letter to him, asking him to forgive Joshua; that blood was thicker than water. Joe had tried on multiple occasions to pray for forgiveness, but so far, it had eluded him. His mother's dying wish was that her boys would reconcile, but alas, the one thing she had desperately wanted before departing from this earth, he was unable to give her.

Jonathan was the brother with whom Joe kept in most regular contact and he had written Joe several letters in the years since he had packed his bags and moved to Colorado. Joe knew that apart from his nephew, he also had a young niece from Caroline's and Joshua's union. He was cognizant that he should not take his anger and hurt out on their children, so he tried hard to find enough forgiveness to allow him to send small trinkets to them at Christmas, because he was determined not to favor his other nieces and nephews with gifts, only to ignore their two children.

Nevertheless, he always got angry with himself regarding the time he took to pick out what he would send them. With his other nieces and nephews, he quickly made or purchased what he thought they would like. With Caroline and Joshua's offspring, however, nothing he could make seemed adequate enough, so he stood in the mercantile and contemplated for what seemed like hours, trying to make sure that he bought appropriate and tasteful presents, but nothing as extravagant as a father would purchase for his children.

He had never gotten an acknowledgment for what he sent, but he did learn through his brother's letters that the gifts were well received by the children and that Caroline and Joshua marveled every year that despite everything that had happened, he still had the grace to include their little ones. Their own guilt about what they did to him made it unfathomable to them that he would be willing to be so generous. In one letter, Jonathan had written that Joshua had recently remarked over a few glasses of shared whiskey that Joe was a decent man, and he was grateful that he did not hold a grudge against the smallest players in their elaborate game.

Sarah and Joe sat in silence for quite a while, each lost in their own thoughts. Eventually, Adam stirred and raised his head a bit. When he saw Joe, he smiled and put his head back down, content and happy, but Sarah took it as the sign that it was time for them to leave. She took the boy in her arms and lifted him up, almost buckling under the weight of him. For the millionth time, she wished that George was still there to offer his assistance. Taking care of a child all by herself was sometimes a heavy burden to bear, literally. Seeing the expression that passed over her face, Joe sadly commented, "I'm sorry I can't help you carry him home, Sarah."

"It's all right. We will be fine."

She took a few steps and had to rearrange him, while Joe helplessly watched her.

"Are you sure you've got him?"

"No, but what choice do I have?" she retorted, and he heard the weariness in her voice.

He said nothing as he watched them walk out. As he heard the click of the door closing behind them, he said quietly, "What choice do any of us have, really?"

Chapter Thirty-Six

Joe continued to heal, though more slowly than he would have liked through the next few weeks. Though his arm was weaker on that side, he was feeling like he was beginning to see the light at the end of the tunnel. His greatest fear was that he was not going to be able to resume his position as the town sheriff and was surprised at the level of sadness it brought him. He hadn't wanted the job; it had never even been something he had considered before that fateful day when the men in town decided he was the best man for it, despite his objections. So, he was surprised to find now, when faced with the possibility he may not recover completely enough to resume his duties, that he couldn't entertain the thought of doing anything else.

He knew that he could always return to mining, but now that he had been able to walk outdoors in the fresh mountain air and talk to everyone he met, he never wanted to be trapped underground like a rat again.

Jacob had come to visit him one day, and Joe had worked up the nerve to ask him if there were any positions with the railroad for him if he didn't recover full use of his arm. Jacob had been kind in telling him that there wasn't really anything in town, but that he could check in Colorado Springs and other larger areas if it came to that. However, Jacob, like everyone else in town, didn't want to consider that possibility at all. Joe was the sheriff, and there was no one better to take his place.

Sarah and Mama D, meanwhile, made him laugh. They carried on like a couple of riled up hens, fussing excessively over him. His stomach never had a chance to even rumble because Sarah kept him so full, and Mama D came to check on him most mornings under the guise of "keepin' him company" between when her girls were done for the night, and her being ready to sleep.

As Joe continued to improve day by day, he became increasingly aware that Sarah was looking done in. She was holding down her storefront, making him three hearty meals a day, and caring for Adam. The exhaustion was visible in the circles darkening the delicate, pale skin beneath her eyes. She never smiled anymore: in fact, it seemed to Joe that she had lost her sparkle. He tried to speak with her about his concerns, but she would blow him off and reassure him that she was fine.

Then, one day, she wasn't. Joe sat up in his bed, wondering, selfishly, where his breakfast was. He had become so accustomed to Sarah's meals and the company that came with them that he lay and waited in anticipation for her for the better part of an hour before he finally rose and got dressed. He then sat in the chair beside his bed for another twenty minutes until he really began to worry that something was wrong. It wasn't like Sarah to not follow through on a commitment.

He went to the back door of her store and found it locked, so he took the spare key he had for the place and opened it. Looking around, he noticed that nothing was amiss, per se, except for the fact that the room was still dark and quiet. Suddenly, fearing the worst, he quickly ran up the stairs. When he entered the apartment, he was surprised to see Sarah and Adam still sleeping together in the bed. His concern continued to grow as the hour was now almost seven-thirty, and Sarah never slumbered so late in the mornings. Ever.

Joe crept forward, lightly touching Sarah's head. She was burning up, and Joe pulled his hand back quickly. He then did the same to Adam and was disheartened to discover that he was in the same state as his mother.

Moving to the stove, he struggled to open the door and put the wood in with his one good arm, all his earlier joy regarding how his healing was progressing quickly leaving him. He looked back toward the bed and was dismayed to see that neither Sarah nor Adam had even stirred, though he certainly hadn't been quiet as he banged things around. Once the fire was started, he filled the teakettle with fresh water, then set it to boil.

When all the morning chores were done, he walked to the table and sat down, just watching the two of them, praying for some sort of sign that they were not as sick as he thought they were, but to no avail. It wasn't until Joe had made a pot of tea and brought the cup to Sarah that she finally opened her eyes.

"What are you doing here?" she rasped.

"I got concerned when you didn't come by the jail today. It isn't like you!"

"Oh!" she exclaimed, trying to rise out of bed, but she was so weakened with fever that she quickly collapsed back against the mattress. "I'm so sorry, Joe! I didn't mean to be late with your breakfast!"

"Sarah, it's fine! You're the one I'm worried about. Where don't you feel well?"

"I'm not sure, exactly… My throat hurts, and I'm achy. I have a terrible headache, as well!"

"And Adam?"

Sarah looked over to her side and saw her sleeping son. She looked perplexed that he was there in that state, so she said, "I'm not sure! He was incredibly difficult last night. He was throwing a tantrum, crying, and being extremely clingy. I thought it was strange, but just assumed he was overtired from playing with friends."

"I bet he has caught whatever you have."

Sarah merely nodded at him, thinking of what to say, but speaking seemed entirely too strenuous at that moment.

"I have made you some tea. I'm sorry that I'm not much more help than that," he said while pointing to the sling that kept his arm immobilized. "I will try to find Doc to get him to stop in and take a look at you, and then I can hopefully get Ginny or Mama D to come in to cook."

"Thanks, Joe," Sarah whispered.

"No problem," he said with a quick grin. "What's that they always say? 'Turnabout is fair play?'"

He placed a cup of tea, laced heavily with honey on the small bedside table. When she took a drink, her eyes opened wide.

He chuckled slightly before saying, "My ma always told us that honey is best for a sore throat."

She looked up at him and whispered, "Did you forget to add the tea?"

He smiled bashfully. "I guess she never did tell me exactly how much to add to a cup. Too much?"

"A little."

"Well, choke down what you can, and then I will add more tea."

She drank about half of the cup before he refilled it and placed it beside her again.

"Better?' he asked once she had taken another drink. She nodded.

"Just rest, Sarah. Let me handle everything. I will make sure you're taken care of."

She settled back in the pillows and closed her eyes. He gently grabbed the blankets and pulled them tight around both her and Adam, tucking them in thoroughly.

The next thing Sarah knew, Adam was crying for water. She tried to get him to go back to sleep because the idea of getting out of bed seemed impossible. However, as he continued to lay there whimpering, she decided that she would have to steel herself to the task in order to bring him relief. When she rose out of the bed, the room began to spin as the floor felt like it was tipping. She struggled to the water pump and sink, only able to manage two thrusts before weakness and exhaustion overcame her. Nonetheless, her exertion yielded half a cup, and she figured that Adam would just have to make do. She somehow made it back across the room to her bed, praying to God the whole way to give her strength. Plopping down beside Adam, he managed to sit up just enough to take a drink. When his thirst was seemingly quenched, she collapsed down beside him, shivering convulsively despite her nightgown sticking to her sweaty body from just the effort of crossing the floor and back.

Sometime before noon, Joe accompanied the doctor to Sarah's room. He took one look at them both and ordered, "You need to stay away, Joe. I think that they are both very ill and in your already weakened state, I'm afraid that you may get it, too."

"Nah, Doc. I'll be fine. I only seem to get hurt, not sick," he added with a smile.

"Joe…" the doctor warned.

"No! Truly, Doc. I only got sick four times in my entire life. My brothers would all come down with something, and I never did."

"Well, then, just stay back and wash your hands well when you leave here, all right?"

"Fine!"

Dr. Miller started with examining Adam. He determined that the boy was ill, but didn't seem desperately so, and thought that with a few days' rest and plenty of fluids, he would be able to pull through just fine.

Sarah, however, was a very different story. After looking over her, he turned to Joe.

"This is bad, Joe."

"Why? What do you think it is?"

"I think that she has scarlet fever."

"And?"

"Haven't you ever known anyone who got it?"

"No," Joe answered, becoming more concerned. "Why do you think that's what she has?"

"Look here. Do you see the red rash starting?" he asked, pointing to the part of Sarah's chest that was exposed above her nightdress.

"And here," he added, pointing to her throat. "See those red lines in the creases of her neck?"

Dr. Miller looked to Joe, who nodded that he also saw what the doctor was referencing.

314

"It doesn't look promising. Thankfully, Adam doesn't have any of the same symptoms, but we will watch him closely."

"Is there anything you can do for her?" Joe asked, worry evident in his voice and expression.

"I can keep her fever down and make her more comfortable, but other than that, no. There has been some experimentation with the use of belladonna to prevent scarlet fever, but the studies haven't been too promising. At this point, the best thing we can do is to keep her hydrated and comfortable."

"So, who is going to stay with them? She's in no condition to be on her own."

"I was just thinking that. I can stay here when I don't have patients. I would ask Ginny, except with her little ones, I don't want to risk her getting exposed and bringing it home to her brood."

"How about Mama?" Joe asked.

"I will have to speak with her, but she might be a good choice."

"I can help, too!" Joe said resolutely.

"No, Joe, really, you can't. We can't risk you getting sick so soon after your little adventure. You're still weakened from blood loss and infection. You really shouldn't even be in here right now."

"But…"

"I know you want to help her, but I am advising you as a doctor, stay away. We can't have you catching this. She's a healthy young woman, and I'm worried. You are not healthy right now, Joe."

"Doc…" Joe tried to object again.

"Truly, the best thing you can do right now is go to Mama's and ask her if she would be willing to sit with them when I can't. I really need to think about hiring a nurse!"

The next few days passed in a blur. Adam, true to Dr. Miller's prognosis, got better slowly, but Sarah was another story. Dr. Miller tried everything at his disposal that he thought might have even the slightest ability to help but to no avail.

Mama D stayed with Sarah and Adam as much as possible, caring for them throughout the nights.

Dr. Miller was not one to easily admit defeat, and he didn't want to give up hope, but as the situation became dire and Sarah's case of scarlet fever progressed to rheumatic fever, he felt panicky. He called a meeting while his patient slept with Mama D, Ginny, Jacob, and Joe the morning after an exhausting night of Sarah vomiting and battling a high fever.

They all met at the jail, and the worry of the situation was deeply etched into everyone's faces. Dr. Miller looked around and jumped right in.

"Things do not look promising right now. I've done everything I can for Sarah, but she's still going downhill. We need to talk about a plan if…" He couldn't bring himself to say the words. Instead, he glanced around the room and saw four equally stricken faces.

"If what, Doc?" Joe asked insistently.

"If… the inevitable happens."

"What kind of plan?"

"I mean that we have to make a decision about what to do with the boy both in the short-term and the long-term."

"What do you mean, Dr. Miller?" Ginny broke in, fear evident in her voice.

"I mean we need to plan on what to do with Adam. Even if Sarah gets better, and at this point, I'd say that's a pretty big if, she still is going to take months to fully recover."

He stopped to take a deep breath, unable to look at any of them, and then continued. "In other words, we need someone to take Adam regardless. Of course, we need to decide who will take him in case of her demise, but also while she recovers if she pulls through, God willing. Her convalescence will be long and hard, and taking care of a child will not make it any easier."

"Do you actually believe she is going to die?" Ginny moaned, her eyes wide in shock.

316

"Sadly, I do. I am so sorry. I'm out of ideas. There is nothing left to try. But Adam is better. So, what do we do with the boy if she passes?"

"Well, of course, Jacob and I will take him!" Ginny exclaimed.

"I figured that's what will happen in the long-term if she passes, but it can't happen for a while yet. I don't want him around your children right now. They're too young, and if they catch this, especially the baby, I don't think they would have any better chance of a good outcome than Sarah is facing."

"I suppose you're right..."

"So, what do we do in the meantime?"

"Well, I can't very well take him to work with me, now can I?" asked Mama D. "I know that Sarah is a wonderful and carin' woman who doesn't judge, but I still can't imagine she would want her little boy livin' in a whorehouse above a saloon indefinitely."

"That's certain!" Ginny added quickly without thinking.

Joe broke into the conversation. "I'll take Adam for the short-term."

"Joe, we already talked about this..."

"I know, Doc. But what other choice do we have? Mrs. McAllister's children can't get sick, and Mama D can't take him. Are you willing to take him?" he asked the doctor, working on a hunch, pinning him down with his eyes.

"No!" the man said too abruptly.

Dr. Miller saw four pairs of eyes dart to him, questioning his emphatic response. "I know nothing about children!" he declared defensively. "I was an only child. I have no idea what I would do with the lad. Plus, I'm out on calls every hour of the night and day. I can't very well drag a tot around with me."

"That's true enough... Can we send him to his grandparents?" Mama D asked.

"My parents would love to have him, I'm sure, but there are two problems I can think of," Ginny said thoughtfully. "First, how do we get him there? I know he can, of course, take the train, but we can't very well send a six-year-old halfway across the country on his own!"

"No, that's a fact!" Jacob agreed.

"Doc, you can't take him because you are needed here, Jacob can't just decide to not work, Mama has to run her business, and I can't take him by myself, not only for my safety but because who then would watch our children? Joe, you're injured…"

"I can still ride a train, for goodness' sake!" Joe exclaimed.

"But…" Ginny continued, ignoring Joe's outburst. "None of that matters because getting him there is the least of our problems. Sarah's husband George's parents will take him, and I know she would not want him to live with them! They threatened to take Adam away from her when she went home last time, and that's why she came back here so abruptly."

"But she's the mother! How could they have taken him away from her? How can they decide where he should live? By law…" Mama D started to argue.

"Her husband's parents are very close with the judge in town. They aren't particularly wealthy people, but they are a long-time established family in the area and are highly respected. My parents wouldn't have the means to fight a battle in court they most likely wouldn't win, anyway, with the judge on George's family's side."

"Joe, can they do that?" Mama D asked in disbelief. "She's the boy's mother! How is that possible?"

"Mama, as much as I would like to say that justice is blind, I have learned that many times it is not. It can often be greedy, as well as self-serving. I wish it weren't so, but people often get what they want because they have money or know the right people. If Sarah is gone, then custody goes to next of kin, and the kin with the highest influence will win that fight. Always!"

"So, where does that leave us, then?" Mama D interjected.

No one said a word for what felt like forever. Finally, Joe spoke with authority. "I'll take the boy for now. Then, we'll just wait and see how Sarah does. If she recovers, then it will be

318

irrelevant, anyway, as he will be returned to her. If she doesn't…" He stopped, unable to complete the sentence, unwilling to accept a world without Sarah in it.

He took a deep breath to regroup before continuing, "If she doesn't, then we will have to reevaluate."

"Poor little fellow!" Mama D exclaimed, her voice dripping in empathy. "I can't even imagine what it would be like to lose both parents before even bein' old enough to go to school. All alone in the world!"

"He won't be all alone!" Joe answered stoutly. "We will all be here for him! If that happens…"

"I know. But I know how it feels to lose all of one's kin. 'Tis not a pleasant experience for an adult. I can't imagine how bad it would be as a helpless child!"

It was decided that Joe would keep Adam with him for the next several days while everyone waited with bated breath to see if Sarah would get better. The little boy was still not entirely recovered, but Joe welcomed the more subdued behavior than normal because he quickly realized that caring for a young child full-time was hard work, especially with a useless, injured arm. He thought many times a day about how much he admired Sarah for all she handled on her own without complaint, and resolved that if she recovered, he would swallow his pride and do more to help her with the boy.

As he collapsed exhaustedly into bed every night, his shoulder still aching slightly with the increased activity, he wondered how Sarah did it. She never complained, but there had to have been days when she was feeling too overwhelmed to want to do anything other than crawl back into bed. Yet she kept going because she had no other option, no one else to fall back on. Of course, Joe knew that he, as well as her sister, had helped care for Adam for brief periods, but he had no idea how she managed on a daily basis with no one else to rely on, having to work, clean, and cook meals, as well as keep the boy occupied and out of trouble.

At bedtime, he wondered if he would be able to keep it up. Then, Adam's warm little body would inevitably seek out the warmth radiating from his own, and he would scoot closer to Joe, surprising him with the overwhelming affection he felt for the boy. The need to protect him from everything bad in the world was overpowering. He thought back to his own father, truly realizing for the first time how much he had done for his sons, and Joe was hit with the realization that he cared more about the boy than he had ever thought possible for any child, but especially one who was not of his own flesh and blood.

Meanwhile, Dr. Miller tried everything he could think of to help her recover, but Sarah continued to hover between life and death until finally he could only hope that the tincture of time would be the best medicine for her. It killed him that he could do nothing more for her. Even though he no longer pursued her because of his own emotional baggage, it didn't mean that he cared any less for her.

Many times, when the doctor or Mama D would be with her, Sarah seemed extremely agitated, but they had no idea what was affecting her feverish mind. She dreamed often of George's parents coming to Colorado and taking Adam while she lay too weak and ill to do anything about it, and would watch helplessly as they took her son, her last connection to George, out her door. Sometimes she would see Joe, Mama D, or the doctor, and even sometimes Ginny, in her delirious fog, but none of them would intervene on her behalf, while she screamed out in protest that only fell on deaf ears. She would thrash and cry, wondering why everyone she thought cared for her would abandon her so completely in her time of need.

One particularly grueling night Mama D and Dr. Miller both worked themselves to the bone. The doctor thought Sarah was past saving and found himself praying and begging a God he wasn't even sure he believed in to save the young woman, surprising himself that in his desperation he turned to faith over science. He watched helplessly as her fever raged and it seemed as if her body had begun to shut down in preparation to depart from the world.

Sarah, however, was completely unaware of the turmoil happening within her, thrilled that her nightmares had come to an end, and she was instead spending time with George, feeling his comforting presence. Somewhere in the back of her mind, she wondered why he was with her if he was dead and she wasn't, but his company was too soothing for her to want to leave him.

She had no idea how long they were together, eventually realizing they were not even speaking, but it didn't bother her: his company was enough. When he did finally speak, she was shocked back to a place of consciousness that disturbed the immense peace she felt, and it irritated her as much as his words did.

"Sarah, sweetheart, it's time to go back."

"No!" she cried. "I want to stay here with you!"

"Sarah, listen to me. It's not your time to be here yet. You're needed back. Our son needs you. As much as I would love to have you with me, Adam needs you too much for you to stay here with me."

"But George!" she cried. "I love you! I don't want to lose you again."

"You will never lose me, darling, but you do not belong here yet. It is time to go back. Your body and mind have rested, and now you have to return to finish your work. I will be here. I'm not going anywhere. I will wait forever for you. But our son needs you, so I have to let you go, even though I don't want you to."

Sarah watched as his presence seemed to move slowly away from her and she began to cry. She had felt incredibly calm and at peace with him, which made her reluctant return to consciousness seem all the crueler. As she became more aware of her surroundings, she felt as though her earthly body was betraying her, with everything aching and hurting. Her heartbeat was rapid with fever, and someone kept wiping her down with a cool cloth. She tried to deny that George was drifting further and further away, unwilling to accept she would not be allowed to stay with him until he was gone completely.

When she opened her eyes, she saw both Dr. Miller and Mama D staring down at her, their faces drawn and weary.

"What happened?" she croaked out, her voice sounding far away to her own ears.

"You, my dear, have been a very ill woman!" Dr. Miller answered, the relief that she was doing better apparent in his voice.

"Where's Adam?" she asked in a panic, trying to sit up, but finding herself too weak to do so.

Dr. Miller quickly placed his hand on her shoulder, "Sarah, relax! He's with Joe. He's fine."

"Joe has him?" she asked.

"Yes. He's had him for over a week now."

"Oh, thank God!" Sarah exclaimed, relief flowing over her like a river. "I thought they had taken him."

"Who?" Dr. Miller asked.

"My in-laws," Sarah told him. "I kept dreaming they came, and no one would stop them!"

Mama D could tell she was getting agitated, so she hoped to reassure her. "He's fine, Sarah, I promise. I've been checkin' in on them every day since Joe is still healin'. The boy has probably eaten more pancakes than most people eat in their entire lives, but other than that, he's just fine."

"Joe's been well enough to take care of him?"

"He's fine, Sarah! Stop worryin'! That's what friends do: we help each other out when we can. You need to continue to get better!"

For three more days, Sarah was asleep more than awake. She felt as though she had walked a thousand miles and couldn't keep her eyes open,

On the afternoon of the third day, after the doctor had listened to her heart, he stood up to put his stethoscope away. "I don't know how you managed, Sarah, but you seem to have come out of this completely unscathed. Your heart is perfect, which was my biggest concern. But everything else seems to be in order, as well. You are a lucky, lucky woman!”

“Well, I guess it had to be my turn for some good luck eventually,” she retorted, trying to keep the emotion out of her voice, when they heard clattering up the stairs.

They turned to look just as Adam burst through the door, Joe closely behind him. The boy slowed to a stop when he saw his mother looking so haggard and weak, and appeared frightened. Needing some reassurance, he melted into Joe. Joe reached down to put a large hand on his shoulder, gently nudging him forward as he leaned down to tell him, “Come on, Adam. Mama’s not going to bite you! Get on up there and give her a big hug and kiss. She’s missed you, I know!”

Adam hung back, still clinging to Joe’s side.

“Come here, my sweet boy,” Sarah told him, opening her arms. Adam looked up at Joe for assurance, which came in the form of a nod, and then ran to his mother, flinging himself into her arms, his tears streaming down his face.

“Shhh…” Sarah cooed as she petted his hair. “I’m right here, son. I’m all right. Did you have fun with Sheriff Joe?”

“Yes,” the boy whimpered.

“Good!” Sarah exclaimed. “In a few days when I’m all better, you can tell me all about it, all right?”

“Yes, Mama.”

Sarah continued to hold her boy close to her as she looked up over his head at Joe. She waited until she caught his eye and then mouthed, “Thank you!” to him. He merely nodded his head.

Dr. Miller watched the whole exchange, fascinated by the easy warmth that existed between the three of them. Joe made accepting Adam look so easy. He didn’t seem to care at all that Adam was another man’s child and even seemed to enjoy spending time with him. The doctor envied how the little boy looked to Joe as someone to rely on. It was obvious that they had a strong bond. With a pang of disappointment, he realized Sarah had been right to call things off between them. Joe was the father figure that Adam needed with seemingly no effort at all.

"I will be off now, then," he said. "Continue to rest, Sarah. Your body has been through a lot, and it still has a long way to go until you have fully recuperated."

"Yes, Dr. Miller," she agreed. "Thank you for taking such good care of me!"

He smiled gently. "My pleasure," he said as he gathered up his bag. Then, as an afterthought, he turned and said sternly, "That means you don't stay too long, either, Joe."

"We won't, Doc, don't worry."

Dr. Miller walked to the head of the stairs when it hit him that Joe had said "we", making it sound as if Adam belonged to him, and felt another jolt of jealousy rip through him. Nevertheless, he also knew he wasn't capable of being what Sarah needed in her life but cared enough for her to realize that she deserved to be happy with someone who could freely accept everything about her. Even still, to accept that he would never be the man she needed and walk away in that moment was the hardest thing he had ever had to do.

Chapter Thirty-Seven

Sarah was still weak, easily fatigued, and her bones ached when she had spent all day in her shop, but she was finally back to a full day's work within a few weeks' time. Adam had come home to her as soon as she was able to care for herself and Dr. Miller had finally stopped continually checking for any lasting effects of the illness on her heart or kidneys. He still marveled that even with how sick she had been she seemed to have recovered unscathed.

Joe, on the other hand, could not say the same thing. Physically, his shoulder was completely healed and his arm out of the sling. Dr. Miller and Mama D had both long since stopped coming by to check on his welfare. However, Adam had entertained and kept him company for so long that when he returned to his mother, Joe felt the loss deeply.

He often found himself thinking of the boy and his quirky little ways, like how he always sat on his knees on his chair at the table in order to reach or how he would kneel on those same small knees, pressing his tiny hands together in prayer before crawling into bed each evening. His home was entirely too quiet without the incessant chatter of the six-year-old, and he found himself wondering how he ever tolerated such silence surrounding him before.

Growing up in the middle of five brothers, Joe was always surrounded by noise and chaos. He never had a moment's peace to himself, and he had to share everything he had with his brothers. His clothes were handed down from his older brothers, and he always received stern warnings that he had to take care of it all, as they had to last through two more boys. Of course, they almost never did, so Jonathan would get new things to be passed down to James. Everything Joe possessed was in the worst condition, his shoes and clothes almost all more patches than original material. He shared a bed with his two younger brothers and at mealtimes he fought off four other boys for his share of the food under his mother's incredulous gaze. Even when he used the privy, there seemed to be a line. When he came to Colorado, he had lived in bunkhouses with other bachelors, so as far as he was concerned, the best perk of becoming sheriff was getting his own space and subsequent silence for the first time in his life.

He had relished in the quiet solitude, too. There was no more roughhousing, boasting, or hiding his things that he had to deal with both during his childhood and at the various flophouses for the mines he had worked in. After Caroline's rejection of him, he comforted himself by figuring that at least now he never had to answer to anyone ever again. He could buy what he wanted, sleep in a whole bed to himself, and even reveled in the fact that his home didn't have the underlying aroma of sweat and tobacco that seemed to permeate any other dwelling he had shared with other men. He convinced himself that he had found his dream life; at least until Sarah had come to town and he started to spend time with Adam.

When he had first taken the boy fishing or hiking, not accustomed to being around small children, Joe had appreciated the calm and quiet of his home when he returned. As the boy had aged, however, he had also begun to cross over to see Joe at the jail during the day. His visits would be brief because Sarah had told him he could go only if he promised to not be disruptive and take up too much of the sheriff's time. Most days consisted of Adam coming in and saying a quick "hello" with a wave, but Joe found himself very much looking forward to those pop-ins.

Then, when he and Sarah had their falling out, she had assumed Joe didn't want to be disturbed by Adam, so he stopped coming around, and Joe once again became accustomed to solitude.

Now, though, when Adam had returned home after coming to stay with him, Joe felt as though his departure had left a huge hole in his life. As exhausting as it was to care for the child around the clock for more than two weeks, Joe marveled in how quickly he had developed a paternal-like affection for the boy. Many times, during Adam's stay, Joe would find himself thinking, *This is what it would be like to have a son.*

Along with those warm and fuzzy feelings, though, came a surge of hatred for Caroline that surprised him. He thought that he had resolved his anger at her after all these years, but she again became the focal point of his rage when he realized all he had missed by not having the opportunity to raise a child from cradle to adulthood. It was the first time that he had allowed himself to truly mourn what he had tried so hard to convince himself he didn't want. Suddenly, quiet and solitude just felt lonely and sad.

If only she wouldn't have chosen his brother over him, he could have been living happily ever after with a household full of children just like Adam in a cabin somewhere in the California mountains for a long time now. Instead, to his astonished dismay, his life at this point just seemed repetitive and predictable, filled with nothing but torturous silence that brought no peace. He thought on how much Sarah missed her husband, and Adam, his father, and he realized with sadness that if he died, no one would mourn him for more than a few days. He had no legacy.

***

Joe was going to Sarah's much more frequently than he would admit. He at first convinced himself that he was only going to check on her. Then, it was to make sure that Adam was all right after the whole ordeal. After that, he ran out of excuses, but still found himself in her presence every afternoon and had quit trying to offer her an explanation because she never asked him for one.

It was during one of his routine visits when Jacob had burst in, out of breath and waving a telegram in his hand.

"Oh, Joe! Good! You're here!"

"What's going on, Jacob?" Joe asked, concerned.

"This telegram just came in for you. I figured you'd be here, so I came here first."

Great! thought Joe, annoyed. *Now even Jacob has picked up on my pathetic need to see Adam and Sarah every day. I wonder who else has noticed I am so predictable?*

"Well, Jacob, give it here, please," Joe requested, holding out his hand.

Jacob handed it over, and Joe's eyes began to scan the paper:

JOE STOP JOSHUA KILLED LAST NIGHT STOP PA HAD AN ATTACK AT NEWS AND VERY SICK STOP HE WANTS YOU HOME STOP TELL US WHEN YOU WILL ARRIVE STOP YOUR BROTHER JONATHAN STOP

"Oh, no!" Joe moaned as he collapsed mindlessly down on a chair in Sarah's shop.

"I'm so sorry, Joe," Jacob said, his voice full of sympathy. "Carl told me right away when this came in. I knew I had to get it to you as soon as possible."

Joe nodded dumbly. "Thanks, Jacob."

"No problem."

"When is the next train out?"

"Tomorrow morning. Want to get on it?"

"Yes, please."

"All right. I will take care of everything. Sacramento, right?"

"At first. Nevada City eventually. But, if need be, one of the boys can get me from there."

"You got it. So sorry again, Joe."

Sarah witnessed the whole exchange but had no idea what was going on. She didn't want to be rude and pry, but her curiosity was getting the best of her.

"Going home?" she asked how she hoped was casually as soon as Jacob had shut the door behind him.

"Uh… What?" Joe answered, obviously distracted.

"Are you going home?"

"Yes…"

"Oh."

There was a long pause of silence as Joe continued to process what was happening and Sarah tried not to ask more questions. When he looked up to see her carefully studying him, he didn't trust himself to speak, so he handed her the telegram. He watched as she read it, and when she looked up from the paper in her hands her eyes were full of sympathy.

"Oh, Joe! I'm so sorry," she whispered.

"Thank you," he answered, his voice shaking slightly.

Sarah handed him back the piece of paper, and he stood to place it in his pocket. Neither of them said anything for a few seconds, but eventually, Sarah opened her arms, and he fell into them. She felt his shuddering breaths as he tried to control his emotions and gently stroked his back, murmuring in his ear that he would be all right. They held each other for a long while, neither of them willing to let go of the other, each relishing the closeness and comfort the other provided. Eventually, he lifted his head from her shoulder and looked at her. Her expression was so inviting, so welcoming, that before he knew what he was doing, his lips were on hers.

The kiss they shared had started out innocently enough, but it didn't take long for it to build in momentum. Joe wrapped his arms more tightly around her, one of them engulfing her waist, holding her firmly to him. She ran a hand up the nape of his neck, her fingers entangling in his hair, stroking him slowly. At one point, she heard herself moan softly and felt when he took advantage as he wrapped his tongue around hers. His hand dropped from her waist, lower to her bottom, and it took all his remaining restraint to not pull her taut against him, not because he didn't want to, but because he was acutely aware of his body's reaction and didn't want her to discover her effect on him.

Eventually, they came up for air. Neither of them said a word as their chests rose and fell with their exhilaration. Joe opened his mouth and said, "I…," then grabbed his hat and left without another word, leaving Sarah standing stunned behind him, wondering what had just happened.

All night, Joe lay awake replaying the event over and over in his mind. It had never been his intention to kiss her, and he was shocked when it registered what he was doing. He still couldn't figure out what had possessed him to do it. Then, there was the kiss itself: that kiss had been amazing. With Caroline, he had never experienced anything even remotely close to the rush he had gotten when kissing Sarah. He shut his eyes tightly and groaned with longing and frustration when he recalled how she had felt in his arms as if she had been made for him, and how he had thought that if he hadn't stopped when he did, he wasn't sure he would have been able to.

Sarah, too, couldn't sleep, gobsmacked by what had transpired. Joe had surprised her with the clinch, and she hadn't even had time to react before she felt herself melting into him. The kiss had awoken in her desires that she hadn't felt in years and had reconciled with herself that she most likely would never feel again. As much as it galled her, she lay and compared the kiss with those that she had shared with George and was surprised when she realized that Joe's kiss had been among one of the most passionate in her life. That knowledge, however, made her feel grossly disloyal to her poor, deceased husband. So, she spent the night trying to justify her reaction, silently apologizing repeatedly to George for her wanton behavior and trying to explain that it was only because it had been so long since she had shared a kiss like that with him that she had forgotten what his had felt like.

Deep down, though, she knew that it was fruitless. The interlude with Joe had been earthshattering. All through the wee hours until dawn, she tossed and turned, feeling immensely guilty that she would allow any other man to caress and hold her when she still loved and missed George so much.

In the morning, Sarah rose and thought briefly about going to see Joe, explaining that it had been a mistake and she never meant to respond to his kiss like that. She couldn't bring herself to do it, though, because deep down she knew that she had wanted it as much as he had, and what was worse, once it happened, she realized that she had wanted it to take place for a long time. Of course, he had kissed her when he was recovering from his wound, but that had been different because she knew it was not meant for her. What had transpired yesterday, however, felt like it had always been written in the stars for them.

Joe, in the early morning, took his pack and shut the jail behind him. One of the men he trusted the most when he needed to deputize help was taking over as acting sheriff until he returned, whenever that would be. He thought briefly about going and trying to explain to Sarah that he was sorry and that the kiss had been a mistake, but as he didn't feel as though it had been, he couldn't bring himself to do it. So, instead, he walked to the depot without looking back and boarded the waiting train.

Chapter Thirty-Eight

It wasn't until Joe had climbed onto the train in Cheyenne that would take him west that the whole situation with his family sank in. He had only focused on his father when he had read the telegraph; the information about Joshua had barely registered. However, as he watched mile after mile of scenery go by, the reality of what happened fully hit him.

His brother, who had been his nemesis for most of his life, the one who had always one-upped him whether he had meant to or not, was gone. There was a time where Joe would have felt exceptionally pleased with the news that fate had taken care of what he had wanted so badly to do himself so many years ago; but now he was surprised to find that he instead mourned, leaving him to wonder when his heart had softened.

Joe's mind flashed back to various stages of their life together growing up, remembering that Joshua hadn't always been so difficult. There was a time when they were young that they were the best of pals. Joe and his two older brothers had played in the woods and by the mines, despite their father's warnings, spending hours exploring their surroundings. Joe, being the youngest then, recalled that Joshua had been the one to stop and help him if there was terrain that he couldn't easily traverse or if he fell. It wasn't until Joe had started school that the dynamic changed.

Joe was actually the better looking of the two brothers, but he never realized it. In fact, he felt invisible next to his two older siblings. Jeremiah was a big boy: he had been five when Joe was born. He was older and intimidating, and there was enough of an age difference that there had never been any competition. Joshua, though, was a ladies' man, even in the early days. Every new town they moved to, every new schoolhouse the three McIntyre boys walked into, Joshua immediately commanded the room. Joe tried to watch and take mental notes of what he did to make him so charming, but whenever he tried the same things, like teasing girls, talking to them about nothing, or talking up the old women, he felt extremely foolish. All the girls from Joshua's age down to Jonathan's had been so smitten that no one had ever even given Joe a second glance.

All that changed when they moved for the last time. When Joe met Caroline, their eyes locked, and he felt as though a jolt of electricity had flowed through him. She had come to bring her father his forgotten lunch, and as she came sauntering up the path it was as if the world around Joe disappeared, and she was all he could see.

When she approached her father, he had been talking to Joe about how he thought they could up production and had his back turned to his guest. Joe's eyes must have widened in surprise, because mid-sentence her father turned around and then back to Joe, with a knowing smile on his face.

"Hi, Daddy!" Caroline had happily exclaimed,

"Hello, my dear. I want to introduce you to Joe McIntyre. He's my right-hand man around here!"

She had demurely stuck her tiny hand out, and Joe took it, paying extra care that he didn't accidentally squeeze her too hard and hurt her. "Nice to meet you," he had surprisingly managed to get out coherently.

She had giggled sweetly before answering, "The pleasure is all mine!"

They stood looking at each other for several seconds until her father had cleared his throat while reaching for the lunch pail, before saying pointedly, "Thank you, sweetheart! That will be all. I don't want you hanging around here just to end up dirty or hurt."

"Oh! Sure, Daddy," she bubbled. "Nice to meet you," she said, looking up at Joe through her eyelashes.

"That's your daughter?" Joe exclaimed in admiration as he watched her sway out of sight, her hips swinging, tantalizing him with every step.

"She sure is," her father had confirmed. Then, he looked sternly at the younger man. "Don't you be getting any ideas there, McIntyre!"

Joe quickly shook his head, "No, sir!"

The thing was, though, that he had already begun getting all kinds of ideas. From that moment on, every dream and fantasy revolved around the man's daughter. To his utter joy or dismay, he wasn't sure which, he couldn't keep his thoughts off her.

Through the next few months, though she never had before, Caroline began to hang around the mine. Before Joe knew what hit him, she was eating lunch with him every day, laughing and flirting with him at every opportunity, and then she began touching him, placing her hand on his arm and, as she got more brazen, his thigh.

Eventually, she invited him to her home for supper on the following Saturday. Joe had been incredibly nervous, donning his Sunday best, and after being carefully coached by his mother, had even stopped to pick some wildflowers that grew along the way.

It had been a great evening. Caroline had cooked an excellent meal, and her father had kept the conversation going. They spoke of their home in Ohio before they headed to California, chasing the same dream that had brought Joe's family West. Her father had been a farmer back East, but like so many before him, he became a miner the minute he crossed over the Sierra Nevadas.

After supper, Caroline's father had excused himself to sit in his chair to smoke his pipe and read the paper while Caroline and Joe sat on the front porch in the darkening evening. She had reached for his hand, and they sat quietly together, listening to the night sounds that rained down around them. At nine o'clock, Joe stood and declared it was time to go. Caroline sidled up to him, kissing his cheek, and he had veritably floated home in a delirium of shock and joy.

They continued to get to know each other, and it hadn't taken long until everyone in town knew that Joe was sweet on

334

Caroline and that they were courting. He was incredibly shy, so she had set the tone of their physical relationship, and very quickly, she had discovered that she could whip him into a frenzy of desire with just a few intense kisses. She would then coyly turn and walk away, back into her house, leaving him staring after her with longing, his desire for her reaching a fever pitch.

At the same time, Joe's mother took a turn for the worst. She had been ill for a few years, but in the fall before she passed, she was in excruciating pain most of the time. One night she had held his hand when he had gone to bid her goodnight.

"Son, I'm not going to live much longer," she had declared.

As much as Joe wanted to deny any validity in that statement, the truth of the matter was that he knew she was not long for their world just by looking at her, so he had instead chosen not to respond.

"I was hoping to live long enough to see you all married, except James, of course. Joe, you're such a kind, responsible, and caring man. I have been so wishing that I would live long enough to see you find happiness with a good woman who would bring out the best in you, but alas, I guess it is not to be…"

"Mama," he had said to her, not having called her that since he was a young boy. "I think that I'm going to ask Caroline to marry me."

Though he had been toying with the idea of asking Caroline to marry him sometime in the future, he hadn't thought much about the timing before that moment. Knowing that Caroline was the love of his life, he figured the downturn of his mother's health was just the push he needed if it would make her feel more at peace about departing from her family.

"Well, then, you need to bring her here for supper so she can formally be introduced to the family. In fact, why don't you invite her father, as well?"

"Are you sure you're up for that?" Joe had asked, concerned.

"Absolutely! This is a reason to celebrate."

So, two days later, Joe had gone to Caroline's father and asked for his daughter's hand in marriage. The man liked Joe and had gladly given his blessing, happy that in a town full of men, his daughter had seemed to find one of the most reliable and responsible ones around.

The next night, Joe had taken Caroline out to supper at the local café, and on the way home, he had stopped along the river to ask her to be his wife under the stars. She had seemed thrilled, though a bit disappointed that he did not yet have a ring. He quickly explained that he had made up his mind to ask her a bit sooner than he had originally intended because of his mother, and when he informed her that he had already spoken with his friend, the local jeweler in town, that very day about making her a ring, she had seemed contented enough.

On Saturday evening, Joe's family's home was ready for company. His mother had directed him on how to cook a simple stew that smelled delicious, and she did her best to put on a brave face to hide her discomfort and pain. It seemed as though it would be a perfect night until about an hour before Caroline and her father arrived, when Joshua had walked through the door.

Joshua had been down in Sacramento, working on the ranch owned in part by Jeremiah and his wife. He had returned unexpectedly, and the rest of the family had been surprised and happy to see him, but Joe had gotten a strange sense of foreboding.

Caroline and her father arrived right on time, and at first, all had gone well. Joe was proud to show off his beautiful young fiancée and to hear the glowing praise her father doled out. It wasn't until later when the conversation at the table hit a lull that the hair on the back of Joe's neck stood up. Caroline had asked Joshua where he had been, remarking that she hadn't seen him around.

"I have been down in the valley, helping Jeremiah run his ranch," he had answered with an easy grin and a wink.

It took everything within Joe's will not to add, "He had to leave town quickly because of an unpaid gambling debt."

336

Caroline then proceeded to ask Joshua all sorts of questions about what it was like in the valley, what he had done on the ranch, and if he spoke Spanish. He replied with some foreign-sounding words, but since Joe didn't speak Spanish, he had no idea that he had called his fiancée a beautiful woman. Nevertheless, when he had looked to Caroline, he could see that Joshua's expression had made his meaning clear as Caroline stared at him with complete adoration. Joe immediately recognized the look, having seen girls gaze at his brother that way for as long as he could remember, so he had quickly steered the conversation away from Joshua, and the rest of the evening had passed pleasantly enough. Caroline had given him an exceptionally intense kiss before she followed her father into the night and Joe sighed with relief that at least this time, it seemed as though Joshua hadn't been able to work his magic.

Joe spent the next couple of weeks trying to stay occupied by procuring a small cabin for him and his soon-to-be bride and fixing the place up. What he didn't know was that Caroline had taken to coming by the house under the guise of looking for Joe, but when she found Joshua instead, she would stay and talk for a while, or they would go for a walk together. They never acted improperly, but the situation raised Jonathan's hackles all the same, and he watched carefully for signs that anything inappropriate was going on. He even confronted Joshua one evening after he had returned from walking Caroline home, asking his brother how long he intended to interfere with Joe's relationship. Joshua had merely scoffed as he walked into the house to gather his wallet, before heading out for another evening at the saloon.

Jonathan had also begun to hear around town how Caroline was receiving fancy gifts. Everyone thought that they were from her fiancé, but knowing the truth, he began to wonder how long Caroline was going to be able to string along two McIntyre boys before the whole thing blew up in her face.

It didn't take long. One fateful morning, ten days later, Joe returned to his cabin to find his beloved fiancée in what was to be their bed, under his older brother, both of them naked and in the throes of passion.

Joe had been so shocked that he had only stood there watching them, not really processing what he was seeing. It took them what felt like hours to realize they were not alone until Joshua, sensing someone was looking at them, had glanced up and exclaimed, "Oh, shit!" before scrambling off the love of Joe's life, putting his hands down in front of his groin.

Caroline, having been so abruptly abandoned, left naked and exposed on the bed, had turned her head toward Joe in confusion. When she saw him standing in the room, a stunned look frozen on his features, she had screeched and reached for the blanket to cover her body; the beautiful, exquisite body Joe had been desiring for several months, while trying to be a respectful gentleman and honor her reputation.

Without a word, Joe had turned around and left, carefully closing the door behind him as if it would shut out the unsightly scene from his memory, but alas, it was to no avail. It had been thoroughly etched into his memory, and as he wandered aimlessly around for hours, he saw the image repeated as vividly as he had seen it the first time.

Eventually, he made it home and went directly to his mother's room, desperately looking for some sort of comfort and reassurance in his despair. His mother had been shocked and devastated for her son, the gentlest and kindest one of the lot. After he had haltingly rehashed the sordid story to her, pushing through the confusion of his inexplicable need to protect Caroline's reputation from his mother's scrutiny, she had merely opened her arms to him, and he had fallen into them, too numb to even cry anymore.

"Do you still love her, son?" she had asked after a time.

"Yes!" he told her resolutely.

"Well, then perhaps things can be mended. Let me speak with Joshua."

Joshua came home a little later, and upon seeing him, Joe walked straight toward the door without saying a word. Joshua opened and closed his mouth before saying, "Joe, let's talk about this!"

"There's nothing to say," Joe replied when he passed by him. "I give up. You win! You always win!" he declared right as he walked through the portal, slamming it behind him.

When he arrived back at his cabin, Joe gathered all the bedding and took it outside. He cleared a large area and then doused everything in kerosene before igniting it into a raging fireball before his eyes. That night, as he lay cold and huddled on the bed frame, now without a mattress, that he thought he would be sharing within a fortnight with his warm bodied fiancée-turned-wife, he still didn't regret his decision to burn everything their naked bodies had touched.

Joe's mother tried to intervene again, begging Joshua to see reason and release any claim he had on Caroline's heart, but by that point, they were already too entrenched with each other to even consider Joe in the equation. She had died about six weeks later, distraught over leaving one heartbroken son while raising another who had proven so callous and heartless.

Joe, in that moment as the train wound its way down the Sierra Nevada Mountains, remembered some of his mother's very last words to him. After giving all her remaining effort to reconcile the huge rift in their family, she had admitted defeat. Joe recalled how hopeful he had been in the beginning that she would be able to talk some compassion into Joshua and that he would see the errors of his ways, but it wasn't meant to be.

His mother had taken his hand in hers, her eyes glistening with unshed tears as she said, "Remember, Joe. What goes around comes around. Family is family, and blood is thicker than water, but sometimes hardheads like Joshua are incapable of seeing it. I know you think she's perfect for you, but I can tell you right now, she isn't. If she did this, then she's as fickle, self-serving, and manipulative as he is, and they will spend the rest of their lives discontented with each other. Two people like that can never find long-lasting happiness, mark my words. They're too busy thinking only of themselves to make the necessary sacrifices to keep a relationship strong. His stealing her away from you may just end up being the best thing that has happened to you in your entire life."

It wasn't more than a few days later that Joe received word while he was at work that his mother was likely to pass that day. He had asked for the rest of the day off from his supervisor, Caroline's father, and given how badly the man felt about what his daughter had done to Joe, he was apt to give Joe the moon if he would have asked for it.

His mother had been incoherent for the entire day, but when Jonathan told her, "I found Joe, Ma. It's all right now," she had opened her eyes and clearly focused on Joe's before telling him, "Remember, my love, the best is yet to come. I promise!"

Joe had smiled slightly at her cryptic message meant especially for him. He had bent down and gently kissed her forehead, saying quietly, "Thanks, Ma."

It wasn't more than two weeks after they had buried their beloved and stoic mother that Joe found out through Jonathan that Caroline was pregnant, and that she and Joshua were marrying without delay. The date was set for two weeks from then, and two nights before the wedding, his normally quiet and distant father had come to his little cabin to see him.

He brought a bottle of spirits, and the two men shared it, using Joe's only cup. Eventually, his father had looked Joe in the eyes and said gruffly, "You aren't planning on going to this damned thing in a few days, are you?"

Joe hemmed and hawed for a few moments, trying to figure out what to say. The truth was he wasn't sure himself what he was going to do. He felt trapped in a nightmare in which he had no control. Not wanting to attend, he didn't want to let Caroline or Joshua know just how much their actions had destroyed him, either. He felt like a shell of a man, and all he wanted was to keep his world from tipping even more precariously.

"I don't know for certain," is how he had eventually replied.

"You know, son," his father started again. "I know I'm not the most loving or attentive father. I always left all this

340

emotional territory to your saintly ma. But I can tell you that I would not begrudge or think less of you one bit if you decided that this would be too much salt in the wound."

Joe had only nodded miserably, the backs of his eyes prickling uncomfortably.

"So, for what it's worth, I think it is perfectly acceptable that you stay away. In fact, I think you should get out. You need to get far away from here and become your own man. Somewhere no one knows you or Joshua. It's high time you get out from underneath that boy's shadow."

As Joe lay awake that night, in his dark, lonesome cabin, he ruminated over what his father had said, and as the eastern sky began to lighten, he decided that the man had been right. The only way he would ever get out from under Joshua's shadow was to go somewhere no one ever knew him.

Joe thought long and hard about it the next day until he coincidentally overheard some men on his same shift talking about how they were going to jump ship. They had talked about going to Nevada, but then a third man told them that he had it on good authority that Colorado may just be opening up for another gold rush. In that minute, Joe's fate was sealed.

He arranged for someone to take over the rent on his little cabin, packed what he could on his back, and took the time to say goodbye to his father, Jonathan, and James, before taking the train to Colorado. The rest was history.

Chapter Thirty-Nine

The train was slowing to a stop at the depot in Sacramento. Joe grabbed his bags and was prepared to jump onto the platform as soon as possible. He was sick of being on the lumbering "Iron Horse" and was looking immensely forward to having solid ground under his feet again after what had felt like years of rocking back and forth.

As soon as he had known the details for his trip, he had sent a telegram to Jonathan in response to his, letting him know that he was coming and what day to expect him. He wasn't sure about the timetable for the connecting train to Nevada City, so he figured he could always stay in Sacramento for a day or two if he needed to; there were plenty of hotels to accommodate him.

As he headed toward the depot, he thought he heard someone call his name, but quickly dismissed it as that he was just overtired. He was almost through the station doors when he distinctly heard it again, this time closer and louder: "Joe! Joe McIntyre!"

Joe turned around and searched in the direction from where he thought he had heard his name. He saw a man further down the platform, waving madly, trying to get someone's attention, but while squinting against the strong California sun he couldn't see who it was or even tell if he was who the man wanted. Deciding to stop, he waited for the man to come closer, until he saw it was his oldest brother, and then took off at a run.

The two men collided with one another in a strong embrace, slapping each other hard on the back. Eventually, they separated and grinned unabashedly.

"Jeremiah! So good to see you!" Joe exclaimed. He couldn't believe how much his brother had changed since he had seen him last. He looked familiar but somehow more distinguished and settled. He even was getting a little grey around the temples, and he had deep lines when he smiled.

"You, too, Joe! You are a sight for sore eyes! We were wondering if we would ever get to see you again."

"Yeah…well…" he stammered, not really knowing what to say, so he decided to change topics.

"How did you know I was coming?"

"Jonathan sent me a telegram with your arrival information after you sent him yours. He has his hands full with Pa, so I said I would come to the station and meet you, and then we could go up together."

"Sounds great!"

Joe grabbed his bag and slung it over his shoulder. "So, what's the plan? I almost jumped ship at Colfax but figured I would have a better shot of finding a room for the night down here. Not having been here in years, I figured it was a safer bet, and then I could hitch a ride on the 'Never Come, Never Go' in the morning."

"That's what Jonathan presumed when you said you would go to Sacramento first. We'll stay here tonight and get a fresh start tomorrow."

The brothers checked into a hotel and then, after eating together at a local restaurant, went to a saloon for a drink and to catch up.

"So, tell me…" Joe began. "How's Rosa? The kids? They didn't want to come with you?"

"Nah," Jeremiah answered, swirling his whiskey around in his glass. "Everyone's good. You're gonna be an uncle again," he added with a smug smile.

"Jesus, Jer! How many does this make?"

"This will be number seven."

"Jesus Christ! How old is the oldest?"

"He's fifteen."

Joe just shook his head. "Don't kill the poor woman!" he stated.

Jeremiah chuckled. "I'm just making sure we are doing our good Catholic duty. Ma would be proud! Don't worry about her: Rosa's strong as an ox. I love that woman!"

"Obviously!" Joe said wryly. "And often!" Both men laughed.

"Aw, come on, Joe. You're just jealous!"

"That you have an amazing woman to warm your bed and bear your many children? Yeah… I guess I am, a little."

There was a lull while Jeremiah tried to think of how to respond. He hadn't meant to bring up his brother's unlucky love life, but he certainly hadn't been expecting that answer after years of Joe's staunch swearing off of anyone of the female persuasion.

Finally, seeing the panic in Jeremiah's eyes as he struggled to find something to say, Joe decided to cut him a break and change the subject. "How are things on the ranch?"

"Great! Juan has taught me so much. He's getting older and finally wants to hand over everything to me. I guess I know enough Spanish after sixteen years to do it!"

"I'm sure you're much better than you give yourself credit for! You were fluent long before I ever left here."

"It isn't just about the language, though. It's about the culture as a whole. To get the respect of the men, I had to understand how things were done in their society."

"I have to say, I was hoping to get to see Rosa!"

"Sorry! She's just a few weeks out now from delivering, and I need to focus on Pa; not my wife and six children underfoot. It would be different if Ma was still around…" His voice faded as they both remembered their mother fondly.

"How bad is Pa?"

"It's pretty bad, Joe. We were all praying you made it here in time. Doc says the attack took out about three-fourths of his heart. Poor Jonathan and his wife and James are doing the best they can, but he needs round-the-clock care."

"Oh." Joe couldn't think of anything else to say. The silence between them stretched further and further until eventually the tension got to be too much, and Jeremiah finally spoke.

"Don't you want to know what happened to Joshua?"

"No. Not particularly."

"Joe…"

"I'm here to say goodbye to Pa, that's it," Joe answered with finality.

"Whatever!"

"Jer, honestly!"

"Sure! It was Pa that dragged you back across half the country… It had nothing at all to do with *her*."

"It didn't!" Joe insisted. Jeremiah only stared back at him, holding his gaze, one eyebrow raised in suspicion.

After a few more seconds, Joe couldn't stand it anymore. "All right! Fine! How is she?"

"Not great, I'm sure. I haven't talked to anyone yet, but I can only imagine that she's not doing too well with the fact that her husband was murdered, and she has three young children."

"Three? When the hell did that happen?"

"You didn't know?"

"No!"

"I assumed Jonathan would have written it to you. They had a third a little over two years ago."

"Oh."

"So, are you going to admit she's why you really came now?"

"No!" Joe insisted. "Truly she isn't! I…" Joe stopped talking while he pondered how much he wanted to reveal. "I sorta met someone…"

"Are you courting someone, Joe?" Jeremiah asked, unable to keep the surprise out of his voice.

"No, not exactly."

"What do you mean by that?"

"I mean… It's complicated."

"Don't want to talk about it?"

"Not really. Especially when I'm trying to figure things out myself."

"All right, then, little brother. Let's just go with that."

The men had a few more shots and then headed up to bed. In the morning, they boarded the eastbound train and started up the mountain, stopping at Colfax, then catching the narrow-gauge railroad for the rest of the way. When they got to the station, Jonathan was waiting for them.

"Hello, boys!" he called out to them as they stepped off the train. The three brothers embraced and held onto each other for several moments before pulling apart. Joe stepped back and clapped them both on their shoulders.

"Where's Jim?"

"At home with Pa. Someone has to be there all of the time. He's not good, Joe."

"I figured he wasn't when you asked me to come home," he said pointedly. Only Jonathan, besides their mother, had really known just how devastating the circumstances were which led to Joe's fleeing so far from home.

"You're right! I wouldn't have sent for you if I didn't think it was necessary. Unfortunately, I think this may be the last day Pa's alive."

"Well then, let's not waste any time… Let's go home."

The three men strolled from the depot to the small house where they had spent a good deal of their childhoods. Along the way, they garnered several second glances as the people in town recognized not only Jonathan, who lived there, but also the two other McIntyre boys who had not been in town in several years. Quite a few young women smiled shyly at Joe, and he felt himself blush. Jeremiah noticed, elbowing him in the ribs.

"Hey, Joe! Looks like you're attracting the attention of the ladies."

"I don't know why," he said, perplexed.

"Ah, come on, Joe!" Jonathan laughed. "Ma always said you were the prettiest of all of us!"

Joe reached around and caught his younger brother in a headlock, scrubbing his knuckles over his head. "You're still my younger brother, you know!"

"Probably more like Pa's been bragging all over the place that you're the sheriff of your town would be more my guess," Jeremiah said with a chuckle.

346

"Oh, no!" groaned Joe. "Please tell me he hasn't!"

"Sorry, big brother," Jonathan confirmed. "But he has been bursting his buttons all over town since your election."

"Election?" Joe muttered. "More like sentencing." His brothers laughed at his candor.

The three men reached the family home, and Joe took a deep breath before walking through the door, unsettled about what was awaiting him on the other side.

Chapter Forty

Nothing anyone could have said would have prepared Joe for what greeted him when he walked through the door. The small home, which had once been shining and clean under the watchful eye of his mother, had now deteriorated into a state of disarray. Joe felt a lump in his throat as he saw newspapers, dishes, and clothing in random stacks across the entire house, before also noticing the multitudes of dust particles floating through the air, highlighted by the sunlight streaming in, despite the grimy windows. He continued on into his parents' bedroom and was shocked even further when he saw the pale, withered old man sleeping on the bed that looked much too large for his shrunken form. Joe wasn't sure for how long he stood, unable to do anything but observe the shell of the man he remembered.

Brian McIntyre had been an intimidating fellow in his youth. He had been tall, dark, and very handsome, and Joe remembered that his mother, a tall woman in her own right, had still only come up to his shoulder. He had grown up working in a coal mine and had decided he hated it with every fiber of his being. So, he had found himself a pretty wife, sold all he had, and made his way West, figuring that if a man can mine coal in Tennessee, he could just as well mine gold in California.

Joe distinctly remembered his father's arms, thick and strong from years of wielding heavy equipment to coax treasure from the depths of the earth. None of the McIntyre boys ever wanted to get a paddling from their Pa: the size of his arms was deterrent enough when their Ma had threatened to send them to their father for punishment.

Always a quiet man, he never said much at all, preferring instead to observe everything and everyone around him. It had always been a little unsettling whenever Pa kept someone in his gaze. He had often told his boys that if they spent most of their time watching instead of jacking their jaws, they could find solutions to ninety-nine percent of the troubles that might befall them.

He had a quick Irish temper but was kindhearted and wanted to believe the best in people. He worked hard, keeping his crew in line when underground, and his men respected him as much as his own children did.

Deteriorating when his beloved wife had passed, he still had been a formidable character. His ability to see a situation clearly and deal with people fairly had led to many of those around him seeking his counsel on everything from financial to marital advice. Clearly, though, the loss of one of his sons had been his undoing, and the daunting man had crumpled.

Joe walked toward him and gently placed his large hand lovingly on the top of his father's head as he said cheerfully, "Hey, Pa! It's Joe. I'm home."

The man did not respond, but he moaned slightly and shifted a bit, so Joe chose to take it as confirmation he knew he was there.

"I'm sorry this happened, Pa, and I'm sorry I didn't get to see you again while you were still doing well." Joe felt his eyes start to tear up and he shook his head.

"I love you, Pa. Thanks for teaching me to be a man. I hope you're proud of me, even though I ran away from my problems. But life has been good to me in Colorado, and I'm glad I went, except for not being here for you."

The man did not stir again, but Joe sat with him in silence for about an hour. He thought about the past memories with his father through the years and smiled occasionally to himself, despite an errant tear falling every now and then. At last, he felt peaceful. If his father passed right then, he would have no regrets. He knew his father loved him, and he hoped his father knew the feeling was reciprocated.

After a while, Jeremiah poked his head into the room. "You all right?'

"Yeah," Joe said, clearing his throat. "Sorry I took so long."

"It's all well and good, Joe. You're the one who hasn't seen him for so many years. The rest of us, even me, have been able to see him much more often than you have."

Joe merely nodded. "Thanks."

"No problem."

Joe went out to the parlor but couldn't sit still. He understood that his father wasn't going to live much longer, and an overwhelming sense of sadness swept over him, catching him off-guard.

Joe was not a man to cry easily. The only two times he could remember since he was a child was the day he spoke to his mother about finding his brother and fiancée in bed together, and then again on the day his mother passed. Therefore, he was surprised by the big sobs that suddenly rolled through his body. He tried to be quiet, not wanting to attract the attention of his brothers, but James noticed. He walked over to put his hand on Joe's shoulder and squeezed. Joe smiled weakly up at him and quickly wiped his eyes. James smiled softly back and moved away. Joe continued to sit, glued in place, with his head in his hands, and was stunned when he felt a sudden, overwhelming need to see Sarah. More than anything, he wanted her to hold him, to comfort him. In that moment, he believed that there was no one else who could bring him peace like she could, not even his own mother.

Prior to the recent events of the past few months, Joe still had thought of himself as a young man. Therefore, whenever he felt lonesome, he had consoled himself with the thought that he still had plenty of time to change his mind and settle down, if he wanted to. Recently, though, even prior to being shot, he had been contemplating the meaning of family in a way he never had before, largely spurred by how fond of Adam he had become, caring for him almost like a son. After having truly faced his mortality for the first time, however, Joe was hit by the hard realization that not only was Adam not his, but also that he had no legacy at all, and the devastation he felt about that shocked him.

Even with knowing that, it was being with his brothers as they rallied around their father in his final days that had really solidified Joe's newfound belief that family was important, not only because he was lonely, but because he was alone. His fear of being hurt again was dissipating as he concluded that constructing a wall around his heart hadn't only cost him companionship; it had also robbed him of building a posterity. He was finally able to calculate the full price of his trepidation in finding a good woman and settling down. It had cost him a rich tapestry of deeply interpersonal relationships, woven tightly together by love and shared experiences, which would then have the power to transcend generations.

Though his understanding had abruptly changed, Joe, after having been set in his ways for so long, hadn't yet discerned all the qualities in a woman he would seek if he decided to let his guard down, other than one whom he could trust to protect his heart if he chose to give it to her. Now, though, when he was longing for Sarah's presence, he had to wonder if he had already found her.

It hadn't taken long, however, for his old doubts to creep in and make him believe that Sarah would never reciprocate his feelings. It was bad enough that he had persuaded himself that she wasn't interested in him, but because it was so painfully obvious that she still loved her deceased husband, he quickly convinced himself she could never be interested in anyone. Even when Doc Miller had tried, she had not appeared to be terribly receptive, so Joe had decided that if she wasn't swayed by the handsome, educated doctor with a good income, he was fooling himself if he thought he could ever find favor with her.

The evening was spent with four McIntyre boys all together for the first time in over a decade, but their reunion was overshadowed by an unspoken feeling of unease. They tried to speak of different things, but it was obvious that each man was half-listening for their father's breathing, resulting in long pauses and dropped conversation.

Eventually, though, as the hour grew late, Jeremiah spoke about the funeral the next morning.

"What time is the service for Josh?"

Jonathan glanced quickly to Joe before answering. "Ten in the morning."

"All right. We'd best all be getting into bed then. Who's staying here with Pa?"

This time three sets of eyes turned to Joe. "I am!" he answered without hesitation.

"You sure, Joe?" James asked. "I can do it. I don't mind."

"I'm sure! There's no way I want to get anywhere near her. I mean there. By the way, why the hell didn't any of you tell me they had another kid?" He glared accusingly around the table. "I looked like an idiot not including that child with their Christmas gifts."

"I don't know, Joe," Jonathan answered levelly. "I guess I didn't want to add any more salt to your wound. For the past few years, your letters never mentioned them anymore, and you seemed much happier than before, so I guess I just figured that what you didn't know wouldn't hurt you. I was hoping that you had moved on."

Joe nodded thoughtfully. Then it dawned on him: Jonathan said that his letters had been more upbeat for pretty much the exact amount of time that he had known Sarah. The realization made him gasp, causing all his brothers to look at him.

"What?" he demanded, unwilling to share his insight. After all the years he had sworn off women, stating that his life was infinitely better by being on his own, he wondered how he would even begin to explain Sarah to the rest of them, especially after he had struggled to define what they had to Jeremiah the night before. Certainly, despite the fact that he and Sarah had spent a lot of time together over the past few years, it wasn't as if they were courting: to be fair, he wasn't even entirely sure that they liked one another. Truth be told, it seemed like they argued far more than they got along. He couldn't deny, however, that whenever they did spend time together and weren't bickering, he felt happier and more relaxed than he ever had before in his life.

He couldn't pinpoint what exactly made him so hesitant to talk about what he and Sarah had, whatever it was called. Was he worried that perhaps his brothers would think he was just lonely, and therefore settling? He was aware that might be a real possibility, especially if he told them she had been married before and had a son. How could he explain to them that another man's boy had begun to feel like his own? Or was it that maybe they would think with his gruff demeanor he wouldn't be a fit father? Perhaps he was self-conscious that they would think she was settling for him out of desperation- was it because she had a child to care for that she was therefore willing to overlook all the flaws that had obviously made him disposable to Caroline? Would they think that the only way a woman would choose to be with him was if she had no other options? His emotions felt like a jumbled mess when he tried to decipher them, and he worried that telling his brothers would mean facing something that he himself had yet to resolve.

"Nothing!" James said quickly, Jeremiah and Jonathan quickly concurring.

"Well, then, if it's all settled, you all will be going to the church, and I'll be here with Pa."

"Well, then, boys, I suggest we clean up and get to bed. Tomorrow's gonna be… interesting!" Jeremiah ordered.

Chapter Forty-One

Joe watched his three brothers as they preened in front of the looking glass that hung beside the door.

"You're all acting like a bunch of girls!" he laughed.

"Well, since the prettiest McIntyre isn't attending, it's up to us to make up the difference!" Jonathan sassed back.

"What can I say? I just don't want to hog all of the attention!"

The three men walked out the door, leaving Joe to sit in silence once more. The house, which used to be so full of life, was now eerily silent and all he could hear was the ticking of the old clock on the mantle. He straightened up the kitchen and washed the breakfast dishes, but he was still antsy and felt like he couldn't sit still. As much as he despised what Joshua had done, it was hard to sit there, trapped at the house, while one of his brothers was being laid to rest. Joe realized that if someone hadn't needed to sit with his father, he would have attended, too, even though he would have seen Caroline. He truly, despite all that had happened, was disturbed by his brother's violent end. He had fond memories of Joshua while they were growing up which he allowed himself to reflect upon for the first time in years. For as long as he could remember, it had been the five McIntyre boys. Now, with one missing, it felt incomplete.

Since his father couldn't attend the funeral either, Joe read to him from the Bible when he awoke, as it seemed the proper thing to do. As he read scripture after scripture aloud, he wondered if he would run into Caroline while he was home. He put on a good act about how he did not want to see her, but he knew that deep down he was lying to himself. What he was unsure of was if he wanted to see her merely for closure or did he see it as an opportunity to gloat that he had done just fine despite her?

Jonathan, Jeremiah, and James all stumbled through the door several hours later. They looked wrung out with the emotions of the day, not to mention the free-flowing whiskey at the wake. Joe reminded himself that even though he was still incredibly hurt and angry with Joshua, his brothers did not have the same history with him, and it was natural that they would find his death difficult.

As his brothers had changed out of their church clothes, Joe set to work cooking supper. He wanted something to occupy his time so that he didn't sit and brood anymore, nor talk to them about the service. Though he would never admit it, the guilt of not attending Joshua's funeral was getting to him, because as his ma had said, blood should be thicker than water. Therefore, being in the kitchen would solve both dilemmas.

When they sat down at the table to eat, very little was said. Joe was relieved that none of his brothers seemed to be in a talkative mood, and he certainly didn't press the matter. He was afraid if he did, his façade would come crumbling down to expose the raw emotions he knew he was suppressing behind his anger.

Eventually, after the kitchen was cleaned and their father had been settled for the night, Jonathan and Joe found themselves alone on the front porch in the cool evening air. They sat together on the swing their father had built for their mother not long after they had moved there. They watched as evening fell around them, listening to the creatures in the woods settling in for the night.

"She asked about you," Jonathan said quietly, breaking the silence.

Joe didn't respond.

"She wondered if you had made it into town and where you were."

"Huh!" Joe grunted.

"She wants to see you."

Again, he said nothing.

"Joe?"

"Yeah? Did she ask you to ask me if I would see her?"

"In so many words, yes."

"Tell her to go to hell!" he said bitterly.

"Joe…"

"What? What is it, John? I don't want to see her!"

"Joe, her husband just died."

"Excuse me?"

"Look, I know that you're still angry that she hurt you. I get it. But come on, Joe. That was ten years ago now. Her husband just died, and she has three young children. She's scared."

"She should have thought about that before kicking up her heels with my brother a few days before our wedding," Joe growled.

"Joe…"

"Listen, Jonathan. She made her bed… No, wait… She made herself comfortable with our brother in my bed; now she can lay in it. I never want to see that woman again in my life! I have no reason to. So, please, I don't want to talk about her anymore."

Jonathan ignored him. "It concerns me that you're still so incredibly angry at her about everything. It's been years."

"Well, let's see how you would feel if you found your fiancée *literally* making babies with your brother in your bed?"

"I know. It was terrible. But you have to give it a rest. She has paid her penance and then some, I promise you!"

"What's that supposed to mean?"

Jonathan paused, then sighed. "Joshua was not a good husband to her, Joe."

"What do you mean? Did he hurt her?"

"I don't think he did physically. But…"

"But what?"

"I shouldn't speak ill of the dead, but Josh was not a good man. He drank and gambled way too much. He would constantly lose all their money. She had to take in sewing and washing just to feed their children, while he would spend hours in the saloons, drunk as a skunk, frolicking with any whore who would talk to him. He had to disappear a few times in their marriage to avoid some creditor or the other, and then things got really tough. James and I, even Pa, would help her out with some extra money.”

“Jonathan, why would you do that? Joshua should have been taking care of his family, not you!”

“We did it for the little ones, Joe. For God’s sake, we couldn’t let them freeze or starve to death!”

Joe was furious at himself because, for all his hatred, he couldn’t help but reflect on the life his brother’s wife and their young children had lived. He didn’t want to feel sorry for her; he had wanted her to suffer. However, when he thought about the innocent children, his niece and now two nephews, it broke his heart. They certainly hadn’t asked to be dragged into the middle of this mess.

“If life was so bad, why did they have another baby, then?” Joe challenged his brother.

“I can’t answer that. You know as well as I do that babies just come with the territory when people are married. We were all surprised, as we had heard through Mrs. Matthews, you know… the town gossip, that Caroline wouldn’t let Joshua touch her once she found out about the whores,” he sighed. “Joshua was not exactly discreet.”

“What about her old man?”

“He died. About a year after you left. He was able to see Gabe, the oldest boy, before he passed. He had left her some money, thinking she might need it to get away, but sadly, Joshua found it and spent it all in a month on booze, gambling, and women.”

“It sounds like you’re expecting me to feel sorry for her!” Joe answered venomously.

“No!” Jonathan declared. “But I do want you to realize that her life wasn’t great. I think there were many times she wished she would have just married you.”

“Just married me… Thanks, John. Glad to know I would have been a good consolation prize. Well, it’s a little late now!”

Joe responded in disgust. "I'm sorry, but this discussion is over. Caroline can just keep on reaping what she sowed. I offered her a good life with me; the best I could give her. What did I get in return? She offered herself to my own brother. Goodnight!"

Joe lay in his bed for several hours, mulling over the conversation he had with his younger brother. He wanted to remain hurt, telling himself repeatedly that if Caroline only would have stayed true to him, none of this would have happened. She could have been happily married to him, with at least two or three little ones, possibly more. He would have had a steady job at the mine and not been nominated to be a sheriff. Life could have been so much easier, but he hadn't been able to make her love him enough.

He thought back to the conversation with his mother before she passed, when she had asked him if he still loved her. He had told her resolutely that he did and would take her back in an instant, despite her having been his brother's lover. Knowing what he knew now, he realized he was so broken then that he probably would have even accepted his brother's fathering her first child if he had known about it at the time. Cringing, he realized that he had so little self-esteem that he would have let her play him like a fool if that was what she had wanted.

"Things have certainly changed," he told himself with what he hoped was finality.

Chapter Forty-Two

The days after the funeral had passed quickly as Joe's father hung in the fight. The brothers were shocked, based on what the doctor had told them and how incoherent he was, that he was still with them. The sons all took turns feeding him broth and turning him in his bed, so he didn't get sores. By the end of the first week after Joe and Jeremiah's arrival, the remaining four McIntyre boys decided that they needed to hash out what would happen next.

The doctor had given them no hope. He had told them that their father's heart was pumping just enough blood to supply his brain and organs with oxygen as long as he lay still. He told them, when asked, that very occasionally, a heart can seemingly repair itself, but based on the fact that their father had been a miner his whole life, first with coal, then with precious metals, and with all of the gases he had breathed while working underground, not to mention how many years the man had smoked a pipe, that they shouldn't hold out hope. The doctor suggested that they keep him comfortable, as the end was inevitable: what wasn't certain was when.

Therefore, the men deliberated the plans to care for the man who had raised them. Jeremiah was direct in asserting his plan to head back down the mountain and home to his ranch in the valley as soon as possible. He wasn't about to miss the birth of his baby, and the others agreed that he had a legitimate reason to leave.

Jonathan stated that he was due back at the mine the next morning. His boss had been kind to give him the week off, but he was unable to take any more time. James, being a skilled mechanic, whose expertise was always needed, had a little more flexibility because his skill set made him more indispensable. He thought he could maybe push for another week, but at the same time he still needed money to live, mentioning that if he could, he would much rather return to work for at least half days so that he didn't fall too far behind.

Everyone then looked at Joe. He sighed, knowing full well what would be expected of him. Figuring it was his due, he accepted that he had not been there for the past ten years while his brothers had borne the brunt of the care of their father during that time. Still, he didn't like seeming so pathetic, having no one waiting on him, so he made a big show of declaring that he supposed his little town could continue on without him for at least a few more days.

Jeremiah returned home the next day after the meeting. He and Joe embraced on the platform, neither of them knowing if they would ever see each other again. Before the events of the past week, none of the brothers had thought much about that as they scattered and maintained their own lives, there was a possibility any one of them could succumb, and the others would never see him again. Goodbye now held a much more sinister connotation in that perhaps it could be the last word spoken between any of them.

Joe then told James and Jonathan to return to work, making sure Jonathan also went home to where his young wife was waiting. Joe knew that his job would be there for him when he returned–no one else was exactly biting at the bit for the position–but his brothers were not so lucky. He told them that he had nothing to do during the days he was there, so it made sense for him to care for their father while they went back to their jobs. It had taken some convincing, but the youngest McIntyre men eventually relented, leaving Joe alone with his invalid father in a disturbingly cluttered house.

Over the next several days, when Joe was not attending to his father, he began to muck out the place. He was shocked at the state of it and had even started a large bonfire by the water pump to burn all the papers and other items that had been stashed in corners for nearly a decade.

Then, when that was done, he took out all the rugs and left them hanging in the warm sunshine while he swept and scrubbed

360

the floors. As they dried, he stood out in the yard, whaling on the carpets with his mother's old beater apparatus, as the clouds of more than ten years of dirt, dust, and grime billowed out around him, every whack bringing him satisfaction as he pictured it was Joshua's face he was beating.

James was flabbergasted when he came home every night, shocked at what Joe had been able to accomplish in just a few days. Both Jonathan and James tried arguing with him that it wasn't necessary, but Joe wasn't about to let them talk him out of his cathartic outlet and told them that with the reality of their father's imminent passing, the house would have to be cleaned so it could be vacated in any case.

Finally, he began to wash the piles of sullied towels, clothing, and bedding that had been largely ignored for Joe wasn't sure how long. He labored over several washtubs full of hot, soapy water, drenching himself in the process. Though he had done his own laundry for years, seeing how much wash a large family could generate, Joe marveled at how his mother had done it all on her own, with five active boys and a husband who worked in the filth and dirt of a shaft underground.

It was on the third straight day of his washing, when his hands were red and raw from the hot water, soap, and the near-constant wind blowing his skin dry, cracking and chapping them in the process, that Caroline had come sauntering up the walk like the last ten years had never happened.

He had felt her before he saw her. Joe had been outside, hanging the sopping wet laundry, when he felt a chill rush through him and the hair on the back of his neck stand up, so he quickly glanced around. He was used to relying heavily on his instincts since he had become sheriff; it had saved his life on more than one occasion. His eyes settled lastly on the path leading up from town when he saw her.

He had to begrudgingly admit to himself that she was still a beautiful woman. Having birthed three babies had rounded out her curves a bit more, but other than that, she essentially looked the same as he remembered.

She came alone. He had no idea where her children were as Joe watched her walk the rest of the way toward the house and then around the side to where he stood frozen in place, his left hand still resting on the line, while the right was poised to place a clothespin.

He had figured at some point, based on the conversation he had had with Jonathan, he would inevitably see her around town at least once, but he never thought she would be brazen enough to come out to the house.

Caroline said nothing for several seconds, just gazing at him with her green eyes, but Joe would be damned if he spoke to her first. They stared at each other until she finally broke and looked away.

"Hello, Joe," she murmured quietly.

He still didn't answer her.

"Aren't you going to say hello?" she inquired sweetly.

"What the hell do you want?" he growled.

"I came to see you," she answered.

He glared at her in response.

"I heard you were still in town, and I figured that one of us ought to be the bigger person and speak to the other."

"I don't see why that's necessary," he retorted.

She chose to ignore his comment and took a step closer. "I heard that you were still in town, taking care of your father."

He finished pinning the sheet to the line and turned to face her straight on, his arms crossed protectively across his chest.

"Have you decided to move home? To come back from Colorado?"

Again, he remained mute.

Caroline sighed in defeat. "I was hoping that enough time had passed that we could speak to one another as friends, but I can see that it is not something you're willing to do. I'm sorry to have bothered you!"

She turned and began to walk slowly away from him. He could tell from her body language that she wanted him to stop her, but he was not willing to play her games, so he simply watched as she moved down the trail out of sight, before exhaling a large sigh.

Joe didn't tell anyone about Caroline's visit. There was no one to tell, except for his brothers, and he was in no mood to be chastised by them because he had dismissed her so completely. Even though he had to admit his behavior had been childish, he didn't want to hear about how he should have been kinder to her, that a lot had changed in ten years, or any of the other reasons they would have given as to why he shouldn't have treated her so poorly.

Chapter Forty-Three

Four days after Caroline's visit, Joe's father passed quietly in his sleep. Joe and James awoke in the early dawn to find that he had succumbed at some point in the night, and Joe was grateful that at least one of his brothers was there with him when it was discovered their patriarch was gone. As sheriff, he had to go to the scene whenever there was a dead body, but for some reason, it felt overwhelming when it was his own kin.

The arrangements were made for the funeral in three days' time, and this time, none of the surviving McIntyre brothers stayed home. Jeremiah had returned, the proud father of a newborn baby girl. The four men were united in the front pew as their father's memory was celebrated and then again, at the cemetery, after having borne the coffin. The remaining sons of Brian McIntyre stood shoulder to shoulder, and each took their turns throwing a shovel of dirt into the grave before their father was commended back to the earth.

Normally, Joe was not a drinking man. He never had been one to hit the bottle, especially to dull emotions, even before he became a sheriff, mostly because he didn't like how it made him feel. He was a man who liked to be in charge of his faculties but had gotten more so since he had become the local law enforcement and he saw how alcohol destroyed lives. Nevertheless, something in him snapped at the wake after his father's funeral, and he drank far more than he ever had before.

It had started with several toasts from his father's friends and former colleagues. Brian McIntyre was a highly respected man and there were many stories shared that day, all ending with a shot of whiskey. Then, as the afternoon wore on, the stories concluded, but the whiskey was still free flowing. By the time evening settled over the town, Joe had lost all track of time and his brothers and was feeling no pain at all.

At some point, Joe realized that he was drunk, ironically when he began to sober up. He decided to step outside into the fresh mountain air to clear his head and try to hasten his senses' return to normal.

Sitting alone on a bench outside the mercantile for quite a while, he pondered over the last few weeks and all that had transpired. Thinking about when he would be able to return home to Colorado, he felt someone slide up beside him. He had been thinking so hard, trying to make his neurons fire in the correct sequence, that he hadn't even paid attention to his surroundings until he felt the heat radiating off her when she came close.

"I'm sorry about your father," Caroline purred first thing.

"Thanks," he mumbled, still too drunk to remember that he didn't want to speak to her. Something primal from deep within his subconscious made him long to be near her, as if the liquor had blocked out all the pain and agony she had caused him.

"Mind if I sit down?" she asked.

He shrugged. "It's a free country," he mumbled. He couldn't recall why, but he was triggered to be wary of her motivations. She sidled up against him.

"How are you holding up?" she asked him.

"I'm all right. You?" he slurred, still not yet recalling how hurt she had made him.

"Things are tough," she admitted with a shrug.

"I'm sorry," he replied. "Wanna talk about it?"

Caroline looked at him strangely but then delved in. "Things were bad, Joe. They were bad for a long time."

"Aw… That's too bad!" he said, his voice dripping with pity. She studied him, wondering if he was being sarcastic.

"I'm so sorry, Joe," she whispered.

Then it clicked. He remembered. Thankfully, though, the effects of the alcohol coursing through his veins tempered his anger considerably.

"S'all right," he relented.

"I wish that I could go back and change time."

"Don't we all..."

"Joe, tell me about Colorado. Are you really the sheriff there?"

"I am," he stated, his chest puffing out a bit with pride. "I got elected and everything."

"I never knew you had any ambitions to be in law enforcement," she said wistfully.

"I didn't, either. The job found me, not the other way around."

"Is it dangerous?"

"Can be! Got myself shot a few months ago. It got really bad. Thankfully, Mama D and Sarah took real good care of me!"

"Oh?" Caroline inquired. "And who are they?" She couldn't keep the jealousy from creeping into her voice, but he was too intoxicated to pick up on it.

"They're my friends there," he said, sounding more like a child than a man.

"Just friends?"

"Just friends!" he confirmed resolutely. "Mama D is a real nice lady who takes care of me like my own ma. Sarah is Ginny's sister, and Ginny's husband is also my friend."

"That's nice," Caroline said, not really caring about who these people were. He didn't seem to be involved with either of them or married, because certainly a wife wouldn't have cared for him like a mother, which made her all the happier.

There was a lull in the conversation as Joe felt himself get sleepy. Caroline reached out and grabbed his hand in hers and to her surprise, he let her. She had been expecting that he would pull away.

"I've missed you, Joe," she said softly.

He squeezed her hand. "I have missed you, too."

"I am so sorry I hurt you!"

"You are?" he slurred.

"Of course! I have thought about nothing but you for years. About how wrong I got it. I will never forgive myself."

"Water under the bridge," Joe drunkenly waved his hand wildly to demonstrate.

"I have never stopped loving you!"

"I never stopped loving you, either."

Joe was drifting in and out of a groggy haze.

"Are you going to stay here now, Joe?"

"I'm not sure," he answered. In that moment, he wasn't. He was home. His time in Colorado felt like a lifetime ago, almost like it was someone else's life entirely.

"I think you should stay," she said coyly, squeezing his hand in hers.

"Maybe I will!" he answered stupidly. At that moment, it seemed completely reasonable.

"That would be wonderful! Maybe we could even pick up where we left off!" she cried. Suddenly, to his shock and delight, she lunged for him, wrapping her arms around his neck before she kissed him square on his mouth.

"Then I'll do it!" he assured her with the intense certainty of a drunk when they came up for air.

Just then, Jeremiah, Jonathan, and James all walked out to find Joe sitting with Caroline, holding her hand. Jeremiah glanced nervously to Jonathan, but he just shrugged. The pair of them looked cozy, and it was obvious that Joe was pleased with the situation as he sat with a satisfied grin on his face, his hand clasped with hers. They had seen the kiss, and it was clear that Caroline had been the instigator, but Joe had obviously not objected. However, his brothers knew that he couldn't be in his right mind if he was sitting there so calmly with her.

Jeremiah took charge, being the soberest of the three, and walked across the street, stopping in front of Joe and Caroline.

"Hiya, Joe. Whaddya you say that we head on home? Party's over and it's time we get back."

"Oh! All right!" Joe answered, somewhat disoriented by the whole ordeal. He stood up and staggered a bit as Caroline grasped at his hand.

"Will I see you tomorrow, Joe? We could discuss your plans for moving back!"

"I s'pose," he answered her. James and Jonathan shared a concerned look.

"Let's go!" Jeremiah ordered, trying to extricate them before Joe agreed to anything else.

Joe did not remember the walk home or tumbling into bed. His brothers made sure that his tie, suit jacket, and shoes had been removed, but he awoke in a cold sweat, a wrinkled shirt, and a spinning room. He wasn't sure what had awakened him, but then one of his brothers spoke out in the main room and it sounded as though he was standing right beside him, yelling in his ear.

"He's still in bed, Caroline. Wait and I'll go see if he is awake."

"Still in bed?" he heard Caroline's voice ring out. "Why, it's almost noon! Lazy man!" she proclaimed affectionately.

Joe panicked. Having no recollection of the night before, he had no idea why she would be there now, but he was in no condition to deal with her right then, that he knew for sure.

He heard Jonathan quietly tiptoe into the room after knocking softly. Joe tightly closed his eyes against the bright sunshine that flooded his bedroom from the parlor as the door opened.

"Close the door!" he feebly cried out.

"Sorry!"

"That's better."

"Sorry, Joe, but you've got a visitor."

"Is it Caroline?"

"Yes."

"What the hell does she want?"

"To talk to you."

"Why?"

"Probably because you and she were cuddling and kissing last night."

"What?" Joe exclaimed. "We did? Oh, no!"

368

He shook his head, making his pounding head hurt worse. "No! No! No!"

"Oh, yes! Don't you remember? You and she were very cozy when we found you after the wake."

"On the street?"

"In plain sight!"

Joe was silent as his foggy brain tried to recall anything about the events to which Jonathan was alluding. He vaguely remembered sitting down in front of the mercantile, but everything else was a blur.

"Jonathan, what am I going to do? I can't see her in this state!"

"I don't think you have much of a choice, do you?"

"Can't you just send her away? Tell her I'm under the weather?"

"No can do! You… How was it that you put it the other day? Oh, yes. You made your bed, now you have to lay in it."

"You are truly the worst brother ever! I can't believe I thought you were my favorite!" Joe grumbled.

"See you in a few minutes!" Jonathan sang as he walked out the door and closed it behind him.

Joe changed his clothes and washed his face, then grabbed his toothbrush and tried to scrub away the whiskey taste still lingering in his mouth. He brushed his hair and put some hair tonic in it to try to tame it. Finally, he took a deep breath and opened the door.

Caroline sat primly on the settee. Her face lit up when he came out of his room, but he could not see her, as his eyes were barely slits against the brightness coupled with the effects of the alcohol still circulating in his blood.

"Good afternoon, Joe!" Caroline sang out, her voice thundering through his head as he used it to guide him toward the settee. When he got there, he had to steady himself against the spinning room before sitting down with a large, "Umph!"

"I would have said good morning, but it's far past noon now!"

Joe smiled weakly at her, leaning his head back against the settee, wondering how he could have been so stupid to end up in this mess.

"I thought that we could continue our conversation about you staying here," she told him.

Joe began to panic. Now much more sober, he had no intention of staying in California. He had a whole life in Colorado. He had friends: Mama D, Doc Miller, Jacob and Ginny, Adam, and Sarah.

Sarah! Joe's heart stopped. What would she say if he decided to stay in California? Then he realized she probably wouldn't care. She was not interested in him romantically, anyway, and after the kiss he had lain on her right before he left, he was sure that he had thoroughly ruined their friendship, too.

"How are you feeling today, Joe?" Caroline asked him sweetly.

"Honestly? A bit rough," he answered, first closing one eye and then the other trying to get some relief from the brightness.

"Still not much of a drinker, Joe?"

"Nope."

"That's a good thing, believe me."

"Good or bad, with my job, I have to keep my wits about me. I never should have drunk so much last night," he sighed.

"It was an unusual circumstance."

"I suppose."

"I can imagine that being a sheriff means that you have a lot of responsibility!"

"It can," he answered her, turning his head to the side to glance at her.

"Well, I think it is marvelous!"

"Thanks," Joe said, somewhat sarcastically.

"How'd you get the job?"

"I had a death wish," he muttered, only half joking.

"Oh, Joe!" Caroline's laugh tinkled.

"I'm not kidding, Caroline."

"Joe, you're so silly!"

"No, Caroline, I'm not. I truly didn't care if I lived or died for years after you decided to kick up your heels with Joshua."

Caroline at least had the decency to stare at the floor and look ashamed.

"I know what I did was inexcusable. I have spent every day ever since then wishing I could go back and change things."

"Well, you can't," Joe stated flatly, not feeling well enough to even attempt to be tactful.

"I know. But, Joe, please… I need to explain to you what happened; tell you my side of the story."

Joe said nothing in response.

"Please?"

He turned his head to look at her. Her eyes were magnified with tears and her expression was one of raw pain. Once again, he cursed his empathetic side. He wished that he could simply remain cold and hard, but he was obviously a sucker for women and their tears. *Perhaps they remind me of Ma*, he thought fleetingly.

"Fine."

"But not here," she said, glancing around to see James, Jonathan, and Jeremiah all trying to appear busy and not like they were eavesdropping, but they were failing miserably.

"What do you suggest?"

"Why don't you come to the house tonight for supper?"

"I guess that would be all right. What time?"

"Thank you, Joe. I never got a chance to explain what happened, not that it excuses anything. But I always wanted the opportunity to apologize to you. How about you come by at six?"

When she left, Jeremiah and Jonathan both pounced. "Joe, what the hell are you doing?" Jonathan cried.

"I don't know!" Joe declared back to him.

"Why didn't you just tell her 'No,' Joe?" Jeremiah asked, his voice revealing his unease.

"I don't know… I guess I want to hear what she has to say."

"I don't think this is going to end well!" James interjected from the kitchen.

"Well, boys, I reckon that since it's my life and not yours, I'll do what I want to do," Joe snapped back as he stood up and marched from the room.

Chapter Forty-Four

At promptly six o'clock, Joe was at the door of his deceased brother's and ex-fiancée's home. The whole way there, he debated with himself about turning around. His head still ached, and he also felt slightly sick to his stomach, but he couldn't tell if that was from nerves or the effects of last night's alcohol binge.

He still hadn't resolved the fight with himself about going or not as he was raising his fist to knock on the door. Figuring that his inhibitions were probably still down from his inebriation, the truth was that he was curious. Point blank, when push came to shove, he wanted to hear what Caroline had to say that could possibly offer an excuse for her devastating treatment of him so many years ago.

As soon as he rapped on the door, Caroline opened it. Joe wasn't quite sure what he would find on the other side, but figured after all he had seen as sheriff, nothing would shock him. However, he was still surprised by the sparsely furnished home. It was clean and tidy, but what little furniture there was looked old and worn, as were the curtains and rugs. There was a clapped-out settee, a threadbare chair, and a table with five mismatched chairs, as well as an old sewing machine, much older than the one he had given Sarah. She saw his eyes scan the room and she smiled slightly.

"Not much, is it?" she asked him sadly. "But welcome."

Joe didn't answer as he stepped through the threshold. He thought that something was amiss, but it took several seconds to sink in.

"Where are the children?" he asked.

'Oh! My friend Julianne took them for the night. I figured that with all we have to discuss it would be better done without the constant interruptions youngsters bring. Besides, this is not a conversation for small ears. Please, sit down."

Joe moved to the settee and sat stiffly as she sank in beside him. Given the condition and size of the settee, they were forced into very close proximity with each other, leaving him feeling uncomfortable.

"Dinner should be ready real soon," she assured him. "I'm sorry it isn't much… Meat is a luxury we can rarely afford, but I was able to get a small roast for the two of us to share."

Joe only nodded. He hadn't really thought about how she would feed him, let alone herself and the three children, for that matter. Hearing that they were struggling for food made his tender heart ache, not to mention it made him extremely uncomfortable. It was yet another reminder that whatever had happened between the adults, the children were innocent in all of it and shouldn't be suffering.

They sat in awkward silence for a while, until Caroline stood up. "Well, supper is just about done. Why don't you sit up at the table while I do the finishing touches?"

She walked Joe over and motioned to the chair at the head of the table. It dawned on him that particular seat had obviously been his brother's, still occupied by him until only a few short weeks ago. He also sardonically recognized that it would have been his seat if circumstances had been different. As she moved around her small kitchen, he scrutinized her unsympathetically as she set several serving dishes on the table, until he realized that none of her dishes or flatware matched. Thinking back to his mother, she had always insisted that her dishes and silverware matched, even when moving from pillar to post while raising five boys. Only then did he feel a momentary spark of pity for Caroline, until he harshly reminded himself that her circumstances were the consequences of her own choices.

When the food was on the table, she joined him, serving him first, and then herself. After a quick prayer and a few moments of silence, she spoke.

"How is Colorado?"

"It's really nice. Beautiful," he answered distractedly, as he noticed the small bed with a trundle in the corner of the main room. He then discerned that there was only one bedroom in the tiny home.

"And you're really the sheriff there?"

"Yup."

"Joe, that's so dangerous!"

"It is! I got shot just earlier this year and it was pretty bad. My friends said that they were afraid they were going to lose me. Doc Miller would never admit it if he thought he would lose the fight, but I think I gave him a run for his money."

"You told me a little about your friends last night," she reported cryptically, making Joe wonder what all he said. "You mentioned someone named Mama D and then a Sarah?"

"Mama D is one of the local madams. She loves me like a son. Her own died when he was just a baby, along with her husband. And Sarah…"

"Is Sarah a whore?" Caroline interrupted, trying hard to keep the jealousy out of her voice, but not succeeding.

Joe was taken aback. "No! Not at all! She's just a woman who had to move to Colorado to be near her sister's family after her husband died. She has a young boy named Adam. He and I pal around quite a bit, fishing and whatnot. She's the local seamstress, and she was a great nurse when I was hurt."

Caroline couldn't help but notice that he was telling her a lot more about Sarah than any other of the friends he had mentioned.

"Are you and she…" she took a deep breath, afraid of the answer, "Are you and she courting?"

"No! We're just friends!" he explained, while he thought to himself that if he said it enough, then maybe he could make himself believe it.

"Oh."

There was a long pause before either of them spoke again.

"Joe?"

"Yes?"

"As I said earlier, I'm so sorry I hurt you! I was so stupid. I was young and thoughtless, and my head was too easily turned by attention and fancy presents. I realize now that it was all smoke and mirrors."

"I get that you wanted more than what you thought I could give you. But did it really have to be my brother? There were plenty of other men in town who would have gladly promised you the moon and not delivered."

"He… he seemed to have potential. Whenever we spoke, he sounded like he had a lot of ambition, constantly talking about getting some claims and trying to go it alone. He promised me a fancy house, fur coats, diamonds…" Caroline paused as she looked around and wryly laughed. "Instead, this is what I got."

"Caroline, all you had to do was to ask any of the rest of us McIntyre boys and we would have told you that Joshua always had his head in the clouds. He talked a good story, but in truth he was nothing but a drunk and gambler."

"Now you tell me!"

"If only you would have given me the chance, I would have told you the night that you met him," Joe said sadly.

"I'm so sorry, Joe. To be honest, I'm surprised that you talked to me at your father's wake, let alone agreed to come to dinner tonight."

"I only spoke to you because I had too much to drink, and I didn't want to come tonight," Joe reported honestly. "But I figure I have spent ten years wondering why. I guess I didn't want to pass up the opportunity to ask you instead of continuing to speculate. As far as I see it, you owe me that much."

"That seems fair. I guess it's the least I can do. If you're finished, let's move back to the settee where we will be more comfortable."

After they had settled into the settee, Caroline looked at him in anticipation, but now that he could ask questions, he didn't know where to start.

Finally, he got up the courage to ask what he had to know. "Were you happy with him?"

She nodded. "I was, in the beginning, when he was still good at holding things together. Then later, there were times when he would straighten up and fly right… for a while."

"When did you know you were carrying his child?"

"Not long after you found us at the cabin."

"Why there?" Joe asked, feeling the familiar constricting in his chest when his mind went back to that day. Ten years later and it still felt as raw as the day it happened; that image would be burned into his brain until he died, he was sure.

"He took me there, thinking it was the only place where we could be alone and not damage my reputation. We couldn't go to the hotel, and he was back at your parents' house. We thought you had gone to work."

"And if I hadn't have discovered you, would you've let me marry you, knowing that you had been with my brother before me?"

"I didn't know how to tell you, Joe," she cried, her frustration setting in.

"I don't know, Caroline!" he retorted quickly back. "How about, 'Joe, I'm sorry, but I'm in love with someone else. I don't want to marry you.' That would have worked just as well and not left me with the visual that still haunts me to this day!"

He could feel himself getting angry and he knew that if he lost his temper, he wouldn't be able to get his questions answered, so he took a deep breath and sighed audibly.

"Joe, I don't know what more I can say. I'm sorry!" she cried. "I'm so incredibly sorry! I was young and stupid, not to mention selfish, only caring about the wrong things and myself. You were too nice, too secure. I felt like I would be smothered by you. Josh was spontaneous and fun and made me laugh. He talked about traveling the world… You talked about building a house, saving money, and raising a family."

He nodded. "I was boring," he stated plainly.

Caroline smiled sadly. "But that's the thing. There's nothing wrong with boring! I wish I realized that ten years ago. I would have been much better off."

"So, what happened to Josh?" he asked her, finally ready to hear the story of his brother's demise.

"He owed money to the wrong people. He always owed money to people," she sighed.

"So, what was different about this time, then?"

"I don't know exactly, to be honest. He was at the saloon and the person he owed money to was there, as well. Apparently, they got into an argument and the next thing I know, Josh is lying dead on the floor, and I have the local sheriff knocking at my door," she said, her eyes tearing up.

"I have had to do those calls myself as sheriff," he commiserated. "They're not pleasant."

"No, I can't imagine they are. I was holding the baby and thankfully, the sheriff grabbed him when I dropped him in shock."

"Why didn't Joshua pay the debt? Or why didn't he ask for help?"

"He had, Joe. Over and over and over again, your father, and even brothers would bail him out. He would square up for a while; even get a job in the beginning, before he burned bridges with every employer in town. But he would start drinking again, then whoring, then came the gambling. Sometimes, it was a long progression, other times it would all happen in the same night. Next, our belongings would start to disappear. He sold anything of any value to anyone. Even my mother's wedding china, hauled all the way here from Ohio, which my father painstakingly saved for me so that I could have it, was gone after a few years. He eventually took my wedding ring, too," she sniffed. "Then, when there was nothing left to sell, he had to start running. He would spend months at a time with Jeremiah down at the ranch, until things would blow over. The only thing he wouldn't sell was my sewing machine. I thought it was because he was trying to take care of the children and me, but then I realized that he knew if he sold it, I wouldn't be able to make money to support his habits anymore. We lived on the money I brought in more often than not – what little I could hide from him, that is.”

“That sounds like Sarah. After her husband died, she had no way to support herself after her in-laws took back the farm they had given him half of before they were married.”

“Oh,” Caroline replied nonchalantly, not wanting to talk about his friend in Colorado.

Joe took the hint and went back to his questioning. “Caroline, I understand the first two children, I guess. But I’m confused about the third. If things were as bad as you say, then why did you have another baby with him?”

“I didn’t want to, Joe!” she cried. “After I found out that he was with every whore in town, I wouldn’t let him touch me anymore, and it worked for years. Then one night about three years ago, he came home drunk. I was asleep in the bed, and the next thing I knew, he was on top of me!” Caroline gave a little sob. “I tried to fight him off, but I was just too weak. He didn’t care. I knew within just a few weeks that I was pregnant again.”

She put her face in her hands and began to weep, her whole body shaking with pain and grief. Joe sat stunned. He had no idea what to say to her when he learned that his last nephew was conceived as the result of a rape. Of course, he knew that as Joshua’s wife, Caroline had no legal rights and was expected to submit to his advances. If she didn’t, he was within his rights to do what he deemed necessary to ensure that she resumed her wifely duty. In his heart, however, he felt it was wrong. He had dealt with sobbing women, battered black and blue, sitting across the desk from him in the jail, begging him to arrest their husbands, and had to tell them that there was nothing he could legally do. He had tried to speak to a few of the worst offenders. The ones whose wives walked around town with blackened faces or worse, their eyes downcast in humiliation and fear, but he had been told repeatedly to mind his own business. It rubbed him the wrong way that when a whore was assaulted, she actually had more rights than a man’s wife.

Instinctively, he reached out and touched her shoulder, rubbing it softly. "I'm so sorry," he said quietly. "I had no idea!"

She looked up at him and gave a watery, weak smile. "What is done is done. I love that little boy with all of my heart, and I wouldn't change having him for anything in the world!"

"That's good, at least," Joe stated, relieved to hear that she wasn't resentful of the little boy.

"They're good children. Very sweet and loving. If I got anything worthwhile out of this marriage to your brother, it was them."

The idea that his brother had fathered children with her, the love of his life, was still hard for him to swallow. He couldn't help feeling that out of everything Joshua had stolen from him, the loss of having a family was still the one thing that he could not move past.

"What is your plan now?" he asked her.

Her head jerked up and she looked him in the eye. "I don't honestly know. My sewing has kept us going, but it has not been a comfortable living. At least Joshua worked sometimes, doing odd jobs for people. Now, I fear I won't be able to feed and clothe my little ones."

"I'll help you," he resolved. "I can send you money every month."

She sighed, before taking a risk. "I appreciate that. But what I really want is a father for them. I want a strong, healthy, male influence in their lives that they never got with their father. He was either gone or taking them to the mercantile and letting them choose whatever they wanted. I was always the bad guy; the practical one who had to say 'No!'"

Joe didn't respond and watched as she snuggled a bit closer to him.

"When you told me last night that you were thinking about moving back here?" she asked him.

"Ummm…" Joe hummed noncommittedly, wondering how in the world he was going to get out of his drunken promise.

"Well, I have to say that I got very happy. I would really like it if you did move back. You would be so good for the children. They will love you so. Already, you're their favorite uncle with the wonderful Christmas gifts you send every year."

"Thanks," Joe replied sheepishly, wondering how he could be their favorite just based on the gifts he had given them. Then he deduced that they were most likely thrilled with anything they got, since his brother certainly did not provide them with any extras and he knew that Caroline could barely keep food on the table, let alone buy toys.

Just then, Caroline put her hand on his knee, causing him to immediately tense up. She felt his response, but ignored it, running her hand higher up his thigh as she looked seductively into his eyes and said, "And maybe, in time, you will learn to trust me again, and we can see about picking up where we left off…"

"Maybe," he squeaked, not really sure what else to say, as he was too busy concentrating on her ever-creeping hand on his leg.

He swallowed hard as her fingers sneaked even higher. "I guess I should be going now!"

"Or you could stay here…" she whispered breathlessly into his ear, as she cupped her hand over his crotch.

"No!" he countered a little too forcefully. "It's getting late. I need to get back."

"Oh! All right… if you're sure," she answered him, and to his relief, she removed her hand.

"I'm sure!" he affirmed, standing up, grateful for the opportunity to rearrange his pants. She handed him his hat with a smile.

"Perhaps tomorrow you could meet the children," she told him.

He answered her with a "Yes," though he was still torn.

"That's wonderful! Would you like to come here for lunch?"

Joe nodded mutely. He reached for the doorknob of the tiny home before finally remembering his manners and was turning back to thank her for supper when Caroline seized the opportunity to kiss him on his cheek.

Mumbling a hasty goodbye, Joe set off into the darkness toward home. He had a lot to think about.

Chapter Forty-Five

When Joe walked back through the front door of his childhood home, he was surprised to find his three brothers sitting and waiting for him.

"What's this?" he stated, annoyed. "An inquisition?"

"Nope," Jeremiah replied. "We were just waiting up for you to make sure you weren't nursing another broken heart."

"I'm fine!" he growled at them. "She's fine! It was fine!"

"Good!" declared Jonathan. "Now you can finally put this whole mess to rest. You can go back to Colorado with all of your questions answered and finally move on!"

"When are you going back?" James asked.

"Where? To Caroline's? I'm going tomorrow for lunch to meet the youngsters."

The three brothers looked worriedly at each other.

"Joe?" inquired Jonathan. "Do you think that's wise?"

"No," he admitted. "But I'm going to anyway."

With that, he walked into his bedroom and shut the door.

At noon the next day, Joe was once again at Caroline's house. This time when he knocked, a young boy opened the door and said, "Hello! Are you my Uncle Joe?"

Joe stood and gaped at the boy. It was as if Joshua was staring back at him from when he was nine years old. Old memories came roaring back, and he wasn't sure he could do this, but then the little boy reached out and grabbed his hand. "Come on, Uncle Joe!"

Joe found himself once again inside the tiny dwelling when a little girl slowly approached. She was a beautiful little thing, and Joe felt his heart ache when he thought about how thrilled his mother would have been to see her granddaughter. She, too, looked like a McIntyre, though she resembled James more than any of the other brothers, including Joshua. She looked at Joe with big, round eyes, filled with equal parts fear and curiosity.

Caroline exited the bedroom, a small boy on her hip. "Oh, good! They let you in. So sorry, I had to change the baby's clothes."

Joe was mute and could honestly not think of anything to say, but Caroline didn't notice and continued speaking. "I see that you have met Gabe and Penelope. This is little Roger."

He knew it would be hard. He was prepared that it would hurt to see his brother's children with the woman who was supposed to be *his* wife. Even so, he had no idea that it would be a crushing blow that would almost knock him to the floor. The older two were a bit easier, because they were not infants, but Joe felt his chest constrict when he saw the youngest boy.

Caroline saw the look that crossed over his face while he regarded his youngest nephew. "Would you like to hold him?" she asked.

"Would he let me?"

"Sure! Why not?"

Joe reached for the toddler, and he stretched his pudgy little arms out to him. Once he was settled in his arms, the little boy said, "Papa?"

Joe looked panic-stricken, unsure of what to say. Thankfully, the oldest boy said, "No! That's Uncle Joe, Pa's brother. Pa's dead, remember?"

"Gabe, that's enough!" Caroline admonished.

"Sorry about that," she said, turning back to face him. "Roger hadn't seen much of his pa for most of his life. He was only back in town, after being gone for six months, for about a month before…"

"Was he with Jer?" Joe asked.

Caroline shook her head. "Not this time. He was working the docks in San Francisco. That's what ultimately got him killed. He played with the wrong people and lost. They had a much farther reach than he ever counted on."

"Did they catch who did it?"

"No. The sheriff said whoever it was knew what he was doing. Came into town that night, played for a while, then killed him. No one recognized him, and he left town before anyone was the wiser."

Joe nodded. "I understand. I've had a few of those myself."

"My ma says you're a sheriff in some town in Colorado," Gabe said to him. "Is that true?"

"Sure is!" Joe answered, ruffling the boy's hair.

"I wanna be a sheriff some day! I'm gonna find the man who did this to Pa!" he resolutely declared.

"Maybe Joe can teach you what he knows, then?" Caroline said, smiling.

"Could you? Could you, please? I'd like that very much!" the boy cried.

"Sure," Joe answered him, not knowing what else to say. He felt disconnected, as if he were in a dream.

They ate lunch, and then Caroline put the baby down for his nap. The older children wanted to play in the yard, so he and Caroline watched them from their seats on an old rickety bench on the porch.

Neither of them spoke for a long time until eventually, she looked up at him and reached for his hand. "I'm so scared," she whispered.

"I'm sorry," Joe replied, giving her hand a slight squeeze. "It'll be all right."

"How am I ever going to do this on my own, Joe?"

"It seems to me that you already have been."

"I have no one. I'm all alone," Caroline whispered before she began to sniffle.

He rubbed her back gently, making what he hoped were soothing noises. He was still uncomfortable around women's tears, having had no sisters or wife, so he didn't know what to do and was instead working purely on instinct.

"What am I going to do, Joe? How am I going to raise these children?"

"Shhh… Caroline, you'll be fine!"

"How could I have been so stupid? How could I have been so foolish? Why didn't I just marry you? Why can't they be yours? You wouldn't have left me alone. You wouldn't have gambled and drunk yourself silly." She paused and took a deep breath before continuing. "I don't think you would've been visiting whores, either."

He smiled wryly. "Well, I do visit whores," he replied.

She gasped, "What?"

"I do, Caroline. I visit them every night."

"Joe McIntyre, you are no better than your broth…"

He cut her off with a laugh. "It's part of my job, Caroline. I visit the saloons and brothels every night. I make sure that everyone is safe."

"Oh!" she said, chuckling a little. "I guess that makes sense."

"Joe?" she whispered, "In all honesty, I'm not sure that I won't have to work in one myself. I don't make enough money sewing, and now that your Pa has passed, he won't be able to help me anymore, and you and your brothers are certainly under no obligation."

"Caroline, I don't think you would have to resort to being a whore," he told her.

"How else am I going to feed these children?"

"I'm sure that you can marry again. California is still deficient in women. You won't be alone for long if you don't want to be," he told her with confidence.

To his surprise, she began crying again.

"What?" he asked, frustrated that he couldn't make things better.

"That would be going from the frying pan into the fire, Joe! How do I know that I won't get someone worse than Joshua? I could end up in a situation where I would be wishing the worst thing that had happened to me after his death was that I ended up a whore!"

He looked at her for the first time in years. Really looked at her. She was still a beautiful woman, though the rough years had worn her down. She was a bit heavier than ten years earlier and her face a little more drawn. He thought about her becoming a whore, trying to find someone to take her children, or worse, having to raise them in a cathouse. She would be far from the only one, but all the same, Joe knew it was not a good environment for little ones.

Then he thought about her marrying some stranger. She was right: she absolutely could go from bad to worse. There was no shortage of cruel men in the world, he knew. She was even more at risk because that type of man would treat her as if he was doing her an enormous favor by taking them on. Joe was well aware of the increased possibility of abuse, especially for the children, in a situation like she was facing. Once again, he cursed his job and the unfortunate things he had learned while doing it.

Looking out across the yard, he watched his niece and nephew playing and knew what he had to do. He thought about how close he had grown to Adam, and they were not even kin, so he figured he could eventually do the same with Caroline's children. After all, they may not have come directly from him, but they were still blood. His mother had told him that there would come a time when he would realize that blood was thicker than water, and it seemed like his time of reckoning was upon him.

Joe draped an arm around Caroline's shoulder and drew her close. It felt wrong, but he told himself it was just because of the history between them, and that ultimately, he would be able to forgive the past hurts, even if he couldn't forget them. Realizing that the welfare of those little ones was more important than his pride, he was willing to forgive a lot if it meant that they would have a safe, stable upbringing for the first time in their lives. He thought that he probably did still love her; it was only the pain of the past that was masking his feelings. Desperately, he wanted to believe that eventually they could move on together.

"Caroline, please don't worry. It will all work out. I have thought about it, and I'm going to resign from my position in Colorado and move back home. I will send a telegram and ask someone to pack up the rest of my belongings and send them West on the train. I will ask Jacob, perhaps, or maybe Sarah…"

At the mention of her name, he felt what seemed like a cold hand squeezing his heart. *Sarah!* Out of all the people he was going to have to tell of his new plans, she was the one he dreaded telling the most. More than his brothers, more than Mama D, he was worried about how she would respond. He then wondered who would take care of her and Adam? Even though they were not in a relationship, he still watched out for her and helped her as much as he could. It dawned on him that even her rent would increase once he stopped paying for the portion he was taking care of every month.

For the rest of the afternoon, Joe was quiet, now feeling torn. He supposed that Sarah, being in the same situation as Caroline, would understand the need for him to help her. Trying to comfort himself with the fact that she had family there, he rationalized that Jacob and Ginny wouldn't let her struggle. Despite this, his guilt continued to nag at him, so he even conceded that Dr. Miller was probably still interested in her.

The thought about Dr. Miller hadn't soothed his soul, however, but rather made him instantly jealous, so he remembered that Sarah had told him in so many words that she was not interested in marrying again. He consoled himself by thinking that Caroline would be happy to have a kind man to care for her children and share her bed, while Sarah had brought her hardship upon herself, as she had made it abundantly clear that she was independent and seemingly had no intention of ever being with anyone else. Instead of making him feel better, though, he still couldn't shake the troublesome feeling deep in his gut that this change would impact her far more than he could admit, and not just financially.

A few hours later, he thanked Caroline, and she walked him to the door. They paused, and she put her hand against his cheek, looking longingly into his eyes. For some reason, though, Joe couldn't bring himself to kiss her mouth as she seemed to be implying she wanted. He chastised himself for being ridiculous and leaned in, but at the last second, he moved his lips up to gently kiss her forehead, and then told her goodbye before starting the walk back to his family home.

As he trekked, he thought about why he had been compelled to kiss her forehead instead of her lips, but by the time he got halfway home, he had convinced himself that it was only because it hadn't seemed proper to kiss her anywhere else with the youngsters around. That issue settled, he turned his focus on how he was going to resign from his position and what he was going to do to make a living in California. He slowed his pace considerably, dreading having to tell his brothers what he was planning.

When he walked in, Jeremiah was cooking supper, and James was reading a newspaper. Jonathan soon came in with an empty laundry basket after having hung clothes on the line. They all looked up expectantly when Joe entered and greeted them, but nothing more was said.

Dinner was a quiet affair, though there was definitely tension in the air, and Joe found himself feeling irritated that no one asked him what had happened. Confused by his reaction, he worried if he was hoping someone would try to talk him out of his plans. When he realized this, he got angry, wondering why he was second-guessing himself.

I'm a grown man, damn it, and I can make my own decisions without having to justify them! he thought defiantly.

Meanwhile, his brothers all warily watched Joe's changing facial expressions as he processed through each thought but knowing just how touchy Joe was about the subject of Caroline, no one dared to break the ice, though they were all dying to know what was transpiring.

Finally, Jeremiah, being the eldest brother, decided to jump in headfirst. "How were Caroline and the children?" he inquired casually.

"Fine," Joe replied between bites.

"What did you think of them?" James asked him cautiously.

"They're children…" Joe answered vaguely, trying to convey he was not ready to speak about the experience yet.

The only noise for a long while was the sound of their silverware on their plates. Jeremiah finally spoke again, hoping to finagle Joe's plans out of him a different way.

"Well, boys, I think now that Pa is laid to rest, I need to get back to the ranch. I think I'll leave tomorrow or the day after."

Everyone murmured their agreement that it was time for him to head back to his own family, but then the conversation died yet again. Joe hadn't taken the bait. Finally, Jonathan had enough.

"So, when are you heading back home, Joe?" he asked poignantly.

Joe met his gaze, and his eyes narrowed in a subconscious warning that he would not be confronted. "I'm not," he answered matter-of-factly.

"Beg your pardon?" Jeremiah asked.

"I'm not going back to Colorado. I'm sending a telegram to Jacob on Monday morning, letting him know that I intend to resign from my position as sheriff."

The other McIntyre brothers said nothing, instead looking sideways at each other.

"And do what?" Jeremiah finally broke.

"I don't know," Joe answered honestly.

"But why?" questioned James, genuinely confused.

"Because I'm needed here."

"By whom?" Jonathan challenged him.

Annoyed, Joe put down his fork with a clatter. "I'm needed here to take care of Caroline and the little ones."

"Joe…" Jeremiah started.

"Save it, Jer. This isn't your decision. She needs help."

"You're right," Jeremiah confirmed, surprising Joe.

"I am?" he asked, confused. He had been reeving up for the fight he thought was coming.

"Absolutely. She needs someone to help her support those children."

"Good!" Joe said, relieved. "I'm glad you understand!"

"What I don't understand is why you're so damned stupid to think that someone has to be you?" Jeremiah pressed him.

"Pardon me?" Joe's temper flared as he pushed himself up from the table with his hands, and then instinctually leaned forward, his stance showing he was ready for battle.

"You heard me," Jeremiah confronted him, standing up as well.

"Oh, no!" James mumbled as he pushed himself back from the table, wary of where this confrontation was going.

Joe glared at his oldest brother for a long time, not backing down, until he suddenly felt exhausted and didn't want to fight anymore. With an exasperated sigh, he announced, "I'm going out for a walk!"

"Sounds good," said Jeremiah, relieved he wasn't going to be fighting his brother that night. "I'm getting too old for this shit!"

"Before you go, Joe, there's a letter for you," Jonathan called out over his shoulder as Joe was almost at the door.

"For me?" Joe asked, completely surprised, wondering who would send him a letter there.

"Yeah. I picked it up in town this morning."

"All right. Thanks."

Joe found an envelope on the desk addressed to him, *Joe McIntyre, General Delivery, Nevada City, CA*, and shoved it into his pants pocket. He slammed the door behind him as he stepped out.

He fully intended to walk far away from the house to try to think in peace, but the letter made him curious. Sitting on the front bench, he opened it and smiled when he unfolded the first piece of paper. It was a crudely drawn picture of a man and a boy fishing. The boy was holding a fish and smiling broadly.

He folded the picture back up and placed it under his thigh, before he opened the second piece of paper.

Dear Joe,

I hope you don't mind, but Adam really misses you and wanted to send you a letter. Since he doesn't write well yet,

*he drew you the picture. Then, he told me what he wanted
to tell you:*
Hi, Joe,

*I miss you! I wish you would come back. I miss you taking
me fishing, or reading me books, and I miss visiting you. I
hope your Pa is better. Please come home soon!*
Your friend,
Adam

*There! Now, I guess it is my turn. Life has been pretty
quiet here. The deputy is doing a good job, but we miss you.
We all are wondering when you will be home!*

*Joe, I never thanked you properly for all you did while I
was ill. Thank you for taking such good care of Adam. I
hope you know how much he loves you.*

*Anyway, everyone here is well. It feels like something
important is missing, though, and then it dawned on me it is
YOU!*

*I, too, hope your father is doing better. Don't forget
about us.*
With affection, your friend,
Sarah

Joe sat with his face in his hands. His head was pounding,
and his heart felt like it was being pulled in a million pieces at
once. He had been completely prepared to walk away from his
life in Colorado until he received the letter. Now, all he could
think about was Sarah.

The door opened, and Jonathan stepped out. He sat down
beside Joe but didn't say a word. Eventually, Joe looked over at
him and grimaced.

"Bad news?" Jonathan asked.

"No, not really…"

"Oh…"

Jonathan could play his next older brother like a fiddle. He
knew exactly how to handle him so that he could get him to open
up before he even realized he was doing it. Long ago, he learned

that if he asked him a question and then waited long enough, Joe would start talking on his own.

"The letter was from Sarah," Joe volunteered.

"Oh. Everything all right there?"

"Yes. Actually, the letter was a drawing from her son, Adam, and then she wrote what he dictated to her, before adding her own note at the bottom."

"I see."

"Got me thinking about how I'm going to tell everyone that I'm not going back," Joe lamented.

"Probably have to tell them sooner than later," Jonathan agreed with a laugh. "Otherwise, I think they're going to figure it out eventually when you just don't come home."

"I know," Joe answered. "I reckon that sending a telegram to Jacob is the best option. He works at the station, so he'll get it right away, and then he will let the mayor and everyone else know, I guess…"

"Sounds like as good a plan as any, I suppose…"

"Then, I reckon I owe Sarah and Adam a letter to explain," Joe said wistfully.

"That'd be nice for them, I bet. I'm sure they will have questions, just like you did when Caroline left you," Jonathan added, cringing inwardly in preparation for the explosion he thought was coming because of reminding Joe about what had happened in the past.

"That's what I was thinking," Joe answered instead, sounding far away.

Surprised, Jonathan pushed on. "So, what are you going to tell them?"

"Just that I came home, and Pa died, I suppose. Then, I will tell them that Sarah is struggling with the death of her husband and needs help."

"Joe?"

"Yeah?"

"Do you realize you just said, '*Sarah* is struggling with the death of her husband and needs help'?"

"No, I didn't!"

"Yeah, you did," Jonathan laughed, patting him on his shoulder.

"I did not!" Joe insisted.

"Yes, Joe, you most certainly did!"

"Well, then it was just a slip of the tongue!"

"Was it?"

"Yes!"

"I thought you wrote me that Sarah had to move there because she lost her husband and needed help?"

"She did," Joe confirmed.

"So, Sarah and Caroline's circumstances are not so different, then?"

"I hadn't really thought about it, but no, I suppose that they're not."

"So, then… what makes you more determined to help Caroline than Sarah?"

"What do you mean by that?" Joe snapped.

"I mean, why are you willing to give up everything to help Caroline, but not Sarah?"

"Because she needs help!"

"But you've said that Sarah needs help, too. I remember in a letter you wrote that you were secretly paying the rent on her shop and living quarters."

"So?" Joe challenged him.

"So," Jonathan pressed on, "what's going to happen to her now that you have decided to stay here and take care of Caroline and the kids?"

"I don't know," Joe admitted. "She's a lot more established now, and she does have her sister and brother-in-law there. They can help her, I suppose, if she needs it. Caroline has no one!"

Jonathan nodded in confirmation. "You're right. She has no one. And Joe?"

"What?"

"I think that she might just be using that fact to her advantage."

"How so?" Joe asked, scowling at his brother.

"Exactly what I said: you have two widows, both of whom you think need your help. Both have little ones and are struggling to make their ends meet, right?"

"I guess, yeah…" Joe agreed cautiously.

"I think that you're once again fighting for the underdog."

"What the hell do you mean by that?" Joe retorted, his head snapping up and looking at his brother.

"Think about it, Joe. You always do this. You're continually there for those who need help the most. Right now, you have two women in the exact same position. Except that they aren't. Sarah has family, and Caroline does not. Which one have you chosen?"

"Jonathan, it isn't like that at all! It is much more complicated than that!"

"Really, Joe? How so?"

"I was engaged to Caroline."

"And then she broke your heart by marrying our older brother…"

"I know!" Joe roared.

Jonathan knew he was on shaky ground, but felt he had to continue. "And now you're willing to go crawling back to her because she says she needs you, only *after* her husband is killed, and you're stupid enough to fall for it?"

Joe took a deep breath and tried to control his own temper, but also his rising self-doubt. "Jonathan, she has no one. I loved her once. I suppose I can learn to do so again. Eventually."

"And Sarah? You think she doesn't need you? Or is she less in need of a knight in shining armor because her husband only died instead of being murdered? Perhaps it's because she has family to help? Maybe it's because she has one child instead of three?"

"Of course not!" Joe countered back, the accusations hitting a little too close to home, making him defensive.

"What is it, then, Joe? Why are you still so drawn to Caroline after everything she did to you? It's no secret she's vulnerable! We all know she has no one. Her husband was murdered. But why was he murdered, Joe? Because he gambled incessantly! So, why are you so quick to give up your entire life for someone who devastated you just because now she doesn't have someone to care for her? I suggest that you really need to think through why you're choosing the woman who broke your heart over the nice, sweet woman who did nothing to you but needed you a bit less?"

"Because she doesn't want me!" Joe roared in anguish.

"I'm sorry?"

"Because Sarah doesn't want me, all right?"

Knowing he couldn't back down now, Jonathan countered. "And you're sure Caroline does?"

"Yes!"

"Do you realize that Caroline has not changed? The only reason she wants you now is that she knows you! She's confident that you would give up everything in order to take care of her if she asked. Meanwhile, I'm not entirely convinced that she truly wants specifically *you*. She only wants to not have to worry about being on her own. I think you're falling for her plan hook, line, and sinker, brother!"

"What are you talking about?"

"Joe, it's so simple. Do you really not see it?"

"She says she wishes that she could go back in time and choose differently," Joe retorted hotly.

"Of course, she does! She wants to go back and pick the responsible McIntyre brother!" Jonathan cried in frustration. "But, Joe, that isn't love. That's self-preservation! The only person Caroline loves is Caroline! She always has had her own best interest at heart, and she always will!"

"I don't believe you," Joe whispered as the words sank in.

"You're so blinded by the fact that she suddenly says she wants you that you're not thinking clearly, brother. You haven't seen her in ten years, because *she had relations with our brother in your bed,* while engaged to you, *and then she married him!* You've heard nothing from her since that day; yet now, after

Joshua was murdered, she's madly in love with you, and furthermore says she's always been?"

Joe said nothing, so Jonathan ventured on, wondering how much further he could challenge his brother before he exploded.

"I don't know Sarah, but from what you've told me about her, she's the complete opposite of Caroline. She's too proud to admit that she needs you or anyone else. She would rather struggle on her own than burden anyone with her troubles. She isn't waiting to be rescued by you. You say she doesn't want you, but at least you can be certain that she doesn't want you only because of what you will do for her."

"You're wrong!" Joe shouted angrily.

"Am I, Joe? Am I really?" Jonathan hollered back. "Has Sarah ever asked you to give up a damned thing for the honor of taking care of her?"

"No, but…"

"But what, Joe? But what?"

"I haven't known her that long! I have known Caroline for years."

"And knowing her longer makes it more acceptable for her to take advantage of you? That she's using you?"

Joe was now silently seething. His face was like thunder and Jonathan knew he had to tread lightly.

"Joe, you're a good, kind man. Women like Caroline see you coming from a mile away! You can always be trusted to fight for those who can't fight for themselves, to maintain order and justice, and to stand up for what is right. Why do you think that you were nominated, then voted in as sheriff?"

"Bad luck!" Joe grumbled.

Jonathan laughed. "Joe, I swear! Anyway, you were chosen because of how you handled the rebellion at the mine. Knowing you as I do, I know you were fair, concise, and made those in power accountable, all without losing your head, right?"

Joe didn't react.

"So," Jonathan continued, "you were chosen because of how you are, but you accepted the challenge to do it because of *who* you are. You will always do what is right, even if it isn't in your best interest. Caroline knows this about you and has since the day you chose to walk away because you thought it was what would make her happiest."

Finally, Joe spoke.

"Even if you're right, and I'm not saying you are, but if you are, that doesn't change the fact that Caroline is alone with three children and no one to help her."

"Joe, it's not your responsibility!"

"She was my fiancée."

"*Was* is the operative word there. She left you. *For our brother*. Don't let her manipulate you!"

"Those could have been my children!"

"But they aren't…"

"It's not their faults. I can't let them suffer because of what she and Joshua did."

"So, don't!"

"What do you mean?"

"If you feel that strongly about it, help her. Helping her, however, doesn't mean that you have to marry and live with her. When you go back to Colorado, mail her some money every month. I'll talk to Jeremiah and James, too, and maybe we all can send her a little something so that she has what she needs for the family. He was our brother, too, and there's no reason why you should be the only one to bear the brunt of that responsibility because you once put a ring on her finger."

Joe started to laugh.

"What?" demanded Jonathan, thoroughly confused.

"I never did put a ring on her finger!" he gaffed. "I had gone to pick it up from Larry when I came home and found them in my bed. I still have that ring somewhere in my desk back home."

"Give it to Sarah, then!" Jonathan teased.

Joe suddenly got serious. "I wasn't laying, John. She's not interested in me. At all! Besides, all we do is argue when we're together… except for the night before I left, after I got your telegram, when I kissed her. Wow, what a kiss it was, too!" Joe added wistfully, as he got a faraway look in his eyes.

"Better than the other night on the bench in front of the mercantile?" Jonathan asked jokingly.

"A million times better!" Joe replied without thinking, so busy recollecting his clinch with Sarah that he was not getting that Jonathan was teasing him at his expense.

"Joe, I'm serious. When you talk about this Sarah, your whole demeanor changes. You're smiling and happy. You look like how I remember you from before all of this happened and made you into a surly, angry man. I think it's time to move things along toward the next step with her!"

"Nope. She's still in love with her dead husband," Joe responded. He added softly, "I can't compete with a ghost."

"Oh, I beg to differ, brother. You just have to remind her of what she's missing. You need to help her recall how nice it is to have a warm, strong man in bed beside her every night," Jonathan said with a grin. "Have you missed her while you've been here?"

"To be honest, I hadn't even really thought about her; not until tonight, when you handed me that letter. Before that, I'd been too busy and preoccupied. It has to mean something that I haven't even thought about her, though, right?"

"I think it's more that it was too painful to think about, so you directed your focus onto something else. You love her, don't you?"

Joe looked his brother in the face. "Yeah," he answered solemnly. "I really think I do, for all the good it does."

"Then, you need to get home to her, big brother!"

"I have a lot to think about."

"That you do, Joe. I don't envy you. Sleep on it, and I'll see you in the morning."

Chapter Forty-Six

Joe stayed out on the porch long after the rest of the McIntyre men had gone to bed. He was in anguish trying to decide what it was that he wanted; what was for the best.

He thought hard about what his brother had said. It was abundantly clear that he truly needed to evaluate the reasoning behind why he was so willing to give everything up to take care of Caroline. What really kept nagging at him, though, was what Jonathan had pointed out: that both Sarah and Caroline were in the same position as widows with children, so why did he feel compelled to choose Caroline over Sarah?

He hadn't lied when he said that he felt responsible for taking care of Caroline and the little ones because they were his blood. Even with all the anger and hatred that flowed in his heart, he still remembered that they were family. He also couldn't shake the feeling that if he and Caroline would have wed, they would have been his children, his responsibility.

After sitting for several hours alone in the dark, Joe eventually concluded that it was his pride that had made the choice for him. His ego was bruised that Sarah didn't seem to want or need him. While she always gave the impression that she valued their friendship, she never seemed to consider the possibility that there could be more. All night long, in his mind he played and replayed the horrified look on her face when he finally pulled back from what for him had been a sizzling kiss. He had so hoped that what he was feeling was mutual, but if her facial expression was any indication, he had totally misread the entire situation and the emotion flowing between them, leaving him deeply embarrassed. Returning home and facing her seemed unfathomable, as he was mortified that he had let his emotions take over his actions with no regard to hers at all.

He also understood, though, that his pride had come into play with Caroline, too. Eventually, he was able to admit that his self-esteem had been hugely inflated by the fact that she finally wanted him: better late than never. After that, he realized that now was the time to force himself to think rationally, and not just react because she was finally saying all the right things to make him feel needed and appreciated. Of course, his battered self-worth wanted to believe that her motivation was genuine. That after all those years, she had come to the conclusion that she had made a mistake, and he really was the man she should have chosen. Deep down, though, he had a nagging feeling that the truth was more that he was familiar, and she felt comfortable with him. She also knew that he was responsible and would provide everything she needed. As much as he didn't want them to, those realizations made him acknowledge for the first time since he had reunited with her that he needed to question her enthusiasm and sincerity. At last, he concluded that Jonathan had hit a raw nerve when he said he was not convinced that she specifically wanted Joe, but instead only set her sights on him because he was a warm, stable, male body with a good work ethic, and she had a family to support.

Joe wrestled back and forth with his dilemma until well past when the eastern horizon began to lighten with the coming dawn. Admittedly, staying in California with his brothers and finally getting to be with the woman who had haunted his dreams felt as if everything he had ever wanted was suddenly coming true.

Nevertheless, when he thought back to his kiss with Sarah, even now, his heartbeat quickened, and his breath hitched. He got a warm, almost intoxicated feeling as the blood rushed around his body. Then, he suddenly recalled the hot summer day when she had come fishing with him and Adam and let out a long, low whistle as he thought about the creamy, delicate skin she had exposed when she opened her buttons to try to stay cool. He recollected with a bashful smile how his body had reacted, as if he had no control, just like when he had been a young man, and how terrified he was that she would discover his desire for her.

Going back even further, his thoughts returned to the very first time he saw her, unconscious, and how he had felt holding her in his arms when Doc Miller had asked him to help get her more comfortable. In that exact moment, he could have sworn that the subtle, sweet scent her body emanated blew by him on the dawn's breeze rustling through the surrounding trees. By the time the coming sun was coloring the dawn sky a rosy-pink hue, he knew what he needed to do.

He ate breakfast with his brothers and, after he washed the dishes, he said goodbye to Jeremiah, who was leaving to go home, then doffed his hat as he walked out the door without another word. On a mission, he didn't want anyone to attempt to dissuade him.

"Where's he off to?" Jeremiah asked, perplexed.

"Not a clue," James answered.

"Three guesses," Jonathan stated, and then it dawned on all of them.

Joe marched along the path from his familial home to the shanty where Caroline lived. He knocked with purpose on the front door and when she opened it, without a word he took her face into his hands and bent down to kiss her. He held nothing back, sending her all the pent-up longing and pain he had harbored for the past decade, and felt her melt into him as their arms wrapped around each other and they deepened the kiss. Joe had no idea how long they embraced, but then he abruptly pulled back.

"Nope!" he stated.

"Nope, what?" Caroline asked as she staggered a bit when he released her.

"I can't do this," he told her firmly.

"Can't do what?" Caroline asked with confusion and a hint of panic. "Joe, what are you talking about?"

"Caroline, I loved you something fierce ten years ago and was prepared to share my life with you. Those little ones in there? By all rights, they should be mine. This house? Well, not this house in particular… This home should have been mine. All of it. I was willing to do everything in my power to love you, care for you, and provide for our family. But you threw it all away because you thought you could do better with Joshua."

"But Joe…" Caroline interrupted.

"No!" Joe said sternly. "You don't get to interrupt! For the last decade, I have cried, pined, and even wanted to die over you." He paused to take a breath.

"But Joe! You can have me now!" Caroline cried.

"But that's just it, Caroline! I don't want you now!" he replied giddily, ignoring her shocked gasp. "I did want you… Lord knows I thought I wanted you so much for the last ten years that I have made myself sick over you! I believed you were everything I wanted, everything I desired. But when I kissed you… When I kissed you, it wasn't the same."

"Well, Joe, of course not! There's been a lot of water under the bridge…"

Joe shook his head. "No, you don't understand. It wasn't like kissing her!"

"Who?"

"Sarah!"

"Your widowed friend in Colorado?"

"Yes!" Joe declared gleefully. "When I kissed her, my world stopped turning. My heart felt like it was going to beat out of my chest! I think I have loved her from the first day she got there, but I was too hung up on you to see it!"

He couldn't help but gush, even though he saw the thunder building in her eyes.

"Joe!" she cried. "What about me? What about us? I thought we were going to give this another shot! I thought you loved me… that you wanted to help me!"

"Oh, Caroline, I will help you, don't worry! In fact, all the rest of us boys will make sure that you receive the means you need to support Joshua's family. But as for me, I don't want my brother's sloppy seconds, especially only because he couldn't be responsible enough to take care of you. I'm in love with Sarah and I have to go home to see if she will have me!"

Caroline began to cry big tears. "But Joe! I love you! I have always loved you!"

"Well, Mrs. McIntyre, you sure had a funny way of showing it! But wouldn't it have been convenient for you if this had worked out? Hell, you wouldn't have even needed to change your last name!"

With that, Joe doffed his hat once more and turned to walk away. After a few steps, however, he turned back and met her furious expression. "Jonathan will be in touch about a stipend we will send for the children. Don't worry, Caroline, I'll still be a slave for you, but this time, you don't get to hold my heart hostage!"

He tipped his hat to her and turned on his heel, practically skipping the first few steps toward home. As he walked down the path, he heard Caroline screaming, "You are a horrible man, Joe McIntyre! You should know better than getting a poor widow's hopes up! There's a special place in hell for you! I never loved you, anyway! You were dull and predictable and a gigantic bore!"

All he did was turn back toward her and tip his hat again, saying, "Goodbye, Mrs. McIntyre! Godspeed!"

Joe practically ran the rest of the way to his family home and burst through the door, surprising his brothers.

"I need to get back!" he happily declared, as he ran to his room. He popped his head back out the door and asked Jeremiah, "What time's the train leaving?"

"In an hour," Jeremiah responded, sounding surprised.

"Great! That gives me just enough time!"

Fifteen minutes later, he emerged carrying his bags. He placed them on the floor by the front door and then turned to his brothers. "Jonathan, I told Caroline you would come by and figure out how much she needs for the household, all right?"

Jonathan only nodded dumbly back at him.

"Great! And, boys, I told her we would all help contribute to the upkeep of those children." He looked pointedly at each of them, and they all nodded their heads somewhat hesitantly.

"Good!" he declared. "I promised her that we would help her do what Joshua couldn't," he told them. "I'll send whatever amount you tell me she needs; my costs are very few."

"Well," said James, "I'm thinking that Joshua made about two dollars a day. When he worked, that is…"

"So, I'm thinking, then, that if we can each spare five dollars month to give her…"

"Is that enough?" James interrupted nervously.

"It should give her enough that she can make up the rest from finding work somewhere. If she needs more, we can reevaluate," Jonathan responded.

"Oh, come on, James!" Jeremiah added. "You know as well as I do that Caroline rarely saw a dime of the money Joshua made. In fact, I think that she will find that quite a comfortable sum after all she has been through in the past ten years, while our brother drank and gambled away practically every penny he ever earned!"

"So, we are agreed, then?" Joe asked them, anxious to get on his way.

"I think that five dollars each is more than reasonable," Jeremiah added.

Joe remembered that his oldest brother had a lot of mouths to feed. While his ranch could provide well for his family, hard cash may prove difficult for him to afford every month.

"John," Joe added, "I'm counting on you to let us know if they need anything else, all right?"

"Sure!"

"Great! Now, come on, Jer! Let's get down off this mountain so we can each get home!"

All four brothers walked solemnly to the station. They waited on the platform for several minutes, talking and laughing before the narrow-gauge locomotive rolled up in a cloud of steam. They all gave each other quick hugs, with slaps on the back, and then the two remaining oldest McIntyre boys were gone.

Chapter Forty-Seven

"What's your plan, Joe?" Jeremiah asked as the train chugged toward Sacramento. Joe had left with his older brother, not wanting to wait another day in his hometown now that he had decided what he wanted to do. His plan was to spend the night in a hotel and head east again on the train in the morning. Perhaps it could be construed as a waste of money, but not only was he excited, he also didn't want to run the risk of seeing Caroline again once he had made up his mind to leave.

"I'm going home. Other than that, I don't know."

"So, what about Sarah? Are you going to pursue her?"

"I don't know. But I want to."

"I think you should. All she can say is no!"

Joe and his brother soon parted, and the next day he began the long journey eastward. The whole trip, he ruminated over what he should say when he saw Sarah for the first time. He didn't know if he should try to apologize for his forwardness when he kissed her and explain that he was caught up in the emotion of the situation, or if he would be better off not saying anything about it unless she did.

As the train hurtled through Utah, Joe, heavily influenced by his shy nature, decided that it would be best not to mention the kiss, and instead play it off as if nothing had happened while waiting to see if Sarah would bring it up.

By the time he arrived in Colorado Springs and was preparing to board the train that would take him on the final leg of his trip up the mountain, he was feeling giddy with anticipation. So, when he disembarked and stepped onto the platform, he wasn't sure what he was expecting but what he found was anti-climactic, to say the least. The station was full of the usual hustle and bustle of his small familiar town, but he had at least expected that someone would notice him. He chuckled when he understood how ridiculous he was being; as if he was expecting someone would be waiting there every day on the off chance he happened to come home, though he hadn't given any notice to anyone about when, or even if, he would be returning. Regardless, though, it felt a little raw when he realized that not only was no one waiting for him, no one even looked up long enough to recognize who he was.

His ego still a bit bruised, Joe decided that he would go see Jacob, letting him know he was back in town. He figured at least Jacob would be pleased to see his friend again. Walking into the station, he knocked on the door left partially ajar and waited for Jacob to utter, "Come in!"

Jacob had his head down over some paperwork on his desk and didn't even bother to look up before he said, "Yes? What can I do for you today?"

Joe smiled wryly before answering, "I just thought I would swing on by to say 'Hi' on my way to the jail."

Jacob's head flew up, and he looked at his wayward friend. "Joe! Oh, my word, it's so good to see you! We were wondering if you were ever going to come back to these parts again! No one has heard neither hide nor hair from you for so long… the mayor was getting antsy, wondering if it was time to elect a new sheriff."

"Well, I'm back now!"

"I see that!" Jacob laughingly told him, while walking around the desk to slap him on the back. "How was California?"

"It was nice. Not much has changed, at least where I'm from. Sacramento keeps getting bigger, though!" Jacob nodded, and then moved on to a touchier subject.

"I'm so sorry, Joe, again, about your brother."

"And my father, too," Joe added sadly.

"Oh, no! We were all wondering. We were hoping that when we hadn't heard anything, he had perhaps rallied after all."

"No, unfortunately, he succumbed to his grief shortly after my brother was put into the ground."

"I'm sorry! I guess that explains why there was a long delay before you came back. We were all beginning to wonder if the call of family and home was simply too great to ignore. Sarah, especially!"

At the mention of her name, Joe felt his breath hitch in his lungs. Trying to act nonchalant, he said, "How is she?"

"She's good. Adam, too. She's finally back to her normal self. That illness really took it out of her."

Jacob was getting into dangerous territory and Joe knew he had to change the subject quickly before he spilled everything to his friend. "Any trouble while I was away?"

"No, not that I know of. Just the usual Friday and Saturday night brawls and drunkards. One of them gave Sarah quite a scare not long after you left by trying to get into her door at three in the morning."

"What?" Joe exploded with worry and anger. "Did they succeed?"

"No, thankfully, she had the door bolted. She wasn't sure who it was. He was slurring his words too much to hear him clearly while he was professing his undying love for her, going on about wanting to marry her. Pretty harmless in the scope of things, but it gave her a fright, just the same."

"Who?" Joe demanded.

Jacob looked at him a bit strangely before answering, "I told you, Joe. She doesn't know. I only heard about it from Michael at the saloon a few days after it happened. He was asking me if Sarah is always so stoic about things. I think he was a bit angry because she didn't tell him about it until several days later. When he asked her why she hadn't reported it that morning after it happened, she told him that it had slipped her mind, but that it wasn't a big enough thing to bother him about while he was filling in for you!"

"How many days later?"

"Jesus, Joe. Why the interrogation? I said I didn't know. I'm only repeating what Michael said. If you want more details, you will have to ask him yourself!"

Joe stared harshly at Jacob, until he realized that he was taking out his frustrations on his friend. "Sorry!" he muttered, still annoyed that Jacob couldn't give him the whole story. "I'm heading home!"

Jacob watched as Joe turned and left without another word. "Goodbye," he called out to his retreating back, and Joe rewarded him with a raise of his hand.

Chapter Forty-Eight

Joe's elation with being home didn't last too long once he got to the jail. His desk, the one place that Sarah hardly ever touched, was in shambles. Paperwork and wanted posters covered every inch as they had been haphazardly thrown around without any rhyme or reason. It was obvious that as acting sheriff, Michael had no idea what to do with the administrative part of the job.

He walked back to his living quarters and was pleasantly surprised that they were much more in order than his desk, and he was glad for it. After throwing his bag on the floor. he wandered back to his desk to sit down and started the long, arduous process of going through and making sense of it all, organizing the papers into piles.

He had lost track of time when the door opened, and Michael sauntered in. He stopped short when he saw Joe at the desk, four big towers of paperwork in front of him.

"Uh… Hi, Joe!" Michael declared.

"Hello, Michael!"

"When'd you get back?" Michael asked as he removed his hat and placed it on a hook by the door.

"Just a little while ago, on the train," Joe answered, seemingly still distracted by the piece of paper in his hand.

"Sorry, Joe," Michael said a bit sheepishly. "I was going to go through all of that eventually. It just… Well, it was a little busy while you were gone, and it took a while to get the hang of all of this paperwork!"

"I know. Don't worry. I didn't exactly take the time to show you that part of the job. Rest of the place looks nice, though."

"Yeah, that's your maid's doing. She made sure that I had fresh linens, meals, and a clean jail while you were gone."

"Who? Sarah?" Joe exclaimed, then caught himself. "I mean, Mrs. Johnson?"

"Yes, Mrs. Johnson! She said she has been doing it for several years in return for the rent you pay on her place."

Joe nodded but wanted to quickly change the subject to the happenings while he was away that concerned him the most.

"So, anything exciting happen while I was gone?"

"Nah… The usual stuff: typical drunkards on Friday and Saturday nights. Adams was caught by Mama D being a little too aggressive with Josephine, so she roughed him up a bit before dragging him out by his ear over here to me. He was just drunk and stupid. Slept it off, then when I let him out, he went straight over on his own volition to apologize to the girl and Mama."

"Anything else?"

"No, not really…" Michael answered.

It was killing Joe not to ask for details about the incident that Jacob had told him about regarding the man trying to get into Sarah's door. He would be damned if he did, though, because he didn't want it to appear as though she was the first thing he cared about as soon as he exited the train, even if it was the truth. So, he waited.

The men stood unspeaking, regarding each other, until Joe realized that Michael was not going to give up the information voluntarily. So, tired of waiting, he probed, "I bumped into Jacob McAllister when I got off the train and he mentioned that Mrs. Johnson had an issue with a man following her while I was gone, saying he even tried to get into her door?"

"Oh! I forgot about that. No need to worry; I handled it," Michael declared boastfully.

Now Joe was really beginning to lose his patience. "Michael, what exactly needed handling?"

"It was nothing! Truly! It was just Walsh, drunk and disoriented. I talked to him after she told me about it, and he had sobered up. There hasn't been an issue since."

Joe studied Michael carefully. Even before he left, he hadn't liked how he had witnessed William Walsh leering at Sarah any time he was in her vicinity. It had made his skin crawl to watch his eyes rake over her body. The man had also made Joe uneasy with how often he happened to suddenly appear wherever Sarah was, so he took it upon himself to observe him more closely on several occasions. Simply by glancing at the man's breeches, it was abundantly clear Walsh enjoyed watching Sarah much more than he should, but eventually, he detected Joe was onto him, so he had backed off considerably.

But obviously when I left, Joe thought grimly, *Walsh felt like it was open season on Sarah again.*

The fact that he was so bold as to attempt to get into her locked door made Joe's hackles rise. It seemed as though Walsh's behavior was becoming more sinister than just a passing infatuation, so Joe vowed then and there that since he was back, he would again pay close attention to the situation.

"So, Mrs. Johnson was all right, then? Not too shaken up or upset?"

"I think it rattled her pretty good, to be honest, but she stayed here for a while, and we drank some tea. She seemed calm enough that I felt comfortable just talking to him and keeping an eye out."

Joe merely nodded, though something about the whole situation was still not sitting right with him.

Several seconds passed, and Michael spoke again. "To tell you the truth, I don't really blame the guy. I think I kinda fancy her myself!" Michael said, dropping his voice lower as if he didn't want to be overheard, even though they were the only two people in the room.

Joe raised an eyebrow. "Oh, really?" he replied, hoping it was nonchalantly.

"Yes!" Michael exclaimed exuberantly. "She's smart, beautiful, kind… To be honest, Joe, I'm not sure how she's still alone."

"Her husband died a few years ago," Joe stated, hoping he would take the hint and back off.

"Oh, I know," Michael confirmed. "She told me all about it."

"She did?" Joe asked, unable to hide the surprise in his voice.

"Sure," Michael answered, looking strangely at Joe. "Does she generally not tell people about that?"

"I don't really know, to be honest. I found out when she first got here, but there were some extenuating circumstances."

"Huh…" Michael exhaled. "Anyway, I'm trying to work up the courage to ask her if she would court me."

"Are you serious?" Joe retorted, harsher than he meant to. He knew he had to temper his reaction, so he quickly added, "Do you think she will accept?"

"I don't know, but I feel like I have to try."

Joe nodded grimly. "Sure! But how do you feel about the boy?"

"Who, Adam?"

"Yeah…" Joe said, trying desperately to sound aloof and disinterested.

"He's all right for a kid, I guess. I've taken him fishing a few times."

"Oh?" This time, Joe couldn't hide the shock in his response.

Michael looked oddly at him before answering, confusion written on his features. "He asked me to take him a few weeks after you left. Said you always took him, but since he didn't know when you would be back, he asked me if I would mind since I was the sheriff now."

"And Sarah just… let you?"

"Sure? Why not? She laughed that Adam must think that taking kids fishing and sledding is part of the job description, but I was happy to oblige. Anything to make points with her. She even came along once or twice."

"Really?" Joe squeaked, before clearing his throat and speaking again. "She did?"

"She did!" Michael confirmed, adding triumphantly, "She even brought a picnic."

"Sounds great," Joe mumbled, trying to sound enthusiastic, but in all honesty, he felt like he had been stabbed in the gut. He had hoped that Sarah had done those things with him because she was interested in him, but apparently she did it with any man who paid her and Adam attention.

"Well, anyway, since you're back, I guess I had better get home and prepare to go back to the mine. Old Man Petersen was kind to give me the time off," Michael said with a chuckle. "But then again, it isn't like there's an overabundance of people banging on his door to take my place. He told me he would make room for me somewhere if you came back. Truth be told, though, I'm kinda dreading it. You've got it pretty sweet here, Joe."

"That I do. I appreciate you keeping an eye on things," Joe answered with a finality that unmistakably demonstrated he was back now and would be reclaiming his rightful position again.

Michael wistfully removed the badge that Joe had left him and slowly moved to put it on the desk between them. "I'm really sorry that I didn't finish that paperwork," he apologized as he picked up his hat and placed it on his head.

Joe smiled wryly. "It's all right, Michael. I appreciate that you were willing to help out!" He stuck out his hand. When Michael grasped Joe's palm in his, Joe thanked him again, and then walked the man out the door.

Chapter Forty-Nine

After Michael left, Joe wandered back to his living quarters and began to unpack. It was obvious that Sarah had been cleaning this room, as there was no trace of anyone having stayed there during his absence. The room still sparkled, free from dust, and the bed was neatly made, with the quilts pulled up tight. Indeed, Michael rented a room above the mercantile, so unless there was an incarcerated prisoner, he had no need to stay there, as he would have most definitely heard any ruckus on the street below from his place.

Joe meandered around and saw that everything was still as he had left it when he had gone back to California. After his inspection was complete, he was pulled to his bed like a moth to a flame, having slept sporadically and uncomfortably on the train for the past several days, not to mention the emotional turmoil of the past several weeks. He surrendered to temptation, telling himself that he was only going to lie down for a few minutes, but his eyes soon closed as he drifted off to sleep.

He had no idea how long he actually slept, but when he awoke, the evening shadows were long and the sky was painted pinky-purple, leaving his room in semi-darkness. Joe scrambled up and searched for some matches to light the lantern beside his bed. After having spent so much time with his brothers, his dwelling felt especially dreary and lonely, so he then also lit a candle and carried it out to the jail in the front room to sit down at his desk and try to make heads or tails of the papers he had sorted earlier.

Working for about an hour, Joe startled when the door opened quickly, the noise pulling him out of his deep concentration.

"Hello?" a soft, feminine voice called out into the room.

The desk was hidden from view by the door when anyone first came in; Joe had wanted it that way, giving him the element of surprise when someone entered, instead of the other way around. Therefore, before Sarah could see who was sitting at the desk, she called out, "Michael? Are you in here?"

"No," Joe answered her and waited.

Sarah stopped short, her hand still on the doorknob. She recognized the voice on the other side but didn't dare dream it was possible. Regardless, she took a deep, calming breath before pushing into the room.

"Joe?" she asked hopefully as she began to close the door behind her. "Is that you?"

He cleared his throat in anticipation before answering, "Yeah, Sarah, it's me. Come on in!"

He waited impatiently as the door closed and she turned to face him. Her eyes opened wide in recognition, and she felt the impulse to rush toward him. After her first few quick steps, however, she slowed down to a more respectable pace as she crossed the floor to where he was sitting, his eyes following her the whole way.

"Well, Joe McIntyre, as I live and breathe! Is it really you?"

God, she is a sight for sore eyes! he thought to himself, fighting every urge to stand up and clutch her to him; to pick her up in his arms and swing her around. Too many things stopped him, though, first and foremost not knowing how she felt about him after their kiss. Instead, he spoke.

"Sure is!" he said and gave her a lazy smile that made her heart skip a beat.

"Well, I'll be! We had all begun to think you had decided to stay put in California, given how long you've been gone," she told him, putting a tray full of food on the desk before her. She self-consciously smoothed her skirts and hair once her hands were no longer occupied. "Or we had given you up for dead!" she added with a nervous laugh.

"Nope. Just had a lot of old business to take care of," he told her. She didn't trust herself not to keep rambling, so she merely nodded in response.

416

They stood staring at each other, the desk between them, for what felt like an eternity.

"But now you're home!" Sarah eventually declared happily.

"I am, indeed," Joe answered, trying not to get his hopes up that she sounded so pleased to see him.

"I hope it was a good trip," she murmured.

"As good as could be expected under the circumstances," he replied with a sheepish shrug. He had so much he wanted to tell her, starting with why he had decided to come home. Somehow, though, the words just wouldn't come out.

"My Pa died," he added as an afterthought.

"Oh, no! Oh, Joe, I'm so sorry!"

"Thank you."

There was a long, awkward silence, before Sarah spoke again, gesturing to the tray she had just put down. "There's some supper if you're hungry. I can go back and get Michael another plate."

"Thank you."

"Not a problem. I was feeding Michael while you were gone. I figured he had enough on his mind."

"So, I heard," Joe answered somewhat ruefully. "I heard that Michael took Adam fishing, and that you went with them, even packed a picnic."

Joe had tried to make his voice sound neutral, but he heard the words as they exited his mouth, and his tone was not one of indifference. He cringed a little inside, wondering if Sarah had caught it.

"Why, Joe…" she playfully taunted him, with a saucy grin, "I didn't know you cared! What with you being halfway across the country and all."

"I don't!" he declared quickly.

"Good! But I have to tell you, Adam still missed you."

Joe smiled. "Good! Because I missed that kid, too."

Sarah dished up a plate from the pot containing his supper, and then handed it to Joe, along with a fork. "He will be thrilled that you're back!"

Joe nodded as he tucked into his meal. "This is really good!" he moaned appreciatively.

She smiled softly at him. "Good! I'm glad that you think so! But then again, hunger *is* the best spice."

Sarah watched Joe eat for a few seconds, until deciding she should go before she said something she would regret. She wanted to ask him if he had seen Caroline while he was there, but the words stuck in her throat because in all honesty she didn't want to hear the answer.

"Well, we are glad to have you back!" she said as a prelude to her goodbye.

Joe looked up and swallowed, not yet ready to let her go now that she was near him. "You're leaving?"

Neither of them made a move, simply continuing to stare at each other, until Sarah gave a quick shake of her head, saying, "Well, goodbye." Then she turned around to leave.

"Wait!" he said earnestly, making her turn around again to face him. "Both Jacob and Michael told me you had a little problem with Mr. Walsh while I was away."

Sarah looked away, her heart hurting that he had only seemingly called her back to talk shop. "It was nothing," she answered, waving her hand as if it was not a problem. "He was just drunk. Anyway, Michael took care of it."

Joe took a sip of water. "I don't like it. He was watching you even before I left. I was keeping an eye out. Please be careful around him!"

"Oh, Joe! Don't be silly!"

Joe placed his fork down on his plate and wiped his mouth with his napkin. He stood up and placed both hands on his desk, leaning forward.

"Sarah, I'm not being silly! This is serious."

"Joe," she cried, "you're being ridiculous! He was just confused because he was drunk!"

"I don't think so."

"Well, what else would it be?"

418

"Sarah!" Joe exclaimed. "Just listen to me! Please! You're about the only respectable single woman in town, and you're also attractive, not to mention unattached. You need to be careful in a town like this!"

Sarah balked at him incredulously.

"I'm serious! You're beautiful, kind, and intelligent!" Joe blurted, feeling his frustration rising. He groaned inwardly as he heard himself expressing too much of his own desire for her, but he shook it off to drive home the point he was trying to make. "The men here… These men are always at least a little drunk and a lot desperate!"

"You're crazy!" she laughed. "No one wants me."

"Believe me, Sarah, you're just the kind of girl men would love to take home to meet their mothers. Sadly, there are even more who would just like to take you home!"

"Joe!" Sarah gasped.

Joe ignored her indignation, imploring her to listen. "Please! Please, promise me that you won't walk alone anywhere anymore and that you will always lock your doors."

"Joe… I always lock my doors."

"You haven't always… I remember having to stand around until you did!"

"Joe… Good grief! I'm not a child!"

"Please, Sarah! Just… Please! I'm begging you to be careful!"

Sarah watched Joe for a long time, observing there was something in his eyes conveying just how grave his concern was, and it spoke to her. She still felt he was being preposterous, though, not to mention overly cautious, so she sighed deeply, displaying her irritation before she spoke again.

"Joe, you're overreacting! No one wants me! Nobody wants to take a twenty-four-year-old widow with a child home to meet their mothers. Who would be crazy enough to want to take that on?"

Joe didn't speak for several seconds, his mind spinning, trying to decide what to do. Finally, he told himself, *Tell her!*

His stomach was in knots. Even though his heart knew he was done trying to hide how he felt about her, his brain was obviously lagging behind. *But,* he wrestled with himself, *if I say something, then at least it would be out in the open.*

It's now or never, he thought, trying to gather his courage, feeling his heart rise to his throat.

Ah, to hell with it! he resolved and took a deep breath. *Just do it!*

"Me, Sarah! Me! I want to take that on!" he beseeched her.

"What?" she gasped, shocked by his admission. "Joe…"

"Sarah! Listen! Please… just let me say this!"

His eyes implored her. She held his gaze for what felt like an eternity until she nodded slightly, compelled to hear him out.

"Sarah, I'm in love with you!" he declared. "Furthermore, I have loved you, I think, since the first day I saw you. I have never felt like this before. *Ever*!" he said pointedly, hoping she would get that he meant even his fiancée who had broken his spirit.

"But…" Sarah tried to interrupt him, but he merely held up his hand and continued.

"I love you!" he cried out fervently, now unable to stop himself. "And, moreover, I love that little boy! Sarah, I love Adam like he was my own flesh and blood!"

He stood and helplessly watched her, as her eyes flooded with tears, her right hand covering her mouth, but he misinterpreted her tears as that she didn't believe him.

"Please, Sarah! Please believe me!" he begged her earnestly. "I love you! I want to kiss you goodnight the last thing I do before I fall asleep, and I want to awaken to you every morning! I want to help you raise that little boy to be a man. So help me God, I love you, and I want you! I want to build a family with you."

At his heartfelt plea, Sarah just shook her head, her tears spilling over. She was unable to speak she was crying so hard. He had almost won her over, until he told her that he wanted a family with her.

"Why don't you believe me?" he asked feebly.

She shook her head as her body trembled with suppressed sobs and Joe's determination turned to anguish. It was as he feared: she didn't love him.

Sarah saw the second his expression changed from expectant to devastated and felt what seemed like cold fingers wrap around her chest, making it hard to breathe. She realized that he must think that once again he was being rejected, and she knew she had to explain before she completely destroyed him. Sensing the immense amount of courage it had taken him to push through the veil of anger, fear, and rejection that he had cloaked himself in for so many years, she knew if she let him go on thinking that her objections lay with him, he would become a broken and bitter man, beyond repair. Still, she couldn't trust herself to speak, so she only held his gaze for a long moment, willing herself to calm down enough that she could explain.

Joe surveyed her with a mix of humiliation and despair, but also concern. He was furious with himself that he allowed his heart to be vulnerable once more, only to be shot down again, but he still couldn't deny that he cared deeply for her. Despite his gut-wrenching disappointment, instead of lashing out and saying something that he would later regret, he let the emotion in her eyes speak to him, telling him not to act rashly, so he forced himself to calm down and give her a moment to collect herself.

Sarah gave a small hiccough, and Joe smiled despite himself. She ventured a tight smile back and then took a deep breath.

"Joe…" she whispered while shaking her head and hugging her arms tightly around her body. "Please don't do this to me! Please!"

He glanced at her in bemusement before shifting his eyes to the far wall. It was too painful to look at her when he was sure of the rebuff that was most certainly coming.

"Joe?" she tried again, knowing that no matter how painful, she had to explain, and her determination to offer clarification then made her voice a bit stronger. "Joe…?"

His expression was closed off and hurt, and when she realized that he was not going to make this easy on her, she sighed in defeat. She thought he was being sullen and stubborn when he did not answer her, not understanding that he was instead trying desperately to keep a tight grip on his emotions. He told himself determinedly that no matter what else happened, he refused to break down in front of her, even though the situation was ripping his heart to shreds.

"Joe…. I just… I can't… Please don't ask me," she started quietly and was surprised to see how immediately his eyes darted to meet hers and how utterly defeated he looked. Nodding slowly, he quickly looked away again.

Of course, she doesn't want me. She doesn't love me, he chastised himself. *What the hell is wrong with me? I obviously have a knack for only loving women who can't or won't love me back.* In that moment, Joe vowed that he would remain a bachelor for his entire life, never risking this kind of humiliation again. Once had been hard enough, twice seemed unfathomable.

In an attempt to try and salvage the last shred of his self-esteem, he took quick stock of his life, trying to accentuate the positive in this situation that at least this time they hadn't been engaged and he didn't find her in bed with another man.

"It's fine, Sarah!" he conceded. "Just pretend I didn't say any…"

"Joe!" she stated sharply, interrupting him. He looked up at her in shock. Sarah was often direct, but she was never rude.

"Please, Joe! Please try to understand! I cannot marry you because…" Sarah took a shuddering breath before squaring her shoulders and continuing. "Because…"

When she didn't say anything for a moment, he asked, "Why, Sarah?" then admonished himself for sounding so desperate.

"Because," she tried again as her tears spilled over. "Because I vowed that I would never marry again."

Joe had braced himself for what he thought he would be hearing; that she cared for him, but didn't love him, or that she could never love anyone else as much as her husband, but he still found his curiosity piqued about what reason she would give.

Finally, when she didn't continue, he was compelled to inquire, "Why?", his tone reflecting his utter despair.

"Because I can't do it again…"

"Do what?" he implored her. Joe wracked his brain about what could have possibly been so bad about being married. She always spoke well of her deceased husband.

She smiled wryly at him. "Joe, you know how you found me on the train a few years ago?"

He nodded.

"That was not my first child lost."

He nodded again. He remembered her sister telling him and Dr. Miller that she had lost other pregnancies, and even a newborn, after Adam was born.

When she didn't continue for a second, he asked her bluntly, "So?" He was too emotionally exhausted to be genial. Honestly not trying to be impudent, he was so out of his depth, he didn't know what next to expect. All he knew was that he was too focused on his own pain to try to discern what she was attempting to tell him.

"So?" she cried out, perturbed at his coldness. "So? I was only able to give my husband one healthy, living child. I lost every other baby I conceived!"

Joe gaped dumbly at her, not comprehending how this related to him. Sarah sighed in abject frustration that he was clearly not understanding and resigned to spell it out for him.

"Joe, regardless of how I feel about you, I could never marry again. Not you or anyone else."

"But why?" he cried out, cringing as he heard himself whining, begging for an explanation. The misunderstanding was so apparent in his eyes that she growled in defeat.

"Because!" she hollered, taking him so much by surprise that he took an involuntary step back. He had seen her angry before, but this was not that: this was complete and utter angst.

Even still, he couldn't help but get drawn in by her obvious raw pain. "I'm sorry I don't understand, Sarah. Please tell me why?" he asked quietly.

"Because," she stated as the tears rolled down her cheeks, "I could never have another man look at me with such contempt and utter disappointment again! I would die!"

With that declaration, she crumpled dramatically to the floor, her head in her hands and her sobs echoing off the jailhouse walls.

Suddenly it all made sense to him. He ran forward and landed on his knees beside her, grabbing her tight into his body, one arm wrapped around her shoulders as she clung to him, weeping. His other hand found the back of her head, holding her against his shoulder as he softly stroked her hair.

"Shhhh…" he whispered to her over and over again, trying to calm her. "Please, Sarah, don't cry!"

They stayed locked together in their embrace until she finally began to cry herself out, and then he spoke again. "Did your husband *say* he was disappointed in you?" he asked in utter amazement. He could not imagine anyone being so cruel.

She sighed. "Not in so many words, no. But after our last child before he passed was stillborn, I asked him if he was sorry that he married me and…" She broke off crying for a moment before she composed herself again. "He answered that sometimes he thought he was."

"What? No, Sarah! You must have misunderstood him! I can't imagine he could have said that…"

Sarah shook her head violently against his chest. "Yes! He did say it. And it broke my heart!"

He stroked her hair as her sobs started afresh. "Shhhh… Sarah. I'm so sorry, sweetheart! How awful that must have been for you to hear!"

424

Sarah continued to weep at the memory but despite all the repressed pain surfacing once more, she also felt compelled to defend her beloved George to Joe.

"It was right after I had delivered our son. He was grieving as much as I was, so I don't fault him for it. But it was extremely hurtful, all the same." She sniffed and continued, "Honestly, it was more what he didn't say. It was the looks of pity, anger, frustration, worry, and most of all, disenchantment that became more and more prevalent after each loss we suffered."

Joe didn't know how to respond, but in his mind, he could not comprehend being so devastated by loss that he would blame his wife. However, on the other hand, he realized from his experience with his job that grief could make people do and say things no one would have ever thought them capable of before.

So, Joe simply held her to him, not saying anything, letting her weep. Sarah felt his silence was strangely empowering, so she quietly continued, her cheeks reddening with humiliation. "He wouldn't touch me for almost a year after we lost our last son. It wasn't until Adam recovered from being very ill that we accidentally came together again one night. He told me after that he had decided to never get me in the family way again to shield both of our hearts from further devastation."

Her eyes welled up again, "He hadn't explained that, though, before that day, so I thought he just didn't love me anymore but felt obligated to stay with me."

Joe couldn't fathom the amount of pain and loneliness Sarah had endured in her married life, but drawing from his own experience, he knew how it felt to be rejected, to feel inadequate. "I'm so sorry, Sarah!"

"It's all right now," she said, giving him a watery smile. "He explained himself and apologized, so everything seemingly went back to normal. But I never could shake the feeling that I had let him down; that he was disappointed in me and wouldn't have married me if he had known."

Joe looked into her eyes before he spoke. He held her shoulder with his left hand and tipped her chin with his right, so she couldn't turn away. "You could never be a disappointment to anyone," he passionately informed her.

"Oh, but I was. I had known George most of my life. He put on a good show, and I know he loved me, but his eyes couldn't hide his disillusionment as the losses went on. I don't think he even realized it, but it was definitely there. It was as if he felt he had settled when perhaps he could have had more with someone else. And don't even get me started on his parents!" she sighed in disgust.

"Why? What did they do?"

"They never let me forget that I was incapable of delivering more healthy children who would help run the farm. George's mother even told me it was the reason he had died; that because he didn't have more help, he was overtired and, therefore, more susceptible."

"But that's crazy!" Joe exclaimed. "Why, Adam was his oldest at just barely four years old, wasn't he?"

"Yes, but that was of little consequence. When I pointed that out to her, she promptly responded that it was the stress, worry, and disappointment over the whole situation that did it."

"She was just looking for someone to blame…" he stated quietly.

Sarah grimly smiled. "That was my feeling about it, too, but it didn't make it any easier to bear."

"No, I suppose not," Joe responded thoughtfully. "I'm sorry, Sarah! No one should have to endure that kind of senseless blame."

"It didn't stop there, either," Sarah added, her eyes now flashing with anger. "When I went home from here, George's parents invited Adam and me to supper every Sunday 'to get to know him better,' or so they said. Then, one Saturday, George's father took Adam fishing, and when we went to supper the next afternoon, they both confronted me on what Adam had been telling him about how we were spending time with you."

"Oh, no," Joe muttered, quickly comprehending this was why, when Sarah had been so sick, Ginny had mentioned

426

George's parents wanted to take over custody of Adam because of her impropriety and would do so if he returned home to Illinois.

"Oh, Joe, yes!" Sarah exclaimed, her demeanor getting more and more agitated. "It certainly didn't help when Adam also mentioned that I slept in your bed," she told him, her cheeks blazing with anger or embarrassment; he couldn't tell which.

"Wait… What?" he exclaimed, his mind racing to understand how in the world Adam would have ever come to that conclusion.

"He meant, of course, when I became so ill on the train, and you took me here to the jail, putting me on the bed in a cell. But they wouldn't let me explain. I tried to tell them that I had been taken to the jail because I got ill and that made them even angrier. All they heard was jail, and you can imagine the conclusions they then drew."

Sarah took a deep breath and continued. "There was no way I was going to tell them I was ill because I lost another baby," she whispered softly. Her eyes filled with tears again, as she added, "The last one I would ever carry."

"Sarah, don't say that! Marry me! You never know what could happen… Please?" he pleaded with her.

"Joe, I can't!" she cried again, her voice sounding shrill, almost bordering on hysterical. "Please, you have to understand… I can never go through another loss again. I'm not strong enough for another one."

"So, I will talk to Mama D, then!" Joe blurted, unwilling to give up now that he knew it wasn't him she was rebuffing. When she looked up at him in surprise, he told her, "There has to be some way to prevent you from becoming with child; only a few of her girls have ever had a baby!"

"Joe, no!" Sarah moaned. "Please! You can't talk to her about this!"

"Fine, then. I'll ask Doc. He has to know!"

"Joe! That's even worse!" Sarah declared, burying her face in her hands.

"Why?" he asked, perplexed. "He's a doctor!"

"I can't believe you would ask people such intimate questions about us!"

Joe was confused by her mortification, as he was thrilled he had found a workable solution to her objection for marrying him. "Sarah, I love you… I'm only trying to find a solution..."

"I cannot believe we are even speaking about this!" Sarah admonished, her face flaming.

"We have to talk about it!" Joe declared unabashedly. "I'm through with losing what I hold dear because of a lack of communication!"

Sarah angrily glared at him before speaking. "Listen, Joe… You can't ask anyone! It's too humiliating! But I know that I can't go through it again! I can't survive the expectation, the hope, the loss, but mostly, your look of discontent as you, too, begin to feel that marrying me was all a big mistake."

"Is that all that is truly stopping you?" he asked her quietly. "Or is it me?"

She raised her head and looked at him, her watery eyes red-rimmed and swollen. He pressed onward.

"All I can think of is that this is all just an excuse. That it *is* me, but you're trying to find a way to not have to tell me, am I right?" he demanded, his own hurt and feelings of inadequacy apparent. He wanted to know the real truth, while dreading it at the same time.

She pulled back and looked sadly at him, wondering how he could have so misconstrued what she had told him that he came to the conclusion she didn't want him. "Joe, I…"

"Sarah, I'm trying desperately to understand. I found a potential solution to what you say is your reasoning behind your blatant rejection of me, but when I offered it, you told me that it was too embarrassing." Joe inhaled a shaky breath before continuing, "I can't help feeling like if you loved me, you would be as determined as I am to come up with a workable solution. You would believe, Sarah, that I love you! Do you hear me? You! If not having children is what we need to do so that I get to have *you* for the rest of my life, then I swear I will do whatever it takes, embarrassing or not."

"Joe, that's just my point!" Sarah wailed loudly. "Even now, you sound like you're having to make a sacrifice in order to be with me. You say it doesn't matter now, but trust me, Joe! I know that one day, even though you don't believe it, you will resent me."

Joe sighed, his weariness from the emotions of the day, coupled with the exhaustion from his trip finally taking their toll. All the fight went out of him.

"Sarah, now I'm asking you to listen!" he implored, his quiet voice raw with both pain and frustration. "Because this is all I will ever say about it again. I will not beg you to do what you obviously don't want to. I love you, and I want you. I could never be disappointed in you. Ever! But I won't force you, Sarah. I've spoken my piece. You do with it what you will."

With that, Joe stood up and walked back to his desk, leaving her in a pathetic slump on the floor. He put his elbows on the desktop, resting his head in his hands, breathing slowly and deeply, trying desperately to control his emotions, his self-pity quickly washing away whatever feelings of self-respect he had left. He didn't know how long he stayed like that, but eventually, he heard Sarah collect her things and quietly walk out the door, shutting it softly behind her.

Chapter Fifty

Mama D found Joe a few hours later, sitting at the bar, talking to Mr. Potter, the barkeep, catching up on any issues that had popped up while he had been away, hoping that focusing on something else would drown his sorrows. Though he knew that Michael had told him that things had been unusually quiet while he was gone, Joe was quickly figuring out that it wasn't because there had been a lull in criminal activity, but because people hadn't reported as many happenings. Michael simply was not Joe and did not carry the same level of respect and trust throughout the community.

Mama's big voice echoed out across the saloon from her perch on the second floor. "Well, if it ain't Sheriff Joe McIntyre, finally decidin' to grace us again with his presence."

Joe smiled wryly at her from his bar stool, swirling his drink around unconsciously. "Hey, Mama," he called out.

He waited while she ambled down the stairs and reached to embrace him. Joe towered over her small frame, but he clung to her in return. When she finally released him, she stood back and held him at arms' length. "Hmmm…" she said after several seconds. "A whiskey? While on duty? Must have been a helluva trip!"

Joe grimaced. "The trip was rough," he confirmed. "The coming home, though…" he sighed.

"Oh, dear. That don't sound good!" Mama D replied as she settled onto a barstool beside him. "What'd you do?"

"What do you mean, what did I do?" Joe bristled.

"Well, I can only deduce that if you're in here drinkin' a whiskey only a few hours after gettin' home, on your own admission that things were rough, somethin' bad has gone down."

"Nothing!" Joe quickly snapped, suddenly not so keen to talk.

Unfazed, Mama pressed on. "Let me guess… Sarah?"

Joe didn't say anything, choosing instead to stare down into the bottom of his empty whiskey glass.

"Ah…" Mama D sighed. "Now I understand. Your homecomin' didn't exactly end with the two of you pickin' up where you left off."

"Wait… What?" Joe stuttered. "You know about that?"

Now, Mama D's interest was piqued. "Know about what, Joe?"

In that moment, it dawned on Joe that she wasn't aware of the kiss that he and Sarah had shared before he left to go home. He also knew there was no getting out of telling her now, short of having a heart attack and dying right there.

"I kissed her," he said quietly.

"You kissed her?"

"Yeah…"

"And?"

"What do you mean, Mama? And, what?"

"Well, you look pretty down in the mouth for a man that just kissed the woman he loves, so I suppose she didn't take it well?"

"I didn't kiss her today!" Joe explained patiently. "It was before I left."

"Oh," Mama said, looking perplexed. "So, why are you depressed today, then?"

Joe didn't answer, still quietly brooding, feeling sorry for himself. Meanwhile, Mama D simply sat quietly and waited, so he knew then the whole story would have to come out, because she wouldn't leave him alone until she knew what happened. He sighed heavily, figuring he might as well start sooner than later.

He took a deep breath and began. "I kissed her when Jacob brought over the telegram about my father and brother. I was in shock, so she held me and I…. I sorta took advantage of the situation."

"And was it a good kiss?" she pressed.

Joe sighed again, this time in appreciation, as his eyes misted over. "Yeah, Mama. The best I ever had."

"So, how did you manage to mess things up on the day you got back if you left on such a high note?"

Joe looked around to see if anyone was listening. He didn't like a lot of people knowing his business, and he was especially concerned about the information making its way back to Sarah, perhaps further hurting her by breaking her confidences.

"When I got home, I almost got back together with Caroline…" Joe started.

"And so, Sarah found out and got angry?" she broke in.

"No! It was nothing like that," Joe hastily clarified, wanting to get back to the story before he lost his nerve. "I didn't tell her."

"Joe, lad, you'd better come out with this story, and quick, because I'm an old woman and you're wastin' what precious little time I have left!" she scolded. "You know, I figured you would go and do somethin' as crazy as considerin' gettin' back together with Caroline… That you would feel some sort of sadistic need to add salt to that old wound… to torture yourself. What changed your mind and made you come back here, then?"

"A kiss…"

"The kiss you had with Sarah?"

"No!" Joe's voice showing his exasperation that she wasn't keeping up. "The kiss I had with Caroline!"

Mama D cocked her head to the side and her eyebrows knitted together in confusion, but she didn't say a word, so Joe continued.

"My brothers tried to tell me that I didn't have to take on the responsibility of Caroline and her children, but you're correct: I sadistically felt that even after everything she put me through, because I had loved her I owed it to her to be there to do everything Joshua didn't." Joe exhaled before continuing. "But Jonathan, especially, was concerned about her motivation, suggesting that perhaps she had apologized now only because she needed me… Well, not me, per se… Just someone, a warm body… And he warned me to be careful.

"Anyway, I'd pretty much made up my mind, but then I received a letter from Sarah. It wasn't anything romantic: Adam had drawn me a picture of us fishing and she added a short message, as well, but I realized how much I missed them… missed her. So, I thought about what Jonathan had said all night while battling my own ego, because Caroline had admitted she had been wrong and wished she had chosen me. I had to assess if I still loved her enough to forgive her, but I also thought about Sarah and how I feel when I'm with her, trying to compare. By first light, I had made up my mind about what I had to do, so I got up and went to Caroline's house. When she opened the door, I gave her the exact same kind of kiss as I had given Sarah the night before I left."

"And?" Mama D prompted when he fell silent again.

"And nothing!' Joe exclaimed. "I felt nothing. Not the same tingling in my arms and legs, the near buckling of my knees, or…" he trailed off.

"Or what, Joe?"

"Or," he lowered his voice to almost a whisper, his cheeks turning red, "the overwhelming urge to bed her right then and there."

"Hallelujah!" Mama D yelled loudly as she slapped Joe hard on his back, turning all the heads in the saloon toward them.

"Sorry!" she roared apologetically, then turned back to him.

Much quieter, she leaned in closer to say, "I didn't think you had it in you, Joe!"

When he didn't respond, only glaring at her, she threw her head back and laughed before continuing.

"So, I don't see what the problem is? You've finally found the one girl with whom you want to frolic, and *that* makes you unhappy? Joe, my lad, I think you may be doin' it wrong!

"We haven't done anything, Mama!" Joe hissed.

"Ah, then, that explains it! Therein lies the problem!"

"Mama D!"

"The problem is that you just need to get that leg over, Joe."

"No, the problem is that I told her I want to marry her."

"What's wrong with that?"

"She said no," Joe quietly told the older woman, feeling his chest constrict all over again.

"Are you sure, Joe?"

"What do you mean, am I sure?"

"I mean, did she actually tell you no?"

"Yes!"

"Hmmm…" Mama D replied, her face contorted in concentration. "I'm sure that girl loves you, so I'm truly surprised. Did she give you a reason why?"

Joe nodded miserably. "Yeah. She said it was because she couldn't have any more children and she thought that I would eventually come to resent her for it."

"Well, would you?"

"No! Of course not!"

"But she didn't believe you, I take it?"

"No! And when I tried to reassure her by telling her I would talk to you or Doc about how to prevent her from becoming with child, she just cried harder and said it was humiliating!" Joe complained bitterly. "I tried everything I could think of to reassure her, but in the end, I gave up and told her that I had said my piece and wasn't going to do anything else to change her mind. She got angry and walked out."

"I see. And now you're here, sittin' on a barstool, drownin' your sorrows, and talkin' to me?"

"Yes!" Joe exhaled, glad she finally understood.

"You're an idiot!" Mama D told him.

He looked up in shock. "Excuse me? What? Why?"

"Joe, I love you like you was one of my own," Mama D expounded, "but boy, sometimes… You're dumber than a box of rocks about women."

Joe gaped at her, unsure of how to even respond.

"Joe McIntyre, that woman has been through hell and back! She lost her husband and buried four children. *Four*, Joe! And

434

you respond by sayin' you will talk to someone about how she won't get in the family way anymore, and then when that doesn't work to convince her, you issue an ultimatum?"

"Well, what should I have done instead, then? I was trying to tell her that I don't care if we never have children."

"Did it ever occur to your thick head to tell her exactly that?"

"What?"

"That you don't care if you never have children."

"It was pretty much implied!" Joe retorted, his indignation growing, despite the emotionally numbing power of the whiskey he had just ingested.

"Joe… Oh, Joe… Implication means nothin'! You should've told her exactly as you told me: that you don't care if you never have children. Instead, you went off half-cocked about spreadin' her personal business from here to London." Mama took a big breath before continuing. "What you really needed to tell that woman is that you will love her no matter what!"

"I did!"

"No, you didn't. You were just a typically dense man, tryin' to fix her problem, rather than listenin' to her."

"But, Mama, I *did* listen to her! That's what got me thinking about that there must be a way to prevent babies. There is, right?"

"Why do you care so much?"

"Because I love her and don't want her to get hurt anymore!"

"Then *that's* what you should have told her, you dunce! Taken her into your arms and let her know you understood. Instead, you tried to fix it so that you would get what you want; you should have worried about her and what her needs are."

"I'm confused. Didn't I do that?"

"No, Joe!" Mama D sighed. "You didn't. You simply wracked your brain tryin' to come up with a solution that would allow you to get into her knickers. Like a cad, too, I might add."

"Dorothy!" Joe rarely used her given name, but that did not stop the older woman from continuing.

"I'm serious! Get your arse off that stool and go over to see her. Tell her that you love her for her and she's the only one for you. Let her know that whatever happens between you, you will manage together, and, for God's sake, don't make her feel like her losin' her children is some defect that needs fixin'. She's terrified that she will let you down, so reassure her that there is nothin' in this world that can happen that would change how you feel about her."

Joe nodded, his head buzzing slightly from the alcohol he had consumed. He was grateful for it, however, because it gave him the courage to try again.

"All right, Mama. If you insist!"

Chapter Fifty-One

Joe trudged down the wintery street, ignoring the few people who tried to stop him to talk, confirming what he had already heard about how crime hadn't slowed down much. There were some who were persistent in wanting to tell Joe something, trying to keep up with his fast pace, talking while they were practically running, but all Joe would say is, "I'm really sorry, but I can't talk about this right now. Come see me in the morning."

He stopped in front of Sarah's building and rapped quickly on her door. He then stood impatiently, jostling from one foot to the other, as he waited for her to descend the steps, cross the floor, and throw the lock so she could open the portal.

"Joe!" she exclaimed, instinctively running a hand over her hair to straighten it, shocked to see him standing before her. "Is everything all right?" she asked, concern flooding her voice.

Joe didn't speak. He didn't move. He stood as though he was frozen in place and if he did anything, he might break the spell. It wasn't until he heard Sarah's anxious, "Joe?" again that he was propelled into action.

He stepped forward and put one hand behind her head, cradling it, as his other slipped around her waist, pulling her to him. His head bowed down until his mouth was touching hers and he felt her melt into him as her soft lips began kissing him back. He smiled slightly to himself when he felt her arms circle around him as he gently slid his tongue alongside hers.

Sarah was unsure how long they stood in the doorway, encircled in one another's arms. At first, she was fighting herself, wondering why she was allowing herself the luxury of feeling wanted, feminine, and special when she had long decided that a relationship with a man was not something that she was willing to entertain. It had been so long, though, and her body quickly betrayed her by remembering how to react to a man's attentions. After a few more seconds, everything but Joe melted away, and all she could do was helplessly feel herself surrender to his ministrations.

As the kiss deepened, her body responded ever more rapidly to his affections in ways that she hadn't experienced in a very long time. She had melted into the kiss with Joe before he had left to go home to California… but this kiss was awakening a hunger in her that she had forgotten what it was to have. She felt her knees buckle and her breath catch as she was overcome by an immense desire to be horizontal, but Joe's strong hands held her frustratingly and firmly upright against him.

When he eventually pulled back, he was pleasantly surprised to hear the whimper Sarah gave in response to the loss of his lips on hers. He bent his forehead down on hers, still panting slightly as he said, "Hi!"

"Hi!" Sarah breathed out.

"Can we talk?" Joe asked.

"All right," Sarah replied. "But Adam is upstairs asleep, so it will have to be down here."

"That's fine." Joe looked around and saw that the candle on the holder Sarah had taken downstairs with her was almost extinguished.

"May I light your lantern?" he asked. Sarah nodded to him.

When Joe placed the glass chimney over the flickering wick of the kerosene lamp, its dim light allowed him to see Sarah better. He noticed her pale face while reaching for her hand and wondered if this was too much for her as he led her to the small settee she used in the room for her patrons to sit upon. Once they were seated, he wrapped his arm around her, pulling her tighter into his body, enjoying the closeness.

They sat silently for a long while in the warm glow of the light, simply relishing in being next to one another, before Joe pushed himself away from Sarah so that he could look into her face.

"Sarah, I have to apologize. I'm so sorry for acting like an insensitive oaf earlier. All I meant to tell you is that I love you!

I want to spend my life with you. I adore Adam. Other children or no children, loss or joy, through it all, we will be in this together."

Sarah sniffed, her eyes shining. "Joe, I can't! I'm so sorry, but I don't think I can ever deal with that kind of pain again."

Joe nodded. "I know," he sighed. "But, Sarah, what I was trying to tell you is that *you* won't be dealing with that kind of pain again. *We will*. Together. Whatever happens, you will not be solely responsible and never alone. Together, we will decide if we want to risk trying to have a baby or not. I love you, and I want to build a life with you. Wherever the good Lord sees fit to lead us, you and I... well, we'll be a team. I could never blame you, especially when what happens lies ultimately in His hands, anyway."

When Sarah didn't say anything, he took her hands in his and looked into her now-brimming eyes. "All I ask is that you not be so paralyzed by fear that you will not take a chance on life. I want you to trust me. I'm willing to accept life's challenges with you because you're worth it. What you need to ask yourself is if you are willing to do the same? Please? Please don't doubt me before you even take a chance! Believe that I will be there for you no matter what."

Sarah said nothing for what seemed like an eternity, while Joe held his breath. She desperately wanted to believe him. She was so lonely… she yearned for him to love her and to love him back.

Please, George, she silently pleaded, *Please tell me if this is right. Is Joe the man you think I should marry?*

Suddenly, she was overcome by a feeling of immense peace. She instantly knew that Joe was telling the truth and wanted her, even with all her faults. It was the confirmation she needed, and finally, with tears running down her cheeks, she quietly whispered, "All right."

Joe had been bracing himself for another rejection, so he only half-registered her acquiescence. Once he processed it, his face became alight with joy. "I… I'm sorry?" he stuttered. "Did you just say, 'All right'?"

Sarah could only nod through her tears. Joe couldn't help himself as he reached for her and enveloped her in his strong arms. He leaned down to kiss her and felt her quickly respond to him, causing his desire to go off like a shot. Her warm weight pressing into him reminded him of the first time he saw her and how badly he wanted to get to know her better even then, and he couldn't help but release an involuntary groan.

Sarah, too, was surrendering to her baser desires, appreciating the feel of Joe's bulk; his strength and masculinity that she didn't even realize she was missing until she had it in her arms, without reservations, once again. Everything about him was enticing her to get closer, so she unconsciously clambered up onto his lap, her hand resting softly on his cheek, his evening stubble rough against her skin. It had crossed her mind that he might be uncomfortable with her boldness, but she couldn't help herself. She wanted nothing more than to get as near to him as humanly possible.

Joe felt his hands begin to wander over her back as if he had lost the ability to control them. As they moved over her, Sarah sank even deeper into him, as if she wanted him to absorb her. He couldn't help but noticed that when she had moved to his lap, the skirt of her dress had hitched up and exposed her calves, clad in thick, woolen stockings to ward off the autumn chill.

Joe found himself getting heady when he looked down and saw the shapely vision before him. His heart felt like it had jumped into his throat as he reached forward and placed a heated palm on her shin, under the guise of moving her body closer to his, as if she would fall off. She stopped kissing him for a moment and looked into his eyes, noticing the wonder contained therein, so she reached down and placed her hand on top of his, guiding it up and under her skirt, coming to rest on her upper thigh, almost on her hip.

He groaned in appreciation as he almost lost himself and had to concentrate hard on his breathing in and out to calm the storm raging within him. Rhythmically, he gently squeezed the flesh beneath, until he felt like he could control himself again. Then he spoke.

"Marry me, Sarah! Please?"

"I will!" she panted breathlessly as she stretched up to capture his lips with hers again.

After several minutes, she pulled back, her eyes heavily lidded in the dim light of the room before she changed her focus from his lips to his neck. As she nibbled and sucked the tender skin right below his ear, she whispered, "When?"

He moaned, so deep and low and feral, it went directly to her core. "Oh, God, Sarah!" he cried. "Now!" he begged, appalled at his suggestion, knowing that it sounded like he wanted to marry her in a hurry only to bed her, but in that moment, it wasn't far from the truth.

She smiled against his neck before continuing her ministrations. "All right!" she agreed, before turning her attention to his earlobe and gently rubbing it between her lips and teeth. She was startled when he stood up abruptly, steadying her to keep her from falling.

"You mean it?" he asked her, his eyes shining. "You want to get married now?"

"Yes, I mean it! What are we waiting for?"

"I don't know!" he laughed joyously. "All I know is that I don't want to wait anymore."

"So, then, go and find the pastor."

"Won't we need some witnesses or something?"

"I'm sure…"

"So, who do you want?" he asked.

"You! I want you!" she told him as she wrapped her arms around his neck.

He smiled in spite himself. "I want you, too. But who do you want to stand up for us?"

"Ginny and Jacob?" Sarah asked him.

"Fine by me. But you know we have to ask Mama D, or she will never let us hear the end of it, and if we ask her, we have to ask Doc." Joe paused for a moment before continuing. "Are you sure you want to do this tonight?"

Sarah's eyes got dark as her pupils dilated. "I'm sure… Are you?"

"God, yes!" Joe answered so quickly it made her laugh.

"Then, go… I'll stay here with Adam. We can get married right here, if you would like."

"I truly don't care where we are married. I just want to be wedded to you."

"I will be waiting."

Joe started walking out the door when he turned suddenly. "What about Adam?"

"What about him?"

"You said he is upstairs asleep already. Where are we going to…ahem…sleep?" Joe swallowed hard.

Sarah smiled knowingly at her soon to be husband. "We can ask Ginny and Jacob if they would take him for the night."

While Joe was out gathering everyone, Sarah was anxious, so to help pass the time, she went upstairs to freshen up. She uncoiled her bun and her braid, brushing her hair until it shone, falling past her rear. After rebraiding it, she then fastened it atop her head, before washing her face and hands, brushing her teeth, and putting on her Sunday dress. She might have been getting married at nine o'clock on a Thursday night in her shop, but she would be damned if she didn't do something to try to make her day extra special. After packing a small bag with a few days' change of clothes for Adam, she went back downstairs to straighten up.

Dr. Miller was the first to come into the shop. He looked at the glowing face of the woman he had thought about pursuing for himself and had to admit that she looked radiant; far better than any other time he had seen her. It was obvious by her demeanor that she loved Joe, and he finally was able to accept that she was perfect for his friend.

"Are you happy, Sarah?" he asked, convincing himself that if she was pleased, he would let it all go as fate.

"Incredibly!" she responded with a glorious smile.

Dr. Miller reached over and pecked her on the cheek. "I'm glad to hear it!"

Ginny, Mama D, and the pastor all burst through the door, laughing and joking with Joe, his face bright red. Sarah wasn't sure if it was the cold wind or the comments of his companions that had made his cheeks so scarlet, but knowing Mama D, anything was possible.

"Jacob had to stay with the children," Ginny apologized as she leaned over to kiss her sister. "He sends his congratulations!'

"Thank you!"

"Are we ready, then?" the pastor asked, his tone insinuating that perhaps he was not as thrilled about the timing of this impromptu wedding as everyone else was.

"They were ready years ago, Pastor!" Mama D interrupted. "They were both just too damned stubborn to realize it!"

Joe didn't even hear the words that the pastor was saying as he stood beside Sarah, her hands in his. It wasn't until Dr. Miller kicked him that he realized that everyone was silently staring at him in anticipation.

"Yes?" he squeaked, before he cleared his throat, embarrassed at being caught not paying attention.

"Well, do you?" the pastor asked him.

"Do I what?" he asked, looking blankly at the man.

"Take this woman to be your lawfully wedded wife?"

Joe saw the look of concern in Sarah's eyes, and seeking to reassure her, he squeezed her hands in his while answering heartily, "Hell, yes, I do!"

Everyone but the pastor burst out in peals of laughter at Joe's signature abruptness.

As soon as the vows were finished, Joe tipped Sarah down in a searching kiss that made her weak in the knees as she clung to him. When they stood upright once again, the pastor said his goodbyes as the witnesses all hugged the couple.

When Ginny embraced her sister, Sarah whispered in her ear, asking her if she would please take Adam for the night.

Ginny gave her sister a knowing smirk and told her Joe had already asked her, and that she would be happy to oblige for a few days' time.

Mama D loudly proclaimed, "I'd better get back to work. I need to make sure my girls are all right, and you two need to seal the deal!"

Totally ignoring that Sarah and Joe stood looking agog at her frankness, she kissed them both and was out the door, and Dr. Miller soon followed.

Ginny turned to Joe and said, "If you could please carry Adam back to my place with me, I would appreciate it." So, Joe quickly turned up the stairs and returned with the limp boy in his arms as Sarah handed her sister his bag of belongings.

Feeling apprehensive and a bit shy, Sarah sat quietly in her dimly lit shop, awaiting Joe's return. As she wrung her hands in her lap, she began to think back on her life with George and had to fight a sense of betrayal that she had married Joe. She spoke to him, hoping that he would somehow understand.

"I love you, George, and I always will. Now that you are gone, though, I'm lonely. I'm a young woman… and Adam needs a father-figure in his life. I hope you can forgive me, sweetheart. Though I love Joe, too, no one could ever replace you…" She trailed off.

Joe had returned and had his hand on the knob when he heard that she was speaking to someone. He was perplexed at first until he realized that she was directing her comments to her deceased husband. Straining to listen, what he heard reminded him that he needed to allow her the space to grieve George and not to feel jealous or slighted when she did. He knew that Adam was entitled to grow up with respect and love for the man who fathered him and promised himself that he would do whatever he could to help foster that.

When Sarah fell silent, he took a deep breath and turned the knob. "Hi," he said reverently, walking up to her.

"Hi!" she responded softly.

When he reached her, he cupped her face in his hands and gazed into her eyes, alive and shining in the lamplight.

"I love you, Sarah!"

"I love you, too, Joe," she replied, smiling gently.

Joe was nervous. He had no idea how to proceed. Knowing what was supposed to come next, he had no clue on how to coax Sarah upstairs to her awaiting bed or how to get her into it. So, instead, he kissed her, long and hard.

Sarah moaned quietly as their kiss deepened and she leaned against him.

"You good for tonight?" she whispered against his lips.

"Umm… what?" he mumbled, dragged out of his reverie.

"You all good for tonight, Sheriff?" she asked him again, this time with a hint of flirt in her voice.

"I'm as good as I'll ever be, I guess," he answered her as his cheeks reddened, misunderstanding her question.

"Oh, I'm not worried about that, Joe. I think you will be divine. I meant are you good with your duties for the night?"

"Oh!" Joe laughed sheepishly. "Yes, I think so. I locked up the jail, and it's a Thursday night, so I'm not anticipating too much rabblerousing."

"Good!" Sarah replied stoutly.

"Should we…" Joe began, his voice cracking. He cleared his throat and tried again. "Should we go upstairs?"

Sarah's eyes sparkled with mirth at Joe's obvious embarrassment. "What's the matter, Sheriff? Are you nervous?"

"Extremely!" he blurted, causing her to laugh.

"There's no need. I don't bite… too hard."

She walked away, beginning to extinguish the lanterns and candles, except for the one needed to find their way back up the stairs, leaving Joe staring after her, his mouth agape and his heart fluttering. He walked to her and took the candle and then her hand, leading her gently to the door of her residence.

Once inside, he looked around the moonlit room, his eyes falling on the table where he had first sat a few years before, imagining how it would feel to be married to her. His eyes then swept over to the bed. The mattress was made up with a pretty, brightly colored quilt, and two large, fluffy pillows. When he saw it, he pictured her laying beneath him in the same way he had seen Caroline so many years ago and swallowed hard with both fear and anticipation.

Sarah had seen the mixture of expressions, both desire and sheer terror, which had come over Joe's face when he looked at the bed. She walked over to him and took his hand in hers.

"You really *are* nervous!" she stated softly.

"Yes…"

"Don't be."

"I can't help it," he answered worriedly.

"Well, I'm nervous, too," she told him.

"You are?"

"Sure!"

"But you have been married before!"

"Yes, but it's been a long time, Joe. I have almost forgotten… I'm sure, though, that I will remember, and so will you."

Joe shook his head. "Nope. I won't. I never have… umm…"

"Never?" Sarah asked him, shocked.

"Don't look at me like that!" he laughed, his cheeks reddening with embarrassment. "I was too young and shy before I met Caroline, and then I wanted to wait to save her honor, for all the good *that* did me. After that fiasco, I was too hurt for a long time, and once I became sheriff, I figured it would be too much of a…" Joe paused to think, before continuing, "conflict of interest if I took up with any of Mama's or the other girls in town, so I never bothered to look at them in that capacity.

"To be honest, though, after everything that happened with Caroline, I just wasn't interested for a long while after that. I wanted nothing to do with women ever again. That is, until you came into town." His voice dropped, and he added huskily, "Then I couldn't stop thinking about it. With you."

Sarah smiled sweetly at him. "Oh, dear! I hope you won't be disappointed."

"Never!" he answered so quickly, she began to laugh.

She glided over to him and began to unbutton his shirt. "So, you have never seen a naked woman before?"

He shook his head. "Oh, I have seen most of this town's working girls in various stages of undress whenever there has been a problem. And of course, Caroline, when she was in bed with my brother, but I was too shocked for it to really register then. Never in this situation, though… never anyone I wanted to…" he paused, clearing his throat nervously, "bed."

"Well, my body is not the same after carrying several babies…"

"It looks perfect to me," he cut her off.

"You haven't seen it yet!" she laughed.

"I have seen more than you know," he told her, ignoring her shocked expression. "Remember how angry you were at me that I had helped Doc get you changed when you first got here?"

"Joe!" she said, hands on her hips. "You told me that I was never fully unclothed and that you didn't look!'

"Well, one of those things is technically correct. But I will admit now I did lie about the other."

"Oh, you!" she told him, stepping toward him, as he scooped her into his embrace, laughing.

"I *am* a man, after all, Sarah. And when I told you I wasn't interested in buying what you were selling, I was telling myself that more than you. Reminding myself that you were not one of Mama's girls, and not to forget it!"

"Thank you," she responded. "I think…"

"I say this now with the utmost respect, but there have been times, Sarah, over the past few years when I wished you were selling, so I could have gotten you out of my head."

"You wanted me out of your head?" she whispered, surprised at his admission.

"I wanted to stop thinking about you like that. There were times when I couldn't even look at you without imagining what it would be like to lay with you. It started that hot day when we all went fishing, and then it only got worse from there."

"I've thought about it, too," she confessed in a small voice.

"What? When?"

"Joe, George and I had… well… we had… an active life together," she told him, her fingers continuing to loosen each button. "To lose that was one of the things that took me longest to get over. I'm still a young woman, and many nights I missed having him in my bed. A man in my bed. But eventually, you began to fill my head more than George did. At first, it scared and angered me. I felt like I was betraying his memory. But after a while, I realized that I was falling for you and that my heart had known it long before my head would acknowledge it."

"I had no idea…"

"I worked hard to keep it that way. At first, I was so disappointed with myself, feeling like I had somehow betrayed George's memory, that I got angry. Then, once I realized that I cared for you and that it was all right to move on, you didn't seem interested in me. So, I hid my longings as well as I could."

She had arrived at the bottom of the shirt she could access before it disappeared into his pants. She looked him in the eye as she gently pulled it out and continued on with her intention. When his shirt was completely open, she ran her nimble fingers up and over his abdomen and chest, before working the shirt down his arms and over his hands to the floor. She then lifted his undershirt, and when his hands raised involuntarily over his head, it was as if he was once again three years old, when his ma used to undress him. When Sarah could no longer reach, he bent forward and kissed her on the forehead before taking over and automatically dragging it off his body to drop unceremoniously onto the floor. He stepped closer to embrace her.

"It worked," he mumbled as he kissed her neck. "When I kissed you the night before I left, I was sure I had ruined everything."

Sarah tipped her head back to give him better access. "No, you just left me confused. I didn't know what to feel."

His lips had whipped the small flame within her into a raging inferno, and she righted her head before entangling her fingers in the hair at the nape of his neck. She gave him a sultry kiss that evoked a deep moan from down in his chest, and his hands found their way to the bodice of her dress. His need only increased as he fumbled with each button until he reached the top of her skirt and gave an appreciative groan at the vision before him as he put his hands inside the sleeves and ran them down her arms. Her blouse open, her breath labored with pent-up yearning, he watched mesmerized as her breasts rose and fell within the confines of her corset.

He had been worried about what to do and making a fool of himself, given that she was experienced in the intimacies of the marriage bed, but as he became more desirous of her, his insecurities left him when he stopped analyzing and allowed his instincts to overtake him.

Quickly, he pulled her blouse the rest of the way off, and it floated softly to the wooden planks below, settling gently around their feet. While they continued to kiss, Sarah worked fervently on the buttons of her skirt, and when it was open, Joe couldn't help but to reach out and push it down over her hips, then gently took her hand as she stepped out of it and kicked it away. Still clasping her fingers, he stepped back a pace and let his eyes rake over her form. He let out a tortured groan of approval.

She moved forward until she was almost flush against his body, her lips thoroughly caressing his, coaxing them open to deepen their clinch. While she kissed him, her dexterous fingers worked at the drawstring of her petticoat, and he felt the heavy material whoosh down her legs. His hand ran up and down the laces of her corset as he vaguely contemplated how to remove it from her. He was not well-versed in a proper woman's underclothing, but in his eager state, his arms wrapped around her, one hand massaging the globe of her bottom, while the other rested on the flat of her back, drawing her closer to him, he figured it was high time he learned.

"Turn around," he ordered gently when he came up for air. She raised an eyebrow at him, surprised by his demand, but he responded with a naughty schoolboy grin as he took her shoulders and gently spun her away from him. He then, before she could protest, began to work on the laces that ran up her back while running his lips along her neck. He had no idea what he was doing, but he remembered from when she had been so ill what the doctor had done to free her from the garment's confines, and his hot, moist mouth more than made up for any fumbling he did.

Once the stays were loosened, he stood dumbly in place, until Sarah recognized his uncertainty and twisted around, her hands already working the clasps in the front, and the visual impact of what he knew was coming hit Joe full bore as he sucked air in through his teeth in anticipation. He was glued in place as he watched her adept hands move lower and lower down her bodice until she was at the last hook. She looked up at him and gave him a radiant smile as the corset was pulled away, free from her torso, dropping with a flourish to the ground.

"Ah!" she inhaled deeply, glad to be free of the restrictive article of underclothing, and stood before Joe, observing his reaction.

She could tell that his cheeks were darker in the dim candle and moonlight, but she wasn't entirely sure it was embarrassment. Her assumption was confirmed when she rose her gaze to his eyes, and they were showing something else entirely: a very obvious hunger. She stepped up to him and slipped her hands behind his waistband and began to unbutton his pants, feeling, more than hearing, his sharp intake of breath as her fingers brushed against his naked abdomen.

Once his pants were opened, he turned his attention back to Sarah, reaching for her and holding her in his embrace. He moaned softly in her ear as he ran his hands up and down her back.

"I want you!" he whispered to her.

"So, take me, then!" she insistently whispered back as she gently nibbled his ear lobe.

Joe didn't need to be asked twice as he gathered her chemise in his hands, bunching it together to pull over her head. Once it was off, he stood back and gave a low whistle.

"Sarah Johnson, you are one fine-looking woman!" he told her.

"It's Sarah McIntyre now. And thank you!"

"I guess it is!" Joe responded with an insolent grin. He reached for her and closed his hand around one of her breasts, enjoying its weight in his palm. Then brushing his thumb across the tip, he watched it bud, unbridled fascination written all over his face. Glancing up at Sarah, he gave her a wicked smile, ignoring the expression of amused indulgence that played upon her features. She was enjoying his innocence, reminding herself that this was his first experience and that she should welcome and encourage his curiosity.

Still caressing her breast, Joe began to kiss down her neck, and lightly brushed his lips along her collarbone. Sarah moaned in response, feeling herself soften into him. Dipping his head lower, he took her into his warm, greedy mouth where his thumb had been just moments before, making her almost collapse with want as a whimper escaped her. Joe smiled against her velvety soft skin as he began to understand more about how she was put together and what areas made her more wanton than others.

He dropped his hands to the drawstrings of her pantalets and looked at her questioningly. She nodded softly, giving him her permission to undo the bow that held them on her hips. His head bent low to better see what he was doing in the flickering lamplight, she gently placed her hands on the top of his head, bending down to kiss the crown. She felt his fingers working against her taut belly, and then the soft caress as the last of her underclothing slid to the floor.

Joe stepped back, and Sarah stood still, resisting the urge to cover her body in order to give him the opportunity to study her. She self-consciously felt his eyes move up and down her form, but then tried to relax as she remembered that in his inexperience he was undergoing the same awakening she and George had enjoyed together. Hearing Joe's respirations increase, she smiled, excited to be the one who got to share this moment with him. One more glance and she could tell he was more than ready to move their interlude to the next level, so she gently took his hand and led him to the bed, leaving him sitting on the edge.

"Are you all right?" she asked him, noticing his flushed face and eyes wide with wonder.

"Uh-huh!" he answered, his mind too preoccupied with what he was seeing and what was coming next to form actual words.

Sarah laughed softly. "I'm glad," she said, running her hands through his hair as he enveloped her torso in his arms. He thought that he had never felt anything so soft and delicate in his life and he turned his head to gently kiss her abdomen until he eventually pulled her down to sit on his lap. Wrapping his hands in her luxurious hair, he inhaled the sweet smell that he remembered from all those many months ago, when he had carried her into the jail cell that fateful night. He took up a lock of her hair and pressed it to his nose, breathing deeply, beginning to relax.

"You smell so good!" he told her.

Sarah didn't respond, and instead began kissing his mouth again, hard. He sucked in a deep breath as he felt her tongue wrap languidly around his, and his heart was once again sprinting. He had no idea that he could feel so good and became almost giddy when he realized what was to come would be even better. It had to be… In his job, he had repeatedly seen just how crazy women made men. It had to be worth all the money and drama men dealt out to lay with a woman, or they wouldn't do it.

Joe felt as if he was floating on air, as though he could no longer sit upright, so he tumbled backward onto the soft feather mattress and pulled Sarah along with him. As she lay on top of him, her expression was a blend of amusement and shock.

"I couldn't sit up anymore!" he explained sheepishly.

"Let's get up on the pillows, then, so you will be more comfortable," she told him sensibly. She turned on her back and scooted up until her head hit the padding, noticing that Joe was following suit.

"Do you want under the covers?" she asked him, unable to read his blank expression as he faced the ceiling. He blinked a few times before he lazily turned his head toward her.

"I don't know… Should we?"

Sarah laughed. "That's up to you. It depends on how much you want to see and how comfortable you will be."

"I want to see!" he said so quickly she couldn't help but giggle at him.

"Don't laugh at me!" he protested weakly, realizing just how pathetic the situation was and how unsure of himself he felt, but he had never wanted anything more than he did right then.

"I'm not!" she protested. "I'm laughing at how endearing you are!"

He turned on his side and slid a hand over her neck and cheek until his fingers rested entangled in her hair. He decided that the only way he was going to have the nerve to do this was if he stopped thinking and just went for it, so he quickly lowered his lips to hers and began kissing her with such ardor, she let out a strangled moan.

"What?" he demanded, instantly pulling back, wondering if he had somehow hurt her.

"Don't stop!" she gasped, and that was all the encouragement he needed.

"Not on your life," he solemnly promised. After a few more minutes, she gently pushed him onto his back and glided over the top of him.

She sat up on his thighs, her pert breasts attracting all his attention while her own hands roamed over his chest and abdomen. As her hands dropped lower, tracing her fingertips over him lightly through his drawers, his pulse sped up to the point he felt like his heart might explode as he looked upon her beautiful form, thanking God for making this ethereal being his wife. He reached for her, and she slid up his body, her naked skin on his, and he almost released right there. He was fighting so hard to maintain control that he was gritting his teeth, but feeling her warm, silky form rubbing against him was almost his undoing. Breathing deeply through his nose a few times, he willed himself to hang on, knowing he would never forgive himself if he surrendered prematurely to his yearning.

As her naked breasts brushed his chest, he was surprised to hear himself release what sounded like a whimper, having never known before what sweet agony it was. Just as quickly as she had come, however, she slid back down and regained her perch across his thighs. She worked her fingers into the knot which held on his drawers and in between trying to undo it, she was placing light, teasing kisses as far down on his abdomen as she could without pulling them off. The hot breath of her exhalations blew on him through the material, making his drawers damp, until he was writhing with need.

"Please?" he begged her, willing her to go further.

"I'm trying, my love!" she assured him.

"It would help if you would just tie a bow instead of a knot!" she gently chastised after a few more attempts, before bending down further and working the nub of the strings with her teeth. Joe couldn't stop himself from rearing his hips up in a wave of pleasure he hadn't even known was possible, as he cursed the thin layer of cotton that lay between her lips and where he wanted them. "Oh, God!" he groaned helplessly.

"Got it!" she yelled triumphantly, sitting up and beaming at her accomplishment. While she sat upon him gloating, he frantically shoved his thumbs down into the material and began to push them down his legs.

"Help me! Oh, God, Sarah, help me! Please?"

She was amazed by his voracity. He had a hunger in his eyes that she had never seen before, not even with George, and it gave her a thrill. In her relationship with her first husband, she had let him take the lead in their marital bed, but she was enjoying being the more experienced one this time, taking control, and driving Joe crazy.

She slid further down his legs, pulling his drawers along with her until they came off his feet. From there, he reached down and hauled her back up on top of him with such force that she gasped.

"Please!" he beseeched frantically in her ear, as he placed feather-light kisses there. "Oh, God, please, Sarah! I'm begging you!" He felt his world was careening out of control and he needed her to ground him.

She couldn't help but tease him further as she rubbed against him, causing him to growl so low and deep it exhilarated her.

"Please!" he pleaded, panting with need, and she nodded to him.

He rolled her over onto her back in one fluid movement and rested between her inviting thighs. He was almost crazy with want as he pushed forward until he was nestled among her warm folds. As if being driven by some unseen force, he pressed onward until, when finally joined together, she moaned quietly in his ear, causing him to groan down deep in his throat in ecstasy. He lay completely still for a few seconds, trying to calm his response as he absorbed the new sensations, hoping to stave off the ultimate ending he knew was quickly building from deep within him, but to which he was not yet ready to surrender.

As her legs wrapped around him, her hands drew him even closer, her nails digging into his back, as she sighed. He alternatingly clenched his jaw and bit his lip, trying to slow the inevitable for as long as possible. Nevertheless, after only a few more seconds, it felt too good, too right, and he could no longer not move. Then, once he felt her begin to respond to his ministrations, he could not help himself.

"Oh, God! Oh, Sarah!" he panted in an unceasing, increasingly helpless litany as his body careened out of his control before spilling inside of her with a triumphantly hoarse roar. Afterward, he lay spent on her chest for a long time as she playfully caressed his hair with her fingertips.

Once he floated back to earth, he lifted his head and placed a soft kiss on her lips. "Thank you!" he whispered humbly, not wanting to disturb the sense of wonder in the room.

"My pleasure!" she said with a soft laugh. "Truly!"

Eventually, he rolled off her to the side, lying beside her as he reached for her hand, intertwining her fingers with his own. He turned his head to the side and looked at her, saying, "I don't know how I have waited my whole life for that. That was… That was…"

"Good?" Sarah quietly responded.

"Amazing!" he enthused. "How could I have lived this long without knowing how utterly astounding that is?"

Sarah smiled sweetly at him. "I'm glad that I was the one who got to experience it with you."

Joe felt increasingly drowsy, almost punch-drunk, as he felt himself floating deeper and deeper into the hazy bliss in his mind. Sarah rolled up alongside of him, jarring him back to the present, and he wrapped his arm around her, pulling her close. "What are you thinking?" she whispered, as she saw the dreamy, faraway look in his eyes.

"That first thing tomorrow, I'm going to get the supplies to build us a bedroom up here. Now that I have experienced this, I intend to enjoy it as often as you will let me."

Sarah laughed softly. "I guess that's the downfall of doing this with such haste. I didn't think about the logistics of where to put Adam now that you're sharing my bed."

"I'll build two bedrooms," he answered. "One on the street side and the other in the rear. We can put Adam in the back, away from the noise below. It's better that I can hear what's going on down there, anyway, because I never again intend to spend another entire Friday or Saturday night on the boardwalk when I have you to keep me warm and satisfied up here!"

456

Chapter Fifty-Two

At some point in the night, Joe was jolted awake when Sarah rolled over in her sleep and drew her leg up over his with a soft sigh. Joe had always been a neat sleeper, staying straight and contained. Having shared a double bed with at least one of his brothers growing up, then graduating to a narrow single bed of his own when he had moved out, he had never been one to splay out across a mattress because he would either get walloped by one of his siblings or fall out completely. The goal of all his brothers was to avoid touching each other in bed as much as possible, so when Joe's eyes had opened in surprise as he felt Sarah's warm breath on his chest, he had to admit that it had taken him a few seconds to register what was going on.

Now awake and stimulated, he stared upward into the darkness as he took his hand and gently stroked Sarah's cool, silky hair. He contemplated how he had ever gone a day in his life without knowing the pure bliss of having her form wrapped around him, limp in her submission to slumber. He still couldn't believe his luck that after all their complicated history, this incredibly strong, courageous woman had chosen him, of all people, with whom to share her life and bed.

His thoughts wandered back to a few hours before, when he finally had surrendered to the love and desire coursing through his veins. Making love to her was everything he had dreamed of, had fantasized about, and more. He worried in the dark that Sarah may have been disappointed by his lack of prowess, but at the same time, he couldn't fathom having shared this milestone with anyone else but her. The connection they had made, the way their bodies had sung together long after words had failed, made him wonder how anyone could partake in that level of intimacy with just anyone. To do so would pale in comparison to the giving and taking of love he had experienced as he lost himself in her. He sighed deeply and shifted slightly under her weight, his body involuntarily responding as he recollected her arms and legs wrapped tightly around him in vivid detail. Shivering, he recalled the way her soft breath had tickled his ear, and how her lips felt like satin on his neck as she placed light, gentle kisses there, all while encouraging him to press on, as if he had needed any coaxing. He marveled that at some point, all coherent thought had left him, making him a slave to instinct as raw, untamed passion had taken over.

People had always described seeing stars after they hit their head or injured themselves unexpectedly. However, no one, as far back as Joe could remember, had ever warned him about the loss of rationality when finally surrendering to desire. He knew that he had been vaguely aware of what was happening but was too lost in the incredible sensations building in him to fully comprehend what he had experienced until his heartrate and respirations had returned to a more normal pace. Even now, the full magnitude of the pleasurable vibrations that had reverberated within him was too intense to remember completely.

Lying awake beneath his sleeping wife, he thought through the events of the past several hours, wanting desperately to recall each calculated and graceful movement in the dance of physical love they had shared. All that came flooding back, however, was the memory of the immense bliss she had given him, making him sigh with sated gratification. This is what he had almost lost in his foolish resolve to be stoic, when he had stubbornly tried to protect himself from further hurt and rejection. Here, laying in such a relaxed and peaceful state, he realized how incredibly stupid he had been to let fear control his actions for so long. He finally understood that his determination to never fall in love with anyone else hadn't hurt Caroline; she had gotten what she wanted. Indeed, he had wasted the last ten years of his life denying himself happiness in an unconscious, feeble attempt to punish her, and it hadn't affected her in the least.

Of course, as Sarah lay entangled around him, he was glad that he hadn't figured it all out until she had come into his life, but he still couldn't help but to begrudge the fact that he had wasted so many years of contentment in both his life and his relationship with her. In that moment, it became crystal clear that he had stopped loving Caroline long ago, if now he would even venture far enough to call his infatuation with her love, but had instead been mourning the loss of what he thought his life would be. Smiling in this newfound knowledge, he closed his eyes and quickly found sleep.

Sarah's hand was splayed across Joe's heart when she awoke a few hours later with a start. For a few seconds, she had no idea where she was or who she was with. Her first inclination was that she was beside George and the last several years had been nothing but a nightmare. However, when she raised her hand to Joe's face and felt the soft stubble on his cheek as he sighed contentedly in his slumber, all her awareness came flooding back.

Sarah smiled as she snuggled closer, grateful for not only Joe's warmth but also the soothing comfort of his bulk beside her. She realized that her leg was swung up over his hip and shifted slightly so that she was now prone beside him. He groaned deeply at the loss but did not fully stir, even when she ran her hand down his strong chest and abdomen, enjoying the masculine cuts and dips of the muscles formed by years of physical labor.

Her hand slipped even lower, feeling his response to her overtures beneath her palm. He shifted slightly and moaned as her hand closed around him, and he lay in a dream-like state until he was aroused enough he had no choice but to awaken.

"Good morning!" he whispered huskily to her.

"Good morning," she whispered back, thrilled at his reaction as she felt her own desire rising.

"Shall we go again?" she asked him, her voice low and throaty.

"Yes!" he belted out much louder into the dark than he had meant to, both in anticipation and enthusiasm.

"Good!" she answered him with a coy smile as she slid up and over his legs until she was resting on his hips.

Under Joe's astonished gaze, she settled down and let her body take over. Joe was mesmerized by both her actions and the vision of her moving over him, her breasts swaying in time to her rhythm and her waist-length hair enveloping her. He had never dared imagine anything quite as erotically exquisite as her body taking its pleasure with him, accentuated by the filtered moonlight dancing through the window. Her skin shone iridescently pearl-like, and she seemed like an otherworldly fantasy he had conjured up in his mind. He fought his body with everything he had to hold out because he was not ready to have his enjoyment come to an end.

This woman is my wife! he thought gleefully to himself, as his large, warm hands rested on her thighs to steady her. *My wife!*

As he writhed underneath her, trying to prolong the ending he knew was coming, he couldn't believe this was his life. If he had only known, he decided in that moment, that Sarah would be his recompense for enduring such pain and heartbreak, he would have waited happily for another ten years.

Way too soon, Sarah cried out, and Joe was so enraptured that he didn't even realize that he was tumbling quickly after her until it was happening. As Sarah fell limp and damp against him, he concluded that there was still a lot he didn't understand about the inner workings of the female body, but now that he had experienced her pinnacle, he was intent on finding ways to reproduce it forever more.

"I love you!" he breathed out, his chest still rising and falling faster than normal due to their recent exertion.

"I love you, too!" she murmured in response, against his neck, already feeling herself drift off, sated and more comfortable than she had felt in years. Joe smiled as he pulled her tighter into him, feeling protective and lucky.

Chapter Fifty-Three

Sarah awoke to the sun streaming in and was reminded of the morning after her first wedding, when she awoke in George's arms, newly aware of all her body was capable of feeling while enjoying the heat radiating off his warm skin. She realized just how much she had missed their time in the mornings, before chores and breakfast. She never thought that she would experience that joy again after having tried to completely wall off her heart to prevent any further pain.

It didn't take long as she lay there, though, for her demeanor to change when it dawned on her that once again she was faced with the possibility of getting pregnant. She struggled to fight her rising panic as she realized there was nothing to do about it now. All she could do was pray that whatever happened, Joe had been telling her the truth when he said that they would face whatever came their way together.

She watched him, his face slackened with sleep, and was shocked by the wave of immense love that washed over her and acknowledged that she had loved him for a very long time. As she really thought about it, she realized that she had begun to care for him from the moment she discovered that he had worried her son may not have any Christmas gifts because of the events that transpired when they first got to town, so he had made him one.

Sarah had to admit that she had known for sure that she loved Joe, though, when he had lain helpless in his bed after having been shot, while she prayed fervently that he be spared. Just thinking back to that awful day made her tear up, unwilling to consider a world without him, even more so now than when it happened.

Joe rolled over and opened his eyes, confused to see his new bride crying before him.

"Oh no!" he whispered, "This doesn't bode well…"

"I'm all right," she tried to reassure him with an attempted smile. "I was just thinking back to when you got shot and how you could have died without knowing how I felt about you."

Joe smiled and gathered her into his strong arms. "Kind of like how I let you go back home, knowing it was a terrible idea."

"But there was nothing you could have done differently," she countered.

"I could have told you I loved you and asked you not to go!"

"But it was too soon!"

"Too soon?"

"Yes! We had just met."

Joe nodded. "You're right. We had. But even then, I knew that I loved you. I just didn't have the courage to try to convince you."

Sarah absently fingered the scar from his bullet wound near his shoulder. "That's how I felt when you got injured. I loved you, but because of my stubbornness and cowardice, I might never get to tell you."

"I'm here, and I'm fine. But I won't object to you telling me now how much you love me," he said with a saucy grin.

"I love you, Joe McIntyre!" she said stoutly, and then laughed as he rolled over her and smiled.

"Oh, yeah? Prove it!" he taunted gently.

"How?" she asked coyly.

"I'm more than sure you can figure it out," he replied as he bent down to capture her lips with his.

"My goodness! For someone who claims he has never experienced this before, you sure have taken to it like a duck to water," she teased him as she kissed his neck.

"Excuse me, but have you felt how good you feel?" he asked her seriously, pulling back and looking into her eyes.

"No, but I know how nice it feels to be felt by you," she flirted.

Several hours later, they awoke again. After their latest romp, they had fallen back asleep, their limbs still intertwined.

As much as he didn't want to, Joe began to carefully extricate himself from her embrace and stood at the side of the bed.

"What time is it?" she asked groggily.

He pulled his trousers up off the floor and dug in his pocket, pulling out his timepiece. Opening it, he answered, "Just after ten o'clock," before finding his drawers and pulling them up and over his body.

"Do we really have to get up?" she muttered, already disliking the empty space left beside her.

"I do," he confirmed. "I have to go patrol around town and make sure everything is all right. I also need to go to the mercantile to get some wood to build a couple of rooms up here and to order Adam a bed. Furthermore, I thought I would stop by and ask Ginny if they would keep him a few more days until I can get everything ready for our new family status."

Sarah nodded at him while yawning. He laughed at her, before leaning down and kissing her on the forehead.

"Get up, lazy bones!" he teased her, and then chuckled at the look she gave him.

"You didn't seem too upset earlier this morning when I stayed in bed!" she taunted him.

"Of course not, sweetheart. I got to stay in it with you then!"

He smirked at her, and she could instantly see what he must have been like as a little boy. She had a fleeting thought, wondering if their children would favor him or her, before catching and reminding herself that it was highly unlikely she would ever know.

Chapter Fifty-Four

The next weeks passed quickly as both Joe and Sarah got back to work and into their new routine. Sarah surprised herself with how often she found her thoughts wandering to her new husband until realizing that she had stopped working to sit idly by, pining for him. Unlike George, who she had always known was working safely in the fields, she found she had a very difficult time not worrying constantly about Joe. She was, of course, aware that farm work could also be dangerous: a few men through the years in her hometown had been injured, or even killed, by equipment or animals. Joe's being sheriff, however, meant a different level of peril altogether. He assured her that he was good at what he did, not to mention that he now had all the more reason to make it home every night, but that didn't stop her from stressing many times during the day about where he was and if he was safe.

Joe, on the other hand, wasn't worried in the least. He hadn't been flippant when he told Sarah that he had too much going for him to be careless. Loving being married, he had slid right into being a husband and father without a hitch. It was obvious to everyone in town that he was smitten with his new wife, and adored Adam, as well. No one could remember a time when he had ever been more pleasant. The long-enduring chip on his shoulder was all but gone while he walked around as if he hadn't a care in the world. The old-timers in the saloons would tease him mercilessly about the cause of his now upbeat and downright cheerful demeanor where a once-sullen man had stood, to which he retorted, "I'm sorry… but have you met my wife?" Joe truly couldn't conceive of how they didn't understand it was impossible for a man to be unhappy with such an amazing and beautiful woman in his life. He would stare at each of them until they dropped their gazes, and would then walk away contentedly, missing the comments that insinuated just how happy those men would be to have such a woman in their beds.

Joe looked forward to evenings most of all. There was nothing he enjoyed more than coming home to Sarah and embracing her tightly, kissing her on the cheek before lingering there just a few more seconds to whisper in her ear how he couldn't wait until bedtime. Stepping back, he would then admire the blush that colored her face.

He relished the time they spent as a family around the dinner table, enjoying Sarah's delicious meals and the company, discussing the events of his days with her and Adam. Then, generally, Sarah would clean up the remnants of their supper while Joe worked sums or practiced reading with the boy, thrilled to spend quality time bonding with his new son.

Once homework was completed, Joe would take Adam to the room he had built on the far side of the apartment from the one he constructed for himself and Sarah and read to him until Sarah joined them for their nightly prayers. On their knees, the small boy between them, Joe couldn't find one fault in his new life.

The nighttime was more than he could have hoped for, as well, and he couldn't believe the joys he had discovered in making love to his wife. She was everything he had dreamed she would be and more. His body reacted with just a thought of her, to the point that he had to consciously keep her from invading his mind while at work, lest he would be distracted to the point of endangering himself.

Joe became so protective of his nights with his warm, supple wife in bed beside him that it became a running joke around town that the only time Joe was gruff and unpleasant anymore was if he was kept or roused from his bed by drunken shenanigans on a Friday or Saturday night. He would get so peeved that the patrons of the saloons and cathouses would warn each other if things were getting out of hand and tried to handle it themselves. It had been quickly discovered that if Joe was forced to go into one of the establishments to deal with an issue, he would just close the place down and send everyone home, regardless of what time it was.

For six months, life moved along nicely. Then, one day, Doc Miller came in to order some new shirts and found Sarah pale and sickly grey. He looked critically at her while she smiled weakly back until he asked her, "How far along are you?"

Surprised, she quickly answered, "I have no idea what you're talking about!"

"Sarah," he reprimanded her gently, "of course you do. Now, how far along are you?"

She held his gaze a long time, trying to stare him down, but he didn't waiver, and so she eventually balked, answering meekly, "I don't know…" before her eyes filled with tears.

Doc nodded. "Sick?"

"Yes," she whispered.

"That's usually a good sign, Sarah!"

She shook her head at him. "Not for me. It doesn't seem to matter…"

"This time could be different…" he started to try to convince her, until she cut him off with a sob.

They sat together in silence for a long while, the doctor just letting her cry, patting her hand now and then. Finally, he spoke.

"Have you told him?" he asked gently.

"No!"

"Sarah…"

"I'm not going to tell him, and neither are you!" she demanded adamantly.

"That's not fair, Sarah, and you know it. That's half his child in there and he loves you. You have to give him the benefit of the doubt!"

"I can't!" she wailed, putting her head in her hands.

"Are you certain he has no idea?"

"Of course! The only pregnant woman he has ever been around before was his mother, but he was young then!"

"That may be so, but you look like hell…"

"Thanks!" she quipped sarcastically.

466

Dr. Miller looked reproachfully at her. "I meant that the man might not be experienced, but he isn't blind. He must see that you're looking poorly. What have you told him?"

"Nothing! I'm better by the afternoon, and he has already left in the morning before I awaken."

"When are you going to tell him, then?"

"There's nothing to tell!" Sarah spat back angrily.

"So, what's your plan? Will you just keep it from him until you lose this baby, too?" Sarah only glared at him, too angry to speak.

"Or do you think you will simply deliver this baby alone and he will never know?"

She still didn't reply.

"The man is not stupid, Sarah! He knows what your body looks like; feels like. Your plan may all be well and good right now and could work if you were to lose this pregnancy early, but if you continue to progress, sooner or later, it will become apparent, and even he will be able to figure it out."

"Please! You cannot tell him!" Sarah begged, sounding panicked.

"Sarah, my dear," Doc Miller asked quietly, "Why are you so worried about having him know?"

"I'm just afraid."

"Afraid of Joe?"

She didn't respond.

"Why?" Dr. Miller pressed again.

"I'm just so happy," she whispered, tears streaming down her face. "I love him so much. I love being his wife. Why did this have to happen, Richard? I love him too much to disappoint him!" Sarah broke down into wracking sobs, her whole body shaking with fear, sadness, and frustration.

Dr. Miller didn't know what to do. He was a frontier doctor who dealt mostly with mining injuries and communicable disease, both viral and those picked up from the local girls in the saloons. He was used to hard women and even harder men. Sarah's tears made him feel woefully inexperienced with how to treat the emotional side of health. Most of the few pregnancies he had dealt with were from the saloon girls asking him how they could get rid of it, not crying about how much they wanted to have it. He patted her shoulder gently, letting her cry.

Finally, she spoke again. "So, will you do it?" she asked quietly.

"Do what?"

"Keep this quiet?

"Sarah…"

"Please?" she begged him, and he felt himself soften under the weight of her duress.

Against his better judgment, he couldn't resist her and nodded slowly. "I'll do what I can."

"Thank you," she whispered.

Dr. Miller spent hours poring over books and medical journals trying to find something, anything, which could help Sarah. He still cared deeply for the woman and considered Joe his best friend, so he was determined to do as much as he could to help her bring forth a healthy baby, but also fought bitterly with himself to respect her wishes to keep it from her husband. Making a point to visit Sarah once a week to examine her, he checked to ensure she was progressing. However, when she began to show a bit of a bulge in her belly, even through her skirts, he had to wonder how his friend could be so oblivious, while renewing his vow to remain mute on the subject until Sarah felt the timing was right.

At home, Sarah was careful to conceal her lower torso with long, gathered aprons and she had begun to go back down to the shop after Adam was in bed to catch up on work, or so she told Joe. Sometimes he would go down to join her and witnessed first-hand the amount of work she had, giving him no reason to doubt her. What she didn't tell him was that she was behind because she spent so much of the day back in bed once he was at work and Adam was in school. Eventually, when he got tired, Joe would go back upstairs to retire, and she would continue to work as late into the night as she could, until she was barely able

468

to keep her eyes open, before crawling into bed beside her sleeping husband. Sometimes he would awaken enough that they would make love, but he was always caught in a dreamlike state, and wasn't paying attention to her growing form.

The only time things got tricky was on bath nights, when Joe would heat water in large buckets for her. She learned to wait to undress and get in until he had filled the washtub and turned his attention to other tasks. Only then would she sink down into the bubbles as quickly as she could, before he could give her a once-over.

Miraculously, Sarah made it past the point of getting sick every morning while Joe was still unaware, much to Dr. Miller's surprise. He wasn't sure how she had managed it, but Sarah had kept Joe completely in the dark… until the day she didn't.

Sarah had been feeling off all morning as if something wasn't right. She was concerned because she recognized the sensations from when she had lost her last child but was trying not to think about it. All she could do was to reassure herself that it had been the right decision to not let Joe know what was happening, so that he wouldn't be disappointed at the loss or worse, her.

Never wanting her to think that he regretted his choice to marry her if it meant he would not be able to have children, Joe was extremely careful about not mentioning anything about them until just a few nights before, when after dinner, they had put Adam down for the night. He had studied the sleeping boy and remarked on how much he had changed in the last year, and how he must be looking more like his father.

Sarah had merely nodded, willing herself not to cry, both because he was right; the boy was looking more like George, but also because of the regret she felt that due to his choice of marrying her, he would never experience having a child who looked like him. As much as she wanted to tell him about the pregnancy in that moment, she hadn't. She figured it would only end up getting him excited over what would most certainly end up being yet another loss. Having been through it several times before, she knew she could handle it without having to disappoint him, especially with Dr. Miller's help.

Dr. Miller always made his house calls to Sarah's shop a little after ten in the morning. Together, they had deduced that was the best time, because Joe was usually patrolling around the mines at that hour of the day, so therefore it was less likely he would come home and discover her secret.

On that particular morning, though, as the doctor walked in, he knew immediately that something was wrong by the expressions of both grief and relief that met him on Sarah's face.

"What's wrong?" he asked, immediately anticipating the worst. "Are you bleeding?"

Sarah shook her head. "No, not yet," she replied quietly.

"Good! Let's get you upstairs and into bed so I can examine you."

Meanwhile, Joe hadn't made it out to the mines yet on that particular morning due to an early morning brawl that had caught him off guard at the saloon. It wasn't often that Mama D's girls got into scuffles, as she ran a very tight ship, but when they did, Joe would have sworn on a stack of Bibles that they were much more vicious than any fight men ever engaged in. Men would hurl drunken punches at each other until one of them either was knocked out or simply passed out. A tooth might be lost, or a black eye given, but most of the time, the slight was forgiven once all parties sobered up and, occasionally, a night was spent in jail. However, as in the case of Mama's girls' fight that morning, female adversaries were typically stone-cold sober, and as always, there was hair pulling, kicking, punching, scratching, and the ripping of one another's clothing. Usually most of the issues stemmed from when someone's "regular" switched to another girl, and it could get rancorous.

Joe had been finishing some paperwork for an upcoming court case when young Katie Sullivan came running in, begging for help. The fight was so brutal that Mama D hadn't dared step in for fear of her own safety and had instead sent her quickest and nimblest girl to fetch Joe.

470

Usually, once the girls heard Joe's deep bass ordering them to stop, they would comply, but on this morning, it was obvious that the newest girl to join Mama D's family wasn't going to back down. It had taken Joe several minutes of coaxing, then yelling, and then even physical restraint to get her to end her tirade, and at some point in the process, Joe's shirt pocket had been pulled off.

Everything finally settled, Joe was now happily thinking to himself about how fortuitous it was that he was married to the town's seamstress and was thankful for the excuse to get to see her in the middle of the day as he tried to push open the door to the shop, only to find it locked. Perplexed, he pulled out his key, disappointed that Sarah had needed to step out at the same time he could sneak a few minutes at home with her.

Finding her shop was indeed dark and quiet, he decided to just go ahead and change, vowing as he marched up the stairs to explain his ripped clothing to her that evening, determined to get quickly back to work since she was not home. As soon as he opened the door, however, he was hit with a horrible sense of deja vu when he looked directly through the open bedroom door and saw his wife laying prone, her skirts hiked up above her waist, with who he thought was his best friend sitting beside her, leaning over her as if to kiss her.

Joe crossed the main room in five long strides while bellowing, "What the hell is going on?" as he drew his hand back and punched Dr. Miller in the face.

He was vaguely aware that Sarah screamed, and that Doc had hit the floor, but he was too enraged to care about either occurrence.

"Pull your dress down, Sarah, and make yourself decent!" he ordered, oblivious to her tears and pleas for him to calm down and listen. Without another word, he spun around and stomped to the kitchen, where he slumped into a chair, his head in his hands, too numb to do or say anything else.

How can this be happening again? he agonized.

Joe was unaware of how much time had passed, not even noticing when Sarah came silently out of the room until she was beside him and put a tentative hand on his shoulder.

"Don't touch me!" he roared, frightening her, which caused her to make a small leap backward as a tiny squeak escaped her lips.

"Joe!" she pleaded with him as she began to cry. He had told himself to stay strong and not be suckered in by her tears and excuses, but when he heard her start to sob, he glanced up and saw her face buried in her hands.

"Why the hell are *you* crying?" he spat out angrily.

"Please, Joe! Listen to me!"

"There's nothing you can say, Sarah!"

"There is!" she insisted. "There is!"

He didn't answer for a long while, instead only glaring at her through narrowed eyes.

He took a deep breath to try to control his seething anger. "What could you possibly say that would justify me coming into my home to find my wife in bed with another man?"

"Joe!" Sarah yelled indignantly.

"What?" he answered her coldly. "Am I mistaken? Because, as you would do well to remember, I do have prior experience with this particular situation."

"I was *not* in bed with Richard!"

"Really?" Joe scoffed. "Sure as hell looked that way to me! I'm not sure why every woman I love turns out to be a wanton floozy!"

Sarah said nothing, too stunned to respond. She stood to Joe's side, tears streaming down her cheeks.

There was no telling how long they would have been locked frozen in this stalemate if it hadn't been for Dr. Miller walking into the room, gently moving his tender jaw.

"Sarah, it's time to tell him…" he quietly began to advise her. As soon as he had spoken those words, Joe shot up and flipped the table over in a fit of rage, anticipating the confirmation of what he was sure was an illicit affair between his wife and his best friend.

"Why?" he cried out, the agony clearly written on his face.

Summoning every last ounce of courage she possessed, Sarah took a deep breath and barely whispered, "I'm expecting."

"Why, Sarah, why? I loved you!" Joe demanded, oblivious to what she had just told him.

She tried again, gathering a bit more strength. "Joe, listen to me: I am expecting!"

"Expecting what?" he asked, his emotions too raw to think rationally.

"A baby."

At the news, Joe fell to the ground, his knees giving out from under him. He had completely misinterpreted what she had said, his anguished mind immediately thinking she meant that she and Doc were expecting.

Sarah looked helplessly to Dr. Miller, unsure of what to do now. He gave her a slight nod and then he spoke up.

"You hear that, Joe? You're going to be a father!" he boomed cheerfully.

Neither of them spoke again as they watched him. He had moved so that his back was against the wall, with his feet on the floor, elbows on his knees, holding his head in his hands. The seconds ticking by from an old clock was the only sound to combat the silence.

Finally, Joe raised his head, his expression flat and defeated. "What did you say?"

"I said, 'You are going to be a father,' Joe!"

Uncomprehending, he looked from Sarah to Doc and back again, his head still not processing what they were saying.

What did he mean when he said I'm going to be a father? How is that possible? How can it be mine when I caught Doc with Sarah in bed...? How long has this been going on?

When he thought about it, he guessed for quite a while. He reflected back on all the nights in the past several months when Sarah had been coming to bed late, claiming she had to work long hours. Angrily, he thought about how stupid he had been, thinking it was because she was so busy, but now he had to wonder how many days she had done exactly what he discovered today, locking up the shop and sneaking upstairs with Doc? It also dawned on him that she had been going out of her way to hide her body lately. Everything now was starting to make sense.

"How am I a father?" he whispered, still not grasping what they were trying to tell him in his devastated state.

"Jesus, Joe!" Doc chuckled, in spite of himself. "I know you were green when you got married, but I figured even you knew how that happens!"

"Are you saying it's mine?"

"Well, of course, Joe!" Doc scoffed. "Who else's?"

"Yours!"

Doc laughed. "Believe me, your wife is a lovely, beautiful woman, and I admit that I do even covet her at times… I have told you many times that you're one lucky bastard… But I promise that as jealous of you as I am that you, of all people, managed to hoodwink such an incredible woman to be your wife, I would *never* betray you like that. And that's just me… I know Sarah feels the exact same way."

Joe turned to his wife, and she nodded. "It's true, Joe. You're the only man for me."

"How far gone?" he asked her.

Seeing Sarah's anguished face, Dr. Miller stepped in again. "She has managed to keep this hidden from you for a little over six months."

He looked at her, the pain evident in his eyes. "*Six months? But why?*"

"Because I didn't want to upset you!" she whispered, her eyes filling with tears.

"Upset me?"

She nodded. "I didn't want you to get excited, since I will most likely lose this baby, too. I thought if I just kept it hidden from you, you would never have to know how badly I will have failed you."

"Failed me? Sweetheart, what are you talking about?"

"Joe, you're too kind a man to ever say anything, but despite what you said when you married me, I know every man wants to have a child of his own. I'm already so lucky that you love Adam, but I know you still would want to have your own flesh and blood if you could. Any man would... Anyway, I didn't want to get your hopes up, only to have them dashed, and I can't handle you blaming me for your disappointment."

"Sarah! I meant what I said when I told you before we got married that I couldn't care less about having my own child. You aren't lucky that I love Adam. I adore that kid exactly as he is because he's a part of *you,* and I love you. Why won't you believe that's enough?"

"Just as I said. Every man wants to carry on his family name. You can try to deny it, but I heard it in your voice that night when you wistfully said that Adam must be starting to look more like George. While you're too kind to ever say it, I know you were wondering if your own child would look like you."

"Truly, Sarah, believe me when I tell you I don't. If you will remember, I never thought I would even get married after what happened with Caroline."

Joe took a deep breath and continued, "I will tell you that I do sometimes feel guilty that I get to raise another man's son as my own while he lies in a grave. It seems unjust and I feel unworthy of such an honor. I'm grateful to George that because of him, I am blessed with a child I never thought I would have. It's a lofty responsibility to be given. I want to do George proud by raising Adam to be a man when he could not. That's it! I swear!"

Turning to Dr. Miller, Joe's mind had already switched gears. "Tell me, Doc... How's it looking? Why are you here? What's going on?"

"So far, she has done remarkably well. She was pretty sick in the beginning. I'm surprised you didn't find out then, honestly. I kept trying to get her to tell you, but she refused. I have been reading everything I can get my hands on and so far, so good. I can't guarantee anything, but I'm pleased thus far. We'll continue to do everything we can to keep her going." He paused before stating with disbelief. "I just can't believe you had no idea!"

"Well, I didn't, so that's water under the bridge. But neither of you have told me why you're here and why you were… I mean she… was in bed."

The doctor and Sarah shared a quick look between them before he spoke. "I have been coming and examining your wife once a week. Measuring and listening; doing everything I can to reassure her that she is progressing. As I told you, everything looks like it's on track right now. However, today, she was feeling unwell, like how she felt in the days leading up to what happened to her on the train when she first came here…"

While the doctor was still talking, at the news she was feeling unwell, Joe quickly rose and gently swept Sarah into his arms, carrying her carefully to the bedroom to put her down on their bed.

"What are you doing?" Sarah asked him.

"You need to be in bed!" he ordered her.

"Joe," Dr. Miller broke in, "I appreciate the concern, but honestly, as far as I can tell, everything is just fine. I think Sarah maybe has a slight infection in her bladder. It can give many of the same symptoms as a miscarriage: bloating, cramping, general malaise. I think the baby is fine and she just needs to take a tincture I will make for her, increase her fluid intake, and make sure she's getting enough rest. I'll be back to check on her tomorrow."

"Oh!"

"So, with that, I will take my leave. Bye, Sarah, and take care!"

"Goodbye, Richard!"

Joe walked the doctor to the door before stopping and shaking his hand. "I'm sorry, Doc, that I jumped to the wrong conclusion before."

476

"Me, too!" Dr. Miller ruefully chortled as he gently massaged his jaw. "You can throw one hell of a punch! Remind me to never get on the wrong side of the law or be clandestinely involved with your wife!"

"Well…" Joe mumbled, now embarrassed about his earlier behavior. "Growing up with four brothers…"

Dr. Miller clapped him on the back and said with a laugh, "You're fine, Joe. To be honest, if I had someone as wonderful as Sarah as my wife and I came into something like that, I probably would've done the same thing!"

Joe nodded stoically. "I know that I am, as you have stated several times, one lucky bastard!"

Joe closed the door and strode quickly back into the bedroom, where he stood beside the bed, gazing down at his wife with a look of absolute awe upon his face.

"What is it?" she asked him nervously after he continued to silently stare at her for several minutes.

"Sarah…" he breathed out.

"Yes?"

"I am so in love with you!"

"You have a funny way of showing it," she answered, still smarting from his earlier accusations.

"May I?" he asked, while gesturing he wanted to sit down on the bed. She gave him an almost imperceptible nod.

"May I see?" he asked, his hand outstretched. Sarah again nodded.

He gently placed his hand on her tummy and rubbed softly. "I can't believe there's a baby in there! We made a baby, Sarah!" he declared, his voice full of reverence and wonder.

"Joe…" Sarah warned as her eyes filled with tears.

"I know, I know!" he exclaimed. "I know not to get my hopes up, but Sarah… you are carrying my baby! I never thought it was possible!"

"Please!" she pleaded, her face crumpling. "Don't get excited! Please, Joe! I'm begging you!"

He pulled her head against his abdomen. "Shhh… Sarah! It's all right. No matter what happens, we're still in this together, I promise. I'm only excited because I never thought this would be a possibility for me, independent of you. I went from thinking I would be alone for the rest of my life, jealous of the families my brothers were building, to getting married, raising Adam, and now, our love has even created this child inside you. Regardless of what happens, you have changed me from a lonely, bitter man to someone I never thought I would get to be, a husband and a father, all because you love me!"

Sarah sobbed, wanting desperately to believe him, but was unable to. The hurt of her experience with her first husband had cut too deeply. Joe moved to lie down beside her and took her in his arms. "Please, Sarah, don't cry. Believe me when I say that I truly only need you to be happy. If we have a baby, that's great, but I'm not going to love you any differently or any less if we don't. You explained all of this to me when I asked you to marry me, and I made the conscious choice then to accept whatever happens in our lives. Darling, no one knows what is going to happen in the future. All I need you to remember is that I chose you; anything else is just a bonus."

Joe lay back and pulled Sarah into his arms. He held her as she cried, feeling particularly protective of her. He knew he shouldn't get excited, but he couldn't help himself. *A father! We made a baby!* echoed in his head as he tried to come to terms with that the woman he cradled was carrying his child. *His*! Of course, he had happily assumed the role of Adam's father figure and loved him as much as if he was his own, but what he hadn't told Sarah was while a genetic offspring who looked like him wasn't important, he did often mourn the fact he hadn't been in Adam's life from the beginning. Feeling as though he missed out on so much in those years that he hadn't known him, he longed to have shared in the excitement leading up to his birth, his first tooth, his first step. What excited him about this baby was that he would have the opportunity to cherish each event and milestone that he had missed with his stepson.

Bending over, he gently placed a kiss on Sarah's head. Her sobs began to fade to silent tears rolling down her cheeks and Joe used his finger to wipe one away. She tilted her face upward, gazing at him. He couldn't contain his desire and bent down to taste her plump lips. She moaned against his mouth, and they were off like a shot.

No words were spoken as they both fumbled to remove their restrictive clothing, their kisses never breaking. His hands roamed over her naked body, taking in her enlarging form, and he wondered how he could have missed it before. Her breasts were heavy and swollen, and he groaned as he cupped his hand around one, appreciating the weight and shape, his desire rising higher with the changes in her body he had helped cause. Pregnancy definitely became her. His mouth was next to her ear as he whispered, "God, I love you, Sarah." She smiled against his neck in response.

His hand wandered lower, resting on her belly, when she placed hers over his, holding him there. Within a few seconds, he felt something gently bump his hand, and his expression showed his surprise and astonishment. He looked questioningly up at her, and she reverently confirmed, "The baby just kicked."

Sarah was surprised at her immediate reaction to his elated amazement. It was as though his knowing had changed her. She could no longer deny the potential of the life she was carrying, made from their love. She hadn't wanted to even acknowledge that she was expecting, but now, while watching Joe, it was as if she was suddenly filled with copious amounts of unsung hope and joy. His eyes gazed lovingly into hers as his lips curled in a radiant smile. "We created this, Sarah... You and me. No matter whatever else happens, I will cherish this moment until the day I die."

She reached up to pull him down for a passion-filled kiss, which grew into many more, until he was laying on top of her, his legs resting between her thighs. She raised her hips to meet him, but just as he was about to delve further he stopped suddenly, his head snapping up.

"Can we do this, Sarah? Will I hurt you? Or the baby?"

She shook her head, biting her lip. She was so ready to show him how much she loved him that her body felt as though it was electrified, humming like a telegraph wire. "It's all right, Joe," she panted in his ear.

"But… you're certain I can't hurt him? Or her? I mean, can I…? Can the baby… see? Or feel? Or…?"

Sarah couldn't help but giggle at him as she took his face in her hands, looking deeply into his eyes. "No, darling, it's fine. The baby is tucked safely away. Besides, we have already been making love up to this point."

"I know… But now that I know, it feels different. How about you? Will I somehow hurt you?"

"No, Joe. I promise both the baby and I will be fine."

"But…"

"Sweetheart, George and I used to make love the whole time I was pregnant. My doctor at home assured us that it would make no difference and that it was perfectly fine, as long as I felt strong enough." When she saw the dubious look on his face, she quickly added, "And he assured us that the losses had nothing to do with our activities."

"And do you feel strong enough?" he asked anxiously.

She kissed him softly, and then lightly pressed her lips onto his closed eyes, before answering, "I do! I want you so much, Joe. Please…"

He didn't need to be asked again. Swallowing his nerves, he carefully proceeded, causing her to nearly go insane with want.

"Are you all right?" he asked her, holding himself as still as possible.

"I'm fine," she breathlessly assured him, moving her body enticingly under him as she gently scratched her nails down the sides of his back and lower over his buttocks, encouraging him to continue. After a few minutes, his fear dissipated as he felt Sarah's even more willing response beneath him until he could hold out no longer. Finishing with a low, loud groan of ecstasy, Sarah immediately tumbled into the abyss after him.

They lay encircled in each other's arms, enjoying the afterglow of their passionate session, but Joe felt as though he couldn't get near enough to her.

"Sarah," he whispered, "I know you don't want me to get excited, but you're carrying *my* baby. *Mine!* I can't even begin to describe how much I love you right now. I'm trying not to get my hopes up, but I can't help it. I want this baby with every fiber of my being, and I will do whatever I can to make it happen."

"Joe," she sighed wearily.

"I know! I know! But darling, that is *my* child in there. You have made me the happiest man alive. Please, let me spoil you. I don't want you to work anymore, at least not so many late hours. If we need your assistant to take on more work, or even hire someone else, we will do it. All I want you to have to focus on is what you need to do to give you both the best chance."

"But…"

"Sweetheart, I know the risks, but today, please, let's just celebrate the news. We can doubt and worry tomorrow… But remember that no matter what happens, I love you. We have Adam and each other. This baby, if we should be so blessed, will just add to our happiness."

She could only nod into his chest, wanting desperately to trust him.

"And," he continued, "if the worst should happen, we will mourn together. You're not alone in this, Sarah. I was there for you last time, remember?" he grinned at her.

As soon as he said that, Sarah felt a wave of peace rush over her. He had been there with her last time, helping to care for her at one of the lowest points in her life, when they didn't even know each other. In that moment, she finally let herself believe Joe meant what he said and was committed to loving her above all else: he had already proven he would care for her when he found her as a stranger laying in a puddle of her own blood on a train several years before.

Chapter Fifty-Five

Sarah's pregnancy progressed over the next few months under the watchful eyes of both her husband and her friend. The two of them were like mother hens, hardly letting her out of their sights. Dr. Miller was forever reading journals and textbooks while sending telegrams to every university and hospital he could think of, attempting to find new potential ways to save the child for his friends. He would excitedly tell them about a new tincture or powder to try, and Sarah had to admit that she had never felt healthier in her life. She glowed with love and the life growing inside of her, and with every day that passed, she dared to hope a little more. Already making it long past the point of where she had lost her last child, she prayed vehemently that things would continue as they should. She couldn't bear to think about the alternative.

Her baby had become a town project, as Ginny was helping with Adam, Mama and her girls made sure that she never had to run to the mercantile, and the young woman in her shop took over more of the workload, allowing Sarah to rest. Joe had assured her that her salary was not necessary to their survival, that he made more than enough. In the next breath, however, he was quick to tell her that if she wanted to continue working, it was her choice. As her middle expanded, he joked that he hadn't known pregnancy shortened a woman's arms, and he began to take over more of the household chores, making sure that she did not exhaust herself.

On a bright Tuesday afternoon, she felt her first twinges but tried to ignore them. It was the first truly hot day of the season, and she tried to convince herself that she was just overheated and dehydrated. She went upstairs to drink a glass of water before laying down and began to count the minutes between her pains. The sun lowered in the sky as she dozed between her contractions until she heard Adam coming up the stairs.

"Hi, Mama!" he yelled, as he put his books down on the table. "I'm home!"

"In here!" Sarah answered him. The young boy walked in and took one look at his mother before his face blanched and he asked, his worry apparent, "Are you all right?" He hadn't forgotten that afternoon on the train several years ago, either, and was concerned by his mother's pale, disheveled appearance.

"I'm fine, darling. But can you please go and find Pa? Can you please tell him that I think it's time?" The boy nodded in response.

"Also, could you ask Pa to take you to Auntie Ginny's?"

"Yes, ma'am."

As her son turned on his heels and high-tailed it back down the stairs and out the door, Sarah changed into her nightgown, gathered clean towels, and put water on to boil. It was slow-going, as she would stop and double over, breathing and counting through each contraction, trying to focus on centering herself to get through what she knew had to be done in preparation for what was to come.

The baby had remained active thus far, reminding her of its presence, which was reassuring. Every time Sarah had begun to wonder how long it had been since she felt the baby move inside her, it was as if it would answer her query with what felt like a somersault in her belly. As she moved slowly about her little dwelling, she couldn't help but get excited.

Dr. Miller found her first, putting her immediately to bed on top of the extra bedding she had put down. Mama D came in next, inquiring if she could be of any assistance, but before anyone could answer, they heard Joe come thundering up the stairs, taking three at a time. He burst through the door looking panic-stricken, and rushed to Sarah's side, his fear reflected in his eyes.

"Are you all right?" he asked as he bent down to place a kiss on her forehead.

"I'm fine right now, but just wait until the next pain," she answered with a rueful smile.

Dr. Miller pulled Mama D to the side and asked her to stay, fearing that Joe was too uptight and worried to be much assistance. He explained that she might need to distract Joe when things got moving, maybe even to remove him to give them some space to work. She nodded solemnly, accepting the challenge.

Mama D then went immediately to work, manning the pots of water on the stove and tidying up around the place. They all watched as she bustled around the kitchen, making soup for their supper while gently humming to herself.

Joe, meanwhile, was beside himself with worry, watching Sarah struggle to bring forth the life they had created. Every cry of pain would find him grimacing with guilt and fear. After a particularly grueling contraction, during which she had held his hand so tightly that his fingers had started to turn purple, he brushed the hair that had escaped her bun back off her face and thought they had to be closing in.

"Doc, is that the worst of it?" he asked, thinking that there was no way he could continue to watch his wife struggle as she was.

"Hardly!" Dr. Miller scoffed. One look at Joe, though, and it was clear he was not amused by his friend's frank answer.

"Joe, my dear lad, babies come in their own time," Mama D interjected from her post near the stove. "Sarah is no stranger to the pains that bring forth life. She's doin' all right."

Sarah's eyes were closed, and her features pinched in agony as the next contraction began to build.

"It's just so damned hard to watch!" Joe muttered.

"Why don't you go and scare up Jacob for a drink, then, dearie," Mama added in a soothing voice.

"There's no way in hell I'm leaving her!"

"Well, all right then, lad. You can't have it both ways, complainin' about how hard it is to watch, but refusin' to leave her side!"

Sarah continued to labor for several hours after the sun had dropped from the sky. She was becoming increasingly more agitated, so Dr. Miller lifted the quilt and felt Sarah's belly. "Sarah, my dear," he said softly, "I think we are ready." The exhausted woman could only nod in reply, the effort to speak requiring too much energy.

"Ready?" Joe asked, unsure of what was going on. "What does that mean?"

No one answered him as Dr. Miller pulled gently on Sarah's legs as she scooted so that she was nearer the edge of the mattress. Mama D rushed over with a stack of fresh towels and bedding, leaving them on the trunk at the foot of the bed.

"Joe, go ahead and prop her up on some more pillows there, if you would," Dr. Miller ordered. Then, he focused his attention back on the laboring woman.

"Go ahead and bend your knees for me, Sarah," Dr. Miller said as he worked his way between them. "Open a little more for me, please, so I can see what's going on… That's a girl."

Joe fought his instinct to object, feeling uncomfortable with having his friend in such intimate proximity to his wife. Only because he had attended the birthing of Sarah's last child was he able to talk himself down enough that he could ask, "What should I do?"

"Well, Joe," Dr. Miller looked up and spoke, "this is when the action happens. Most men feel the need to step out now if they haven't yet."

Joe looked to his wife, torn between wanting to be there for her and fear of what was to come, and softly asked, "Shall I go?"

"No!" she cried, grabbing blindly for his hand. "Please, I can't do this alone."

He clutched her sweaty palm in his and was surprised at the amount of force with which she held it. Staring at her face, he only barely registered Doc's voice when he ordered, "Here we go, Sarah! *Push!*"

She grimaced, and Joe watched helplessly as her body went rigid with every muscle working. Eventually, she exhaled loudly while laying back in relief. She waited, breathing hard with her eyes clamped tightly closed for a few minutes, until the whole ordeal began again.

Joe was unsure of how long the process repeated itself, but after what seemed like forever, Sarah fell back against the pillow again, her face grey with exhaustion, tears streaming down her face.

"I can't!" she cried. "I can't do this anymore. Something is wrong! I can't! I can't!"

Joe whipped his head up in surprise and caught Doc's eyes. "Sarah…" the older man began, "Sarah, listen to me. The baby seems to be a little stuck. Joe's a big guy, and I think this little one takes after its pa. But listen to me. You can't give up! You're almost there. I know you're tired, but just a few more pushes for me, all right?"

"I can't!" she whimpered. "Please! I can't do this again! I can't do it all over! Something's wrong, I know it! Please, Joe, do something!" She looked at him, her eyes begging him to help her.

"I…" he began but was completely unsure of what to do or say.

"Joe, why don't you let Mama over there take her hand. Now, I want you to get in behind her…" Joe looked questioningly at the doctor as he climbed up on the mattress. "That's right… Just like that. I want you to get in behind her and help brace her from behind. When the next pain comes, I want you to help prop her up to see if we can get a bit more force out of her."

Joe braced himself behind his wife, and his legs splayed out with hers in between them. She visibly relaxed as she lay against him until the next contraction came. As he felt her tense and struggle, he sat forward, supporting her, which caused her to bear down even more. He held her up until the pain passed, when she fell limply against him, her head lolling onto his shoulder.

"Good!" Dr. Miller declared happily. "That helped! We got some give that time."

486

Joe took one of his hands and brushed the hair off Sarah's forehead, and then cradled her in his arms. "Good job, sweetheart! You're doing great!"

"No!" she moaned. "Something is wrong. I don't feel it moving! Joe, something's wrong… I can't do this!"

"Darling, it's all right. Just try to res…"

"Joe!" she screamed hysterically. "I can't! I can't! I'm scared it's…"

Joe caught Mama D's gaze, and she nodded slightly.

"Sarah! Sarah, look at me!" He waited until she opened her eyes and focused her gaze on his. "You don't have a choice, darling. This baby has to come out. You're doing what needs to be done. Regardless of what happens, this baby needs to come out. Use me to help you. I promised you wouldn't have to do this alone, and you aren't. I'm here, right behind you!" He felt her nod against his shoulder.

"All right, Sarah, here we go…" Dr. Miller cajoled.

Joe sat up again and braced his wife as she pushed with everything she had. This time, he heard the doctor sigh with relief.

"What?' he demanded.

"I see the head. Finally, she's making some progress!"

Once again, a contraction came, but Joe was so focused on propping Sarah up that a scream cutting through the air shocked him.

"What? What is it?" he asked, his voice reflecting his panic.

"Great job, Sarah! The head's out! The baby is staring at me!" he laughed with relief. "That's what was taking so long. Baby's face up, not face down. Just give me one more really big push, and you're all done!"

Gathering every ounce of strength left that she possessed, Sarah cried out in pain and release as she felt the baby slide free from her body. She collapsed against Joe, sobbing with both fear and relief.

Joe watched out of the corner of his eye as Mama D rushed in to take the babe into a towel. Something was missing, but he wasn't sure what it was while his eyes darted from Sarah to Dr. Miller to Mama D, trying to grasp what was happening. Suddenly, the most beautiful sound he had ever heard rang out into the silent room. The little bundle, safe in Mama D's arms, began to wail.

Stuck behind Sarah's limp weight, all he could do was watch as Mama D carefully rubbed and dried the child, before bringing it to place on Sarah's chest.

"Congratulations, my dears," she exclaimed happily. "You have a beautiful baby boy!"

Joe watched his son's face, enraptured. He looked so much like his younger brothers had when they were newborns it was uncanny. The baby opened and closed his eyes a few times, before opening his mouth in a wide yawn, and settling in against Sarah's breast. Joe could no longer control his emotions from the ordeal and tears began coursing down his face.

"Our boy!" he whispered into the top of Sarah's head before placing a gentle kiss there. "Our son! He's amazing!"

Sarah's arms tightened around the little boy as he began to root around near her breast until he latched on. Joe watched his baby suckling and thought he had never seen anything as beautiful as the sight before him.

"All right, Sarah. You're almost ready…" Dr. Miller's voice cut through the awed silence in the room. "Just stay where you are for now, Joe, while we finish up. Once she's done with this part, you can get up, but for right now, just enjoy holding your family." He caught Joe's eye and gave him a wink.

Several hours later, Joe held his precious son while he watched his wife sleep. He had never known he could experience such utter peace and contentment. In the room on the far side of their dwelling, his stepson slept peacefully, after excitedly meeting his baby brother. Sarah had cried for him, so Dr. Miller had given the okay for the boy to come home once Sarah and the baby were declared healthy and fit. Still not believing all that had transpired, Joe had pulled his old friend aside to double check everything was truly well before he left, and the man had assured him that as far as he could tell, their baby was as whole and healthy as any he had ever delivered.

The baby whimpered, and Sarah stirred awake, opening her eyes to see her big, strong husband looking completely smitten with their tiny boy. His gaze moved to hers and his mouth widened into a big grin. "Good morning, beautiful," he said quietly.

"Is it really morning?" she asked, surprised.

"Yes and no. Technically, it's five in the morning, but it's also the middle of the night. How are you feeling?"

"I'm all right. A little stiff and sore. How's the baby?"

"He's perfect!" he answered, looking lovingly down at the bundle he held, and she smiled.

"Have you put him down at all since I fell asleep?"

"Nope."

"You will learn quickly, darling, that it's best to sleep when they do."

"That may be, but right now I'm enjoying him too much. He's amazing!"

"Just like his pa! Speaking of which, what do you want to name him, Joe?"

"Me?" he asked, looking up at her in surprise.

"Yes."

"Why me?"

"Because I've gotten to do this before; you haven't."

"I… I don't know! What if I name him something he later hates?"

"Well… what was your father's name?"

"Brian."

"Brian McIntyre. How about that? I like it!"

Sarah looked up to see Joe staring intently at her. "What?"

"And I love you!" he answered. She smiled sweetly in return.

"What about his middle name?" Joe asked, his voice barely above a whisper.

"I think he should be named for his pa, don't you? Brian Joseph McIntyre. I think it's a very fitting name."

"Sarah…" he started. "You don't have to name him after me."

"Why not?"

"I don't know. I'm nothing special."

"Joe McIntyre, you're the most wonderful man in the world!" Sarah cried, interrupting him. He gave her an incredulous look in response.

"Honestly, Joe," she insisted. He sighed in acquiescence, knowing he would not change her mind, while praying he would never do anything to change her opinion.

The boy rooted around, opening and closing his tiny mouth, before Joe stated, "I think he's getting hungry." When Sarah nodded her agreement, he leaned over to present his son to his wife, kissing her on top of her head once he carefully laid him in her arms.

"And wet!" Sarah quietly laughed and motioned for him to grab a clean diaper and some pins. He watched as she adeptly changed the boy's diaper and then settled him onto her breast.

"I'll not forget this sight as long as I live," he whispered, playing gently with his son's small toes. "He's absolutely perfect!"

Sarah just yawned in response and settled in against Joe's broad, strong chest. Carefully, Joe settled them all back into the bed, where they slept until the sun had climbed high in the sky.

Chapter Fifty-Six

The baby grew big and strong, and after a few months, Sarah finally allowed herself to relax. The boy was alert and happy, crying only when hungry. Once she healed, Sarah had begun to take him down to her shop every morning. Even the roughest, gruffest miners were smitten with the small boy, making Sarah chuckle quietly at the men, covered in soot and grime, who would bend over her son's bassinet, cooing and babbling at him, as the boy smiled joyfully back at them.

Dr. Miller had been correct when he stated that the boy seemed to take after Joe, as he was big. Even Sarah eventually agreed that Dr. Miller no longer needed to come every day to examine Brian and let him fall back to every other day, then every third, to eventually just once a week. The doctor could never answer why Sarah was able to birth such a robust and healthy son after her many losses and could only explain it as the children had different fathers. It was as much as he dared to say, not wanting to insinuate that there may have been something unhealthy about her first husband. He wasn't convinced that the trouble had lain entirely with George, either, but instead suspected that perhaps it was the combination of the two of them that was somehow incompatible. Needless to say, whatever the reason was, based on how well their son was thriving, it did not appear to be an issue between Joe and Sarah.

The family settled into a routine, and Joe realized he had never been happier. He was so incredibly in love with his wife and his two sons. An outsider who didn't know their family's story would never guess that Joe was not Adam's biological father. The two of them would often pal around town together in the afternoons while Sarah and Brian slept, Adam strutting beside his sheriff father, the pride beaming out of him. He told everyone who listened that he was going to grow up and be just like his pa, and no matter how many times Joe heard it, he would still feel the prickling of emotion in his eyes.

When Brian had turned six months, Joe was awoken in the middle of the night. He sat straight up in bed, glancing briefly at his wife, who was still slumbering, and then at Brian in his crib. All seemed well.

He listened intently, wondering if whatever noise had jarred him from his sleep would repeat. Waiting for little more than a minute, he heard pounding on the door to Sarah's shop. There was no other commotion outside. Usually, when he was aroused from his bed, he could often hear the raised voices and overexcited jeers of men who had been in a saloon. This time, however, it was dead-silent, which both concerned him and made him curious about what was going on, but more than anything, he worried that the repeated noise would wake his family.

Throwing his denim pants on over his long johns and a flannel button-down over his shoulders, he grabbed his boots in one hand and walked stealthily down the stairs. He saw the person's hand up, ready to knock again, so he threw open the door, startling the young woman on the other side.

"What the hell is going on?" he hissed quietly, noticing immediately that the girl flinched and stepped back at his flare of temper, and he decided he had better back off a bit.

"I... I'm sorry, Sheriff!" the girl stammered an apology. "Mama D told me to run over here and fetch you!"

"All right, Hattie," he answered, trying to hide his annoyance.

If Mama sent her alone in the middle of the night there must be a good reason, he supposed.

"Let's head on over."

When he walked into the saloon, the place was surprisingly empty, even for a Wednesday night. Though the real ruckus in town didn't generally start until Friday, some of the regulars liked to get a head start. He glanced quickly at the clock, which read it was twenty after one. When he looked in the direction of

492

the bar, he caught the eye of the barkeep, who gave him a grim, tight smile. Not having any idea what was going on, he quickly followed the young girl up the stairs.

"I'll leave you here," she whispered almost reverently.

"All right," he answered, still confused. He pushed open the door, unsure of what would be waiting for him on the other side.

The lights were dim, and it took a few seconds for his eyes to adjust, but when they did, Joe saw Mama D standing in the corner, cradling something, with tears in her eyes. He then looked to his right and saw a young woman stretched out on the bed, with the signs of what seemed to have been a massacre around her, her bedclothes bloodied and wrinkled. His eyes were drawn to where Dr. Miller was sitting at the far side of the woman, looking exhausted and defeated.

"What the hell is going on in here?" Joe asked.

"I lost her!" Dr. Miller responded dejectedly.

"Huh?"

"Joe," Mama D began, "we lost Kitty tonight. Her child survived, thanks to Doc, but she did not."

"Kitty was pregnant?"

"Aye," Mama D answered.

"How long did you know?"

"For about two months. The little minx was careful to hide it from me before that. Thought I wouldn't let her keep it, silly girl."

"Would you have?"

"Of course! A baby's a gift from God, Joe! You know that! It doesn't happen often, but I have worked with some girls who kept their babies through the years. But she didn't make it."

"And now what? You said the baby survived?"

"She did," Dr. Miller confirmed.

"The baby is a girl?" Joe asked softly, moving closer to Mama D, who held the baby away from her so Joe could see. His paternal instinct taking over, he reached for the girl and gazed into her big, blue eyes. She immediately settled into his warm chest, having no idea what was happening around her or that her new life was already fraught with so much peril.

"What are you going to do now?" he asked, absentmindedly stroking her soft cheek.

"Don't know. I have always let my girls keep their wee ones here with them when this has happened before, but there ain't no one who's got time for a little bastard without a mama." Joe cringed a little at Mama D's harsh wording.

"So, what do you need from me?" Joe asked. "Though this looks like a crime scene, it obviously isn't. Doc doesn't need my help with this." Joe's annoyance about being awoken and summoned out of his nice, warm bed beside his even nicer, warmer wife was beginning to resurface.

"Actually, Joe, I'm the one who asked you to come," Dr. Miller answered.

"Why? We could have dealt with this in the morning…"

"Well, as Mama said, there isn't really anyone else who can take care of this little one. No one here can."

"And? What do I have to do with that?"

"Joe," Mama broke in, "We were talkin', and Doc pointed out that Sarah is still nursin' young Brian. There aren't any other women in town who are nursin' right now, and none of us whores have the knowledge or the time to figure out how to feed a baby without its mama's breast. We were hopin' that Sarah would be so kind as to feed her for us."

"You want my wife to care for this woman's baby?"

"Yes," Dr. Miller broke in. "She's the only one in town who can easily do it."

"Easily? You do realize that we have our own baby to feed, she has Adam to care for, as well, and works in her shop, right? Do you have any idea how difficult it is to care for a newborn?"

"Joe," Dr. Miller interrupted, "Without Sarah's help, this little one could very well die!"

Joe sighed. "What about any family? Kitty must have some kin somewhere?"

494

Mama D just shook her head. "Nope. Her ma died in childbirth with her, and her pa died when she was thirteen. Found her way to me not long after, with not another soul in the world to look after her. You know that I had her as my house girl until she was sixteen, when she saw that the other girls were makin' triple what she was just layin' on their backs, and well… that was that."

Joe had known that Kitty had come to Mama D early, and that the woman had fought to keep the girl out of the profession for as long as she could, but he didn't know much else about her backstory before now. He had learned a long time ago that the girls' backgrounds were often just too heartbreaking, and it was generally better not to ask unless necessary.

Mama D had been watching Joe snuggle the little girl, unwittingly caressing her face and rocking her in his arms. She decided there had been enough talking and she went in for the kill.

"Careful, Joe, your tender side is showin'. Once a father…" she said quietly.

He looked back at her for a moment, and then down at the soft, pink bundle in his arms, unwilling to admit that his head was coming around to the idea his heart had obviously accepted. He sighed deeply.

"She's adorable," he answered, as she snuffled a bit in her sleep. "But I can make no guarantees. It's Sarah's decision, and I won't hear another word about it, understood?"

Dr. Miller and Mama D nodded obediently, both biting their lips, trying to keep from smiling.

"That's reasonable," Dr. Miller agreed, hoping to get Joe and the little girl moving along before she woke up, searching for nourishment. "Why don't you head on home with her, and Mama and I will clean up around here."

The doctor and the madam stood shoulder to shoulder on the top landing of the stairs in the saloon as they watched the large man descend with his precious cargo.

"Lord, I hope this works!" Mama prayed quietly.

"What do you mean? He's taken her, hasn't he?"

Mama D shot him an incredulous look. "Men!" she said in a huff.

Dr. Miller rolled his eyes in contempt. "What did we do this time?"

"He ain't the one I'm worried about. 'Tis her!"

"Sarah?"

"Of course, Sarah!"

"Why are you worried about Sarah?"

Mama D swore and shook her head. "I swear to God above, a whole room full of you men still ain't no smarter than one woman alone!" She paused when she saw Joe stop by the door and rearrange the blankets around the newborn before exiting into the frigid night.

As the door closed behind him, Mama D turned to the doctor with a large smile on her face.

"I knew it would be like shootin' fish in a barrel with Joe. He's a changed man. As I said, it's Sarah who worries me!"

"But why? I don't understand. I thought all women loved babies?"

"Yeah, you numbskull… *their* babies!"

Seeing the confused look on the doctor's face, she sighed and continued. "I guess I have to spell it out for you. I wasn't worried one iota about Joe. Marriage and fatherhood have made him soft. Look how he took to Sarah's little boy immediately, as if he were his own flesh and blood! That woman and her child finally broke through the exterior shell he had been cartin' around for so long, not that it wasn't needed mind you, and it has only gotten better with the birth of that boy! She's the one we have to worry about convincin'. She's still carin' for their own wee lad. Mothers get protective of their resources when their own children could suffer." Mama D paused and took a deep breath before continuing. "Of course, that doesn't even bring into account the fact that she may refuse based on how this baby was conceived. All we can do is pray that Joe can help her grow to love and take care of this little girl by remindin' her that

496

bein' kin doesn't matter, like how he has done with young Adam."

"I sure hope so, because if not, I honestly don't know what we will do."

"If need be, we can always scare up some goat milk. Had to do it before I came here for the neighbor down the lane. Ten children, and she dies birthin' the eleventh!" Mama reminisced, her eyes taking on a far-away look. "But I don't think it will be needed. I guarantee you that durin' his journey across the street, Joe has already planned how he is gonna convince Sarah to keep her. For all his objections and airs, he was smitten with her the second I put her in his arms."

Chapter Fifty-Seven

Mama D's predictions were spot on. As Joe opened the door to the shop and made his way up the stairs, he was already running through all the things he could possibly say to convince Sarah that they were this tiny girl's only hope.

Once inside, he didn't know what to do, as he had no place to lay her down. Brian was in his cot and Adam was in his room, so the only place to sit in the main room was the table. The bedroom door was ajar, and after he lit a candle, he could barely make out Sarah's form snuggled deep within the blankets and had to fight the overwhelming urge to join her. Instead, though, he only sat until the baby in his arms began to whimper.

At first, he tried to quiet the little girl, but then he realized that the faster Sarah awoke, the sooner they could have the looming conversation.

As the cries grew louder, Sarah arose; he saw when she sat up. She listened for a moment until she stood up and peered out into the main room.

"Joe?" she called out quietly, obviously confused. "Is everything all right?"

He didn't answer her, wanting instead for her to come out to him, while allowing her eyes to adjust to the light. He counted silently in his mind as he watched how long it took for the scene before her to register.

"Joe!" she demanded, her voice sounding concerned. "What's wrong with Brian? Why does his cry sound different?"

How in the hell can she tell that? Don't all babies sound the same? Joe wondered as she stumbled out of the bedroom. From there, it didn't take long until she was fully awake and her eyes wide open. "Who's this?"

"She's just been born."

"And?" Sarah asked with a yawn.

"You know Kitty, right? One of Mama's girls?" He waited until she nodded dumbly before continuing. "Apparently, she was pregnant. Didn't tell Mama a thing about it until two months ago. Anyway, she delivered tonight and for some reason didn't survive. Mama sent Hattie over to get me a few hours ago..."

Sarah interrupted. "Why didn't you wake me?"

"I didn't know what was going on then."

She didn't say anything, so he cautiously continued.

"Doc and Mama were there, and it looked like a murder scene, Sarah. I had no idea what I was walking into until I saw Mama holding this little one."

"That's all well and good, Joe, but what's she doing here?" Sarah's frustration was beginning to show.

"Well, that's where you come in..."

"I'm sorry?"

"Sarah," he began, trying to tread carefully. "Mama D and Doc want to know if you would be willing to feed her, since her mother is gone and can't."

"How?"

"What do you mean, how?" he asked, perplexed.

"I mean a newborn needs to eat all of the time! You certainly remember how exhausted I was when Brian was born!"

"I do," he agreed, realizing in that moment this little girl was for sure destined for their family, but that he would have to do some serious convincing to make that happen.

"And it hasn't even been that long, Joe!" she continued, sounding exhausted just thinking about it. "He has only been sleeping for more than three or four hours at a time for about the last two months."

"I know," he confirmed.

"So... am I going to be expected to walk across to the saloon every time she needs a feed? Because I won't wake up several times a night, get dressed, and then stroll into a saloon at all hours!" Sarah's voice was rising in volume and intensity with each word she spoke until she sounded very near hysterical.

"We haven't talked about specifics yet, sweetheart," Joe answered her quietly, trying to keep his emotions in check as to not frighten the little girl in his arms. "But, sweetheart, she's crying. Could you feed her now? Please? She's starving, and there's nothing anyone else in this whole damned town can do about it at two-thirty in the morning but you!"

With her husband's heartfelt plea, Sarah was able to calm down enough to hear the soft yet insistent newborn wails and nodded her head. No matter what else she was feeling, there was no doubt the poor little thing had been through an ordeal and was in need of nourishment, as well as comfort. She wearily pulled out the chair and readied a breast, then Joe handed the child down, and while softly stroking his wife's hair, watched as the girl struggled at first to latch on. Sarah gently coaxed her, and after several attempts, he exhaled the breath he didn't even realize he was holding when he heard the recognizable snuffles and soft grunts of a baby being suckled.

Sarah was at first very stiff, but after a few minutes, she began to relax as she had done while feeding her children. Joe said nothing as he watched the scene in front of him, vehemently praying that his wife would be willing to accept the awesome responsibility presented to them. His eyes followed her fingers as she began to gently run them through the girl's dark locks.

Sarah looked up and caught him staring at her. "She's a little beauty."

"I know."

"She has Kitty's hair. And eyes. They're so blue they're almost violet."

"That they are." Hope swelling in his heart, Joe didn't even want to blink and risk breaking the spell in the room.

Neither said a word as Sarah pulled the little girl from one breast to settle her on the other side. "I can't let her get too much," she explained. "I'm making enough milk for a six-month-old, not a newborn. I don't want to drown her." Joe merely nodded in response, still praying.

500

Each lost in their own thoughts, they both stopped talking and simply watched the baby feed for a while.

"I always wanted another daughter," Sarah wistfully mused as she pulled the child free from her breast and propped her up on her shoulder to burp her. Joe wordlessly reached over to grab a clean dish towel and handed it to his wife.

"Is there any other family?"

"No," Joe answered. "Kitty's ma died when she was born, and her pa when she was about thirteen. Mama was the closest thing to a mother she's had."

"Poor little darling!" Sarah cooed as she placed the baby into the crook of her arm, where she slept, warm and sated.

"I guess I could help feed her for a while," Sarah acquiesced with a sigh.

"Thank you!" Joe gushed, his overwhelming relief evident in his expression.

Sarah studied him for a few seconds, before exclaiming, "Joe McIntyre! I think this baby girl has wrapped you around her little finger already!"

Looking sheepishly at her, he responded, "Guilty as charged."

"Well, how are we going to do this? Will she stay overnight with us? Because we have no place to put her! Brian is still using the crib right now," Sarah reasoned.

"Nothing says we can't have two cribs."

"And where do you propose we put two cribs?"

"Brian is old enough now that he can sleep in Adam's room. As you said yourself, he rarely wakes up anymore. I'll go get him if he does."

"You promise?"

Joe nodded solemnly. "I swear on it!"

Sarah looked down into the tiny face before her. "Any idea who the father is?"

Joe shook his head. "Not a clue. Mama doesn't, either. Kitty had a few 'regulars,' but she was open to anyone, just like all the others. Mama said that even if we could find out who the father was, he most likely wouldn't want to keep her."

"Why not?" Sarah exclaimed. "She's beautiful!"

"She is! But how's a miner going to keep a baby alive out here, Sarah? No wife or family... Most of these men are pretty hard-living and aren't exactly family men."

"I guess that's certainly true." They lapsed into another silence.

Eventually, Sarah spoke once more, while still studying the baby's face. "Don't Mama and the girls want to keep her?"

"And do what with her? Mama claims they haven't got the time to fuss with her."

"Hmmm…"

More quiet. Joe felt like he was going to burst, but he kept his mouth shut, not wanting to say anything that could change the course of where he felt this conversation was heading.

Sarah glanced up at her husband while stroking the infant's supple cheek with her fingertip. "Could we keep her? Legally, I mean?"

"I don't see why not," Joe replied, trying unsuccessfully to hide his elated grin. "I'll talk to Judge Hastings next time I see him and ask if there's anything we would have to formally do. But as she has no known kin and there's no abundance of families looking for children here, I can't imagine it would be much of an issue, either way."

They both heard a door squeak as Adam pattered out of his bedroom. "Ma?" he asked sleepily. "What time is it?"

"It's a little after three in the morning," Joe answered.

"Who's that?" Adam asked when he noticed who his mother was holding.

"Ummm…" Sarah was at a loss on what to say.

"Adam, that's a baby that one of Mama D's girls had. Her mother didn't make it, so your ma is helping out."

"Her ma died? Like what could have happened to you on the train?" Adam asked, his eyes big and round.

"No, I lost a baby, but I was never in danger of dying," Sarah hurriedly explained. Joe didn't agree with her statement but knew it was not the time or place to argue.

"So, she has no ma?"

"No."

"What about her pa?"

Sarah shot an exasperated look to Joe for guidance on how to handle this very delicate subject.

"Her pa can't take care of her," Joe simply explained, and the boy was thankfully satisfied with the answer.

"So, then, I guess we will have to take her!" Adam stated with determination.

"Would you like to?" Sarah asked tentatively, unsure of what his answer would be.

"Sure! I think it would be swell to have a baby sister!"

"It would mean big changes around here," Joe interjected. "We would have to move Brian into your room and put her in with your ma and me."

"That's all right! Brian's getting old enough now that he's kind of fun!"

"He still might cry and wake you up…" Sarah warned him.

"It'll be fine. He doesn't wake up as much as he used to. She's so cute! What's her name?"

Joe and Sarah looked to each other. "Did Mama tell you her name?" Sarah asked quietly.

"No. I think we can call her whatever we want."

"What do you have in mind?" Sarah asked him.

"Since her eyes are so blue they look almost purple, I was thinking… How about Violet?"

"That seems fitting," Sarah agreed. "But don't you think we should call her after her ma?"

"But, Ma, won't you be her ma?"

"I mean the woman who bore her."

"Well, I'm not even sure of her name, other than Kitty," Joe stated. "What's Kitty a nickname for, anyway?"

"Katherine or Kathleen, I suppose," Sarah told him. "With you being a McIntyre and Brian having an Irish name, what do you think of Kathleen?"

"Violet Kathleen," Joe said, trying it out.

"Violet Kathleen McIntyre," Sarah added.

"So, you want to keep her, then?"

"I don't see how we couldn't, Joe."

Chapter Fifty-Eight

True to his word, the next week, after telling Mama D and Dr. Miller that he and Sarah would keep the baby and raise her as their own, Joe had gone down to Colorado Springs and spoken with the judge. It was just as he had predicted. The judge had assured him there were no issues with the McIntyres raising the baby since there was no other family, after which he thanked and commended them for their caring and generosity.

In the months that followed, life in the McIntyre household was hectic, with two babies under the age of one, a school-aged boy, and two working parents.

Sarah had tried to work as much as she could, but soon found it was impossible to keep up, so she hired a second young girl to work for her after school and on Saturdays, which helped lessen the load quite a bit. It was meant to be temporary, but Sarah had no idea when it would potentially end. With Brian now newly mobile and Violet becoming more alert and awake, she was so busy catering to their needs that on most days she could barely poke her head down the stairs to ensure the young women in her employ were doing all right.

One particularly sweltering summer Sunday afternoon, Joe and Sarah couldn't take their stuffy apartment over the dress shop for another minute. The temperature was high while the wind was still, and everyone within their four walls was cranky. So, they took the children to the creek bank in an attempt to escape the oppressive heat.

Recently, Sarah had been nagging Joe because she was worried he had been working too much every day, while as of late he had also been awoken most nights to deal with issues in their town. In the summertime, his workload always picked up, as the miners relished the warmer and longer days by drinking harder and more frequently, often combining it with games of poker and frolicking with the town's working girls. Summertime also meant that more people were coming and going through the town, leaving or looking for work. He hadn't really noticed or minded before he was married: it had given him something to do to occupy his time. However, now with his nights beside his wife being constantly interrupted and the babies awoken too many times by commotions outside, he had enough. He was exhausted and welcomed the opportunity to escape to the peace and quiet by the creek.

Joe had fished with Adam for a while, before coming back to Sarah, who was on a blanket in the shade. He carefully lay down between his slumbering son and daughter, with his hands under his head, looking up at the blue sky and fluffy white clouds filtered through the green leafy canopy of the trees.

The next thing he knew, the sun was considerably lower in the sky than it had been before, and Sarah was looking at him, her face lined with worry.

Before she could speak, he told her, "Before you say anything, Sarah, I know what you're thinking…"

"You do?"

"Yes! You're going to complain that I'm working too much."

"Well," she started indignantly, as she quickly glanced at the bank of the creek to check on Adam, who was still contentedly fishing. "You work all day, every day, and then you keep having to get up at night, too, and…"

"I know," he cut her off. "You tell me this all of the time!"

"It's only because…"

"Sarah, will you let me finish?"

She arched an eyebrow at him but then barely nodded.

"I was going to say that I know I'm working too much. I agree! That's why I wanted to bring you out here today. To talk to you." Joe carefully eased himself up to a sitting position, as to not wake the children, and moved until his back was supported by a tree trunk, so he could better see his wife.

Sarah didn't speak, so he continued.

506

"I spoke to the mayor last week. I told him that I want to deputize Michael to be in the Sheriff's office with me full-time. I explained how I'm never getting a full night's sleep anymore, and with a family, I never have a chance to catch up, especially since the town is growing again. To my great surprise, he agreed. We are going to be a two-man operation now! Michael will be splitting duties with me and taking most of the overnights. And what's even better is that I don't lose any pay. The mayor agreed that the town is getting to be too much for one man to safely handle."

"Oh, Joe!" Sarah cried happily. "That's amazing! But I know you, and I have to wonder how you're ever going to be able to sleep when there's a commotion going on in a saloon or the street below us?" Sarah asked.

"You do know me too well," Joe laughed. "Now, if you would just be patient for one more minute… That's the second part of this conversation. As you said, I'll never be able to sleep, even if I know Michael is taking care of it, listening to everything going on down there. So, I'm going to build us a house."

"A house?"

"Yes! Not only have we outgrown our living arrangements, but it's also too enmeshed in town for me to be able to properly relax. You don't have time to work in the shop much anymore, so there's really no reason for us to stay there. Therefore, I think it's time we build ourselves a house. And," he paused for dramatic effect, "I bought the property that we are sitting on right now!"

"Oh, my goodness," Sarah exclaimed. "How did you manage that?"

He just shrugged, looking sheepish. "I was a single man making a decent wage for most of my life. My expenses were few, my needs even fewer. I just socked most of it away for a time I could use it. I figured that time is now."

"Oh, Joe!" Sarah cried in delight. "That will be wonderful!'

"I'm sorry I didn't ask you, but I wanted it to be a surprise. I know you've been trying to get me to slow down and spend more time with the family, however I knew that would never happen if we stayed in town. I would just be too accessible. So, I figured this was close to Ginny and Jacob, and town, but not in it. Not to mention that we already have a lot of memories here. Besides, the kids are only getting bigger and will need more room to run."

Sarah nodded her agreement but didn't have a chance to answer, as Violet awoke and started crying. She unbuttoned her blouse and got their daughter situated before looking up to continue their conversation.

But instead, Joe was studying his wife and grinning.

"What's that smirk for? You seem like the cat who's gotten the canary!"

"That's because I have!" he flirted.

"Oh, yeah?" She let her eyes sparkle at him. "How so?"

"I was thinking back to so many summers ago when we came to this exact spot, and you got so warm, you unbuttoned some of the buttons on your dress. I fantasized about how magnificent your breasts were for a long while after that and dreamed about taking you back here at some point in time to hopefully get to investigate them further."

He winked before leaning over and kissing her gently on her cheek, as to not to disturb their daughter who was still nestled against Sarah's chest. "Not exactly how I imagined it happening, but they are just as outstanding as I thought they would be, so my fantasy's come true."

Sarah quickly glanced at her husband and children, then laughed. "I guess in life, we do tend to get what we think we want if we want it badly enough, even if it isn't in the way we thought we would!"

"Well, I wouldn't have it any other way!" Joe leaned forward to tell her, his tone earnest.

Sarah put her hand on his cheek in a soft caress. "Nor would I!"

"I love you, Sarah McIntyre!"
"I love you, too, Sheriff Joe!"

About Majken Selinder Nilsson

After a particularly difficult year, Majken (pronounced "My-ken") Selinder Nilsson started writing novels as a way to safely and legally deal with an extremely stressful period in her life, finding during the process that she really enjoyed and had a knack for it. This was not surprising, however, as Ms. Nilsson has always had a vividly active imagination, having not only one but two imaginary friends as a child. Even as an adult, her characters come to life in her head and their personal stories often flow out faster than she can type. In just nine months, she had written two full-length novels, including extensive research, and started a third.

A native Nevadan from a small town, who also spent some time living in her ancestral home of Sweden, Ms. Selinder Nilsson is now a transplanted Southerner, where she lives with her very understanding family, who accepts that she stays up way too late writing, and all of whom are now used to calling her name several times to get her attention whenever she is in front of her computer. They are also accustomed to her bringing her laptop everywhere there could possibly be a few minutes' wait and have even stopped teasing her about her ever-changing facial expressions while she is writing dialogue.

Ms. Selinder Nilsson strives to develop a strong sense of place blended with complex characters with whom people can relate, while utilizing succinct, developed dialogue. Their personas become like close friends, often surprising her with the twists and turns in their lives as much as her readers. She connects with her characters on a deeply personal level and is known to mourn them when their stories come to an end.

Social Media

Facebook:
https://www.facebook.com/MajkenSelinderNilsson/

Website:
http://majkenselindernilssonbooks.com

LinkedIn:
https://www.linkedin.com/in/majken-selinder-nilsson-43b31112b

X (Formally known as Twitter):
https://X.com/MNilsson_Author

Blog:
https://majkenselindernilssonwritesblog.wordpress.com/

**If you enjoyed this story, check out these other
books by Majken Selinder Nilsson:**

A Good Kind of Crazy

Kat, the epitome of a middle-aged Southern housewife, had been
feeling as though she had lost herself even before her husband's
infidelity comes to light. Needing to make a change she simply
drives away to visit her childhood friend, Jen, the owner of a
successful Hollywood catering firm.

When a last-minute family emergency keeps Jen from traveling to
her next job on the shoot of a TV show in Canada, she convinces Kat
to go in her place. There, Kat is blindsided when she meets the
younger, handsome Irish star of the show, Ian Gregory, who is
standoffish at first, but later takes Kat into his confidence. Then
things get complicated.

Can Kat and Ian cook up a successful romance or will her trepidation
mixed with his indecision ruin the recipe?